THE SUN
BEHIND THE CLOUD

THE SUN BEHIND THE CLOUD

BASAVARAJ NAIKAR

ATLANTIC

ATLANTIC PUBLISHERS AND DISTRIBUTORS

Published by
ATLANTIC PUBLISHERS AND DISTRIBUTORS
B-2, Vishal Enclave, Opp. Rajouri Garden, New Delhi-27
Phones : 5413460, 5429987

Sales Office
4215/1, Ansari Road, Darya Ganj, New Delhi-110 002
Phones : 3273880, 3285873, 3280451
Fax : 91-11-3285873
web : www.atlanticbooks.com
e-mail : info@atlanticbooks.com

ISBN 81-269-0126-8

Typeset at
APD Computer Graphics, Delhi
Printed in India at
Mehra Offset Press, Delhi

DEDICATED TO

my son

Sivakumar

PREFACE

Bhaskararao Bhave of Naragund popularly known as Babasaheb was one of the earliest freedom fighters of India, in the latter part of nineteenth century. Although the notion of India as a whole was not yet in vogue in the colonial period, a separate nation called Hindustan was slowly emerging at that time. It was on account of the emergence of new awareness of their identity that the patriot kings of princely states tried to fight against the British people in the first war of independence in 1857. The negative policies of East India Company reached their climax during the days of Lord Dalhousie, Governor General of India then. The Disarmament Bill, the Doctrine of Lapse and the general imperialistic attitude of the British in India aggravated the problems for the Indian kings who had to lose their property, military strength and self-respect for various reasons. Unable to tolerate the British oppression any longer, Nanasaheb Peshwa rebelled against them and tried to inspire the other kings of princely states in India to do the same. Bhaskararao Bhave who belonged to the Peshwa dynasty was a fiery patriot who suffered from heirlessness and other allied problems. He initially sought permission from the Company Government to adopt a son from among his relatives. But when permission was refused to him by the British authorities, he rebelled against them and finally declared war against them. The British authorities cleverly used the "Divide and Rule" policy and weaned some of Bhaskararao's officers to their own side. Thus Bhaskararao was betrayed by his own men like Baniya Bapu and Krishnaji Pant. Rendered helpless by the emergency Bhaskararao ran away from Naragund. The British authorities searched for him and finally arrested him and passed a death sentence on him. But again due to the quirks of his fate, he escaped from death when one of his confidants courted death by impersonating him. Thus the novel depicts the story of colonial conflict between Indians and the British and the other related matters. The story of Babasaheb easily brings to our mind Okonkwo of Chinua Achebe's *Things Fall Apart*.

I have entitled this novel as *The Sun Behind the Cloud* to highlight the solar image and to suggest the contrast between light and darkness symbolically present throughout the novel. The name of the protagonist, Bhaskararao means "the sun" who shines brightly and then is hidden behind the clouds as it were. Similarly the East India Company or the British Government which believed that the sun never sets in the British Empire was behind a cloud as it were until it annexed the kingdom of Naragund and began to shine brightly. The solar image in the novel happens to be quite ironical.

The special reason for my writing this novel (which is my first one) happens to be the political connection of my own ancestors with Bhaskararao Bhave's rule in Naragund. My great grandfather Virabhadranayaka happened to be one of the army officers of Naragund and a confidant of Babasaheb. He fought heroically in the war with the British and lay down his life for his master.

As a young boy I was inspired by my parents' narration of the heroic feats of Babasaheb as well as of Virabhadranayaka. The theme of the novel was kept alive in my mind for the past thirty years. I made a systematic study of the topic by reading the major recorded material in print and tried to reconstruct the history of the colonial encounter in a realistic manner without resorting to sentimentalism or glorification. In writing this novel, I have drawn relevant material from the research findings of Sri A.S. Hugar of Naragund, Dr. Channakka Pawate of Dharwad and Dr. Ashok Bhave of Pune (the great grandson of Bhaskararao Bhave) and oral instruction by many of my relatives, friends and scholars.

Writing a historical novel is not so easy as that of a contemporary novel. The novelist has to do a lot of research and locate a logical thread in the mutually contradictory pieces of information thereby reconstructing history in a convincing if not a pleasing manner. I have done my bit in this novel and wait for the reactions and responses from historians and literary critics to guide my writing career in future.

BASAVARAJ NAIKAR

IN 1800 Appasaheb Sarkar was ruling over the princely state called Naragund. The hill of Naragund lay northwest and southeast across the vast plain. The sturdy hill of about eight hundred feet had the grand look of a sleeping lion. The capital city called Naragund was situated on the top of that lionine hill. Apparao Sarkar was walking up and down in his court and feeling rather fidgety. "What shall I do if I get a female child? I only hope that Lord Venkatapati will bless me with a male issue." Apparao Sarkar bowed down to his family deity and mumbled these prayers. Now he would go to the window and stare at the sky, now he would come back to the spot where the tiny idol of Lord Venkatapati stood and reverentially bowed down to it. "Lord, if by your grace I get a son, I can spend my lifetime without any worry about my kingdom. My whole life depends upon your mercy. Float me or drown me". Again he walked to the window and gazed at the golden crest of the spire of the temple.

There was a hustle-bustle going in the harem. The cry of children, the fussing of women and the moaning of the queen could be heard quite clearly in the interminable silence. The guards were peeping into the court occasionally. The sun had risen an elbow-length from the horizon. At last a maid-servant called Hemalata dressed in immaculate white sari and blouse rushed into the hall and bowed to the King and said with a beaming smile on her face,

"Sarkar, at last Rani sarkar is delivered of a male child." Appasaheb was overjoyed to hear the happy news. He raised his hands up in the air and said,

"O God, Lord Venkatapati, you have blessed me with a gem of a son. Your kindness is indeed very great."

Hemalata stood there with her fingers clasped ın front of her. Appasaheb called her,

"Come here, my dear Hemalata."

Hemalata walked towards him with fear mixed with hope. She said,

"Sarkar order me what to do."

She stood there biting her lips. She covered her chest properly with the hem of her sari. Appasaheb said,

"Hemalata, take this ring. As a reward for the happy news that you have brought to me this morning."

He instantly slipped a ring off his finger and held it out for her. Hemalata joined her palms before the King. Appasaheb leant a bit and dropped the ring into the hollow of her palms. The diamond in that ring dazzled her eyes and she forgot herself for a moment. As the King coughed a little, she recovered her presence of mind. She folded the ring tightly in her palms and said,

"Victory to you, Sarkar."

"Tell the matron that nothing should be lacking and ask her to make all arrangements for the mother and child."

"Yes, Sarkar."

Hemalata bowed down to him once again and walked out of the hall briskly.

Appasaheb relaxed on his throne with a sense of satisfaction. He closed his eyes, leant his head against the cushion and fell into a nap. Another half an hour went by. A few sardars and ministers came in and sat silently in the hall and did not want to disturb the nap of the King.

Another maid servant namely Kanakangi entered the hall with the new born baby in swaddle cloths placed on a silken cushion. She was followed by other maids. All of them said in a chorus :

"Sarkar."

Appasaheb was suddenly awakened from the tranquil sleep. As he opened his eyes he saw a bevy of maids standing before him. Before he could say anything to them, they said in a chorus :

"See, Sarkar, here is your princeling."

They lifted the baby and placed it on his palms. Appasaheb balanced the baby on his palms and gazed at it affectionately. He lifted it carefully and kissed it on the cheeks. The sardars also took the baby in their hands and scanned its features.

"Sarkar, the baby has all the royal features. He is going to be a grand king in future" said one of the sardars.

They gave back the child to the maids. Appasaheb turned at the Minister and sardars gathered there and ordered,

"Dear minister, please arrange for a grand service to Lord Venkatapati and distribution of coins, cereals, cloths and cows to the poor. Let the entire population of Naragund be fed at my palace."

"Everything shall be arranged as you wish, Sarkar," said the Minister.

On the occasion of the naming ceremony, all the relatives and dignitaries of the Samsthan had gathered in the harem. The Rani had adorned the child with a golden chain, rings and waist-bands. The matron and other maid-servants were making a lot of fuss in the hall there. They were all clad in their new garments. The priest walked into the hall and the maids supplied all the items of the ritual. All the others made way for him. The saffron scarf slung on his shoulders was shining in the morning light. The priest took the holy water from the bowl and sprinkled it on the child lying in the cradle. The child, of course, seemed to be thrilled by the lively gathering. The priest applied the sandal paste and saffron powder on the child's forehead and adorned its head with a wreath of jasmine and chrysanthemums. He said,

"The child-gem is born in the womb of the Rani. He is named as Bhaskararao as per the desire of Appasaheb Sarkar. Let the child shine like the sun whose name he bears and give light to the entire world."

Appasaheb walked up to the cradle, put a tiny golden ring studded with a gem on the child's finger, caressed the cheeks and looked at it affectionately. Then he walked back making room for the women-folk of the harem. They huddled against one another around the cradle and began to sing the lullabies in a chorus. The mellifluous sound of their voices filled the hall and soothed the hearts of all the people gathered there. Appasaheb was beaming with ecstatic joy.

* * * * *

Bhaskararao grew up in a luxurious atmosphere. Every morning the brahmin teachers used to visit the palace and teach him Sanskrit grammar, logic and astrology etc. In the evening, the royal teachers used to take him down the hill and coach him in sword-fighting and horse-riding. The teacher would whip a naked horse and train the young prince Bhaskararao mount on the back of the running horse. Occasionally he used to go to the royal pond called *Puskarini* and swim there. He used to practise diving and nictivating. Thus Bhaskararao grew into a smart young man of sixteen.

Young Bhaskararao was irresistibly smart. His bow-like mustaches, his biceps and the cuts of his virile body used to drive young women mad. The maid servants were eager to massage his body with coconut oil and bathe him after he returned from his daily exercises like horse-riding and sword-crossing. They would wipe his body with towels and comb his hair nicely. They were so eager to see the bewitching smile on his rosy lips. Even when he ordered them to go away from him they were so unwilling to part from him.

Appasaheb Sarkar thought of marrying a beautiful girl of good family to his young son Bhaskararao. He sent words to many of his relatives for a suitable bride. Many royal families sent their proposals. At last Appasaheb Sarkar selected Savitri, daughter of Manjrekar family of Ajare of Western ghat area as the suitable bride for Bhaskararao. The wedding was celebrated on a grand scale in the palace of Naragund. The chiefs of all the neighboring princely states were invited to the royal wedding. Thousands of natives, relatives and friends were fed with a veriety of dishes and hundreds of cows were given away to brahmin priests. The natives of Naragund remembered the grand royal marriage for many days and appreciated the royal family and its glory. As for Bhaskararao, he spent most of his time in playing and dallying with his pretty wife. Locked in her arms, he would never think or remember any difficulty or problem of the state.

Bhaskararao spent five years without any worry or anxiety. He used to spend half of his time in military exercises and the other half in the arms of his pretty wife. His father Appasaheb Sarkar was looking after the administration of the kingdom. Bhaskararao used to accompany his father to the temple of Lord Venkateswara and watch the holy service there. The father and son and the entire family would gather before the holy shrine of Lord Venkateswara. The brahmin priest would first wash the stone deity in water and milk; then clothe it with silken garments and the golden crest, arm bands and wristbands. Then he would apply sandal paste and saffron powder on different parts of the deity's body. Then he would pour some *aksata* on its head. He would put a fistful of incense powder on the burning coals in the bowl and wave it before the deity in a circular fashion. The sweet smoky aroma of incense would spread out in curls and soothe the minds of the people gathered there. The simultaneous chiming of bells also would create an intoxicating effect on them. Then the *panchamrita* would be symbolically offered to the deity. The priest would then place the deity on the palanquin which is decorated with silk, brocade and golden tassels. Two servants would lift it and slowly walk around the main temple. The palanquin is preceded by seven temple dancers who would stop at regular intervals and perform a few postures and gestures. The whole palanquin procession would circumambulate the temple five times before the holy service is concluded. Appasaheb and Bhaskararao would distribute coins to brahmin priests at the end of the holy service and return to the palace with a sense of supreme satisfaction. While the holy service was going on in the temple, the temple-musicians would play on *nagaswaram* clarionets and big drums the Karnataki tunes near the main gate to the temple precincts.

One day Bhaskararao was chatting with his father in the durbar-hall after dinner. They were discussing the arrangements for the fair of Lord Venkatapati during *Navaratri* festival. Bhaskararao was curious to know the origin of the fair. He asked,

"When exactly did you start this fair and car-pulling, father?"

"It was not I who started the fair. It was my father who started it after an interesting event happened in his life-time," said Appasaheb.

"What's that interesting event, father?" asked Bhaskararao.

"O, that is a very long story," said Appasaheb.

"Please tell me that, father, I am very curious to know it," requested Bhaskararao.

"Then, listen to it carefully." Appasaheb sat erect against the cushion, spat the globule of pan and betel in the silver spittoon and cleared his throat. The guards, men-servants and maid-servants cocked their ears and stood behind the doors and curtains to listen to the story that Appasaheb was about to narrate. Bhaskararao also grew alert, put a pillow upon his squatted knees and leant his elbows on it. Appasaheb began the narration :

"In my father Ramaraya II's time, an interesting event happened. He used to visit the temple of Lord Venkateswara at Tirupati every year. Once in the month of *Pausya*, he left Naragund for Tirupati with his limited company consisting of two camels, five horses and fifty persons in all. The camels were loaded with cooking utensils, ropes and tents. The five horses were ridden by sardars and others were cooks, servants and palanquin-bearers who used to carry it by turns. They went southward covering the plains, mounting the hillocks and crossing the brooks. At last they reached the river Tungabhadra. But they could not dare to cross the river as it was overflowing with water everywhere. The usual banks of the river were not visible at all as the water had spread over a vast stretch of area beyond the banks. The dark water was rushing torrentially, swirling loudly. The bubbles of various sizes used to float on the waves and burst out occasionally. The trunks of trees, thorny hedges and leaves used to float swiftly before their eyes. The pilgrims could not identify the usual ford on which to cross the river. Ramaraya II exclaimed,

"Oh God! We are in such a hurry to reach Tirupati, but this flood is so big that we cannot cross it, we have got to reach there by tomorrow somehow or the other."

He was really worried as to what to do about it. He consulted one of his sardars,

"Do you think, sir, this flood will subside within a couple of hours? Shall we wait until then?"

The sardar looked at the flood once again and said,

'Sarkar, I don't think it would subside so soon. It may require at least a day."

Ramaraya said,

"We cannot afford to wait for the whole day. We have got to reach Tirupati tomorrow. I don't want to miss the holy service."

"What shall we do then, Sarkar?"

"Sir, please send a few servants to search for a boatman around here." The sardar, accordingly despatched half a dozen servants to go about in different directions. King Ramaraya and his retinue waited under the shade of a big banyan tree. As the King thought of the holy service, the sardars gazed at the parrots on the branches. The other servants were busy counting the hanging roots of the tree. After half an hour went by, the servants brought a cowboy who had laid a black woolen blanket across his shoulders and held a staff in his right hand.

The cowboy said,

"I bow down to you, Sarkar. Why did you send for me ?"

"See, brother, we have to cross the river, but this flood is too much. Will you help us to cross it? Or is there anyone to boat us across it? We'll pay you amply for the help," said Ramaraya.

The cowboy looked at the flood and pointing his staff in that direction, said,

"This flood won't go down today, Sarkar. Why not stay here for a day and start tomorrow ? Otherwise you have to lose your life in it."

"No, brother, we have got to cross it today itself. Somehow or the other. And go to Tirupati. We are not too many. Just two camels, five horses and fifty members in all. Do something to help us cross it."

"Why do you bother about God so much? You will have to lose your lives. Do you think your God Venkatapati will save you?"

"Don't say like that, brother. That will be sacrilege. Nothing happens in the world without Lord Venkatapati's grace. By the way, what's your name, brother? What are your parents?"

"My name is Venka, Sarkar. I lost my parents long back. But a man of Reddy community has brought me up and has been feeding me. I'm therefore, tending his cattle."

"See, brother Venkappa, please do something to help us cross the river."

Venka was rather puzzled. He scratched the back of his head with his right fingers and remembered something. Then he said,

"Then, Sarkar, you will have to follow me for a distance of two miles downward. There I shall show you a sort of ford."

"All right, come on, let's go," said Ramaraya to his retinue. They followed him slowly along the river-side fields. The camels, the horses and the people walked slowly and produced a slushing sound. An hour had passed by now. At last they came to a relatively hard and rocky spot. The cowboy stood and pointed his staff at the rocky bank and said,

"See here, Sarkar. Here is a flat stone of three elbows' length, though it is hidden beneath the waves. I'll walk ahead and you have to follow me in a single file. You have to hold one another and walk very carefully on the slab. If you misplace your steps even a bit, you'll reach the bottom of the river. Later you cannot complain against me. 'Will' it be OK now?"

The entire group agreed to his suggestion. Then the cowboy said,

"Sarkar, you have to get off your palanquin and walk behind me by holding the tail of my blanket. The others may follow you in a similar fashion."

Accordingly Ramaraya got off his palanquin and held the tail of Venka's woolen blanket. The others also formed a single line. The cowboy walked upon the stone-slab overflowing with water. As they moved, the water swirled around their feet. The camels, the horses and the palanquin-bearers also walked very carefully. After a quarter of an hour or so, they reached the other bank of the Tungabhadra. They heaved a sigh of relief. They washed their faces, hands and feet and quaffed a little water just to ease their parched throats. Again they went to the big Benjamin tree and relaxed for a while. Ramaraya was beaming with a sense of satisfaction. He called the cowboy and asked him,

"Dear brother, I thank you profusely for this help. I want to give you something in gratitude. Tell us, what you want. Do you want gold or gems?"

"What shall I do with gold or gems, Sarkar? Robbers may come and thrash me to death and take away all of them from me."

"Do you want thousand square yards of land?"

"What shall I do with the land, Sarkar? I have neither wife nor children. I don't want anything."

"How is that possible brother? I must give you something in gratitude. Otherwise my conscience pricks me. Please tell me what you want."

"In that case, Sarkar, do you have the temple of Venkatapati at your place?"

"Yes brother, we have the Temple of Venkatapati at Naragund. We have an establishment of sixty-three employees there."

"Do you conduct the fair there?"

"Yes brother, we conduct the fair every year in *Navaratri.* We celebrate it with great pomp and glory."

"In that case, Sarkar, when you return to your place, please distribute two paise to each one of your temple-servants in my name. That's all I want from you."

"Is that all you want, brother?"

"Yes, Sarkar, that is all I want."

"All right, then. I shall do accordingly."

Ramaraya thanked the cowboy profusely. Then the entire group of pilgrims continued their journey. The next day they reached Tirupati and took rest in the *dharmasala.* In the evening Ramaraya entered the temple and had a *darsan* of the deity and prostrated before it. He then asked the priest,

"Will you perform the *abhiseka* tomorrow?"

"Why not Sarkar? By all means. Please come here in the early morning. Shall I ask twenty brahmins to attend the lunch?" asked the priest.

"By all means. Tomorrow I shall be here in the early morning. Please take these gold coins for the expenses."

Then they went back to the *dharmasala* located not far from the temple of Lord Venkateswara. King Ramaraya, the sardars and servants rested in different halls of the *dharmasala.* The chorus of frogs and the sharp and shrill sound of crickets lulled them into sleep. As they were tired on account of the long journey, they slept like logs. The camels and the horses were also tired and slept soundly.

As the cocks began to crow Ramaraya got up and coughed for a couple of times. Immediately all the sardars and servants got up. The servants heated the water in cauldrons for their bath. After completing the morning ablutions, Ramaraya dressed up and sat on the palanquin which the bearers carried to the temple of Lord Venkateswara. They attended the holy service.

The priest began to wash the idol with water and chant the *mantras*. Ramaraya sat right in front of the shrine. Then the priest poured the mixture of *panchamrita* containing milk, curd, ghee, honey and urine of cow over the head of the deity and rubbed it clean with a mini red towel. Then he decorated the deity with dots of sandal paste and saffron powder on different limbs. He decked the idol with jasmines, roses and chrysanthemums after keeping the golden crest on the head. The gem on the crest of the deity was resplendent and used to dazzle the eyes of the spectators. The priest burned the incense and waved it around the deity. The combination of a variety of sweet aromas created an intoxicating atmosphere in the *sanctum sanctorum* of the temple. Ramaraya sat drinking in the beauty of the deity with his eyes. As he stared at it for long, he felt a bit confused because now he saw the deity, now he saw the face of Venka, the cowboy who had helped him to cross the river Tungabhadra. The two pictures went on alternating before him. He was flabbergasted so much that he felt a sudden blackout of consciousness. He fell to the floor and received an injury on his forehead. Drops of blood trickled on the ivory floor of the *sanctum sanctorum*. Immediately the sardars who were seated in the central hall of the temple rushed to the spot. The servants lifted and carried the unconscious king to an open air verandah and laid him on a silken carpet and removed his jeweled turban. A maid-servant began to fan him with a bunch of peacock-feathers. Another man-servant started rubbing his feet with ash. One more servant brought a pail of water and poured it on the head of the unconscious King at regular intervals. As they stimulated his feet and fingers continuously, Ramaraya began to stir. He opened his eyes slowly and grew conscious of the surroundings. After a few minutes went by, one of the sardars asked him,

"Sarkar, what happened to you? Why did you fall unconscious? Is anything wrong with your health? Shall we send for a physician?"

The King said in a faint voice, "Don't you worry. My health is all right."

"How can that be, Sarkar? Otherwise you would not have fainted like this," said one of the sardars.

"No, I am all right. While the holy service was going on, I saw a miraculous sight. Now I saw the idol of the Lord, now I saw the face of the cowboy who helped us to cross the river yesterday. How unfortunate that we could not recognize and bow down to the Lord who had helped us to cross the river yesterday! How unfortunate that we could not recognize and bow down to the Lord who had come to us in the guise of a cowboy! That was the reason why I fainted."

"Oh, how wonderful! How strange are God's ways! We never know when God comes to us and in which guise!" exclaimed the sardars.

Ramaraya sat through the whole *abhiseka* ceremony of the Lord and amply distributed alms to all the brahmins including the head priest. He felt a new enthusiasm in life and a renovated faith in the Lord of the Mountain. He beamed with a great sense of satisfaction. The next morning he had his *darsan* of Lord Venkatapati once again and returned to Naragund with the retinue of his sardars and servants. In the month of *Pausya*, he got a towering chariot (*mukuta vahana*) of a beautiful shape and colours for Lord Venkatapati in memory of his last visit to Tirupati and ordered it to be used regularly in the *Navaratri* fair at Naragund.

"This is how my father arranged for the chariot-procession in *Navaratri* every year," said Appasaheb.

"Father, this is a very interesting story indeed! I did not know that the Temple had so much history behind it!" exclaimed Bhaskararao.

"Yes, my dear son. But this is only the later half of the story."

"Is that so, father? Is there a first half also to this story? Then why not tell me that also?"

"It's already past midnight, son. Now you go and sleep. Savitri might be waiting for you. I shall tell you the remaining part of the story on some other days."

"All right father. I did not know that it was so late. You take rest now."

Then they dispersed to their respective rooms.

After a fortnight they had another occasion for chatting. As usual they returned to the durbar hall after dinner. A maid servant clad in white brought *pan*, betel, lime, cloves and cardamom and kept them on the tripod. As they began to chew *pan*, another maid-servant brought two silver spittoons and placed them by their side. Then young Bhaskararao reminded Appasaheb,

"Father, last time you left the story incomplete. I would like to know who first got the Temple of Lord Venkateswara built at Naragund and when and why?"

"Dear son, you have asked not a question but a chain of questions. Don't you worry. I shall tell you all that."

Appasaheb Sarkar spat a big globule of *pan* into the spittoon and quaffed a glass of water. He cleared his throat and began to narrate the story.

"Dear son, this holy shrine of Lord Venkatapati was founded by my grandfather. My father had told me this story when I was of your age."

Bhaskararao sat upright on his seat and cocked his ears to listen to the history of the establishment of the shrine. Appasaheb continued,

"Of course, I have forgotten many details, but can remember the broad outlines. In my grandfather Venkataraya I's regime there was no shrine of Lord Venkatapati in the kingdom of Naragund. Venkataraya, therefore, used to go on a pilgrimage to Tirupati every year and offer service to the deity there in *Navaratri* period. He used to go there along with many sardars and soldiers. He would have *darsan* of the shrine of Lord Venkateswara and arrange for *abhiseka* and distribute gold coins to brahmin priests and beggars. After he was done with the holy service there at Tirupati, he would leave all his company behind and ask them to return to the Kingdom leisurely, while he would come back to Naragund only with a few sardars and bodyguards. But when the soldiers left behind by the King, returned leisurely, they used to destroy the crops and plunder and rob the way-side farmers of Tirupati. Venkataraya I did not know this at all. This robbery happened to be a regular affair. The farmers, therefore, grew tired of this regular loss and inconvenience. They discussed this among themselves and prayed to Lord Venkatapati of Tirupati,

"Lord, there is a King from Naragund who visits your shrine every year. He is said to be your fast devotee, but his soldiers plunder our homes and farms. Lord, kindly give him some reason and sympathy so that we can be spared the regular loss and inconvenience." The farmers used to repeat this request to Lord Venkatapati both in the temple and outside it. At last the Lord seems to have heard their prayers.

One day Venkataraya had his sumptuous dinner and relaxed on his bed. As he closed his eyes, he fell into a sound sleep. He had gone for a stroll near the *puskarini*. There a bright mass of light seemed to dazzle his eyes. He blinked his eyes for a couple of times and saw Lord Venkatapati of Tirupati move towards him with a compassionate smile on his face. Venkataraya, without knowing what he was doing, had prostrated at the feet of the Lord. He requested the Lord, "Kindly bless me Lord, I am coming to your shrine next month and donate a golden crest for the idol." The Lord said, "Don't you worry, child. Don't take the trouble of traveling all the way to Tirupati every year. Your soldiers unnecessarily pester the poor farmers there. Henceforward you need not come there for my sake. I will come and settle there at Naragund. You establish a shrine there. On the day of *Garuda Vahana* I shall give you *darsan* by playing like a bee before the idol. I will leave there five footmarks of a child, which should be enough for you to know my arrival there. Keep it a secret and don't tell anybody." Venkataraya said, "All right Lord, I shall do as directed by You" and prostrated once again to His feet. When he lifted up his face, the Lord had disappeared in the air. Venkataraya suddenly woke up and heard the sweet notes of the cuckoo which soothed his heart. He got up with a sense of glee and engaged himself in the morning ablutions.

After his breakfast, he sent for his ministers and sardars. While the servants went away, Venkataraya tried to visualize the picture of the shrine that he wanted to erect. When they came to the durbar and sat down on their seats after bowing down to the King, he addressed them,

"My dear sardars, I have decided to establish a shrine of Lord Venkatapati here at Naragund itself."

"Sarkar, that is a very good idea. It is indeed a long felt need," said one of the sardars.

"Please make all the arrangements for the same. Send for a few sculptors and architects from wherever they are available."

"Yes, Sarkar. I shall attend to it immediately. But I would like to know the spot on which to erect the temple."

"That shall be to the east of *puskarini*. I shall show you the exact spot where the shrine has to be erected."

Within a couple of months the temple was ready. The shrine of Lord Venkatapati was founded with all the ritual discipline. A big pot of golden ornaments, gems and jewels was buried in the earth below the shrine. The idol was carved exactly in imitation of that of Tirupati. The tall spire of the temple was adorned with a golden crest.

Innumerable service-men and temple dancers were invited from various places and were appointed for various duties in the temple. They were all given land grants appropriate to their duties. Thus the temple of Lord Venkateswara was formally inaugurated."

When, Appasaheb completed the story of the establishment of the temple of Lord Venkatapati, Bhaskararao was excited beyond measure by what his great grandfather had accomplished in the past in keeping with the dignity of the royal family.

"Father, our great grandfather has done such an excellent job by bringing the Lord from Tirupati to Naragund!" exclaimed Bhaskararao.

"Yes son, our duty is to continue the tradition established by our forefathers. Our father had granted so much of land to the sixty-three service-men of the temple. He has left thousand acres to the goudas (*i.e.* palanquin bearers), four hundred acres to dancers, four hundred acres to instrumental musicians, two hundred acres to flower-vendors and fifty acres to the torch-bearers of the temple. He has written in the royal grant-order that the temple-service should continue as long as the sun and the moon remain in the universe. Isn't it our duty to fulfil his desire, son?"

"Yes, father, we must. Not only that. We must add to the tradition as much as we can," rejoined Bhaskararao.

"It is getting on for twelve o'clock, son. Go and take rest." Then they dispersed and went to their respective rooms with sleepy eyes.

*****

A few years went by. One day Appasaheb fell ill. The news was brought to Bhaskararao by a servant. Immediately Bhaskararao sent for the royal physicians who came to the palace with their herbs and roots and administered them, to Appasaheb. But the medicines could not compete with old age. Appasaheb grew weaker and weaker every day. His queen Yamunabayi always sat at his feet and nursed him around the clock. His daughter-in-law also sat near his head and attended to him. Appasaheb's voice became rather faint. One day he called Bhaskararao to his side and said,

"My son, I may not survive for long. You'll have to bear the responsibility of the Kingdom of Naragund."

"Please don't talk like that, father. You'll recover soon," said Bhaskararao assuringly.

"No, son, we can't violate the Law of Nature. My days are over. Remember what I tell you. Don't be afraid of anybody or anything in life. Never be a slave to anyone. Nothing is greater than self-respect. Never forget these *mantras*."

"No, father, I'll never forget them."

Afterwards Appasaheb lost his power of speech and within a few hours life ebbed away from him. The entire royal household began to wail and cry. The entire population of Naragund Kingdom mourned the death of the King. The funeral was, of course, conducted with all the royal pomp and dignity. But before that the golden crown of Appasaheb was ritually placed on Bhaskararao's head and Bhaskararao was formally declared as the King of Naragund on that day in the year 1835. As the funeral procession went near the hillside cemetery, Bhaskararao carried the earthen urn before the cadaver of his father.

When the funeral procession reached the cemetery, the relatives performed *puja* to the royal cadaver and placed it on the funeral pyre made of jungle wood. Then at the beckoning of the priest, Bhaskararao lit the pyre with a burning wooden stick. As the jungle wood caught fire, soon the flames began to rise high and lick the whole mass of faggots. Bhaskararao and other relatives went round the pyre for five times. The wood cracked mildly for a few seconds. Then they could hear the cracking of the skull of the cadaver. Gradually the mass of burning wood diminished in size as it was reduced to ash. Then Bhaskararao, his relatives and all the ministers and sardars returned to their respective homes, took their bath and rested for the night.

After three days, the ash and the bones of the late Appasaheb were collected from the burning ground by Bhaskararao and thrown into the nearest river. On the eleventh day Yamunabayi was taken to a nearby well where her head was shaven by a barber and her bangles were broken by the women of the royal family. The dot on her forehead was wiped out and the ornaments like ear-rings, nose-rings and toe-rings were all removed from her person thereby making her aware of her widowhood. Yamunabayi was so much distressed by the demise of her husband that she did not care for her beauty or ornaments any longer. Besides, she was too tired to speak anything, in the presence of the death of her lord, she felt that the entire Kingdom looked a big blank to her. The post-funeral pacification, *puja* and lunch were arranged in the palace. Several cows and golden utensils and coins were gifted away to the brahmin priests. All these days went by only in mourning the loss of the beloved father.

After the post-funeral ritual was over, Bhaskararao began to feel the responsibility of the Kingdom though slowly. He felt sad at the sight of his widow stepmother and, therefore, asked his wife Savitri to take special care of his stepmother Yamunabayi. As days went by, Yamunabayi began to spend more and more time in the temple of Lord Venkateswara meditating and saying prayers to the deity.

Now the ministers and sardars started visiting him regularly and reminded him of the political situation in the neighbouring states. At that time Lord Dalhousie was the Governor-General of India with his headquarters at Calcutta. The East India Company was situated at Madras then. Although Bhaskararao was puzzled by the presence of foreign rulers in the Indian continent, he could not do anything about it as he had no occasion to rub with them. He began to inspect all the sections of his kingdom like infantry, cavalry, weapons, temple-service, lands, taxes etc. Sometimes it was his habit to go on the horseback to the nearest village

Hirekoppa and practise weight-lifting there with a huge round boulder and then return to his palace to have his bath and *Puja*.

Babasaheb used to take a round in the city every morning and pay his homage to the deity Uduchamma situated at the west end of the city. When the women heard the clop-clop of the horse's hooves, they used to go into their houses out of respect for the king, whereas the children used to wait curiously for the sight of the king and his beautiful stallion.

One morning Babasaheb was on his daily round in the city. It happened to be a Holi Festival Day. The citizens of western part of the town had worshipped the effigy of Lord Kama in the middle of the square and set fire to it. As the flames began to leap, the citizens began to flap their mouths with their palms thereby producing a mourning shout. As Babasaheb rode his horse there he saw the road blocked by the burning effigy and wooden pieces around it. People suddenly stopped their ritual mourning and stood watching the King with curiosity. As the road happened to be blocked by the fire of the effigy, the people thought that Babasaheb might return and follow another path. But their expectation was falsified. Babasaheb took an instant decision and whipped his horse sharply. The animal whinnied, broke into a canter and high jumped right across the burning effigy and continued its regular trot. The onlookers looked at Babasaheb and wondered at his heroic and adventurous spirit.

After the death of Appasaheb, Bhaskararao Bhave took over the administration of Naragund Kingdom. Bhaskararao had a very bitter experience with Raghopant Limaye who had been an opportunist and who had succeeded in spoiling the relationship between Bhaskararao and his father. As soon as Bhaskararao took charge of the kingdom, he decided to cut Raghopant Limaye to his size. He also contemplated of forgiving him and giving him humanitarian help if Raghopant Limaye confessed his past crimes and sought his pardon. But he saw that Limaye did not show any sign of relenting. He, therefore, decided to teach him a lesson by compelling him to go out of his Kingdom. He ordered his soldiers to demolish the big house of Raghopant

Limaye. When the soldiers went to his house with rods and hammers, Raghopant Limaye grew scared and left his home along with his wife and children and ran away from Naragund. After his house was vacated, the soldiers demolished the walls of his house and reduced it to the ground. The onlookers watched everything mutely and thought that there must be some misunderstanding between the new king Bhaskararao Bhave and Raghopant Limaye. The next morning when Bhaskararao rode his horse through the lanes of Naragund and saw the house of Raghopant Limaye being demolished, he felt a sense of relief on having got rid of a trouble-shooter of his own community. After a couple of days, he ordered his subordinates to arrange for the construction of a *chavadi* in the Kasaba area of the city. Accordingly the masons and carpenters busied themselves in using the stones, mud and wood of the demolished house of Raghopant Limaye and began to construct an imposing *chavadi*. Within a months' time the *chavadi* was ready with white wash and paint.

Meanwhile Raghopant Limaye had taken his wife and children to Jalihal-Hosur and kept them there and he himself began to stay at Dharwad. He heard the news from Naragund that his house had been completely demolished and the materials of his house had been used for the construction of the *chavadi* in the Kasaba area. He grew very vindictive and began to hate Bhaskararao from the bottom of his heart. He remembered how he had enjoyed the special confidence of Appasaheb when the latter was alive. He thought that Bhaskararao had reduced him from the status of somebody to that of nobody. He introspected, "Just as Bhaskararao has destroyed my house, I must destroy his Kingdom somehow or the other. I must give him tit for tat." He gnashed his teeth and wrung his fingers in anger.

As days went by, Raghopant Limaye began to strengthen his friendship with the officers in the Deputy Commissioner's Office at Dharwad. After gaining their confidence, he began to slander Bhaskararao and prejudice them against the Kingdom of Naragund. He submitted an application to the Deputy

Commissioner of Dharwad complaining against Bhaskararao. He had complained that his wealth had been forcibly confiscated by Bhaskararao; his house had been demolished and he was rendered homeless and banished from Naragund. He had requested the Deputy Commissioner of Dharwad to inquire into the matter and prayed for justice. In course of time, his file began to move from table to table. He used to meet the key officers and carry tales against Bhaskararao Bhave and his so-called ill-will against his family.

When Raghopant Limaye's application was taken up by the officers for consideration, they asked for Bhaskararao's opinion also about the case. Accordingly Bhaskararao Bhave sent his views on 30-7-1847. He had written to the officers, "Raghopant Limaye has been engaged in underhand dealings like fraud and instigating the sepoys and merchants to go out of Naragund. Further he has misappropriated the annual grant of Rs. 1326/- from the Company Sarkar to the temple of Sri Venkateswara. He has not submitted the said amount to the treasury of the temple. He should, therefore, be sent back to Naragund along with the temple-grant of Rs. 1326/-."

Raghopant Limaye felt embarrassed by the complaints made by Bhaskararao against him. He, therefore, began to lie before the British officers to save his face. But he continued his efforts to slander Bhaskararao Bhave.

*****

One day, when the holy-service was going on in the temple of Lord Venkateswara, Bhaskararao saw a young dancer who caught his fancy. She danced there before the palanquin of the deity. He happened to observe the details of her beauty very keenly as he had never done before. Her hairbun secured on top of her head, the mischievous light in her eyes, her drooping shoulders, her shapely breasts, tapering fingers and her protuberant posteriors charming in themselves assumed an additional beauty when twisted into different postures and gestures. His eyes were riveted into her seductive smile on her rosy lips. The amorous jerks and turns of her bewitching limbs distracted him deeply. He therefore, heaved a sigh of agony. Nonetheless, he went through the formalities of the holy-service and returned to his palace. The instrumentalists were still playing on *nagaswaram* and bell-shaped drums. Even when Bhaskararao was having his dinner with his queen Savitribayi, the image of the young dancer seemed to haunt and tease him. He spent a rather sleepless night thinking about the damsel of his dream.

The next day, Bhaskararao sent one of his servants to fetch the danseuse to his private room in the palace. He waited restlessly for her. After an hour's duration he heard the echo of the jingle of the dancer's anklets in the courtyard. His heart began to flutter with excitement. The servant entered the room, bowed down and said,

"Sarkar, I have brought the danseuse."

Then the servant walked back immediately. The pretty dancer entered the room, joined her palms in reverence and said,

"Salutations, Sarkar. May I know why the Sarkar sent for me?" Bhaskararao was enthralled as much by her beauty as by her melodious voice. He took a long breath to control his excitement and said,

"My dear young lady, please be seated on the cushion there." The dancer walked to the cushion gracefully and sat on the cushion in front of the king expecting his words.

"Younglady, I liked your art of dancing immensely. I have enjoyed the sight of your dance every Monday. I had a very strong desire to talk with you personally. That's why I sent for you."

Bhaskararao stared at her passionately. When her eyes met his, she felt a little shy and lowered hers and said,

"I deem myself lucky to be noticed by the Sarkar."

"By the way, what's your name, lady?"

"I am called Bhimasani, Sarkar."

Bhaskararao walked slowly near her, caressed her chin and said, "What a sweet name you have! Darling, you are my breath. I cannot live without you."

He locked her in his arms and smothered her with kisses.

"Please leave me, Sarkar, lest the servants should see us."

"Don't you worry about that, my dear. My servants are sensible enough to be away from my room whenever some lady is with me." Bhimasani's heart was fluttering with secret joy. Still she said modestly,

"Sarkar, I am too poor a woman to be fit for you."

"Don't bother about it at all. I shall provide for all you need in your life. By the way, where do you stay?"

"I stay in a rented house behind the Temple of Lord Sankaralinga."

"All right, I shall arrange for a storeyed building for you there, so that I shall be able to see you standing at your balcony."

Bhimasani was overwhelmed with excitement at the unexpected turn of her luck. She dreamt of bright days in future. Tears trickled in her eyes. She wiped them quickly and folded her palms in salutation and stuttered,

"As you wish, Sarkar. I am at your service."

She seemed to remember something. She made bold to say, "Sarkar, I have another request. If you don't mind."

"Tell me what it is. Don't hesitate at all," said Bhaskararao.

"Sarkar, I have lost my parents, a few years ago. I have no well-wishers except my Guru Keshar Prasad. He is like a father figure to me. Sarkar I can stay in Naragund and be in your service only if you can give shelter to my guru also. I can have some emotional security if he stays in this city itself."

Bhaskararao understood Bhimasani's problem and decided to help her have security in life. He assured her,

"Don't worry about it at all, darling. I shall give shelter to your guru also. I shall give land and arrange for the construction of a mansion for him. I shall arrange for similar security for you also."

Bhimasani felt a sense of liberty as the king took her into confidence. He steered her to the silk covered bed and lay her there. Bhimasani surrendered herself whole-heartedly to the king as she had never before to anyone. He tumbled upon her, explored her innermost beauties and sported with her until the fire of his burning was quenched. Then both of them got up with a sense of satisfaction and slipped into their garments. He gave her a final patronizing kiss as she took her departure from him.

Bhimasani was extremely happy to occupy it. She thanked God for her good luck. When she stood in her balcony, she could easily see the King standing in the balcony of his palace. Since the distance between the two buildings was only quarter of a furlong, they could easily beckon to each other and communicate with gestures. Bhaskararao was thus happy to give the security of a permanent home to his mistress Bhimasani. But he could not visit her mansion publicly lest it should offend the sensibilities of the neighbours of Bhimasani. She used to visit him now and then in his own private room in the palace after midnight. But Bhaskararao did not want to continue this practice for long. He immediately thought of an alternative plan. He arranged for the construction of an underground tunnel connecting his palace with Bhimasani's mansion. The masons accordingly struggled for nearly two months for building the underground tunnel. They used huge boulders, steel rods and mortar. Hundreds of servants including male and female were employed for the construction work. The underground tunnel ran from north to south and remained invisible to the pedestrians of Naragund. The presence of this tunnel was not known to many in the Kingdom. Bhaskararao began to visit her once or twice a week according to his mood and convenience. It was his usual practice to go to her house through the tunnel around midnight. He was accompanied by only two torch-bearers and two bodyguards who waited in the tunnel itself until the early morning when the King returned from Bhimasani's mahal after the rendezvous with her.

This became almost a regular habit with the King for his nocturnal entertainment and relaxation. A mansion was built for Keshar Prasad also who occupied it with a sense of gratitude to Bhaskararao Bhave of Naragund.

*****

Lord Dalhousie was the Governor-General of India at that time. His rule in the country had not directly affected Bhaskararao in any way. Another fifteen years went by in peace. Bhaskararao spent those years in royal luxury and merriment. Although he had heard about the British ill-treatment of other Indian kings, he had had no occasion to be disturbed by the alien rulers.

In spite of all the peace and plenty in his Kingdom, Bhaskararao had a secret worry gnawing at his soul. His first child died immediately after its birth. Afterwards he had no issue at all in spite of his normal matrimonial life. Savitri was not as sportive as Bhimasani in bed, but she was no less artful than the latter. In spite of being a very homely type of a wife, Savitri would not hesitate to surrender herself to him, but yet she failed to conceive for the second time. Bhaskararao consulted many a physician and took a number of aphrodisiac medicines concocted from a variety of roots and fruits. They all added to his amorous enjoyment but, unfortunately, did not help him to procreate any issues. Bhaskararao and Savitri worried about the problem silently.

One day he sent for an astrologer who had come from the northern part of India. The astrologer was ushered into the royal chamber by a servant. He bowed to the king and squatted on the wooden seat covered with a silken blanket. He joined his palms in salutation to the King and said in a mild voice,

"Sarkar, I am at your service. What is the problem, let me know." Bhaskararao clapped his hands and beckoned to the guard who understood the meaning of the royal signal, withdrew from the chamber and closed the door behind him.

"Punditji, I don't have any issue so far in spite of being married for the last so many years. Please see whether I am designed to have any issue or not. If yes, when?" Bhaskararao asked. Then the astrologer asked for a number of details like the janma-nama, date of birth, name of the father, mother and wife, time of birth etc., and noted them on a slate. Then he drew the horoscope on the slate with a piece of chalk and marked the location of each planet. Then he counted on his right fingers. He studied the *lagna* and counted the zodiacal houses all over again and confirmed the result of the combination of planets in it. His face grew serious because he found Jupiter the planet indicating procreation nullified by the presence of Rahu. He lifted his face up and looked at the King who was eagerly waiting for the former's answer. He asked him,

"What does your calculation indicate, Punditji?"

"Sarkar, you have got me here with deep faith in my ability to read the horoscope. I'll tell you the truth only if you promise not to misunderstand me."

"Punditji, please tell me whatever is indicated in the horoscope. Don't have any hesitation. I shall not mistake you."

"Sarkar, your horoscope indicates that you'll have no issues at all as Jupiter is rendered ineffective by the presence of Rahu". Hearing these words of the astrologer, Bhaskararao naturally grew pale and took a deep breath. After a few seconds he asked again,

"You mean, I'll have no issues at all throughout my life?"

"That's what the horoscope indicates, Sarkar."

"Then, thank you very much, Punditji, for your frankness. You have confirmed my doubts. My own court astrologer had not told me quite clearly."

"Sarkar, kindly pardon me for being so frank."

"No, Punditji, you have done your duty sincerely and alerted me about the future."

Then Bhaskararao clapped and asked 'who is there?' Immediately a servant appeared at the door. He ordered,

"Ask the treasurer to offer *daksina* to this Punditji."

Within a few minutes the treasurer came and offered a purse of gold coins and a dhoti and a silken scarf as royal gift to the astrologer. The astrologer saluted once again to Bhaskararao and took his departure from there.

*****

Three months went by. Bhaskararao was busy with nothing but the routine exercises and administration. One day, he returned from the morning service at the temple of Lord Venkateswara and sent for his Diwan Raghopant Kulkarni. The minister came within fifteen minutes and saluted to the King by joining his palms,

"Sarkar, why did you send for me? Is there anything urgent?"

"Please take your seat."

The Diwan sat in his chair and looked askance at the King. Bhaskararao cleared his throat and said in a confidential tone,

"See, Diwan sir, Lord Venkateswara did not bless me with a son so far. I am deeply worried about it. For the last so many days, I have been disturbed even in my sleep. I do not know how to solve this problem. What do you think I should do about it?"

The minister remained silent for a moment and knit his brows. He had understood the gravity of the situation. But suddenly something flashed across his mind. Then his face relaxed again. He said,

"Sarkar, why do you worry about it? If Lord Venkatapati has not blessed you with a son, it is He alone who would show the way out. Why not think of adopting a son from among the relatives?"

"I am also thinking along the same line. I have some boys among my relatives in Pune. My family line will continue and my kingdom will have a heir if I adopt one of these boys. What do you think about that?"

"Obviously that is an excellent plan, Sarkar. In fact that is the only way out of the situation. You may adopt one of those boys and solve all these problems. Everything has to go according to Lord Venkatapati's design."

"Yes, minister sir, let's leave everything to Lord Venkateswara. Let's wait and see what is there in our destiny!" sighed Bhaskararao with a sense of temporary relief.

Then both of them discussed the routine problems of the kingdom for some time and dispersed.

*****

It was in 1845 that the Disarmament Bill was passed by the East India Company when Mr. Dalhousie was the Governor-General of India. A copy of the bill was sent to Babasaheb of Naragund also through the Deputy Commissioner of Dharwad. When the order was handed over to the Diwan of Naragund, Babasaheb was informed about it. He asked his Diwan to read the contents. Accordingly the Diwan tread out the contents of the letter which were as follows :

"All the heads of the princely states of India are hereby ordered by the Governor-General to surrender all their military weapons such as guns, rifles, swords and spears etc., to the Government within three months failing which they are to be severely punished. The heads of the princely states are not supposed to retain any military equipment as it is the responsibility of the Government to protect them."

Sd/-
Governor-General
East India Company
Calcutta

Babasaheb was exasperated beyond measure when he heard the contents of the Governor-General's order. He said to his minister,

"What do you feel about this, Diwan sir?"

"My blood boils when I hear this news, Sarkar. Why should these red-faced fellows try to disarm us like this? What do they think of us? Do they think we have put on bangles on our wrists?"

"Don't be upset about it, Diwan sir, we have to think coolly before doing anything."

"What right have they over us? Do they think that our military weapons are their parental property? Sarkar, we should not yield to this pressure."

"You are absolutely right in your opinion, sir. But we have to think of the consequences. Supposing we refuse to obey them, it may lead to a lot of bloodshed."

"Sarkar, what shall we do then?"

"That's what worries me so deeply."

"Just now I get an idea, Sarkar. We shall defeat the red-faced monkeys in their own coin. There's still three months time for surrendering the weapons. We shall not oppose the British government openly. But before they come to our Samsthan for confiscation, we shall ask our subjects either to destroy or, to hide in the earth or throw in the wells and rivers all the weapons they have with them."

"Wonderful! It's indeed a very good idea! That's how a Diwan's brain should think. Please have this order promulgated tomorrow itself in the lanes of Naragund. Let our subjects do it at their earliest."

"Yes, Sarkar. I shall have the order promulgated tomorrow itself."

"That's good. It's only now that I have some peace of mind."

Diwan Raghopant Kulkarni bowed to Bhaskararao and took his departure from him.

*****

The next morning, the promulgator went about in the lanes of Naragund, with a small drum slung across his chest. He had braced his dhoti around his knees and twirled his mustaches in a bow-like fashion. He stood in the corner of a lane and sounded his drum half a dozen times *dhum, dhum, dhum, dhum, dhum, dhum* and attracted the attention of the spectators who gathered around him with curiosity to know the royal announcement. Then he raised the pitch of his voice and promulgated loudly,

"Listen to me, citizens of Naragund, listen to the orders of Babasaheb Sarkar carefully. The Ingreji Sarkar has demanded that all the citizens of India should surrender the arms like swords, spears, maces, rifles and guns etc., to the *firangi* Sarkar. The *Ingreji* soldiers may come to Naragund anytime to confiscate the arms. But Babasaheb Sarkar has hereby ordered all the natives of Naragund either to destroy or hide in the earth or throw in the wells or rivers whatever weapons they have in their houses so that the *Ingreji* soldiers should not be able to find any when they come down to raid our city." *Dhum, dhum, dhum, dhum, dhum, dhum.*

As he promulgated the royal order, the people cocked their ears and listened to him carefully, and began to murmur among themselves. As he walked into the next lane, those who had heard his message began to discuss the matter loudly and openly. He walked from lane to lane. He had begun from the Ambabhavani temple through the Red-Gate lane, market and brahmins' lane upto the western tank. As he was exhausted by the repetitious shouting he was panting for breath. He went down the stairs of the tank and drank some water by cupping his palms. Then he walked back to the high bank of the tank and fell into a nap under the cool shade of a big banyan tree.

*****

There was quite a stir in Naragund as the news circulated fast among the citizens. The civilians who owned some weapons for self protection felt very sore at having to surrender them to the British Government. They all felt that the order promulgated by Babasaheb Sarkar was quite justified. Most of the farmers took their swords, axes and knives in bullock-carts to the farms and buried them in deep pits. Some people took out their weapons and threw them into deserted wells. Some others who were too lazy to go far, buried them in their own backyards. They felt safe now that they had made their own private arrangements.

*****

A month had gone by. The natives of Naragund began to hear the rumour about the British soldiers marching from place to place confiscating the arms and weapons of the civilians. One day they heard from the local spies that the British soldiers were just twenty miles away from Naragund and that they would reach Naragund the very next day.

The next morning most of the farmers and merchants locked their houses and shops and went to work on their farms. The whole town was tense with fear. Some elders of Naragund thought it wise to please the British soldiers before they could enter the town so that there would be less trouble for them. They, therefore, collected huge quantities of jowar-breads, wheat-breads, vegetable curry, milk and curds from the natives and stored them on large pans and pots and stocked them in a large tent outside the town. They piled the breads in large wicker baskets and curds and water in large cauldrons. Half a dozen volunteers stood there quite eager to please and satisfy the British soldiers.

Around eleven o'clock when the sun was growing hot, the volunteers in the tent heard the hooves of horses clop-clopping in the distance. They cocked their ears and stared into the direction from where the sound came. They could descry a shadowy patch marching slowly along the cart-track. As the soldiers came near the tent the cloudlets of dust were raised. They were very thirsty and hungry and thought the tent to be a sort of a canteen. They rode to the tent and looked with desire at the food kept alluringly there. The volunteers offered them cool water from earthen ewers. The soldiers who stood in a queue and quaffed the cool water felt a very happy but preliminary satisfaction. Then the volunteers served them with jowar-breads, wheat-breads, vegetable curry, curds in leaf-plates. The soldiers devoured the delicious native food like hungry wolves. After they finished their meal, they were served with mugful of buttermilk with salt and garlic in it. The soldiers who ate bellyful of food and drank very tasty buttermilk, belched with satisfaction and thanked the natives of Naragund profusely. Then they lay under the mango trees nearby and smoked their hookas. The volunteers felt happy to note that the soldiers were quite pleased with their food and service. They wishfully guessed that the soldiers might not indulge in unmentionable activities like looting or raping at least in their town.

The soldiers rested for a couple of hours under the cool shade of trees. Then they all got up and entered the city of Naragund for confiscating the weapons from the natives. They went on visiting the houses one by one and took into their possession whatever swords, lances, rifles or guns they could lay hands on. They just knocked on the doors and when the doors opened they walked into the houses and searched around for weapons, without caring for the feelings of the owners. They entered even the puja rooms with their heavy boots on not knowing or not caring to know that they were committing sacrilege according to Hindu belief. Many houses were unfortunately locked for them. But they entered other houses wherever the tenants were present and searched for the arms and took them into their custody. As they crossed the potters' lane, they saw a big house behind a white-washed temple. One of the soldiers asked a passerby as to whom the big house belonged. They were answered that it belonged to Virabhadra Nayaka who was connected with Babasaheb's army. The soldiers walked briskly towards the house and knocked at the door. There was no response. They knocked for the second time. This time it was heard by the inhabitants of the house. Virabhadra Nayaka peeped through the tiny window from the side wall and confirmed that it was the soldiers who were knocking. It took him not a fraction of a second to guess as to why they had come. He beckoned to his servants and whispered something into their ears. The servants went to the middle hall of the house and carried all the swords and spears silently to the backyard and threw them into the deep well-like lavatory. They did this with utmost care and diligence. Then they beckoned back to Virabhadra Nayaka. The women folk huddled together in the kitchen. Virabhadra Nayaka went to the kitchen and asked them not to be nervous and assured them that nothing harmful would happen. Then the third knock was heard from outside. Now Virabhadra Nayaka walked towards the main door of the house and took out the wooden bar from the sideholes and opened the door. Suddenly one of the soldiers said,

"We've come for the weapons. Give us all the weapons that you possess."

"We have no weapons worth the name. Except a few small ones. You may search by yourselves in the house," said Virabhadra Nayaka.

The soldiers entered the house and went on inspecting the different rooms. The inmates of the house tolerated the tap-tap of the boots of the soldiers as they walked leisurely across the big house and searched the nooks and corners of the house. The small children, on seeing the strange-looking soldiers, set up a loud cry and snuggled into their mothers' arms. First, the soldiers searched in the front room and found nothing. Then they went to the cattleshed adjacent to the front room and rummaged beneath the trough and behind the cattle. The cattle seeing the strange figures moving around them bellowed loudly and registered their protest. Then the soldiers walked to the middle hall and found two big swords hung on the wall across each other. One of the soldiers walked straightway towards them and took them with him. The blades of the swords sparkled even in the dim light of the middle hall. Then they walked to the back rooms of the house and found nothing but piles of bags bulging with corns and cereals. Then the soldiers walked back mechanically to the front door and asked Virabhadra Nayaka,

"Are these the only weapons you have with you?"

"Yes, saheb, these are the only ones we have with us. You saw with your own eyes."

The soldiers grunted helplessly and walked to the next house. Virabhadra Nayaka stood on the doorstep of his house with his left arm akimbo and right hand twirling his bushy mustaches. The womenfolk of his house heaved a sigh of relief, yet they dared not come out of the house to peep at the strange soldiers for fear of the terrific Virabhadra Nayaka. That day there was a rather gloomy atmosphere in the whole city. In the evening, however, Virabhadra Nayaka learnt from his servants that the soldiers had left Naragund and gone towards north. He was also happy to know that they had not tried to harass the farmers or loot the houses or molest the womenfolk of Naragund. Virabhadra Nayaka thought it was all due to the nice treatment and supply of delicious food to the hungry soldiers at the entrance of the city. That night and the next morning there was a lot of gossip among the citizens of Naragund about the confiscation of the weapons by the British soldiers. They were happy to note that they were not treated roughly by the enemy soldiers and that they had tricked them very intelligently by hiding or destroying their weapons.

The next morning Virabhadra Nayaka rushed to the palace and met Babasaheb and joined his palms in salutation to the Chief of the Samsthan. He said,

"Namaskar, Sarkar. Have you heard any report about the Ingreji soldiers?"

"Virabhadra Nayaka, you are the first visitor to me this morning. You have to tell me whatever you have heard from people."

"That's the reason why I rushed to the palace, Sarkar. Yesterday the Ingreji soldiers were searching the houses of the civilians and confiscating the weapons from them. In fact, they had come to my house also. They could find nothing but two swords. The rest of the weapons I had arranged to be thrown into the lavatory in our backyard. Sarkar, your plan was very successful. Most of our natives have hidden the weapons in the fields or backyards or haystacks. That's why the soldiers could not get many weapons from our city."

"Very good, Virabhadra Nayaka, our people have carried out our plan very successfully. We have to defeat the firangi fellows in their own coin. Otherwise they would have looted all our weapons and other things. Hope nothing unpalatable has happened yesterday?" asked Bhaskararao concernedly.

"Absolutely nothing, Sarkar. We had arranged for nice food and water for them at the outskirts of the city. The soldiers were extremely pleased with the arrangements. So was I told."

"Very good, Virabhadra Nayaka, we have to resort to all these tricks just to save the lives of our people. Please see me in the evening. Now it is time for my visit to the temple." Virabhadra Nayaka bowed himself out of the chamber.

*****

It was in the month of February that Manson came to India and met the Governor-General at Calcutta who ordered Manson to officiate as Political Agent over the sixty-three princely states of South India and establish his headquarters at Kolhapur. Accordingly Manson went to Kolhapur and took charge of the office and began to acquaint himself with the details of the problems he had to deal with. Rajaram Maharaj was ruling at Kolhapur then. Manson had no idea of the nature of the sixty-three princely states that he had to control. He, therefore, sent a circular to all the kings to attend a general meeting at Kolhapur. He had specially ordered them to go to him with all their pomp and glory.

A messenger came and handed over the circular to the Minister of Naragund. The Minister gave it to the clerk for reading it out. Bhaskararao sat on his throne and cocked his ears to listen to it. The clerk stretched the paper up and read out the contents loudly. According to the letter, all the sixty-three kings of South India were requested to attend the general conference at Kolhapur on the first Monday of March. They were also requested to go to Kolhapur with all their pomp and glory. The messenger was sent back after being treated hospitably by the officers of Naragund. Meanwhile Bhaskararao consulted his Minister and other confidants and decided to attend the conference at Kolhapur.

Babasaheb set out for Kolhapur on horseback. He chose, only eight cavalrymen with him as bodyguards. Vira Sarnayaka also accompanied him. Bhaskararao had great faith in Vira Sarnayaka's loyalty and heroism. All the ten of them rode on horseback, crossing wide stretches of land, mountain ridges and meandering brooks and rivers. They used to travel upto evening and camp at night in tents erected by the soldiers. They would resume their journey again at sun-up. Thus they took about five days to reach the boundaries of Kolhapur. They were attracted by the bewitching beauty of the greenery around them. They erected their tents there on a hillock and rested. They had one more day's time at their disposal. Bhaskararao stood on a rock and ran his eyes at the skyline of Kolhapur. He wanted to confirm whether the other kings had been coming to Kolhapur or not. He, therefore, called Vira Sarnayaka to his side and said,

"Dear Sarnayaka, would you mind riding upto the city and confirming what arrangements have been made and whether other kings have come there and if so how many?"

"As you wish, Sarkar, I'll go there right now."

Vira Sarnayaka jumped instantly on his horse and rode towards the city. As he went nearer the city the houses and temples looked clearer. He saw the gigantic pandal erected by the Political Agent for the next day's conference. The entire pandal was decorated with multicoloured cloth, festoons and tassels. Four big gates were erected at all the four sides of it. A few workers were still at work attending to the inner decoration. On the whole, the arrangements appeared to be quite grand to Vira

Sarnayaka. But he was puzzled by one thing in particular. Each main gate led to three inner gates one smaller than the other. Thus the fourth gates on all the sides were smallest of all, with the result that when somebody on a horseback could just ride through the main gate quite easily, had to duck his head while crossing the second gate. When he came to the third gate, he had to virtually get off the horse and actually bend himself in order to cross the fourth gate before entering the auditorium. He made a mental note of it and rode back to the camp where Bhaskararao was waiting for him. Vira Sarnayaka reported everything that he had seen there. Babasaheb knit his brows a little and asked him,

"Do you think Manson has erected the sixteen gates deliberately to insult us the kings?"

"I think so, Sarkar. I suspect he has some plan in all that clever arrangement."

"Sarnayaka, should we attend the conference or go back from here? I don't like to be insulted like this."

"Don't you worry, Sarkar. We have come all the way from Naragund to attend the conference."

"But what if we are insulted?"

"I shall solve that problem, Sarkar."

"How'? Let me know "

"We shall enter the first gate quite easily. Sarkar, I shall be going ahead of you there. When we have to cross the second, the third and the fourth gates, I shall shatter them with my sword so that we need not have either to get down from horses or to bend ourselves."

"All right Sarnayaka. But what if Manson gets irritated over that?"

"Why to worry Sarkar? Let him be angry. We shall answer him properly and silence him."

"All right Sarnayaka. We shall do as you have suggested."

The next day, Babasaheb, Vira Sarnayaka and the bodyguards completed their morning ablutions and had their breakfast of sweetballs, hot chapatis and vegetable curry. They mounted their horses and rode towards the city of Kolhapur. They were really invigorated by the fresh breeze of the morning. Their eyes feasted on the trees, creepers and rocks of bewitching colours. As they entered the city, they could feel the sense of jubilation in the natives there. As they rode through the lanes, the men and women and children used to rush out of their homes and stare at them with dumb admiration. At last when they came to the huge pandal with four main gates in each direction, they stood for a moment and had a better view of it. Vira Sarnayaka said to Babasaheb,

"Sarkar, I shall go ahead and do as I told you. Don't you worry about that."

"Yes, sir. We remember that. Please go ahead."

They crossed the first gate. First Vira Sarnayaka went in. He was followed by Babasaheb on horseback and his bodyguards. Since the first gate was quite high, they had no problem in crossing it. After a few yards, they had to cross the second gate. Though that was smaller than the first one, it did not obstruct their entry through it. Again they passed through it in the same order. They rode a few more yards. When they came to the third gate, they found that they could not pass through it without ducking their heads. Babasaheb beckoned to Vira Sarnayaka who drew his large sword from his sheath. As he went near the third gate, he lifted his sword with a flourish and struck at the beam with such force that the beam cracked and splintered into pieces and fell on the floor. Now that the beam was cut off, all the five of them passed through the gate without any difficulty. They rode another few yards and came to the fourth and last gate. They found that they could not pass through it without dismounting from their horses. Again Vira Sarnayaka lifted his sword dexterously and struck at the beam with such force that the beam parted into two and fell off to the floor. Now they passed that gate without having to get down from their horses.

As they entered the central pavilion, the other kings and their followers began to look at them with a little amazement. A few of them whispered among themselves,

"What a shame that we had to get down from our horses in order to come through these gates! We wish, we had done like this heroic king."

By this time word was sent to Manson about how the last two inner gates were smashed by the King of Naragund. Within a few minutes Mr. Manson walked up to the spot and asked for the king who had smashed the gates. An assistant officer pointed towards Babasaheb who was by now settled into one of the chairs along with his men. Mr. Manson walked up to him and thundered at him,

"You, King of Naragund, why the hell did you smash the gates? Who permitted you to do it? I do not tolerate this kind of arrogance." Babasaheb stood up in a stylish fashion and answered him,

"Do you remember the order sent to us? You have asked us who are like your sons, to come here with all our glory and discipline. Do you like your sons being insulted like this by being made to pass through the gates with bent heads? I don't think it becomes a father to insult his own children. It is not in my nature to bend down like that. That is the reason why I asked my Sarnayaka to smash them."

Mr. Manson, was disarmed by the unexpected answer. He did not know how to react to it. For a moment he stood silent there because of the sense of puzzlement that he felt. But immediately alerted by his diplomatic sense, he changed the tone of his voice and said to him,

"O that's very good, Babasaheb. I very much appreciate your dignified behaviour and courage. I admire your respectability." He stretched his hand towards Babasaheb and shook hands with him with a broad smile on his face. Both of them stared into each other's eyes. Vira Sarnayaka was beaming with a sense of satisfaction.

Mr. Manson went back to attend to other details of the conference. When the function began, it was presided over by Maharaja Rajaram of Kolhapur. In the course of the programme, Mr. Manson addressed the royal gathering as follows :

"My dear Rajas of all the sixty-three princely states, I have called this meeting mainly to acquaint myself with all of you. I am happy to bring to your kind attention the fact that I have been appointed by the East India Company as Political Agent over the sixty-three princely states of South India. I am extremely happy to meet you all. In fact I called this meeting only to acquaint myself with your pomp and glory. Since I am appointed to be your protector, I request you to extend all help and cooperation. Your loyalty to the British Government will be highly appreciated."

When Mr. Manson finished his speech, Maharaja Rajaram of Kolhapur answered the toast from his presidential position. He spoke on behalf of all the kings of the princely states. The kings, in spite of a deep sense of embarrassment in them, were impressed by the general atmosphere of amity and goodwill engendered in the programme. After the formal meeting was over, they were conducted to a separate palace where a grand feast of innumerable dishes was arranged. All the kings were quite happy about the culinary arrangements. In the evening a number of entertainment items like singing, instrumental music and dances were arranged. The entire programme went off so well that the kings could not help appreciating it.

Next morning Mr. Manson visited all the kings and bid farewell to them, after giving them some mementos and shaking hands with them. When he came to Babasaheb, he said,

"Hullow sir Babasaheb, yesterday I was very happy to note your behaviour which speaks of your dignity and respectability. The East India Company really needs the support of kings like you. As a token of my appreciation of your heroic behaviour, I am giving you a special drum-set. Please accept it."

Then Mr. Manson ordered his assistant to arrange for the same. Within a couple of minutes, the drum-set locally known as

Dunk-Nagari was brought on a horse-back and symbolically presented to Babasaheb by Mr. Manson. The servants transferred it to one of Babasaheb's horses. Vira Sarnayaka was all appreciation for that. It was a special set of drums set parallel to each other and could be fixed on the two sides of a horse. The drummer could sit on the horseback in between them and play on both the drums simultaneously with his hands. He was, of course, protected from the sun by a silken umbrella fixed on top of the two drums. Babasaheb also liked the new type of drum-set and asked his servant to try his hand at it. Babasaheb shook hands with Mr. Manson once again and took his departure from him.

*****

A couple of months went by. Bhaskararao was busy with his daily service at the temple of Lord Venkateswara, exercises and administration. Although he used to be preoccupied with the diurnal duties, he would worry about his heirlessness whenever he happened to be alone. He consulted his confidants and well-wishers about the same. Sometimes in the afternoons his mother would see him and remind him of the need for doing something about having a heir for the kingdom. He would assure her that he would definitely do something about it. He, then consulted his minister and Vira Sarnayaka and others. After long deliberation he ordered his minister to send a letter to Mr. Manson asking for permission to adopt a son for the kingdom of Naragund. The minister immediately sent for the scribe and dictated the letter. The scribe read out the letter for Bhaskararao to hear it.

"Honorable Sir Manson, hope this letter finds you in good health. We would like to bring to your kind attention the fact that we do not have any issues of our own. But we need a heir to take care of our kingdom after us. We, therefore, request Your Excellency to kindly permit us to adopt a near relative of ours as our legal heir to the Kingdom of Naragund. We hope to hear a favourable reply from your end at the earliest."

The letter included the other epistolary formalities. As soon as Bhaskararao approved the contents of the letter, the Minister asked a messenger to take it to Kolhapur and hand it over to Mr. Manson. The scribe rolled the scroll, put it into a cylindrical box and gave it to the messenger who kept it in his clothbag, mounted his horse instantly and set out for Kolhapur. After ten days he returned to Naragund after having handed over the letter to Mr. Manson. Bhaskararao waited patiently for one, two, three months, but there was no reply at all from the other end.

Another three months went by. Bhaskararao began to grow restless over the issue. He remembered that there were many other kings who, like him, had no heirs and who were equally worried about the same. He, therefore, sent out messages to Bhimaraya of Mundaragi, Desai of Hammagi, Yasavantaraya of Jamakhandi and Virarani of Chitradurga asking them to gather at Jamakhandi to discuss the problem of adoption. Within a few days he received messages from all of them that they were glad to attend the meeting. Later they jointly requested Mr. Manson to preside over the princely council. Fortunately for them Mr. Manson accepted the invitation.

Mr. Manson attended the meeting at Jamakhandi. All the five princely chiefs had made up their mind to thrash out their problems. The meeting began in the morning about 10 o'clock. Bhaskararao stood up and said,

"Sir, all the five of us do not have issues. We, therefore, request you to grant us permission to adopt somebody from among our nearest relatives."

There was a look of indifference on the face of Mr. Manson. He scanned all the five chiefs from one corner to the other. Then Bhimaraya of Mundaragi stood up and said,

"Sir, Bhaskararao has spoken for all of us. We are deeply worried about our heirlessness. We must be allowed to adopt our nearest relatives."

Then the Virarani of Chitradurga sat erect in a dignified fashion in her chair and said,

"Manson saheb, you must permit us to adopt our heirs from among our relatives. Otherwise the consequences will be serious."

All the chiefs looked at one another meaningfully and began to wait for Mr. Manson who was a little irritated. He licked his lips with his tongue, sat upright in his chair and said in a firm but slow manner,

"Lady and gentlemen, I have noted the contents of your requests both oral and epistolary. But I must confess before you that I am not empowered to grant the permission that you have so solemnly sought. I can understand your problem quite well, but I cannot do anything about it. I assure you that I shall definitely refer the matter to the higher authorities in London and let you know the result after I hear from them. Beyond that I cannot do anything. You will have to wait patiently until then." Manson leant back in his chair. The five chiefs were not happy about what he said. They began to whisper among themselves. Bhaskararao was fuming with anger. He thundered,

"You must give us permission in your regime. We have got to take care of our states. We do not want to listen to your pretexts." Manson was irritated by the words of Bhaskararao. He raised his voice and shouted,

"Dear Mr. Bhaskararao, please don't be in a hurry. We have received orders from our East India Company. According to that, all of you should surrender your army and ammunition to our government. Besides, permission regarding the adoption cannot be granted. Therefore all the property belonging to the heirless states should be handed over to our government. Everyone from king to farmer must submit themselves to our authority."

Manson was excited when he was speaking these words. His palms were folded in fists. He spoke his broken Kannada in an artificial and stylized fashion. All the kings and the queen were angered by Manson's words. They began to look daggers at him. Bhaskararao could not control himself. He jumped on to his feet, stood with his right hand on the hilt of the sword and shouted,

"You cannot say like this Manson saheb. Our country is called Hindustan because we believe in Hindu religion which has allowed the privilege of adoption for the heirless all through the history. You cannot take away that privilege from us. That would be sheer injustice. Please think over it."

Bhaskararao was so angry while speaking out these words that he did not sit. He continued to stand only. Manson was also exasperated. He jumped up from his sitting position and shouted back at Bhaskararao in a rather contemptuous fashion.

"You arrogant fellow! How dare you talk like this to me? I say get out!"

Bhaskararao was angered deeply and shouted back,

"Are you born to Hindu semen, bastards? How are you connected with our Hindustan? You should abide by certain ethical principles. You shouldn't rob us of our property by denying us the privilege of adoption. Everything will be all right if you grant the permission. Otherwise,..." He drew his sword from its sheath and rushed towards Manson to strike him. Manson, who was not prepared for such an unexpected encounter was taken aback. He shuddered at the sight of Bhaskararao's sword. But the other kings dissuaded Bhaskararao from attacking him. The normality of the function was upset in that conflict. Bhaskararao's anger knew no bounds. He stood up once again and took an oath,

"Mr. Manson, please remember that you cannot take my kingdom except through war. I will fight for my kingdom and against the British rule until the last breath of my life. Come what may!" Manson who listened to the fiery words of Bhaskararao trembled at heart and could not have the courage to see him in the face. He managed to sneak out of the palace and rushed on horseback to his office at Kolhapur. He thanked his stars for saving his life from the unexpected danger that had cropped up in the meeting.

Bhaskararao and the other four kings exchanged confidences among themselves and dispersed. Bhaskararao returned to

Naragund and immersed himself in the routine matters of administration.

*****

Gangadhar was one of the leading merchants of Naragund. He used to deal in grocery and cereals. He had a great landed property, oxen and bullock carts in his household. Because of his wealth and personal dynamism he was respected by one and all in the city of Naragund. Another important reason for the people's reverence for him was that he was on very friendly terms with Bhaskararao. Whenever Babasaheb was free from the serious matters of administration, he used to send for Gangadhar and both of them would go for a walk in the evening. On different days they used to go in different directions. Then they used to chat for an hour or two.

One day; both of them were walking along the eastern side of the hill. On the right side of the road there was a well from which men and women used to draw water and go back. When Bhaskararao cast his glance at the crowd, his eyes were riveted on a beautiful younglady who was carrying a brass pitcher on her head and going back towards the city. Bhaskararao observed her rhythmic gait, pretty face and maddening curves competing with one another. Babasaheb's mouth began to salivate. For a moment he forgot the topic he was discussing with Gangadhar. But somehow he regained his composure and resumed his talk with him. Gangadhar had noticed what had happened to Babasaheb but kept quiet about it and tried to divert his attention to some other matter of the royal life. They walked another mile and sat on a huge, flat rock. The purple and rosy clouds were slowly drifting in the eastern sky. The regaling wind was blowing gently. The cuckoos in the distant trees were cooing melodiously. Babasaheb seemed to have lost himself in observing the beautiful Nature around him. A sweet pain was inundating his heart.

Gangadhar said, "This year jowar and wheat crops are abundant everywhere. The farmers are quite happy about it."

These words jolted Babasaheb and brought him back to the world from his trance.

"Ah, yes, yes. The farmers of Naragund are quite happy," said Babasaheb and again grew absent-minded.

"This year, there'll be absolutely no problem for our cattle. But the preservation of the extra cereals and paddy will be a problem, sir," said Gangadhar.

"Yes, yes, it would be a problem," said Babasaheb rather absentmindedly.

Gangadhar understood that Babasaheb was thinking about something else, but he could not make it out. He made bold to ask Babasaheb,

"What has happened to you sir? Today you are not your usual cheerful self. Is anything wrong?"

Babasaheb felt a bit embarrassed by the direct question. But yet he made a clean breast of his wish. He lowered the pitch of his voice and said to Gangadhar,

"Dear friend, you know you are my close friend. I cannot hide anything from you. Just a few minutes ago while coming this side, I happened to see a beautiful younglady carrying a water-pitcher on her head. She had such wonderful features that I have never seen the like before. I must have her. What's the meaning of this life if I cannot enjoy such a beauty?"

When Gangadhar heard these words from the king-friend, he was shocked beyond measure. The younglady that Babasaheb referred to happened to be none other than his own (Gangadhar's) daughter-in-law. But at the same time he did not want to betray his feelings. He pretended ignorance of the lady and said,

"Have you liked her so much, sir?"

"Yes, yes. Very much."

"How could you find such beauty in an ordinary girl? Don't you think your temple dancers and courtesans are hundred times better?"

"What you say is correct. But this, this kind of serenity I have never seen in any of the courtesans."

"Is that so? I don't think. I suspect, sir, something has happened to your taste."

"I cannot help it friend, I must have her. Otherwise life will be incomplete."

Gangadhar grew more and more shocked inwardly, although he pretended not to be upset at all. He tried to engage Babasaheb in conversation and tell him some other news of the commercial life. By now darkness had descended everywhere, they got down from the rock and walked towards the palace. The bodyguards were following them at a distance. They crossed the Red Gate and the market lane and reached the palace. Gangadhar bowed to Babasaheb and took his departure from there.

Although Gangadhar pretended ignorance before Babasaheb, he was deeply worried inwardly. He was very much concerned about the family honour. What if the king tried to possess the younglady by secret persuasion or force? What would the whole city say if his daughter-in-law is the object of the king's carnal desires? What would his son do if he comes to know that his young wife is desired by Babasaheb? Can he ever allow her to be an adulteress? Or can he give her up to the king? He simply shuddered to think of these ideas. What would be the consequences if they refused to surrender their daughter-in-law to the king? The present friendship between the king and himself will turn into enmity? All right, if he made up his mind to become the enemy of the king, would it be possible to survive there in the kingdom? Gangadhar thought about the various possibilities and could not get a solution. After incessant thinking he came to a decision. He thought of putting an end to the problem by taking away the life of his daughter-in-law Annapurna.

He called his son Rudrappa and said, "Dear son, tomorrow you go to Bailahongala and bring ten large lumps of jaggery, five bags of rice and some cardamom and cloves for the year. We must have a good stock of these things. You may take a servant also with you."

"Yes, father. I was also thinking about that. Shall I go on horseback or by bullock-cart?"

"It's better if you took the bullock-cart."

"Yes, father. Shall I take the cart with those two white and hefty bulls?"

"Why not son? You need the hefty bulls to carry the heavy load."

"Yes, father. I shall start early in the morning."

That night Rudrappa had his sumptuous dinner and went to his bedroom. He stuffed his mouth with betel, *pan*, lime, cardamom and clove and began to chew it leisurely. He enjoyed the sweet aroma of the ingredients of the *pan* in his mouth, and felt a new freshness in the mouth. Annapurna was still having her dinner with her mother-in-law in the kitchen. Rudrappa was eagerly waiting for his sweet wife as he wanted to talk with her to his heart's content before he left for Bailahongala on a long tour. At last when he heard the tinkle of bangles and rustle of the sari, he felt happy. Annapurna bolted the door from inside and gently walked towards the bed and sat beside him. She was also chewing *pan* and betel and her lips were incarnadined and appeared ruddy even in the dim light of the wick-lamp. He gently drew her to his side and enfolded her in his arms and pressed his cheeks against hers. He whispered into her ears,

"My dear, I am so reluctant to be away from you. But what to do? Father has instructed me to go. Therefore, I must."

"Shall I also come with you?"

"No. What about our family-honour? We cannot allow our womenfolk to go about with us for these routine matters."

"In that case, I'll stay back. But you try to finish your work as early as possible and return home."

"Of course, I shall come back very soon *i.e.*, within a fortnight or so. But even that period looks so long to me."

Annapurna was silent as she could not prevent his departure the next morning. He drew her to his side and smothered her with kisses. Then he caressed all her curves passionately until he could no longer control himself. He entered her moist softness and locked himself into her thighs. He penetrated into her and started the gentle strokes rhythmically for a few moments and forgot everything about the world around him. Slowly the sweet pleasure overwhelmed his body thereby appetizing his desire further. She was moaning and grunting with satisfaction. He increased the speed and hardness of his strokes gradually and felt that he was climbing the tower of heavenly pleasure step by step. Finally when he reached the peak of orgasm, he felt a great relief in his veins and filled with a sense of fulfilment. His wife was inundated with the sweetness of milk and honey as it were which was far beyond expression. They sank into a deep sleep undisturbed by any cares or worries of the world.

*****

The next day Rudrappa woke up early in the morning and set out towards Bailahongala in his bullock cart. Annapurna stood in the verandah and waved him farewell with a smile, although she was rather unhappy inwardly. She began to feel lonely even before his bullock cart disappeared in the corner of the lane.

Gangadhar appointed two servants to dig a pit of ten feet in the backyard of his house. The servants took two days to dig the earth. Gangadhar had given them sufficient money to keep the secret. A huge copper cauldron was placed in the pit. Gangadhar's wife had told her daughter-in-law Annapurna to be ready for the worship of Goddess Laxmi. That day Gangadhar sent for a priest to perform the holy service. All that was part of a machination. Annapurna believed that the whole thing was a genuine religious affair. In the evening, the priest came to their house and made all the preparations for the holy service. As the night descended on the earth, the noises of the city began to die down slowly. Everybody in the family was waiting for the midnight hour. There was pindrop silence all around, except for the occasional croaking of frogs. Gangadhar's wife asked her daughter-in-law, "Annapurna, now you go and perform the worship of Goddess Laxmi."

"Yes, madam, I am ready now."

Gangadhar then beckoned to the priest who placed a small bamboo ladder and descended into the pit and placed all the items of worship like flowers, incense, wick-lamps and a tiny idol of Goddess Laxmi. Then he asked Annapurna to descend into the cauldron which was placed in the pit. She gently climbed down the rungs of the ladder and squatted in the cauldron. The priest instructed her to worship the tiny idol of Goddess Laxmi. Accordingly, Annapurna bent her face down and began to wash the idol with water. The priest who was waiting for this moment, instantly placed the copper lid on the cauldron and kept a big stone on it. He could hear the muffled crying from within the cauldron, but he hardened his heart deliberately as he was paid heavily for the inhuman task. Then he hurriedly climbed up the ladder. The servants who were ready with their spades, began to fill the pit with the mud. Although Gangadhar's heart was thumping like hell, he controlled it with a strong will and stood watching the whole situation. His wife who could not control her sorrow, had been crying loudly in the kitchen.

The entire week was spent in crying and wailing. Gangadhar had to use all his talent to silence his wife,

"My dear, you have to bear this sorrow in the interest of family honour. You must see that this news doesn't reach even the neighbours. I have warned the priest and the servants also to keep mum about it. Otherwise it would cost them their lives."

His wife managed to ask him in-between her sobs, "What'l! you tell your son when he returns from Bailahongala?"

"Don't you worry about that. We shall select another bride for him. Now at least I am happy that Babasaheb cannot tarnish the honour of our family. He cannot get Annapurna even if his spies search for her. A great burden is off my chest now."

He wiped the tears off his wife's eyes and tried his best to console her.

*****

Bhaskararao sent for one of his confidential spies and asked him to search for the younglady whom he had seen near the well. The spy did not know why the King wanted the lady, but said,

"Sarkar, I shall try my best to search for her. May I know her name and her family name so that I can easily locate her?"

"Fool, don't you have any commonsense in you? Had I known the name I would have sent my servants directly to her house."

Now the spy seemed to guess at the whole thing. He could understand that something confidential and emotional was involved in it. But he could not question his own King about it. However, he made bold to ask,

"Sarkar, kindly let me know some details of the lady — I mean her appearance, height, complexion, and the possible age."

Although Babasaheb felt embarrassed at his plight, he managed to describe the younglady,

"See man, she is about twenty-five years old. She is tall and strapping. Fair complexion. I saw her near the well outside the Red Gate. Try to locate her at the earliest. I shall reward you properly if you could do this favour to me."

"I shall do my best to locate her, Sarkar," said the spy and bowed himself out of Babasaheb's chamber.

*****

The spy was strictly warned by Babasaheb not to divulge any details of the task to anyone including even the other spies. So he had to do it all alone. Everyday he began to observe the people around the well near the Red Gate and try to identify the younglady who had caught the fancy of Babasaheb. He sat at a safe distance from the well and watched all the men and women coming to and going from the well with their pitchers. Whenever he saw a beautiful woman from the distance, he would feel happy thinking that she might be the younglady he was looking for, but grow disappointed after noticing the sagging folds and wrinkles of her body from the vicinity and go back to his vantage-point. He sat there from morning till evening and developed an ache in the eyes staring at the visitors to the well. Though he felt bored by this kind of espionage, he was happy at the prospects of earning a fat reward from the King. Anyway it was part of his duty and he had no reason to grudge it, thought he. He did his duty very meticulously but could not spot the younglady described by his Sarkar. He thought the lady might have gone to her relatives' house and might return after fifteen days or a month. Thus he waited for her for more than three months but could not get any idea or news about her. At last he grew desperate and gave up the idea of earning some fat reward from Bhaskararao. One day he met Bhaskararao and described the futility of his search for more than two months and got rid of the whole affair for good.

*****

Bhaskararao had received the secret letter from Nanasaheb which he read and felt enthused to carry out the instructions given therein to all the patriots of the Daccan and Karnataka area. It read as follows :

Proclamation

From Dhondo Pant Nana Peshwa, Pant Pradhan to all the Suranjamadars, Jagirdars, Deshmukhs, Deshpandeys and other Jameendars, Patels, Kulkarnis, Naikwads, Shetsandees and the whole of the population of the Deccan and the Carnatik. It is ordered to be proclaimed that the English who are "Kaffirs" came to this country under the pretense of carrying on trade. Afterwards instigating sedition among our Suranjamadars and practising treachery they seized all the Hindu and Mohammadan kingdoms, imprisoning some of the descendants of the former kings and driving others to beggary; they themselves enjoy the country. This is well-known to the whole of you.

The Kaffirs upon the strength of their acquisition of the empire have turned very arrogant and keeping up outward appearances of justice, have most unjustly destroyed and acquired wealth and property. They have been endeavouring to delude and convert the population of this country inducing them to abandon their own religion and caste but having failed by mild means to do this they were about to use force.

Tyranny, wickedness and injustice having been much practised by the Kaffir (English) on the faithful and sin-fearing, I have been commissioned by God to punish the Kaffirs annihilating them and to re-establish the Hindu and Mahammadan kingdoms as formerly and to protect our country as I have conquered the country north of the Narmada river.

To submit to and live under such wicked Kaffirs is very disgraceful. So immediately on the perusal of this proclamation you are bravely to take up your swords and without mercy destroy the Kaffirs. By this you will gain merit and show your manliness and your courage will be proved.

Ye heroes! this is the best time for you to avenge the wrongs and wickedness perpetrated by the Kaffir English on your land and on your kings. By allowing such an opportunity to escape do not suffer the stain of being effeminate and foolish to attach to the people of the South. At the present time the English having disagreements among themselves about their religion are quarreling and fighting and killing each other. The French and the Russians who entertained from a long time a hatred against the English and a design to turn them out of Hindustan have thought this a proper time to carry it out and with this intention they have been sending armies by sea these three months past. The Chinese also have declared war against these Kaffirs and the latter having no army to send against the Chinese are much alarmed. The Persians, Afghans and Ballochees moreover, are ready with their armies collected to aid us. In short, this is the golden time to root out completely the English from this country.

The Kaffir English in order to discourage the population, fabricate false information of their having taken Delhi and other places and having defeated us and make it known among the public, but such ought not to be believed. If you allow this time to escape, all of you will be liable to punishment from us and for that guilt whatever jageers, lands and other subsistence you may possess will be brought under attachment. This proclamation is published by the order of Ullu Shah Bundeegah Ullu Hozoor, the Emperor of Delhi.

By Rao Pant Pradhan Peshwa

After reading this letter Bhaskararao felt a new enthusiasm and felt hopeful about his own kingdom as well as the other ones. He had heard the news that similar messages had been sent to other kings and Desais of the Deccan. That was the reason why they were all coming together to fight for the common cause of saving their country and honour from the British people.

*****

Three months had elapsed now after the meeting with Mr. Manson at Jamakhandi. Babasaheb was smouldering with anger at the red-faced fellow. He felt that he must do some thing about it. He, therefore, sent out his messengers to fetch all the four friends like Bhimaraya of Mundaragi, Kenchanagouda Desai of Hammigi, Yasavantraya of Jamakhandi and Virarani of Chitradurga. Likewise he sent letters to the Desais of Soratur, Govinakoppa, Dogaludosi Inamdar and Srirangaraya of Anegundi.

*****

Bhimaraya of Mundaragi and Kenchanagouda of Hammigi dismounted from the horse carriage in front of the *wada* of Desai of Soratige. Servant Sinappa who was drawing water from the well, saw the guests. He, therefore, hurried into the house and conveyed the news to the Desai who had been wiping his mouth after having his breakfast and a bowl of milk. He rushed out of his room to know who the guest must be. He was a bit surprised by the sight of two guests *i.e.* Bhimaraya Nadiger and Kenchanagouda Desai of Hammigi seated in the front hall. They exchanged amicabilities. Kenchanagouda embraced the Desai of Soratige and said, "Whoever knew that your house be looted like this? Everything is part of Lord Shiva's will !" Bhimaraya added, "Nothing happens according to our wish. We have to follow the path prescribed by the Great Lord."

Then the servants brought in the luggage of the guests from the horse carriage. The Desai of Soratige ordered his servants to make arrangements for hot water for the guests. Accordingly the guests finished their bath. Kenchanagouda completed the morning duty of *istalinga* worship and put it back into the golden casket hung around his neck by a golden chain. Bhimaraya completed his morning duty of Vaidic worship. Then they were offered sumptuous breakfast of sweetballs, *uppittu* and milk. They swallowed the items with gusto. All the while the Desai of Soratige was inwardly worried about why those guests might have come to his house. He could not even guess it properly.

When they sat together after the breakfast, Bhimaraya stared at the face of Desai of Soratige and asked him, "You look worried about something, perhaps about our unexpected visit to your home. We shall tell you the reason privately in the room on the first floor." "As you please," said the Desai of Soratige. "I inferred that there must be some serious purpose behind your unexpected visit." Then he took them to the room on the first floor.

Bhimaraya bolted the door from inside the room, and said, "This is an ideal spot for confidential discussion. Our words will not be overheard by anybody." Then Kenchanagouda and Bhimaraya sat leaning against a big pillow. Soratige Desai sat blinking his eyes at both the guests. Bhimaraya was impatient to convey his message. He twisted the ends of his bow-like mustaches and said, "I am not able to hide anything from you, both the Desais of Hammigi and Soratige are like two elephants in the forest called Hindustan. But the Company Sarkar has been acting as a lion to these and such elephants. You know the signet of the Company Sarkar contains the picture of two lions who seem to be bent on hunting the elephants. Should we tolerate such an insult ? Babasaheb of Naragund who is senior to all of us has invited all of us to a special confidential meeting at Naragund. I have come here as his messenger. Babasaheb will explain to you all the details when you attend the meeting there." Bhimaraya took out a sealed cover from his inner pocket and gently handed it over to Soratige Desai, whose face had already been wet with perspiration. Kenchanagouda was watching the two with keen interest.

Soratige Desai broke the wax-seal and opened the cover with tremulous hands. He took out the letter which was addressed to him by Babasaheb of Naragund. He poured his eyes over the sentences and grasped the sentences. The summary of the letter was as follows : The people of the East India Company came to India with the pretext of carrying trade here, but later they began to rule over us. Thus we Indians have become impotent fellows. They have been taking advantage of our personal and communal defferences and conflicts, and sitting over our heads. When they attacked Mallasarja Desai of Kittur, we kept quiet. Similarly we kept quiet when they attacked and insulted the Maharaja of Jamakhandi and Jahagirdar of Nippani. Now the Raja of Surapur and the Raja of Ramadurg have got into trouble. All these trouble is due to the Company Sarkar which is striking root in Hindustan. In the Northern Hindustan, the kings of Lucknow, Kanpur, Allahabad, Kashi and Aligarh have rebelled against the Ingreji people and ousted them and captured Delhi. The rebellion was led by Dhondopant Nanasaheb Peshwa himself who finally succeeded in enthroning Bahadur Shah in Delhi. The Ingreji people have taken a lot of care to prevent this news from reaching the common people of Hindustan. But Nanasaheb Peshwa has issued a *farman* in the name of Bahadur Shah of Delhi and ordered all the Desais, Deshpandes, Jahagirdars, Patils, Kulkarnis and other Shetsanadis of Southern part of Hindustan to rebel against the British people. We have enclosed a copy of the *farman* for your kind information. It is your bounden duty to bow down to the order of Nanasaheb Peshwa. If you wish to cooperate with us in this matter, you please attend the meeting which will take place at the palace of Naragund on Tuesday evening. If you don't attend the meeting, we shall consider you as the supporters of Ingreji fellows and as per Nanasaheb's order we shall punish and insult you as treacherous people."

The letter ended with the signature of Bhaskararao Bhave of Naragund. Then Soratige Desai began to read Dhondopant Nanasaheb's *farman* with deep interest. When he completed reading, his silken shirt was wet with perspiration. His face grew pale and his throat grew parched and he seemed to have lost his power of speech. With tremulous hands he folded the letter, kept it back in the cover and sat silent with his head bent down. Bhimaraya and Kenchanagouda appeared to be two ugly emissaries of Lord Yama.

Bhimaraya said to Soratige Desai, "You seem to be quite scared. But you need not become nervous. We wish you to be bold," and offered him his scarf for wiping off his perspiration. Soratige Desai rubbed his face and neck with the scarf and began to fan himself with one end of the scarf. Then he said in a low pitch, "This is a very serious matter. Presently the Company Sarkar is our rulers. We have great respect for Dhondopant Nanasaheb Peshwa although he has lost his kingdom. Likewise we cannot disobey the words of Babasaheb of Naragund. I only request you to give me some time to think coolly about the matter. I shall take the decision as directed by God."

Bhimaraya understood the oscillation of Soratige Desai's mind. He, therefore, tried to enhearten him. He held his palms, stared into his eyes and assured him, "Please remember that none of us has any wish to harm you. We have sought your help only in the interest of our country. The meeting is scheduled for tomorrow evening. We shall give you time upto this evening. You may let us know your decision by then. We shall be happy if you decide to attend the meeting. Kenchanagouda has a horse carriage in which you can go to Naragund and return from there.

As for me I have my horse." Then Bhimaraya and Kenchanagouda lay down for a bit of relaxation.

Then Soratige Desai walked down to the ground floor with a heavy heart. For a moment he wanted to tell his wife everything, but feared that she might be scared beyond measure by the news. He, therefore, entered his puja room and sat there with a blank mind. The death of his relative Chinnappanayaka had saddened all the members of his family. Then he mechanically went through the motions of puja and prayed to God whole-heartedly to help him out of the dilemma. He walked out of the puja room and entered his wife's room.

Sitabai was reciting a religious narrative connected with *Sola Somavar Vrita*. He stood silently there until she completed her recital. When she looked at his perplexed face, she asked him, "You look serious, What's the matter? What news have the guests brought?" "I have come to consult you about the very same thing," said he. Then he narrated to her all the details of Babasaheb's call for the meeting and significance of Nanasaheb's *farman*. He further explained to her his dilemma, "We will be dubbed as treacherous people if we do not attend the meeting called at Naragund by Babasaheb. If we attend the meeting, we will definitely be harassed by the Company Sarkar who are our present rulers. I do not know what to do in this matter. I am told that women have a pure intuition. You have just finished the holy recitation and your mind is very pure now. Therefore you tell me what decision I must take so that I shall do accordingly." Sitabai sat with closed eyes for a few moments and her lips were moving. After a little while, she opened her eyes and said to her husband, "I feel that you must respect Babasaheb Sarkar's invitation and attend the meeting at Naragund. I am directed by God to say so." Soratige Desai's dilemma was solved at last. In the evening he sat in Kenchanagouda's horse-carriage and journeyed towards Naragund.

Soratige Desai and Kenchanagouda reached Naragund at around midnight. But Bhimaraya had reached Naragund two hours before them by riding his horse fast. He had met

Babasaheb and reported all the important details. He was happy to learn that the Raja of Surapur and the Nawab of Savanur had already come to Naragund.

The arrangements for the accommodation for the guests were made on the first floor of the palace and in the adjacent office vacated for that purpose. Soratige Desai and Hammigi Desai were sent into a room where the Jahagirdars of Gajendragad and of Sondur had already settled. A separate room was assigned to Raja Venkatappanayaka who was accompanied by his Mussalman secretary and his vassal Desais. Another room was assigned to the Nawab of Savanur and the Jahagirdar of Nippani. The Desais of Mudhol, Jamakhandi had not come to Naragund, but sent word to Babasaheb that they would abide by any decision taken by the secret meeting and that their coming there might arouse the suspicion of Ingreji officers and create premature problems. Most of these dignitaries were tired from their journeys and therefore, fell into sound sleep after partaking of their dinner.

They were all awakened by the sweet notes of *nagaswaram*, drums and cymbals played at the turret of the temple of Lord Venkateshwara on the hillside. They got up and completed their morning ablutions and had cold water bath in the early morning. By that time a servant came there and announced humbly, "Babasaheb Sarkar is ready to go to the temple and requested the willing ones to accompany him."

By that time a bugle sounded in front of the palace. Babasaheb stood ready with his wife Savitribai. He was clad in an immaculate white dhoti and an embroided woolen shawl across his shoulders. He held in his hand a silver basket full of puja items. Savitribai was clad in a green bordered sari and bare footed. She held in her hands a wicker basket full of flowers and tulsi leaves and a silver container filled with turmeric and vermilion powders. When the bugler sounded the bugle twice the members of the royal family stood behind Babasaheb. Hammigi and Soratige Desais walked down together. Behind them came the Raja of Surapur and his retinue. So did the Nawab of Savanur and the Jahagirdar of Nippani.

As the bugle was sounded for the third time, the members of the royal family of Babasaheb and his honourable guests moved towards the temple, to the accompaniment of the music of drums and pipes. The guests observed many familiar as well as unfamiliar faces in the group. They mounted innumerable stone-steps and reached the big yard of the temple. Babasaheb's love of discipline could be seen in every detail of everyday activities. Then they entered the temple. Babasaheb and his wife sat facing the deity in the *sanctum sanctorum.* Inside it were five brahmins who began the holy worship by reciting the Vedic mantras. When they completed the course of puja and began to wave the holy *arati*, the sun in the east was rising. Then the priest offered *prasad* and *tirtha* to Babasaheb and fruits and flowers in Savitribai's hem of sari.

By that time Bhimaraya came near Babasaheb and whispered something in his ears. Babasaheb, therefore, led Raja Venkatappanayaka of Surapur by the hand and took him upto the door of *sanctum sanctorum*. Raja Venkatappanayaka fell prostrate in front of the deity to offer obeisance. Then the priests offered him fruits and recited benedictory verses in Sanskrit. Then the other guests walked to the *sanctum sanctorum* one by one and offered their homage. When the Nawab of Savanur received his fruits from the priests, Bhimaraya suggested to the priests to recite royal benediction to the guests. Accordingly the priests recited the Vedic mantras and blessed the Nawab of Savanur who felt very happy. Bhimaraya was watching every detail very carefully. After the morning puja Babasaheb, his family and guests returned to the palace to the accompaniment of drums and pipes.

By that time breakfast was arranged for all the guests. All the guests sat on the wooden plank seats in a row. Babasaheb and Bhimaraya were supervising everything. First some sweets were served. Cashewnut and Kerubeeja were also kept in front of the guests. After *uppittu* was consumed, masala milk with excellent flavour was served in silver bowls. When everybody was through with his breakfast, Bhimaraya announced that Babasaheb Sarkar would have an interview with every guest separately.

The interview was arranged in the office adjacent to the palace. Three seats with cushions were kept in the office hall. Raja Venkatappanayaka of Surapur sat in the centre and Babasaheb Sarkar and the Nawab of Savanur sat on both sides. A cushioned seat was kept in front of them for the guests to be interviewed. Bhimaraya called in the guests one by one and introduced them to Babasaheb Sarkar. All the interviewers used to congratulate them for their willingness to attend the meeting and exchanged amicabilities. After the formalities, Babasaheb Sarkar used to explain the reason for calling the secret meeting, in response to the *farman* received from Dhondopant Nanasaheb Peshwa and request for military and financial help from the guests. He also explained to them how he would report the names of all supporters and nonsupporters to Nanasaheb who was likely to vanquish the Ingreji people in Southern Hindustan and establish the Hindu empire.

When the interview was over, it was past midday. Every interviewee kept quiet about the details of the interview and did not discuss them with one another. They had their sumptuous lunch and relaxed in the late afternoon.

The evening meeting was scheduled to be conducted in the templeyard. Hence the priests completed the evening puja before sunset and vacated the templeyard. The royal servants took charge of the templeyard and made seating arrangements. After the sunset, the guests were conducted to the templeyard in the light of torches. On an elevated platform were kept ten guns in a row. Behind each gun stood a golandaj. As Bhaskararao Bhave mounted the steps of the temple, along with Raja Venkatappanayaka of Surapur and the Nawab of Savanur, the bugler sounded his bugle thrice. The guests followed the three kings. All of them stood in front of the guns. Then the golandajs thundered the guns one after the others. There was a series of bangs thereby exciting all the kings gathered there. The sound echoed from the hill for a few seconds. The smell of gun powder wafted in the air.

After appreciating the charge of cannons, the guests entered the place of meeting and occupied their cushioned seats. In the central place sat Raja Venkatappanayaka of Surapur who was flanked by Babasaheb Sarkar on the right side and by the Nawab of Savanur on the left. Raja Venkatappanayaka was clad in his royal dress. He had put on a long gown of panther skin, loose trousers and Pune slippers. His head was decked with a gem studded cap with silver brocade. Babasaheb Sarkar was clad in his normal dress. He had put on a white dhoti, and an orange coloured gown. His head was decked with a red *pagadi*. He had slung a woolen shawl on his shoulders. The Nawab of Savanur was clad in his usual Muslim garments. He had worn a loose white pyjama and a white gown. His head was decked with a turkey cap. Most of the other kings, Desais and Jahagirdars were clad in white dhotis and gowns. Some of them wore gold-brocade-turbans on their heads in a very stylish fashion.

Babasaheb Sarkar stood up and welcomed all the guests very heartily. He said, "My dear friends, I have already acquainted you with the main points in the morning interview. Now I have nothing new to add. But I shall mention only a couple of points. In this war with the Ingreji people, we have to accept the leadership of Raja Venkatappanayaka of Surapur Kingdom. He is a leader not only for Karnataka, but for the whole of southern Hindustan, which was once upon a time, part of the Vijayanagara Empire. Since the kings of Surapur were the close friends of the Emperors of Vijayanagara, now they represent the forgotten empire. Here I have a personal letter from Nanasaheb Peshwa sent on behalf of the Bahaddur Shah of Delhi. Nanasaheb Peshwa has suggested that Raja Venkatappanayaka of Surapur should preside over this function. He has also ordered that after kicking out the Ingreji people from our country Raja Venkatappanayaka of Surapur should become the Emperor of southern Hindustan." All the kings gathered there clapped loudly in appreciation of Nanasaheb's orders.

Then Babasaheb Sarkar praised the heroic tradition of the King of Surapur, his learning in Sanskrit, Parsi and English, his patriotism, love of freedom and sense of justice. Finally he requested Raja Venkatappanayaka to offer his presidential remarks.

Raja Venkatappanayaka of Surapur stood up and began to speak eloquently in his wonderful voice. His speech appeared like the roar of a lion. He spoke fluently for one full hour, "We must all get ready to fight the Ingreji people and kick them out of our holy land called Bharatakhanda. We must be ready even to lay down our lives. We are certain of achieving success in this war of independence. If we die on the battlefield, we shall attain heroic heaven. If we succeed in vanquishing the British people, we will be able to rule our country. I, therefore, appeal to you to be patriotic and participate in this war. Those who help and cooperate with us will be deemed as our friends and those who shy away or back out from this war will be deemed as our enemies and punished accordingly after establishing the native rule in our land." Bhimaraya who had sat in the back row of the audience suddenly clapped his hands. Consequently others also clapped loudly. The loud clap of hands echoed mildly from the hill.

Raja Venkatappanayaka continued his speech, "Every King and every patriot has a right to participate in the liberation movement of our mother country. How tó help and what is the nature of help and such other details are known to our close friend and patriot Sri Nadiger Bhimaraya. Therefore everybody should obey him. We have authorized him to punish those who are either indifferent or disobedient to him. We have also requested him to act as the Chief Commander of this war of freedom." As these words were spoken, there was a loud clapping again which echoed from the hill. Babasaheb Sarkar stood up, walked upto Bhimaraya, hugged him and patted his back. He said in high pitch, "Our Nadiger Bhimaraya will be the right hand man of Raja Venkatappanayaka as Tatyatopi is the right hand man of Dhondopant Nanasaheb." Again Babasaheb Sarkar's exhortation touched the hearts of the patriot kings deeply. They, therefore, clapped their hands loudly.

Then Raja Venkatappanayaka exercised his presidential right and requested Nadiger Bhimaraya to speak a few words. Babasaheb Sarkar led Bhimaraya by the hands to the stage. Again there was loud clapping. Bhimaraya bowed down to the kings in the audience and started his speech. "My dear fellowmen and patriots, I am an ordinary servant of our motherland. I am compelled to talk a few words in response to the order given by Raja Venkatappanayaka, the great patriot, scholar and lover of freedom. He has already described how our country has been caught in the clutches of the Anglian *raksasas*. This is not the time for us to sit idly like cowards. We have great heroes like Raja Venkatappanayaka in our country. We have to search for them and organize our strength. Whereas the Mughal Badshah is the Emperor of the northern Hindustan, Raja Venkatappanayaka should be the emperor of the southern Hindustan. We cannot wear bangles like women at this juncture. We have to awake now and inject new life in our fellow-men. The Ingreji fellows take our cotton to England and sell the cotton goods back to India. Hence the starvation of our weavers. You prevent this cotton being sent out of Hindustan. Some of our own merchants have been helping the Ingreji people in this business. I, therefore, advise you to burn all the cotton bales wherever you see them. Similarly you shoot the Ingreji people wherever you meet them. For this war of independence we want both money and people in large quantity and quality respectively. I appeal to all the rich people to help us with money and we can collect a large number of poor people to fight as soldiers. When we combine money and man power, we can easily kick out the Ingreji people from our motherland. Once our Raja Venkatappanayaka becomes the Emperor of southern Hindustan, you will be amply rewarded with money and wealth. If you are not cooperative in this righteous war, you will have to die."

When Bhimaraya completed his speech, bowed down to the audience and returned to his place, there was loud clapping again. The golandajs filled the cannons once again and fired them. Everyone felt as if the war had already started.

The next morning Bhimaraya and Babasaheb Sarkar met the guests one by one. When Soratige Desai met them, Bhimaraya welcomed him cordially and asked him to be seated. Then he praised Soratige Desai's wealth to impress upon Babasaheb Sarkar. He, then, said to Soratige Desai, "We do not expect any money from you. I can bring it from anywhere by robbing the rich people. But what we really need now is your patronage. We request you to be a supporter for all the freedom-fighters. We have some problem in feeding our soldiers. We, therefore, send a hundred *lambani* people from Jalawadi village. We request you to collect foodgrains in your village as well as in the neighbouring villages and send them to us through these *lambanis*. You have to do us another favour *i.e.* you must give shelter to the freedom fighters and the members of their family if required. I hope you will agree to these." Soratige Desai felt that his throat was parched. He went on nodding his assent to Bhimaraya's requests.

In the afternoon, a servant went to Gangadhararaya and informed him that he was requested to see Babasaheb Sarkar. As Gangadhararaya entered the hall, Bhimaraya asked him to be seated and said to him, "You are a gentleman. We will not count you among the rich ones gathered here. We do not expect any money, or fighting, or shelter. But you have to do us an important favour *i.e.*, you have to go to Surapur along with the Maharaja who will give some letters. You will have to take those letters to Hyderabad and meet some people there. Since you are a thorough gentleman, nobody will suspect you. That is why we wish to make use of you. From today, you have to obey the secretary of the Maharaja of Surapur." Gangadhararaya mechanically agreed to the request and took his leave.

Thus all the guests were invited separately to the office hall where Babasaheb Sarkar and Nadiger Bhimaraya requested each one of them to render a particular kind of help. Most of them promised to help in the best of their capacity. In the evening, all of them took leave of Babasaheb and went back to their respective cities in the horse-carriages.

*****

The news of the meeting of five kings and a queen reached Chandralal Deshpande who was a native of Navalagund which was twelve miles away from Naragund to the south-west. Chandralal Deshpande had a grouse against Babasaheb of Naragund. Now he did not want to miss the golden opportunity of betraying Babasaheb to the East India Government. He, therefore, sent a messenger namely Ramu to Mr. Manson and briefed him about the confidential decision of united fighting that the five Desais and the Rani had taken at Naragund.

Mr. Manson was a very clever British officer who used to visit all the native princely states of his jurisdiction once in six months and gather latest information and intelligence about them. Ramu met him confidentially and told him how he had been sent there by Chandralal Deshpande of Navalagund to inform him that Babasaheb of Naragund had been consolidating his military forces in order to fight against the British Government. On hearing the news Manson knit his brows and contorted his face with anger. He said to Ramu, "Thank you very much for the news. Please convey my thanks to Mr. Chandralal Deshpande. You wait here for a day. Tomorrow I shall give a letter." He then sent Ramu to the guest room and arranged for his boarding and lodging.

Manson was so angry with Babasaheb and his activities that he wanted to put an end to them at his earliest. He remembered the courage that Babasaheb had shown in the Kolhapur meeting. He also remembered the arrogance and defiance that Babasaheb exhibited at the Jamakhandi meeting. He considered Babasaheb as a potential enemy and thought of crushing him as early as possible. He said to himself,

"I must kill this snake Babasaheb by hook or by crook. Otherwise he can be very dangerous. I must put an end to this."

That night Manson thought of a plan for his future action. He thought of enervating Babasaheb by using his own men against him. The next morning he called Ramu to his room and gave him a sealed pocket containing a letter in it and instructed him,

"Mr. Ramu, please, take these letters to Mr. Baniya Bapu and Krishnaji Pant secretly. You must see that nobody should know this. Here is the reward for you."

He gave Ramu a small bag of gold coins. Ramu who was a very poor fellow was overjoyed to have the gold coins. But immediately he remembered another difficulty and asked Mr. Manson,

"I am ready to obey you whole-heartedly, Saheb. But what if I cannot get entry into Naragund? You know, Saheb, it is surrounded by a big wall and is strictly guarded at the gates."

"O I see. I have given you this money precisely because of the risk you have to take. Frankly speaking, I cannot guide you as to how to accomplish this. You must do it somehow or the other. Why not disguise yourself and seek entry into Naragund?"

When Ramu heard the suggestion offered by Manson, he thought it to be a very good plan and felt confident of himself. He thought he could do it very successfully. He said,

"Yes, sir. I shall take the guise of a fortune-teller and do the work."

"OK. Thank you very much."

Manson rose from his seat and shook hands with Ramu and bid farewell to him with a smile.

*****

Lieutenant Thomson had joined service as Police Superintendent of Dharwad district. Six months had gone by. He was trying to familiarize himself with all the local details. He used to visit various towns and villages in the Dharwad district and keep an eye over the public life which required law and order.

One day he put on his professional outfit and hat on his head. He mounted his horse and whipped it gently. The horse went ahead slowly and descended the hill of the collector's office. He took the direction of Hubballi. The horse began to canter. He tilted his hat to his right side to shield his face from the glare of westward sun. When he reached Unakal Tank, he saw a few native Indians and a couple of Britishmen. Goaded by his professional curiosity, Mr. Thomson directed his horse towards them. As he went near them a British officer saluted him and said, "How do you do?" Then Mr. Thomson responded to them with a gesture of his hand and said gently, "May I know who you are all and what business you have been carrying on here?" The Britishman replied, "You have asked me the right question. We the whitemen who have come far away from our country have got to know one another and should not stand on formalities. I happen to be a representative of a British company called Bryce and Co. in Mumbai. My duty is to purchase American cotton here and send it upto Kumata. Besides, there are about four or five white officers here who happen to be representatives of different companies. The owner of our company Mr. Nigel Bryce himself has come today. We purchase the American cotton or Kumata cotton supplied by the local farmers and arrange to send it on ox-back to Kumata through the Devamani pass. Then our company arranges for its transport in ship from Kumata to England. I am sorry I did not tell you my name. I am Mr. William Smith. Please come on with me. I shall introduce you to the other white friends." He took Mr. Thomson through the narrow path between the rows of bullock carts loaded with cotton bales.

Mr. William Smith took Mr. Thomson to a tent where many native Indians and white men were seated on wooden stools and discussing business matters. Mr. Smith said, "I want to introduce you to these whitemen, but I am sorry I did not ask your name at all." Then Mr. Thomson introduced himself, "I am Lieutenant Thomson. I joined as the Police Superintendent of Dharwad district six months ago." Then all the whitemen stood up and came forward to shake hands with Mr. Thomson and introduce themselves to him. One of them was Mr. Michael Stone, another was Robert Davidson and the third was Nigel Bryce. Mr. Thomson did not remember the other two whitemen.

Then Nigel Bryce stared at Mr. Thomson and requested him, "Kindly take your seat and rest for a while. I am sorry I cannot treat you better in this tent." Thomson replied, "Don't worry about any treatment. I have had a heavy lunch at Dharwad a little while ago. But my horse seems to be hungry, I request you to feed him a bit." Then Nigel Bryce beckoned to William Smith who took Thomson's horse to the temporary stable and offered it a little fodder.

The whitemen began to discuss their business with the native agents in Kannada. Thomson felt uneasy and apologized, "I am sorry I am disturbing your business." Nigel Bryce replied, "Not at all. Our representatives will take care of the business. I have come here only for supervision." Then Thomson asked him, "Could you please tell me when you came to India and what you have been doing here all these years?" Nigel Bryce replied, "My elder brother Mr. A.C. Bryce runs a company called M/s Bryce and Co., which has several branches in different parts of India and which has started many experimental farms and encourage the farmers to grow cotton of new breed *i.e.* American cotton. I came to India four years ago. Our Company buys cotton from the native farmers and arranges to send it to England." Then a native servant brought a brass bowl of tea and offered it to Thomson. Nigel Bryce requested him, "Please have the tea. You seem to be tired. May I know which town you are riding to?" Thomson said, "It is sure that I am tired. But after talking with you all, I feel quite relaxed now. You asked me about my destination. This morning I have ridden my horse from Dambala to Dharwad. Now I wish to ride back to Gadag. But my horse seems to be very tired. It may not excuse me."

Nigel Bryce thought for a while and said, "If that is the case, why not stay at Hubballi? Or you may stay at the guest house of our experimental farm at Kusugal. That guest house is built specially for Europeans. Two or three of our friends will give you company there." Thomson felt satisfied by this suggestion. He thought it to be a good opportunity to know the life of people of his district. He, therefore, said, "I am very lucky to enjoy your hospitality for the night," and thanked Nigel Bryce by shaking hands with him. "It's good that you have agreed to be our guest for the night. We shall finish our business within an hour. Then we shall ride back to Kusugal. Until then you may relax yourself by listening to our business talk," said Nigel Bryce. He took Thomson to a row of bullock carts loaded with cotton bales. Thomson listened to the dialogues between William Smith and Sivbasappasetti, who had brought cotton bales from Hubballi.

"I swear by Lord Siva that this is the cotton from Gadag. I am not cheating you," said Sivabasappasetti.

"I swear by myself that this cotton is not from Gadag. The yarn of Gadag cotton is not so short. And it has a better shine. You have brought it from Raichur and lie to me that it is from Gadag," said William Smith.

Sivabasappasetti was really surprised at William Smith's business acumen. He thought inwardly that the whitemen were very intelligent and efficient both in trade and in administration. He did not know how to convince the Englishman. He felt frustrated and sat down on the ground by keeping his palms over his temples.

Then Shamarao Sirurkar came there, higgled haggled with Sivabasappasetti and bought his cotton bales at a relatively cheap rate. Sivabasappasetti grew helpless, sold his cotton and returned to Hubballi with a sense of disappointment.

Lieutenant Thomson who was watching these business deals felt amused by them. As the evening set in, they completed their quota of business for the day and began to ride their horses towards Kusugal farm. On the way Thomson grew very curious to know more about the cotton crop in India. He asked Mr. Nigel Bryce, "By the way, when did you start growing American cotton here in India?" Then Nigel Bryce replied, "The credit of popularizing the American cotton in India goes to an American planter called Mercer. That was the time when there was a great enmity between the British and the Americans. At that time Captain Bylace went to America and brought a few American cotton planters and some variety of cotton seeds stealthily to India. He conducted many experiments in cotton growing in India, but most of them turned out to be unsuccessful. Captain Bylace was deeply frustrated in his efforts. But the American farmer Mr. Mercer enheartened his master Bylace and came to the plain land of Dharwad district for his experimentation. He conducted his first experiment in Kusugal farm of about ten acres. He grew two types of cotton *i.e.* upland Georgian and New Orleans. His experiment was very successful. Consequently he encouraged the farmers of Navalagund, Naragund, Gadag and Ron talukas to grow those varieties of cotton. So cotton was grown in one hundred thirty-five thousand acres of land. But this year it has decreased by ten thousand acres of land."

Nigel Bryce was a talkative man who narrated the story of American cotton in India continuously. Thomson listened to him very patiently. Their horses were moving ahead with normal speed. Thomson was suddenly seized with curiosity about the last sentence of Nigel Bryce. He, therefore, asked him, "Why did it decrease suddenly this year?"

Nigel Bryce felt enthused by Thomson's curious question. He was eloquent in explaining the details. He said, "Sir, you may not know that we have made arrangements for encouraging the growing of American cotton in the Company Sarkar area. The Mamledars go to the villages and pressurize the farmers to reserve certain portion of land for growing cotton. Until the last year also we had arranged for the American cotton-growing in Naragund area. But this year the ruler of Naragund has ordered that no farmer in his land should grow American cotton. Hence the farmers have grown only jowar and wheat and a bit of

Kumata cotton. But, you know, our Manchester Mills require only the American breed of cotton *i.e.*, either upland Georgian or New Orleans one."

As they crossed Hosur and rode ahead, Thomson noticed a big cart with a heavy load pulled by eight oxen moving northwards. About eight to ten drivers were goading the oxen ahead by twisting their tails. Thomson grew curious, and rode his horse fast and went near the moving cart. He observed the peculiar garments of the cart-drivers and guessed that they did not belong to Dharwad district. He, therefore, asked those cartmen, "Gentlemen, where do you come from and what are you transporting in this cart?" Then one of the cartman stepped forward and replied, "We are from Mysore area. We have our smithy in Chikkamagalur. The King of Naragund had ordered us six months ago to supply ten guns. Therefore we are taking them in the cart to Naragund."

Thomson and Nigel Bryce felt surprised by the cartman's answer. The cartman counter questioned them boldly, "You seem to be *Vilayati* men. In our Mysore region we don't see the like of you. But in these western villages, your people can be seen almost everywhere. By the way, what's your profession? Agriculture? Business? Or Government service?" Nigel Bryce replied, "Ours is cotton business. We grow *Vilayati* cotton in this part and we have our experimental farm in Kusugal." Bryce would have said something about Thomson also, but the latter beckoned to him to be silent. Then the cartman joined his group and began to goad their oxen forward.

Nigel Bryce and Thomson continued their horse ride. Lieutenant Thomson who had heard and seen something connected with Bhaskararao Bhave of Naragund had grown alert about his duty as a Police Superintendent of Dharwad district. He saw the seeds of rebellion and non cooperation in the behaviour of Babasaheb of Naragund and wanted to bring it to the notice of higher authorities and also to arrange for a more intense collection of intelligence about the chief of Naragund. He did not wish to reveal his professional secrets to Mr. Nigel Bryce. He, therefore, said to Nigel Bryce, "I am very thankful to you for your invitation to the farm-house at Kusugal. But you know, I am a Government servant and therefore, have to attend to many things. Now I have got to go to Navalagund. Please guide me as to how to reach there via Kiresur. I will be very thankful to you for that." Niger Bryce was a bit surprised by Thomson's decision and stared into his eyes for a moment. He did not make any comment on him. He took him upto the road leading towards Kiresur village and showed him the north-eastern direction of Navalagund. He also pointed out to him the blue haze of the semi oval shape of the hill of Navalagund in the north-eastern horizon. Thomson saw the distant hill and confirmed the spot of his destination. He thanked Nigel Bryce and rode his horse a bit fast. His horse had fed well on fodder at Unakal and also rested for a while. Being refreshed now, it seemed to understand his rider's intention and began to canter thereby raising cloudlets of dust.

Four hours had gone by when Lieutenant Thomson reached Navalagund. He rode straight to Dak-Bungalow and ordered the watchman to bring Mamledar Moreshwara. Then he rested in a room for a while. After a few minutes Mamledar Moreshwara came there along with the Hawaldar and few sepoys. Instantly he arranged for Thomson's bath and dinner. It was past midnight when Thomson had his bath and sumptuous dinner. The Mamledar sat blinking his eyes in front of Thomson. The Hawaldar and his sepoys were dozing. The Lieutenant called Mamledar Moreshwara to his side and whispered his orders to him. "I am assigning a special responsibility to you. You please make a note of it in your diary. You send a few spies in disguise to Naragund and report all the activities of Bhaskararao Bhave to Oglivey, Magistrate of Dharwad every day. And send me the copies of the same report simultaneously. This is my strict order and you have to do it very seriously." Mamledar Moreshwara had no choice at all. He replied, "Yes sir, I shall do my best in this matter." Then Thomson lay down on the woolen mattress on the wooden cot. As he was utterly tired, he fell into sound sleep and began to snore loudly. Mamledar Moreshwara walked out of the room, ordered the watchman to arrange for boiled eggs and tea for Lieutenant Thomson in the morning. Then he returned home worrying about the heavy responsibility placed upon his shoulders.

Lieutenant Thomson came to know from people that there was a severe famine in some talukas of Dharwad district. He, therefore, decided to roam the countryside and familiarize himself with the condition of villagers. He remembered that he had promised the villagers of Melodi that he would visit their village once mainly for hunting the wild boars. So he sent a servant to Melodi in the evening and asked him to inform the gouda of the village to arrange about 25 or 30 hunters and some hounds the next day.

The next morning Lieutenant Thomson took his gun and rode to Melodi. But he was surprised to discover that no preparations were made in the village in spite of his instructions sent previously. He saw the *Gouda* and the *Shanubhoga* sitting in the *chawadi* and waiting for him. When Thomson enquired them about the preparations for hunting, the Gouda replied in a lachrymose voice, "Saheb, most of the houses in the village have been vacated. There has been a severe famine in this area this year. People have started starving. They have been deserting the village and going in search of livelihood in the rainy areas." Then the *Shanubhoga* also seconded the gouda. Lieutenant Thomson felt rather disappointed. But yet goaded by his professional curiosity, he enquired an old messenger about a number of details. The old messenger told him how many villagers died of starvation in the village, how many of them have how much provision in their house, who belonged to which caste and sub caste and how many people left the village for the rainy belt. Lieutenant Thomson interrupted him, "Is there any guarantee that the people who go to the rainy belt will certainly get their livelihood?" Then the old messenger replied, "Not all will go to the green belt, huzoor. The young and healthy ones have joined Bhimaraya's army and been living happily." When

Thomson heard the name of Bhimaraya, his curiosity was aroused instantly and therefore, he began to make detailed enquiries about the same.

The old messenger narrated all the details about Bhimaraya's army that he happened to know. He told Thomson how many young men from his village had joined Bhimaraya's army in the past fifteen days, how Bhimaraya used look after the soldiers like a father and provide them with two full meals of roti and *dal* and a bowl of milk everyday and how he had employed about forty to fifty maid servants to cook the food for the soldiers.

Thomson asked the old messenger, "Can you tell me the place where Bhimaraya's army has been camping?" The old man replied, "Saheb, I do not know it. In fact nobody knows it for certain. Some people say that it has been camping on the Kappattagudda hill. Some other say that it is either this side or that side of the river.

Then the gouda took Thomson around in the village and showed him the different lanes where people had deserted their homes. Finally the gouda took Thomson to his house and showed him half a bag of jowar and asked him as to how to face the situation. Thomson suddenly remembered something and asked him, "In my last visit to your village I had met a brahmin youth in the *chawadi* and given him a gift of five rupees. Where is he now?" The gouda replied, "Saheb, he is Martanda, son of Subbannabhatta, who left for Pune a week ago. They have only two *chitti* of jowar in their house. Martanda is deeply upset about the poverty." Lieutenant Thomson expressed his desire to see the brahmin boy. Immediately the old man went and brought Martanda. Thomson saw the two of them coming from a distance. The gouda whispered to Thomson, "This fellow wanted to leave his mother alone in the house and join Bhimaraya's army. It was a big task for us to make him change his decision."

By that time, Martanda came there along with the old man and saluted to Lieutenant Thomson, by joining his palms. Thomson shook hands with him and patted on his back affectionately. Then he said, “Mr. Martanda, we don’t like your joining the army of Bhimaraya. Instead we shall appoint you as a sepoy in the Company Government. You will have to work at Dambala office. Every day you may travel from your village. Do you agree to this?”

Martanda hesitated for a few moments. Then he requested, “Huzoor, I am ready to obey you, but if I join your service as a sepoy in a place nearest to my village, the natives of my village will laugh at the plight of a poor brahmin like me. I shall gladly accept the job if you can place me at a place away from my village.” Thomson laughed mildly and questioned him, “Are you ready to serve at Naragund? Then who will look after your mother here?” Martanda replied, “Navalagund will be all right for me. There is nobody who knows me. I need not worry about my mother because I shall take her with me to Navalagund.” Thomson said, “If this is agreeable to you, you come to the office at Dambala and meet me. By the way, we did not ask me about the salary. We shall give you a monthly salary of fifteen rupees. Is it agreeable to you?” Martanda felt swollen with joy. He said enthusiastically, “I shall accept whatever salary you pay me, huzoor.”

Though Lieutenant Thomson was disappointed about the cancellation of the hunting programme, he felt satisfied to learn many details about the social and economic condition of the villagers, the side effects of the famine and a few hints about Bhimaraya’s army. He said good-bye to the gouda and Shanubhoga. He patted the back of Martanda and said jocularly, “Hence forward we shall not give you any gift of money. On the contrary we shall give you regular salary.” Then Lieutenant Thomson mounted his horse and rode towards Dambala in the afternoon.

*****

Lieutenant Thomson tried to locate the army of Bhimaraya but could not succeed in it. Every thing appeared to be mysterious to him. But he wanted to confirm some facts and therefore wished to visit Naragund and talk with Babasaheb who was said to be a friend of the Company Government. He wanted to visit Naragund as the Police Superintendent of Dharwad district and gather information about the anti Government activities and arrangements made by the king. He wrote a letter to Babasaheb about his visit.

When Lieutenant Thomson reached Naragund on horse back, he was received warmly by Babasaheb. He was given a nice treatment in the palace. He observed every thing minutely in Naragund. He did not find any cannon mounted on the palace walls. Nor did he find any soldier walking the streets of Naragund. He remembered the details informed by the Mamledar of Navalagund but could not confirm them by first hand verification. He had himself seen some cannons being brought to Naragund from the southern part of the country. He wished to see where those cannons were mounted. He asked Babasaheb, "Mr. Babasaheb, may I have a look at the temple of Venkateswara?" Babasaheb Sarkar agreed to it instantly and said, "Why not? I shall send an officer with you who will show you the temple." Immediately an officer took Lieutenant Thomson to the temple and showed him different parts of the templeyard. Thomson observed everything very carefully and found no cannon. But when he came to the eastern gate of the temple he found a cannon of medium size and felt enthusiastic. He went near it and touched it. He asked the officer, "Why have you kept this cannon here?" "We have a tradition of firing the cannons on the occasion of special *puja* to the deity," replied the officer. Thomson questioned further, "How many more such cannons do you have at your disposal?" "This is the only cannon we have. There are no other cannons," replied the officer rather hesitatingly. "How long has this cannon been here?" asked Thomson. "It seems to be here since long ago. Perhaps Babasaheb's grandfather or great grandfather had kept it here. I don't know anything more about it," replied the officer. Thomson wanted to cross question him further, "Where have you kept the ten cannons brought from the south?" The officer felt puzzled and replied flatteringly, "Which cannons are you referring to? I don't know anything about them."

Thomson did not continue the enquiry. He returned to the palace along with the officer on horseback. He told the officer, "I would like to see Mr. Babasaheb instantly." The officer accordingly sent a message to the king in the palace but received a reply that Babasaheb Sarkar was busy in his puja and could not allow anybody to see him at that time. Lieutenant Thomson felt helpless. He took a piece of paper and scribbled a message to Babasaheb that he should send the cannon kept in the templeyard to Dharwad and wished to know where the other nine cannons were hidden. He asked the officer to hand over the letter to Babasaheb. He mounted his horse and rode back to Gadag.

When Thomson entered the Mamledar's room at Gadag, he was surprised to see Mr. Oglivey seated in the central chair and directing the subordinate officer about something. Thomson saluted the Magistrate Mr. Oglivey and said, "I thought I was the only person capable of giving surprise visits. Now I understand that you also are capable of it." The Magistrate asked him to be seated and told him why he had come to Gadag a couple of days earlier than he had planned. After half an hour Mr. Oglivey completed his office work and signed a number of papers. He said, "Thomson, let us go to Dak-Bungalow directly. I had to discuss with you a number of issues." Both of them rode their horses slowly. They remained silent until they covered some distance. As they came near the Dak-Bungalow, Mr. Oglivey said, "Thomson, you are a Superintendent of Police. You know more about public life than I do. I will come to know tomorrow what you know today. You have warned me that something dangerous is going on in this district, but I neglected it then. Now I have started realizing the truth of it." Then both of them mounted off their horses. The servants tethered the horses in the stable.

Mr. Oglivey and Thomson entered a room in the Dak-Bungalow and bolted the door from inside. Mr. Oglivey informed the details of the information that he had received from the British resident in Hyderabad like the preparations of war against the British being made by Raja Venkatappanayaka of Surapur and coming together of many important people like Babasaheb of Naragund, Bhimaraya of Mundaragi and many officers. Mr. Oglivey said, "Mr. Thomson I suspect that some conspiracy has been going on against the British. We can see only the smoke of it now, but the fire is not visible yet. I have not got any proof against either Babasaheb of Naragund or Bhimaraya of Mundaragi. I learnt from Moreshwara, the Mamledar of Navalagund that Babasaheb of Naragund has recently bought about ten cannons. I, therefore, sent my personal secretary Mr. Karkhanis of Naragund to enquire about the same. But I learnt that Babasaheb had kept those toy-cannons by way of family dignity and to use them at the time of holy service to the family deity Venkateswara. He was even willing to send them to Dharwad if we wanted them. He said to have told Mr. Karkhanis, Ingreji Sarkar is like a big ocean whereas Babasaheb of Naragund is like limited water in a well. That Babasaheb should wage a war against the Ingreji people might be a mere joke indulged by the loose talkers to kill their time. As for Nadiger Bhimaraya, he is an ordinary person. How can he have the courage to rebel against the British Government?"

Thomson listened to Magistrate Oglivey very patiently. Then he replied, "My impression is contrary to yours. I strongly suspect that Bhimaraya of Mundaragi must be behind the rebellious activities of Babasaheb, or of Raja Venkatappanayaka of Surapur or of any other King. When I analyze the unhappy events happening in this part of the District, my suspicion about Bhimaraya of Mundaragi has been growing stronger. This is too serious a matter to be neglected. I have been collecting as much intelligence as I can in this respect. We have already collected more information than the one collected by the British resident at Hyderabad."

Mr. Oglivey was nonplused by these words. He did not know how to react to them immediately. However, he recovered his composure and said, "Mr. Thomson, you please bring to my notice the details of your enquiries. My only suggestion is that we should not unnecessarily suspect our own subjects who are loyal to us. Let our suspicion not result in hatred. I do not doubt your extraordinary ability or honesty. Your loyalty to the Company Government is undoubtable. But let us not unnecessarily suspect or trouble the civilians. If you find solid evidence of any conspiracy against our Government, then please bring it to my notice. I shall not hesitate to punish them no matter who they are." Both of them had their dinner and slept in their respective rooms.

The next morning Mr. Oglivey rode on horseback to Dharwad whereas Mr. Thomson rode his horse to Dambala.

Ramu rode his horse towards Naragund. As he was three miles away from the city, he went to a small village where a friend of his lived. He borrowed a black gown studded with cowries and a percussion-instrument. He then rode in the direction of Naragund. While he was half a mile from Naragund, he dismounted from his horse and tethered it to a banyan tree with a long rope so that the animal could have ample freedom to move about. He took off his shirt and put on the black woolen gown with cowries studded on it. Then he tucked the dhoti-fold behind him running it between the thighs. He applied ash on the different parts of his arms and forehead and a vermilion dot on the centre of his forehead. He wound a pale yellow turban around his skull. He took out a small percussion-drum and shook it right and left thereby producing a rhythmic rattle. He tried it for a couple of times and rehearsed the set-phrases of a fortune-teller. After a couple of repetitions, he gained some confidence and slowly walked towards the southern gate of the city of Naragund.

Two guards stood with long spears at the gate. They used to enquire every entrant into the city about his whereabouts and the purpose of his visit before allowing him into the city. If they suspected the visitors they would even search their bags and bundles. A few visitors were permitted into the city after much enquiry. The fortune-teller walked towards the gate. As usual the guard held his spear against him and thundered at him,

"Who are you, fellow and where do you come from?"

The fortune-teller replied rather meekly, "I have come from Banahatti, sir. I am a fortune-teller and have come here to earn a little in this city.

The guard looked at him rather contemptuously and inspected his clothbag slung across his left shoulder. Not finding any harmful thing in it he ordered the fortune-teller, "All right, you may go in."

The fortune-teller thanked his family-god inwardly, crossed the gate and slowly walked into the city. He turned back a few times to see if the guard was still watching him suspiciously. After going out of sight from the guard the fortune-teller grew confident of himself and walked ahead quite boldly. He stood before the first house he saw and began to rattle the percussion-drum in a very dexterous fashion. First he would play it in a slow tempo and then suddenly speed it into double speed. Simultaneously he would accompany it with set phrases in a stylized fashion. The street urchins would gather around him in a circle and gape at him with delightful curiosity. He would say, "Goodluck is going to befall on you. Goodluck is going to befall on you. Before the next Full Moon, your daughter is going to get a good bridegroom," and rattle his percussion-drum in a double speed. The mischievous urchins would delight in miming his gestures and imitating his phrases.

Then he would skip a few houses and stand before another big house and play his percussion-drum. Like this he went on telling the fortune of people. He then crossed the vegetable market and the Sankaralinga Temple. He walked slowly through the brahmins' street and stood before the house of Krishnaji Pant which was situated a short distance behind the palace of Babasaheb. It was midday and the hot sun was licking the earth. The entire city was quiet as most of the people were taking their lunch or having their siesta. The fortune-teller started rattling his percussion-drum in a dexterous manner. There was nobody around. Krishnaji Pant stood at the main door of his house and waved his hand at the fortune-teller to go away. But the fortune-teller looked around him and confirmed that nobody was watching him. He entered the gate rather cautiously and walked towards Krishnaji Pant who grew angry and shouted at him,

"You fool, who asked you to enter the compound? First, get out from here, or else I shall thrash you."

The fortune-teller smiled mischievously and beckoned to him, "Sir, don't be angry with me. I have came on some confidential purpose. Manson saheb has sent me to you."

On hearing these words, Krishnaji Pant grew quiet and began to show some interest in him. He took him to his bedroom and asked him what the matter was. The fortune-teller said, "Manson saheb has asked me to give this letter to you secretly." He thrust his right hand behind into the pocket of his black gown and took out a sealed cover and handed it over religiously to Krishnaji Pant who took it and opened it. He saw the beautiful handwriting which he guessed to be Manson's own. It read as follows :

Dear Mr. Krishnaji Pant,

Hope this letter finds you in good health. I will be camping at Munavalli in January 1856. I, therefore, request you to come there with Baniya Bapu to see me personally without fail to discuss some very confidential matter. Please keep this as a top secret. The rest in person.

Thanking you.

Yours cordially
Manson
Political Agent
East India Company, Kolhapur.

After reading the letter, Krishnaji Pant felt flattered for being called by no less an officer than Manson. He asked the maid-servant to offer some food to the fortune-teller. The maid-servant went into the kitchen and brought some jowar rotis, curds, rice and pulse and kept them before the fortune-teller. Being ravenously hungry the fortune-teller fell upon the food greedily and ate it up rapturously. He then lay on the mattress in the room for an hour or so.

That night Krishnaji Pant went to Baniya Bapu's house and told him all about Mr. Manson's letter. Both of them decided to go to Munavalli camp and see Manson there privately. The next day they sent a letter of reply to Manson through the fortune-teller who returned to Kolhapur to hand it over to Manson. Krishnaji Pant and Baniya Bapu did not want anyone in Naragund to know about their secret meeting with the British officer. They continued to attend to their normal duties.

Krishnaji Pant and Baniya Bapu were working as clerks under Raghu Prahlad Diwanji, Chief Secretary to Bhaskararao Bhave of Naragund. Both of them were in charge of the military goods like gunpowder and weapons etc. Their duty was to supply gunpowder, swords and spears to the soldiers. They had been given permanent landed property for their service. Babasaheb had great faith in their loyalty to the kingdom and therefore, used to keep them in good humour. Besides they also belonged to the caste of Babasaheb. They used to visit the temple of Lord Venkateswara regularly.

According to the schedule, Manson went to Munavalli and camped there with all his office staff in the month of January 1856. He waited for Baniya Bapu and Krishnaji Pant in order to hatch their secret plans. One day Krishnaji Pant and Baniya Bapu went to the palace and met Babasaheb and requested him,

"Sarkar, we request you to grant us leave for a week."

Babasaheb was puzzled a little and yet he could not afford to displease these clerks who held key positions in the military affairs of his Kingdom. He asked them,

"Why do you want leave? What's the reason?"

"Both of us have got some personal work to attend to, Sarkar. We just want a week's time," requested they.

"All right, men. You may take a week's time, but don't exceed it."

"No Sarkar. We'll definitely return after a week."

They saluted Babasaheb and walked out of the royal chamber. The next day they set out on horseback to Munavalli in the early morning. But whenever they chanced to see some acquaintances on their way, they used to lie to them that they were going to some village for some personal work. They passed Achamatti, Chulki and reached Munavalli. They saw the cluster of big tents erected near the hillock. They rode upto the hillock and dismounted from their horses. They went to the tank and washed their faces, hands and feet. Then they walked upto the main tent of Manson and sent word to him through the guard. Manson asked the guard to take them in. Krishnaji Pant and Baniya Bapu entered his tent gently and saluted him in the traditional Hindu style by joining their palms. Manson stood up for a moment and welcomed them by shaking hands with them. When the robust fingers of Manson squeezed the soft brahmanical palms of Krishnaji Pant and Baniya Bapu, they felt a crushing pain in their palms and even felt a little embarrassed by the touch of the mlenchha British officer though they managed to hide their feelings. Manson said in his stilted Kannada,

"So I suppose you are Mr. Krishnaji Pant and Mr. Baniya Bapu."

"Yes, saheb. We are the persons."

"Please take your seats and feel comfortable," Manson pointed to the chairs opposite to him.

Both the visitors walked gently to the chairs and sat on them meekly.

Krishnaji Pant asked gently, "Saheb, we got the confidential message that we should meet you. May we know the reason for it?"

Baniya Bapu also asked, "Why did you send for us, saheb?"

"That's very kind of you. Does your king Mr. Babasaheb know about your meeting with me?" asked Manson.

"No saheb. We have not told our King yet about our arrival here. We excused ourselves on the pretext of attending to our personal work," Krishnaji Pant replied.

"I appreciate your practical wisdom. You have done the right thing."

Baniya Bapu and Krishnaji Pant were watching the coat and the bow tie of Manson very curiously. They were both awed and thrilled by the sight of the British officer. His pronunciation of Kannada sounded very artificial and alien to them. Manson said to them,

"I have some very important matter to discuss with you. Before that let's have a few snacks. Just a minute."

He excused himself for a couple of minutes and went out of his tent to the next one. Baniya Bapu could not help making his remark on the British officer. He turned to Krishnaji Pant and said,

"Dear friend, doesn't he look like a patient of leucoderma?"

"You mischievous fellow.... You have made the right observation. But don't express them here," Krishnaji Pant cautioned him with a smile.

By then Manson returned to the tent followed by a servant with a tray of snacks and glasses. The servant kept the bread and butter, fruits and glasses of tea on the table and arranged them in three plates. Manson said to them, "Please help yourselves."

All the three of them sat around the table and ate the light tiffin with real gusto. As Baniya Bapu and Krishnaji Pant were very hungry on account of their tiring journey, they enjoyed every bit of the tiffin offered by the British officer. After the tiffin was over, Manson conducted them to his private chamber and requested them, "Mr. Krishnaji Pant and Mr. Baniya Bapu, you must help us in our administration."

"How to help you saheb? Please tell us how." Manson lowered the pitch of his voice and said, "You must supply us the news of all the activities of your king Babasaheb. Later if we have to fight with him, you have to work on our side and see that he is defeated."

For a moment Manson stared into their eyes. They felt embarrassed. Krishnaji Pant made bold to ask him, "How can we work against our own King? It is against our ethics."

"Why do you bother about ethics? Does your king give you anything other than salary? If you help us to defeat your King, we shall give you some jahagir of which both of you can be Lords. You can enjoy all the glory and grandeur of life. Why do you rot in the humble position of clerks in Babasaheb's kingdom? Think over the problem and let me know your decision."

Krishnaji Pant and Baniya Bapu looked at each other meaningfully. The prospects of their future lordship thrilled them. Krishnaji Pant nudged Baniya Bapu and said to Manson,

"All right saheb. We shall do as you wish. Hope you'll keep your word about our share of the kingdom."

"Mr. Krishnaji Pant, don't you worry about that, I mean about my promise. You will be future lords of two jahagirs. You must help us whole-heartedly."

"Don't you worry about that saheb. We shall do our best to help you."

"That's very good. You are the best friends of the British Government. I thank you very much," Manson walked up to them and shook hands with them.

Krishnaji Pant and Baniya Bapu whispered into each other's ears and said,

"Now, please allow us to go back to our place."

"How can you go so early? You are the guests of the imperial Government. You'll have to partake of our hospitality tonight."

That night both of them stayed there at Munavalli camp. An hour after sunset they were taken to a big tent-hall where they were offered wine in glasses. As they sipped their wine they felt a strange kind of sleepiness. Manson also gave them company. The other British officers were also busy sipping their wine with their wives and sisters. Baniya Bapu and Krishnaji Pant were, in spite of the influence of liquor on them, were gaping at the red-faced and buxom ladies in their skirts. Their mouths began to salivate at the sight of nearly half naked foreign women. An hour passed in drinking.

Then a few instrumentalists brought a pair of banjos, a pair of cymbals and a couple of guitars and settled themselves in a corner. Then they began to play upon them slowly and rhythmically. Krishnaji Pant and Baniya Bapu cocked their ears and started listening to the alien music. It was something they had never heard anywhere in their life. The sharp rattle of the banjos and the thrumming of guitars seemed to captivate them. It was something different from the *nagaswaram* notes and beats of horizontal drums played at the temple of Lord Venkateswara at Naragund. The rhythm of Western instruments was creating ripples of new enthusiasm in their veins.

As the tempo of the instrumental music increased, the ladies and gentlemen in the tent-hall got up and began to form into innumerable pairs. Each man took the hand of a lady and began to move rhythmically. Manson took the right hand of a lady, and put his left hand upon her shoulder and started waltzing with her slowly. As he beckoned to two young foreign girls in bright coloured skirts, they stalked towards Krishnaji Pant and Baniya Bapu, held their hands and gently drew them into the dancing crowd. They said, "Come on dear ones, let's dance." Krishnaji Pant and Baniya Bapu felt shy and embarrassed at the strange invitation, although secretly they thanked their stars for the unexpected pleasure.

The British girl held the hand of Krishnaji Pant and directed him by her own movements. For a moment Krishnaji Pant's hairs stood on end and he perspired mildly. She stared into his eyes and smiled mischievously at him. He also reciprocated her smile. Although he could not step rhythmically, he was trying his best to keep pace with her steps. He was amused at the sight of green cat-eyes of the girl and was observing the contours of her moving, swinging and swirling body. Likewise the other girl also captured the attention of Baniya Bapu. The ball was followed by a grand dinner. That night Krishnaji Pant and Baniya Bapu could not sleep at all because of their obsession with the sweet figures which danced with them so bewitchingly.

The next day they took their departure from Manson and rode back towards Naragund. On the way they did nothing but dream about their grand future. Krishnaji Pant said to his companion,

"If we help Manson, we'll be able to be lords of half of Naragund. I'll be the king and you can be my minister."

"Yes. How wonderful will that be! Why should I be your minister? I can as well be a king myself," said Baniya Bapu.

"How is that possible? How can two kings rule the same kingdom?"

"That is not possible. But we can always divide the property between ourselves and be lords over our portion."

"That's wonderful. You are very clever in these matters."

Both of them went on fantasizing about their grand future and rode back to Naragund rather slowly. They went home and settled down to their routine official work. The next day they met their King Babasaheb and pretended ignorance about Manson.

*****

Manson went from Munavalli camp to Kolhapur quite happily. He felt a sense of satisfaction at having hit upon a good plan of enervating the arrogant Babasaheb of Naragund. He was accompanied by his army. The soldiers had to climb many hillocks, ford across many rivers and brooks and cross vast stretches of land before reaching the undulating region of Kolhapur.

*****

Krishnaji Pant and Baniya Bapu went on supplying all the important information about Babasaheb and his activities to Manson regularly and confidentially. But Babasaheb did not somehow suspect the bonafides of his clerks, because after all, they belonged to his own caste. Every time they supplied intelligence to the British officer they used to get a purse of golden sovereigns as reward. Time and again they used to imagine themselves to be the future lords of jahagirs and fantasize about the future happiness.

*****

Babasaheb was deeply worried about his hairlessness. He thought of a number of ways of solving the problem. One day he called a confidential meeting of all the officers and enquired about the military prowess that he had. As per the royal order Vira Sarnayaka also attended the meeting at night. Vira Sarnayaka whose real name was Virabhadra Nayaka was popularly called Vira Sarnayaka. He was working as the head spy in the kingdom. He used to take different guises and go into market places, temples or gymnasiums where people usually gather and chitchat or discuss public affairs. It was the duty of Virabhadra Nayaka to gather and supply information of vital importance to the King. Babasaheb had developed a special trust and confidence in Virabhadra Nayaka because of his sincerity, extra-ordinary courage and loyalty. Babasaheb asked him,

"My dear Virabhadra Nayaka, could you tell me how many soldiers are at your command now?"

"Sarkar, I have about seven hundred soldiers."

"Are they well trained and ready to face the enemies?"

"Why not Sarkar? They are at my beck and call. They are ready to die for their king any moment."

"That is really very heartening news to me. Virabhadra Nayaka, please keep them in training, because we may have to launch a war against Manson any time. Please give them additional salary so that they can keep up their high spirits."

"As you command, Sarkar," Virabhadra Nayaka replied with his usual confidence.

Then Babasaheb announced his decision to the confidential gathering of royal officers,

"I cannot put off the problem of adoption any longer. I, therefore, have decided to fight with and capture that red-faced fellow called Manson and forcibly extract his permission for adoption. You must make all the arrangements for the same."

"All right, Sarkar. We'll do as you wish. All our soldiers are ready for action," replied Raghopant Kulkarni who was the Commander of the army. Then all the officers dispersed.

*****

One day Baniya Bapu met Babasaheb in privacy. He saluted Babasaheb by joining his palms and said, "Sarkar you have been making preparations for the fight with the British people. I am not against this patriotic zeal. But I would like to bring to your kind attention the practical difficulties involved in the war. You know Sarkar, the insurgence started by Nanasaheb in the north has been suppressed successfully by the British people. The Company Government has a highly organized military system. But we are not in a position to defeat them as we have to depend upon the inexperienced recruits and untrained villagers. Our army is not as well organized as the Britishers'. During the regime of Tippu Sultan our late Sri Venkatrao Sarkar fought against Tippu Sultan continuously for nine months because he had the strong support of the Peshwas. But now we don't have such support from any side. Don't you remember Sarkar, how the Raja of Surapur fought against the Company Sarkar and miserably failed? Had we declared the war against the Britishers a year ago, we could have succeeded in it. But now the context is very different. As per the order of the Company Sarkar and your permission, we have sent most of our weapons and gun powder to Dharwad on 7-5-1858. Now again the Company Sarkar has sent order that we must send the remaining weapons. I request you to permit me to send them away so that we can be free from the worry. Sarkar you don't listen to Raghopant whose motives are suspect. If you don't like my suggestions, Sarkar, kindly follow the suggestions offered by Srimant Ramadurgakar. Sarkar you may even consult your *matosri* or your *vahini*. I am requesting you, Sarkar, with all humility. So far I have never dared to speak before you, Sarkar. But since I happen to be the Diwan of the Samsthan, it is my duty to express my views frankly. If there is anything wrong in my suggestions, Sarkar may order for my death. I shall die happily."

Babasaheb listened to him patiently and said, "Diwanji, what you say is true. We should have behaved that way earlier. But now that time is over. The circumstances have gone beyond our control. I cannot back out now. I have to fight the enemy or die. That is my nature. I have understood the nature of Raghopant Limaye completely. But what can be done about it? Now I am caught in dilemma." Baniya Bapu listened to Babasaheb's words and felt helpless.

*****

One day in winter, Lieutenant Thomson felt bored at Dambala and therefore, rode to Gadag. The cold was severe. When he reached the Dak-Bungalow, he saw a white man to whom he introduced himself. The white man introduced himself as Mr. Meadows Taylor and further told him that he had come from Hyderabad and was on his way to Dharwad and that he had halted at Gadag for the night rest. He then said rather sternly, "Hope there is peace in your area. As for Surapur, it is burnt down. Now it is the turn of Naragund. You have been killing innocent people under the pretext of maintaining peace." Lieutenant Thomson did not understand the significance of his words. He did not know anything about the destruction of Surapur. He wondered why the white man was speaking to him so bitterly. But still because of his professional patience he went on listening to him.

Meadows Taylor narrated, "The Company Government declared a war against Surapur rather unnecessarily. It was a terrific war. My hairs stand on end when I remember it. The war started on 7th February and ended on 10th. But within those three days, it wrought havoc with the life of natives. The British people had brought armies from Lingasugur, Kaladagi and Raichur. But the natives of Surapur being great lovers of freedom fought heroically in the battle and a majority of them laid down their lives. You must have heard of what happened to Captain Newbury. He was punished properly for his arrogance. A patriot of Surapur shot him to death." Lieutenant Thomson felt irritated to hear a white man commenting on the English Government. He could not control himself. He, therefore, burst out, "What you are telling me is a serious matter. I listen to it with great patience. But before that, I would like to know who you are and your background."

Meadows Taylor continued, "I have already told you my name. You may remember it. By profession I am a teacher. I have come to India fifteen years ago. I had undertaken the task of tutoring Raja Venkatappanayaka right from his childhood. He used to respect me as a son could do to his father. But that beloved disciple is no more now." With these words Meadows Taylor began to sob loudly. "Did he die in the battle?" asked Thomson. "No, when he was sure of being defeated by the English people, he went to Hyderabad to seek the help of Rohils and Arabs. But he was caught by the English people. But he could not stand the insult. He therefore shot himself to death to save his honour and dignity," replied Meadows Taylor and wiped the tears from his eyes.

Lieutenant Thomson felt pity for the exceptional white man and sensitive teacher, Meadows Taylor. He asked him, "Why are you going to Dharwad? Do you have any relatives there?" Meadows Taylor replied, "There are no kith or kin or close friends for me in India. I wish to go to Kumata via Dharwad and from Kumata to England." Lieutenant Thomson said, "All right, you return to your home country. Wish you all the best." Then he rode his horse to the Post and Telegraph office and sent a telegram to Mr. Oglivey asking for the details of Surapur war. Then he returned to the Dak-Bungalow, had his lunch and relaxed. By that time he received a telegraphic reply from Mr. Oglivey, "No details of Surapur war available. Keep an eye on the activities of Naragund and Dambala. Be watchful."

Lieutenant Thomson had begun to visualize the future picture of the rebellion of the native Kings. He felt he would have discovered all the details of Bhimaraya's army if he had been allowed by Mr. Oglivey. But Mr. Oglivey used to say, "Let's wait and see." Thomson feared that Bhimaraya would definitely rebel against the English Government and possibly Babasaheb of Naragund also might follow suit. He was not sure if the king cobra called Raja Venkatappanayaka of Surapur was completely killed or, still active. Lieutenant Thomson wanted to nip everything in the bud.

He, therefore, rode to Navalagund and sat in the Dak-Bungalow. He felt that the atmosphere was very peaceful there. Moreshwara, the Mamledar of Navalagund came and saluted him. He told Mr. Thomson that the political atmosphere was not so tense now as it was about two months ago. He further reported that a week ago Babasaheb of Naragund and Bhimaraya of Mundaragi had been to Dharwad to meet Mr. Oglivey and declared they were the friends of English Government and that some malicious fellows were trying to malign and misinterpret them to the British authorities.

By that time a sepoy came into the chamber and saluted Lt. Thomson. Moreshwara, the Mamledar pointed to the sepoy and said, "This boy appointed by you is a very smart one. He has already acquainted himself with a number of brahmins at Naragund. We can collect all kinds of intelligence through him." Then Lt. Thomson scanned the face of the sepoy carefully. The young sepoy burst into a smile and said, "Huzoor, don't you recognize me ? I am Martanda, son of Subbanna Bhatta of Melodi village." Martanda saluted once again in the military style. Lt. Thomson walked upto him, patted his back and said,

"Oh I had clean forgotten you Mr. Martanda. I have to discuss many things with you. You must stay in the Dak-Bungalow tonight." Martanda was only too happy to oblige the British officer who had given him his livelihood in the form of a regular job.

In the Dak-Bungalow, Lt. Thomson lay on the wooden bedstead. Martanda sat on a mat on the floor. Thomson began to ask him many subtle questions. Martanda went on answering them very sincerely and frankly. Thomson asked him, "Do you think that Babasaheb of Naragund intends to raise a war against the British Government?" "Yes, Huzoor," said Martanda, "I feel like that. Not only I, but even Krishnaji Pant Joshi and Baniya Bapu think like that. If Babasaheb does not intend to wage a war, why has he mounted the cannons on the palace parapets? Why has he loaded gun powder in the magazine? Why has he appointed three hundred cavalry men?" Lt. Thomson felt happy to learn many concrete details about Naragund. Next, he asked Martanda, "If he wants to wage a war, when do you think he might do so?" Martanda replied, "Huzoor, I do not know the right answer to this. You have to ask this question to Baniya Bapu who always moves around with Babasaheb. In fact I have already posed this question to him. Do you know what he said?" "What did he say?" asked Thomson. Martanda continued, "Baniya Bapu says that it will take some time for the war to begin; that a lot of preparation has yet to be made; that the army of Nanasaheb Peshwa is expected from North Hindustan, and that Bhimaraya was eager to begin the war. Further, Baniya Bapu made bold to suggest to Babasaheb that they should wait until the end of summer and onset of the monsoon."

Lt. Thomson was very happy to learn many secrets of Naragund. He sat upon his bed and asked Martanda to sit by his side. Martanda got up from the mat and sat on the bed by the side of his officer. Then Thomson whispered many things into his ears. Then he promised to Martanda, "You must do it at the right time. If you do it, we shall recommend a big reward for you." Sepoy Martanda felt elated to be taken into the confidence of his high officer and decided to please him by obliging him.

The next morning Thomson rode back to Gadag and sent a telegram to Mr. Manson, Political Agent of South India. Likewise he sent the same message telegraphically to Oglivey, Magistrate of Dharwad; Mr. Taylor, Deputy Commissioner of Raichur and Mr. Pelly, Magistrate of Bellary. Then he wrote a detailed letter and sent copies of it to all these officers.

*****

Lieutenant Thomson camped at Gadag for the whole week. During that period, he felt disturbed by two things. As instructed by him Moreshwara, the Mamledar of Navalgund had started sending copies of his letters to Magistrate Mr. Oglivey. Moreshwara had done his work very cleverly. He had sent two of his peons in disguise to Naragund to collect intelligence from there and send it to him. From Moreshwara's letters, Thomson learnt that the main gates of Naragund were guarded by about twenty guards who used to make detailed enquiries before allowing any visitor into the city; that about twenty-five to thirty *golandajs* had come to Naragund from outside and some of the *golandajs* had come from Ratnagiri area and spoke Urdu. He also learnt that a few small detachments of soldiers used to parade in the main streets of Naragund just to awe the common people; that the cannons bought and brought from the south had been laboriously carried up the hill slope and parked at the vantage points of the palace parapets and the parapets of the temple of Lord Venkateswara and that cannons were fired at the time of holy service to the deity.

Moreshwara had revealed many other details in his other letters. As Thomson studied those letters, he learnt many things about the secret activities going on at Naragund, like, *e.g.*, that the king of Naragund had started collecting jowar and rice in a big way; that when the merchants of Bagilukote were taking their merchandise in oxen carts to Hubballi via Naragund, the soldiers of Naragund bound and thrashed them and looted their goods.

Thomson, further, learnt that recently there was a misunderstanding between Naragundkar and Ramadurgkar. Moreshwara had also intimated that Joglekar of Yavagal mahalkari maintained close relationship with Babasaheb of Naragund and that a special watch had to be kept on the former.

From all these diverse details Thomson could guess that there were signs of war in the locality though he could not visualize its nature or intensity. He was especially eager to know what kind of relationship existed between Babasaheb of Naragund and Bhimaraya of Mundaragi.

*****

The next day Krishnaji Pant and Baniya Bapu came to know the decision that Babasaheb had taken. They, therefore, made haste to intimate the same to Manson who in their view, was a king-maker. Krishnaji Pant called a confidant-servant and gave him a letter to be handed over to Manson. The servant assumed the guise of a beggar and sneaked out of the eastern gate of Naragund. But before he could do that he had to answer a number of questions asked by the guard.

"Who are you?"

"I am a beggar, sir."

"Where are you going?"

"I am a beggar, sir. I am going to the next village for begging."

"Why are you going to the next village?"

"You can as well beg here," said the guard and thumped his spear on the ground.

"I have exhausted all the houses in this city, sir."

"All right, you can go." The guards removed their spears which they had held crosswise and allowed the beggar to pass through the Gate.

The beggar's heart was thumping with tension when he was questioned by the guards. He walked slowly and tried to ease the tension by telling himself that he had cleverly managed to cheat the guards. He took quite some time to recover his normal poise. He walked up to the nearby village and visited his close friend and rested there for the night. The next morning he borrowed a horse from his friend and rode towards Kolhapur. He reached Manson's residence after a week's time and confidentially handed over the secret letter from Krishnaji Pant and Baniya Bapu. Manson read the letter hurriedly and was shocked to learn that Babasaheb had decided to declare war against him. On knowing this Manson began to boil inwardly. But he tipped the messenger and sent him back with a request to supply intelligence like this regularly about Babasaheb's activities. "I must teach that arrogant fool the lesson of his life," he said to himself and clasped his right fist into his left palm, "I must overtake him before he attacks me," he muttered to himself gnashing his teeth. He paced up and down in the hall with his palms clasped behind his back.

*****

Manson ordered two hundred cavalrymen to be ready. The soldiers got very good stallions to withstand the rough and rocky area. After completing their morning ablutions and having their lunch, the soldiers mounted their horses and rode towards Toragal. They were led by Manson who was seated on a palanquin carried by four bearers. The rhythmic clop-clop of the hooves of horses aroused the curiosity of the villagers on the way. The horses usually would kick up a cloud of dust behind them. Most of the horses were of dark brown colour. They reached Toragal and rested there for a while. Then they started towards the hilly region of Ramadurg. It was quite a task for the soldiers to ascend and descend the circular ridges of the hills studded with prickly trees and bushes.

In Ramadurg, Manson was received warmly by the King of Ramadurg. As his soldiers were all tired and hungry, they were badly in need of food and rest. The King of Ramadurg understood their plight and arranged for their treatment. The royal cooks and servants were all pressed into service. Within two hours the local food was ready. The sweet aroma of the delicious items made the nostrils of the tired soldiers dilate with hungry expectations. Soon the soldiers were invited into the banquet hall of the fort of Ramadurg and served with innumerable delicacies which they could neither name nor remember. They fell on food with ravenous hunger and ate the countless items until they began to belch with surfeit and satisfaction. After their food, the soldiers began to doze and therefore, they rushed to the large halls and slept like logs on the mattresses provided by the King of Ramadurg.

The next morning Manson thanked the King of Ramadurg profusely for the nice hospitality shown to him and his tired soldiers. Although the King of Ramadurg happened to be a cousin of Babasaheb of Naragund, there was some kind of rivalry and jealousy between them. Babasaheb had sent a letter to him asking him to join the battle against the British people like Manson and fight for their freedom and autonomy. But the King of Ramadurg did not join his cousin Babasaheb. He knew that the British Government was a big force and thought that he could benefit a lot by ingratiating them and by betraying Babasaheb of Naragund to them. He, therefore, took Manson into his private chamber and showed him the letter written to the former by Babasaheb of Naragund requesting him to join hands with the native kings for fighting against Manson and others. Manson's blood was up as he grasped the contents. He heaved a sigh of anger. He was confirmed in his belief that Babasaheb was a very independent-natured fighter and determined to bring him down very systematically. He thanked the King of Ramadurg for providing intelligence about Babasaheb and proceeded towards Sureban on his way to Dharwad. His cavalry followed him across the hilly region. At last they came to a valley near a village called Sureban. Since it had grown dark by that time they camped there. Manson wanted to camp there for a couple of days so that he could plan the strategy of attack on Babasaheb by getting the additional army from other parts of the country. His soldiers were very tired. He, therefore, had to break his journey there at Sureban before proceeding to Dharwad. It was 29th May 1857. The bearers lowered the palanquin on the raised platform of a resthouse. Manson stretched his limbs and eased his nerves. His soldiers kindled a bonfire and sat around it for warming themselves. The cooks prepared a hurried meal. Manson and his soldiers ate their meal with ravenous hunger and slept like logs in their tents. Manson slept in the palanquin whereas his guards who sat around his palanquin also fell into a deep sleep because of their fatigue of the preceding journey.

*****

The spies of Babasaheb brought him the news that Manson had come to Sureban and camped there and that he wanted to attack Naragund within a couple of days. Babasaheb was taken aback by the unexpectedness of Manson's arrival there. He easily suspected that Manson must have kept an eye on the activities going on in Naragund. Nevertheless he did not feel disheartened. He wanted to rise to the occasion and show his heroism and solve the problem of adoption. He, therefore, called Virabhadra Nayaka to his palace and asked him,

"My dear Virabhadra Nayaka, our spies have brought news that that the red-faced fellow Manson has come with army and been camping in the valley of Sureban. That fellow must be contemplating to attack us unexpectedly. But we do not have exact information about his army."

"How to get the exact picture of that, Sarkar? Shall I ride up to the spot and study the situation?" said Virabhadra Nayaka.

"That will be ideal, my dear Virabhadra Nayaka," said Babasaheb with satisfaction.

"There's no time left now. I must rush to Sureban."

Virabhadra Nayaka took his departure from the King, went home, told his wife about the trip. After having his lunch, he mounted his dark brown horse and rode towards Ramadurg and rested in the *dharmasala* outside the city. The passers-by were discussing the camp of British soldiers near Sureban. Virabhadra Nayaka slept on the floor at night.

The next morning he got up quite early and went through the morning chores and had his bath in the pond near the *dharmasala*. Then he took out the costumes of a *jangama*. He wore a knee-length white dhoti and a shirt of half sleeves. He smeared horizontal triple marks of *vibhuti* on his forehead, chest, belly, arms and wrists. He tied an *istalinga* in a cloth-band around his neck. He also put on a rosary of *rudraksi* around his neck. Then he took out a big cloth-bag and slung it from his left shoulder. He held a walking stick with a silver ferrule at the bottom and a bunch of mini-bells fixed at the upper half portion of it. Now he looked like a *jangama* and whoever saw him felt like bowing down to him in reverence.

The *jangama* went on tapping the earth with his walking stick and producing a tinkling rhythm in keeping with his gait. He went into the village of Sureban and started begging from door to door. As he stood in front of a door and said, "*kanthi-bhiksa nidri*," one of the inhabitants brought two *rotis* with some vegetable curry upon it and placed it on the palms of the *jangama* who carefully kept it in the clothbag. Like this he took a round in the village and went to the side where the army of Manson had camped. He pretended to collect some flowers from the bushes and studied the details of the camp. He saw around fifty or so military tents and around two hundred horses tethered near the tents. The soldiers had got up late and were attending to the morning chores. They were going out one by one and cleaning their bowels behind the bushes. The *jangama*, although pretending to be picking flowers, made a mental note of all the details of the enemy and walked towards the Maruti temple outside Sureban. He took out all the *rotis* and vegetable curry and ate them and laid down on the cool floor of the temple for a couple of hours. In the evening he woke up, washed his face, hands and feet in the nearby tank and walked briskly to Ramadurg. There he took off his guise of *jangama* and put on his usual civilian dress and rode back to Naragund. He met Babasaheb forthwith and narrated everything that he had noted.

*****

No sooner had Babasaheb heard the details of Manson's camp than he began to fume with anger and restlessness. He instantly sent for his Commander Visnu Kulkarni of Hirekoppa. The servant rushed with the royal message. After two hours Commander Visnu Kulkarni entered the royal chamber and saluted to Babasaheb. "Namaste, Sarkar. May I know why the Sarkar sent for me?" Babasaheb's wrought up face relaxed into a wan smile and he said,

"Commander sir, please be seated. We have to face everything now. I hope all your soldiers are well-fed and well-trained."

"Yes, Sarkar. They are kept in readiness. May I know the royal wish?"

"What is the exact strength of your army now?"

"We have about five hundred soldiers at our service now. Most of them are seasoned fighters."

"Commander sir, we have gathered the latest information that Manson has camped his troop near the valley of Sureban. You must take your army there tonight and capture him, so that we can forcibly take his permission for adoption. You must do this before Manson can bring his army to attack us here. I also shall accompany you there."

"You need not come there, Sarkar. I shall go there and manage everything."

"Don't worry about that, Commander sir. I had sent Virabhadra Nayaka to collect sufficient information about Manson and his army. I shall myself come there and we have our Virabhadra Nayaka to guide us about the location of the enemies."

"As you wish, Sarkar." Commander Visnu Kulkarni saluted and walked back from the royal chamber.

*****

In the evening Commander Visnu Kulkarni sent orders to his soldiers to gather on the ground in front of the hill. The soldiers rode their horses slowly and gathered. They had put on their uniforms of knee-length trousers and half shirts. Their sheaths were tied at the left side of their waists. There was a general mood of excitement in the atmosphere. The soldiers stood on their horses in clusters and were discussing the forthcoming fight with the British soldiers. The hustle-bustle of the soldiers came to an end as soon as the Commander stood on a raised platform and shouted his orders :

"My dear soldiers. Please fall in line."

All the soldiers hurried into their platoons and stood in an orderly fashion. Murmurs and whispers gave place to pin-drop silence. The Commander shouted at the top of his voice :

"Savadhan. My dear jawans, we shall go to Avaradi first where we shall have our food. From there we shall go to the valley of Sureban and attack Manson and his troops. Let us swear that we shall fight for our King at the cost of our lives. "*Babasaheb Maharaj ki Jai.*"

All the soldiers raised their voice to the highest pitch and repeated the slogan "*Babasaheb Maharaj ki Jai.*" The loud chorus of the slogan sent up a wave of enthusiasm in the soldiers. Then the Commander descended from the platform, jumped on the back of his stallion and whipped it into movement. As his stallion started its rhythmic march, the soldiers followed him in a row. The Commander directed his horse to the north-eastern direction. He was followed by Babasaheb and the rest of the soldiers. Virabhadra Nayaka rode ahead of Babasaheb.

*****

They reached Avaradi where they took out their packets of food and fed themselves well and rested for an hour. They had to travel for another hour to reach Sureban. When they resumed their march, it started darkening everywhere. Commander Visnu Kulkarni suggested to his servants to light the torches. Accordingly half a dozen servants took out the torches from their bags, poured the groundnut oil on the cloth balls wound around the edge of iron spikes and lighted them with the help of two flint stones. Two servants carried two torches and rode before the Commander and the other torchmen rode in-between the platoons. After an hour's march they reached the valley of Sureban. Immediately the Commander gave order for a standstill and consulted Virabhadra Nayaka about the strategy and the route to be followed. Virabhadra Nayaka explained the details of the location and suggested the way to be followed. Babasaheb asked them to stand in a circle around the valley and slowly close in and attack Manson's army suddenly. Likewise the soldiers of Naragund distributed themselves around the valley and waited for the signal from the Commander.

The soldiers of Manson's troop were sleeping in their tents peacefully without any suspicion about any possible attack. Manson was snoring in his own palanquin quietly. The guards also were dozing in their own places. Crickets were singing their continuous chorus in a lulling tone. Stars twinkled in the sky without any dimness caused by the clouds. The horses which were tethered to the bushes and trees were also dozing peacefully. Small candles were flickering in same tents.

As soon as the Commander gave a shrill whistle, Virabhadra Nayaka advanced with his group of soldiers. Other soldiers also began to march ahead over the bushy land. As they went near the tents, they cut the ropes with which the horses of Manson's troop were tethered and released them. The horses ran away from there whinnying and neighing confusedly. The Commander ordered them to start fighting. The soldiers of Naragund began to wield their swords at the enemies indiscriminately thereby killing many sleeping and half awake soldiers belonging to Manson's party.

There were many sounds of shrieking and howling heard. The ones who had not been struck by swords sprang to their feet in alarm and groped for their weapons, tried to comprehend the situation and think of what to do next. It was very dark all around the valley. They were at a loss as to what to do. Soon the bugle-man took up his bugle and blew it loudly to alarm his troop. Manson was flabbergasted by the unexpectedness of the whole situation. Nevertheless he ordered his soldiers to fight the enemies in spite of the darkness. By this time the soldiers of Naragund had killed many British soldiers and their horses. Although nothing was clearly visible, the swish of swords and the clanking and thudding sounds of swords could be easily heard. The British soldiers did not know how to face the situation. Manson could not manage the situation because he could not see anything clearly in the darkness, nor could he communicate his orders to his soldiers properly. But somehow he could make out that the strength of his army was dwindling moment by moment. He learnt that his loyal servant and friend Puran Singh was also killed. He used to hear the frequent cries and groaning of his dying soldiers. For the first time in his life Manson began to lose confidence in himself because of the quick loss of his soldiers. He knew his total helplessness. He, therefore, jumped on to his horse and rode in the darkness and away from the battle. In the confusion of fighting on the other side of the camp, nobody noticed his escape from there. The fight continued between the two groups. Virabhadra Nayaka was actively fighting and hacking the British soldiers. He also used to be alert about the safety of Babasaheb and Visnu Kulkarni. At last when more than half of their soldiers had died, the British soldiers began to run away from there for life. When the battle was over Commander Visnu Kulkarni found out that he too had lost a few of his soldiers. But he did not bother about that, because his sole intention was to capture Manson. He, therefore, began to search for Manson under the ragged and ravaged tents where he might have hid himself. But after much searching they found out that Manson must have escaped from there into the nearby village of

Sureban. Commander Visnu Kulkarni took a few soldiers with him and went into the village of Sureban and searched every nook and corner throughout the night. But they could not locate him in the darkness. They were bent upon capturing him.

The morning star appeared in the eastern sky. The rosy tint enveloped the eastern horizon. The Commander and two soldiers were waiting at the outskirts of Sureban. Cocks began to crow and sparrows started spattering. A door of a big house opened suddenly. It was the house of a local Setty. An old woman came out with a small pitcher and began to sprinkle water on the front portion of the house. Commander Visnu Kulkarni looked at her and recognized her. She also recognized him and asked him,

"Why my son Visnu, why are you waiting here? Fcr whom? That too so early in the morning?"

"Mother, a *firangi* officer has escaped from our hands. That's why we have been searching for him in the entire village."

"Is that so, my son? A little while ago when I came out of my house for nature call, I saw somebody with tap-taping boots running towards the Maruti temple. I think the fellow must be hiding himself in the temple itself."

"Thank you very much, mother. We snall see you later." Commander Visnu Kulkarni lost no time in his search. He rushed towards the temple just about a hundred yards from there. With him were two soldiers called Marya and Raya. They reached the precincts of the temple. Commander Visnu Kulkarni wanted to enter the temple. But the two soldiers who happened to be brothers, forbid him from doing so. The elder of the two said to him,

"Commander sir, please don't go into the temple alone. The *firangi* fellows are very clever and cunning. That fellow may shoot you down. You please stand here outside and we two will enter it. Even if we are to die, there is no loss to the kingdom. But your life is very precious for the kingdom." The younger brother also seconded the opinion of the elder brother.

Visnu Kulkarni was convinced by their suggestion. Marya and Raya took a torch and tapped the only door of the temple. They also pushed it a couple of times but it did not open. They guessed that it must have been bolted from inside. They, therefore, kicked the door with all the force in their veins one after the other. After half a dozen attempts, the door was broken and dislocated at the place where hinges were fixed in them. They took out the fragments of the broken door and threw them outside. As they peered into the *sanctum sanctorum* they could not make out anything as there was pitch darkness inside. They, therefore, took the torch and cautiously entered the temple and searched for Manson in every corner. They went round the idol and focussed the light of the torch behind the nook of the door, but saw none there. They were disappointed a little and even felt puzzled. They walked out of the temple and told their Commander that there was nobody inside the temple. But Visnu Kulkarni told them again,

"There are a few big stone lintels high up in the wall. He must be hiding there. Please check up once again."

The two soldiers felt enthused by this suggestion and rushed back into the temple. They held their torches high towards the ceiling and saw something glittering on the stone lintel. As they walked near it, they found out that they were the heels of Manson's boots. They instantly caught his heels and dragged him ferociously to the stone floor. Manson fell on the floor and felt very insecure. He lost no time in triggering off the double-barrel gun at the soldiers. Bang went the bullet. And lo, the bullet hit Raya in the chest. Suddenly Raya sagged to the floor unconscious. The death of his dear brother enraged Marya beyond measure. He, therefore, jumped on to Manson and knocked his gun off his hands and threw it outside the temple. He, then, held the hands of Manson and went on kicking him out of the temple. He felled Manson on the ground, sat on his belly and began to pound his chest with all the might he had in his fists. Manson was completely helpless and was pleading for his life,

"Dear man, please leave me alive. You may take me to your king, but don't kill me."

But Marya could not forget his dear brother who was shot dead mercilessly by the British monster. Commander Visnu Kulkarni shouted from a distance,

"Marya, don't kill him, don't kill him please. Only bind him up." Although Marya heard the words of his Commander, he was not in a position to care for them. Mad anger raged in him. He lifted up his large sword and struck it heavily on Manson's neck. Lo! The head of Manson was severed from his trunk and fell a little distance away from there. Blood spurted out from the mangled parts. The trunk of the British officer lay there still writhing with convulsions. As Commander Visnu Kulkarni rushed to the spot, the story of Manson was over. They threw away the trunk of Manson in the camp fire there. Then Marya lifted up the severed head of Manson and pierced it on the tip of his sword and went on exhibiting it to the people in the village of Sureban. Commander Visnu Kulkarni was very proud of his soldier Marya.

Commander Visnu Kulkarni rode to the camp. He dismounted from his horse and entered the tent. He saluted Babasaheb formally and said enthusiastically,

"Sarkar, we have brought the head of Manson."

Babasaheb was shocked by the news and exclaimed, "O God, you have brought danger to my head, Visnu. I had asked you to capture Manson and bring him alive. But you have killed him. That will have very serious consequences for our Kingdom. The Company Sarkar will not keep quiet about it."

Babasaheb was deeply worried and sat with his forehead resting on his palms for a while. Commander Visnu Kulkarni felt guilty but could not help for what had already happened. He explained to Babasaheb how Manson had shot Raya and, therefore, Raya's brother Marya had taken revenge upon Manson by severing his head off his trunk. Babasaheb listened to him patiently and sighed out at last,

"You have brought down the huge mountain upon my head. All right I shall do as directed by Lord Venkatapati."

They cheered themselves and shouted joyfully and rode back to Naragund. As they entered the city, the natives began to gather around them and wondered at the strange and weird sight of the red-face. They went ahead and stopped at the Red-Gate. Marya pulled the face of Manson from the tip of the sword and tied a cord to the bunch of hair on its head. He, then, climbed the steps of the Red-Gate and hung it from the beam of the Red-Gate. The tongue of Manson was lolling out and blood was trickling slowly. Soon there was a large gathering of natives wondering at the strange sight. The flies were swarming and buzzing in a chorus around the cadaverous face. The eyes were popped out of their sockets as it were. Soon the news circulated from one corner of the city to the other. The natives of Naragund started coming in groups and gaped at the face of Manson hanging from the beam of the Red-Gate. The children who saw the popped out eyes in the hanging face were frightened by the ghastly sight so much that they were inflicted with fever and remained bed-ridden for many days. Many expectant mothers were scared even at the memory of the sight in the advanced years of their pregnancy.

Babasaheb, then, rode to the Red-Gate where Manson's severed head was hung for public exhibition. He felt both pity and hatred for the dead British officer. He knew inwardly that this event was the beginning of disaster, although he could not visualize all the details. He thought that the snake of British power, which he had wounded now, would bite him to death any time in future. He returned to his palace and spent a sleepless night. The other officers like Commander Visnu Kulkarni, Minister Raghoji Pant, the soldiers and the natives of Naragund jubilated over the murder of the British officer and felt proud of their king Bhaskararao Bhave for the courage shown in facing the British enemies.

*****

After a week's time, Babasaheb called a meeting of all the Deshapandes, farmers and leading merchants of his kingdom. All of them gathered in the court-hall of his palace and sat in their respective chairs. It was a strictly confidential meeting. Babasaheb addressed them, "My dear citizen-friends, you all know that our soldiers have killed Manson. We have thus, enraged the snake called the Company Sarkar. We don't know when the snake will take revenge upon us. We must, therefore, be prepared to wage a war against the red-faced fellows. For that purpose, I need your cooperation. You must help us with soldiers, horses, grains and weapons which will definitely add up to our strength. I would like to know how best you can contribute to this war with the British people."

All the leaders of Naragund were bubbling with patriotic zeal. They felt inspired to declare the kind of help they would be able to extend. First, a Deshapande got up and assured,

"Sarkar, I shall take the responsibility of collecting all the arms of the natives and supplying them to your soldiers."

"That's very good of you, Deshpande," said Babasaheb.

Then Virabhadra Nayaka stood up and promised,

"Sarkar, I have about seven hundred private soldiers at my command. I shall try to collect another three hundred. This is the best that I can do."

"That's very good Virabhadra Nayaka. I always rely upon you in emergency," replied Babasaheb.

Then a leading farmer stood up and promised, "Sarkar, I shall collect as much cereal as I can from the farmers of Naragund and send it to the palace."

"Yes, that will solve the problem of food for our soldiers," said Babasaheb.

Then a leading merchant stood up and declared, "Sarkar, I shall supply the grocery-provision by collecting it from other merchants of Naragund."

"Dear Setty, I am really proud of having such patriotic people in my kingdom," said Babasaheb thankfully.

Likewise other admirers of Babasaheb promised to contribute their mite to the palace to meet the unexpected emergency in their kingdom. They all felt that it was their moral duty to support their king when he had asked for it. Babasaheb, thus, discussed all the details connected with the war that he was going to wage against the Company Sarkar. He thanked all the native leaders for their active interest in the patriotic cause. He felt enthused to go ahead with his plan of rebellion. He also believed inwardly that the grace of Lord Venkatapati would be there on him. All the leaders of Naragund took their departure from the palace that day and busied themselves in attending to their respective responsibilities. There was a general atmosphere of excitement in the city.

*****

Meanwhile Baniya Bapu and Krishnaji Pant sent secret messages to Mr. Malcolm who had taken charge of the office after the assassination of Manson by the rebels of Naragund. Mr. Malcolm who had been deeply enraged by the loss of the precious life of his predecessor took a vow to exterminate Babasaheb from the face of the earth itself. He, therefore, began to ingratiate Baniya Bapu and Krishnaji Pant more meticulously. He sent word to them through his secret messengers that they should inform him about every activity going on inside Naragund. Accordingly Baniya Bapu and Krishnaji Pant confidentially informed him that Babasaheb was making preparations for the war against the Company Sarkar. Mr. Malcolm was terribly upset by the arrogance of Babasaheb. He, therefore, wrote to the Head Office at Calcutta for the supply of additional soldiers and arms. He wanted to compensate for the loss of Manson's life. At the same time, he kept on ingratiating Baniya Bapu and Krishnaji Pant and requested them to supply intelligence regularly.

*****

The British Government was very suspicious of Babasaheb's behaviour. The British officers knew that he was a very influential chief in the southern part of the Maratha country and could, therefore, wield a lot of influence on the neighbouring chiefs who were equally disgruntled with the British Government and their exploitative policies like Arms Act and the Doctrine of Lapse. Sir Malcolm wanted to ascertain the fact about Babasaheb of Naragund. He knew that Naragund was situated on a high hill and protected by a very sturdy fort. Fighting with Babasaheb who had certain geographical advantages was rather a bit difficult even for the well-organized armed force of the British. Sir Malcolm, therefore, wanted to know what preparations were being made in Naragund by Babasaheb and his supporters so that he could defeat him by foul means if not by fair ones. He sent a secret message to the Mamledar of Navalagund to keep a watch upon all the activities going on inside Naragund and report the same to him regularly. The Mamledar of Navalagund could do the duty very easily as the distance between Navalagund and Naragund was only about twelve miles and there were many officers in Navalagund who used to visit Naragund frequently either for official purposes or for meeting their close relatives residing in Naragund. He did his duty meticulously to please the British authorities so that he could get some benefit like a quick promotion. He appointed his subordinate officers to visit Naragund regularly in disguise with some pretext or the other and gather intelligence about the war preparations made by Babasaheb and his machinery. On 27th May 1858, he sent the following report to Sir Malcolm :

"I have received your order of 26th May calling upon me to report respecting the Naragundkar. Before receiving your order I had sent a Havaldar and peon to find out what was going on, but they have not yet returned. Lest they should meet with any opposition, I gave them a letter requesting payment of the balance of revenue due on account of Konnur — the Havaldar moreover is in disguise. I have also sent other people who reside near Naragund. I have ascertained that some people have left

Naragund and have gone to other villages, and that some Sawkars are preparing to leave, but that the authorities will not allow them to quit the place, and ask the reason of their departure. They are moreover summoning some of their Shetsundies and have returned to them some of the weapons which they had taken from them. They only allow persons to pass in and out of the town and palace after much questioning. Two or three thailees have been sent from the Huzoor (probably Mr. Manson) summoning the Chief to attend but he excused himself on the plea of sickness. The meaning of this is that the Jamakhandikar was taken and placed in confinement and he is doubtful lest he should be treated in the same manner, he is desirous of either remaining in his own territory or of going to Benares. Such is the report — I have not yet heard whether the Dummul people are in league with him or not. I have sent all the balance in the Treasury to the Huzoor."

The next day the Mamledar of Navalagund sent a report dated 28th May 1858 about the latest activities of the natives of Naragund. He had offered a few more details thereby making the British authorities more alert about Babasaheb :

"I sent Ayyappa Setty to Naragund to find out what was going on. He returned today at 6 o'clock, he reports that three guns were brought back from Jagapur and mounted today on the fort. Besides these, ten or twelve guns have been mounted on the tower. Golandazes have been presented with coats and turbans and means have been taken to prepare powder and balls and about two thousand five hundred people have assembled and more are being summoned. Today puja is to be performed to the arms and tents are to be pitched outside. Means are being taken to purchase grain. The Shetsundies have been presented with 50 sheep. The Ramadurgkar has been summoned but has refused to come, but it is said that the Naragundkar will not rest till he has brought him. It is reported that Bhimarao Mundaragi is to come in two days and his assistance is to be sent from Surapur. It is necessary that some people be sent here for our protection. I sent the Treasure yesterday to the Huzoor. I hear that a force is coming from Kaladagi. On the road there is a pass where there is a Desai who intends to dispute it. Some Bagalkote merchants have brought some rice to Naragund on their way to Moorut. The Naragundkar wished to buy it but on their refusing to sell it he seized it by force. He also bought supplies from the merchants."

On 28th May 1858, the Mamledar of Navalagund sent the following report :

"I sent Havaldar Abdulla Khan and Dharam Chand Sawkar to Naragund. They returned yesterday and reported that there were 40 Shetsundies at the three gates of Naragund. They examined all persons approaching the town but permitted the Police on their producing the letter to pass in. Today preparations are being made. This is all the news they have brought. Kelakeri belonging to this district is close to Naragund. I have sent the Kulkarni of that village to Naragund; he has returned today to say that the Naragundkar yesterday did puja to his arms and feasted Brahmins. He intends setting out today or tomorrow. He has entertained some recruits promising Sepoys 5 Rupees and sawars 7 Rupees per month. It is said that the Ramadurgakar is coming. The Kulkarni also says that someone is to come from Bhimarao Mundaragi today. It is evident that he intends to make a disturbance. Formerly there were only 10 people at the gate of Naragund and there appears no reason why there should be now 40 and from the Naragundkar saying that he intends to set out and to hunt, it appears that there will be a rising similar to what has taken place in Dummul. The Foujdar went yesterday to Naragund but would not let him, enter without an order. He says that they examined all persons and passengers in and out with much caution. I have sent today the Police Setti Ayyappa as he has relations within the town. It is said that the guns which were sent towards Dharwad have been brought back to Naragund."

On 29th May 1858, the Mamledar of Navalagund sent the latest report about the activities going on in Naragund :

"I reported yesterday what had happened at Naragund up to last evening. Last night 5 guns were fired from Naragund fort at eleven o'clock. I do not know whether it was in consequence of his palki being paraded or as an acknowledgment to God that all the guns and ammunition had been successfully carried up to the fort. After this no thailees or letters ought to be sent to the Naragundkar. He has rebelled against the Government and it only retains to send a force here."

*****

Babasaheb had asked Commander Visnu Kulkarni and Virabhadra Nayaka to make all the preparations for the fight with the enemies. The entire city was seething with excitement and also some kind of fear. Womenfolk began to leave Naragund for other villages overnight in bullock carts to seek shelter with their parents, brothers or sisters. The whole city seemed to have come under the influence of *Rahu*. Malcolm sent an envoy to Babasaheb to intimate the date of war. Babasaheb accepted the invitation and was prepared to wage a war with the British army. He sent for Commander Visnu Kulkarni and asked,

"My dear Commander sir, hope everything is ready?"

"Don't you worry, Sarkar. I have made all the preparations. Virabhadra Nayaka has been training nearly a thousand soldiers," assured Visnu Kulkarni.

Babasaheb said further, "They are expected to attack us on Tuesday. We have hardly four days left at our disposal. I hope the cannons are kept ready on all the sides of the hill-top."

"Yes, Sarkar. I have personally inspected the installation of cannons on the hill-top. I have got them arranged in all the four directions. Today I have asked my subordinates to keep the gun-powder ready."

"Please see that nothing is lacking. The hill-top is nearly four hundred yard high. If we shoot at the enemies from that height, they will be simply leveled to the earth," said Babasaheb with confidence.

*****

When the sun went down in the western horizon, darkness descended everywhere. Krishnaji Pant and Baniya Bapu asked three servants to carry two bags of *ragi* and ten pots of sweet oil to the hill-top. The three servants loaded them on the backs of four oxen and goaded them up the hill along the narrow path. As there was not much traffic there at that time, nobody noticed it. The servants took nearly an hour to reach the hill-top. They unloaded the bags of *ragi* and oil near the compound of the powder magazine hurriedly and returned home. As they had received ample money from the clerks, they did not bother about the reason why the bags had been carried up the hill top.

The two clerks *i.e.* Krishnaji Pant and Baniya Bapu were eagerly waiting for the opportune time. As a few hours went by, the noise of the city decreased gradually. They waited patiently for a little more time. As the night advanced, dead silence overwhelmed the city occasionally punctuated by the barking of dogs in the distant lanes. The nocturnal silence was intensified by the shrill chorus of cicadas. Baniya Bapu and Krishnaji Pant started chewing pan, lime and betel to kill their time for a while. When Krishnaji Pant snapped his thumb on the middle finger and winked at Baniya Bapu, the latter stood up and ready to go. Both of them silently mounted their horses and rode along the hill path. They avoided the spots where guards stood and followed a shortcut to the powder magazine. The stars in the sky were glittering. But they were perspiring profusely in spite of the pleasant breeze blowing around them. They dismounted from their horses and tethered them to the iron rings of the compound.

Baniya Bapu opened the door of the powder magazine and both of them carried the bags of *ragi* and oil into the building. The gun powder stored in the large stone pit was giving a very strong and sharp smell. They felt disgusted with the acrid smell so much that they spat their sputum repeatedly by coming out of the door. But they had to do their duty which they had promised to Malcolm and get an unforgettable prize. Krishnaji Pant took up a leather bag of oil, opened its lid carefully and poured the oil on the gun-powder which created a mild swishing sound.

Baniya Bapu followed suit. Both of them exhausted all the bags of oil. Then Krishnaji Pant opened the bags of *ragi*. Both of them lifted up the bags one by one and poured the soft tiny grains in the gun-powder. Both of them were perspiring heavily while doing the treacherous act, but they could not lose any time. They brought in two sturdy bamboo sticks and stirred the mixture of gun-powder, sweet oil and the grains of *ragi* until they felt that the three items were amalgamated properly. Immediately they moved out of the store room and locked it. They mounted their horses hurriedly and rode back to their homes. They heaved a sigh of relief and slept like logs until the next morning.

The next day, they sent a secret messenger to Kolhapur to inform Sir Malcolm about their nocturnal accomplishment. Sir Malcolm was very happy to learn the news. He was supposed to attack Naragund on Thursday, but he wanted to overtake Babasaheb two days ahead and that too unexpectedly. He, therefore, ordered his army to be well prepared. That very evening he set out towards Naragund. The soldiers sat on their horses and rode swiftly towards their enemy. Their guns were slung on their backs. As the horses marched ahead, they raised a cloud of dust behind them. They reached Amaragol and camped there at night. Sir Malcolm wanted to attack Naragund the very next day.

Babasaheb was waiting for the help from the sympathizers like Desai of Hammigi, Bhimaraya of Mundaragi and the Virarani of Chitradurga. Messages had been sent to all of them who had promised to join him in their common fight against the British. There were still two days time for the beginning of war. Babasaheb and his patriotic companions were making preparations of all kinds, like weapons, foodgrains and uniforms etc. On Tuesday Commander Visnu Kulkarni got up early in the morning and went for a stroll on the hill-top. He stood near a crag and looked around at the horizon. The rosy tint was slowly spreading across the eastern sky. The disc of the Sun was slowly rising out of the skyline. As he turned right, he descried white dots a few miles away from Naragund. It took no time for him to guess that the British soldiers of Sir Malcolm had camped there. A cold wave ran through his spine and his heart began to throb with anxiety. He rushed down the hill, mounted his horse and rode towards the palace. He left his horse at the main gate and rushed into the royal chamber, met Babasaheb and burst out,

"Sarkar, we are in for trouble. Sir Malcolm's army has already camped beyond the Hirehalla river. They were supposed to come here on day after tomorrow. What to do now, Sarkar?"

"What?" exclaimed Babasaheb. "They were expected to come here on Thursday. How could they come before that? Are you sure that they are the British army?"

"I am very sure, Sarkar. I suspect some conspiracy going on against us in our own city."

"All right, Commander sir. We have to face all the unexpected emergencies in life. Please send for Virabhadra Nayaka and ask him to collect his troops in the templeyard."

"Yes, Sarkar. I shall attend to it immediately."

Commander Visnu Kulkarni rushed from there and rode towards his office near the templeyard. He sent a messenger to Virabhadra Nayaka to join him immediately. Soon the soldiers gathered in the templeyard and awaited orders from the Commander. Within a short while Virabhadra Nayaka rode into the templeyard with extraordinary speed. The other soldiers made way for him. Commander Visnu Kulkarni stood on the high platform and shouted his orders,

"Attention please. Dear Virabhadra Nayaka, you are the leader of a big portion of the civilian army. You shall stand in front of the palace and protect Babasaheb Sarkar from the enemies. You may have as many detachments as you wish to be with you."

"'Yes, sir.' I shall do that. I'll not require more than a hundred soldiers for that," replied Virabhadra Nayaka.

Then Commander Visnu Kulkarni shouted orders to the other troops standing to attention with their swords in their right hands.

Their swords flashed dazzlingly in the morning light of the sun.

"Troop number one shall go to the hill top and attend to the cannons. The cannons should be fired only when I send orders, but not until then. Troop number two should wait near the Red-Gate. Troop number three should wait behind the hill. And all other troops should guard the other gates of the city. We shall be ready to lay down our lives for the sake of Babasaheb Sarkar who has taken care of us.

On 2nd June 1858, Babasaheb was eagerly waiting in the palace. He was feeling rather restless. Bhimarao of Mundaragi had sent a letter to him saying that he could not rush to Naragund instantly as he was busy fighting with the British people at Koppal and that he would certainly send his army to Naragund within four or five days. Babasaheb was also waiting for the help promised by Kenchanagouda of Hammigi and the Virarani of Chitradurga. But so far nobody had been able to come to his help as the battle had been unexpectedly preponed by the cunning British officers. He was so restless that he could not sit up for long on his throne. He was pacing up and down in the court hall. He would go to the window, hold the bars and peep out at the outskirts of the city and walk back to the throne and sit for a moment. Then he would quaff a little water from the silver bowl and go to the other window and stare at the spire of the temple of Lord Venkateswara and exclaim, "I'm at your mercy, lord. Nobody can save me except you." Suddenly he heard the bugle and trumpet sounds answering those of the enemies. Babasaheb cocked his ears and heard the war cries in the distant outskirts of the capital.

*****

The soldiers of Sir Malcolm rushed to the main gate of Naragund where the soldiers of Naragund were waiting. As the bugle was sounded, the native soldiers gave a war cry and fell on the British ones. They struck the British soldiers with their large swords, but the British soldiers shot the native soldiers with their guns from a distance of ten feet. The tussle continued for some time. A few British soldiers were mangled to death and fell in the bloody pools. Likewise several native soldiers were also shot dead by the enemies, sagged to the earth and died heroically for their master Babasaheb. The gun-powder that was available in Naragund was soon exhausted. The soldiers of Naragund lost their lives very rapidly. The surviving ones began to run for life. The soldiers of Colonel Malcolm were many times bigger in number than the small army of Naragund. Commander Visnu Kulkarni realized the gravity of the situation. He felt that his soldiers with their primitive swords and spears could not be equal to the British ones with their guns. Besides, the army of Colonel Malcolm had spread itself in all the four directions of the city of Naragund. The native soldiers were concentrating on the main gate. Commander Visnu Kulkarni felt that face to face fighting was not of much avail. He, therefore, asked his subordinate officers to blow the loudest trumpet thereby signaling to the soldiers in charge of big cannons to fire at the enemies. He waited for several minutes to hear the bangs and booms of the cannons. But he heard only the hissing sounds. Soon a messenger ran to the Commander Visnu Kulkarni and told him between gasps,

"Commander sir, we are in trouble. Our cannons are not working at all. They are giving out only hissing sounds."

"Where are the store keepers Baniya Bapu and Krishnaji Pant? Go and bring them here."

"No, master. We searched for them at home and at the hill-top. But they are not to be found anywhere. Besides, we saw...."

Commander Visnu Kulkarni was able to guess what might happen to Naragund. He rushed to the main gate where face-to-face fight was going on. He learnt that most of his soldiers had been killed by the enemies and felt that their kingdom would be seized by Colonel Malcolm within no time. He felt ashamed of himself for accepting the anticipatory defeat. But his practical sense awakened in him and made him think of the safety of his beloved master Babasaheb. He could somehow compromise with the shameful situation and the pitiable condition of Naragund, but he could never imagine Babasaheb to be killed or ill-treated by the British officers. He, therefore, rushed to the palace where Virabhadra Nayaka stood guard, along with his troop. Commander Visnu Kulkarni went to him and whispered something into his ears and rushed into the palace after dismounting his horse quickly. Babasaheb was eagerly waiting for the news of the progress of the war. Commander Visnu Kulkarni said with a lachrymose face,

"Sarkar, we are in for trouble."

Babasaheb stared into his eyes and could make out that there must be something unpleasant. He was impatient to hear the news. He, therefore, said,

"Come on Visnu, what's the matter. Tell me quick."

Commander Visnu Kulkarni controlled his inner fluctuation and said,

"Sarkar, our soldiers are overpowered and killed. The British army is many times bigger than ours. Besides, our gun-powder stock is completely exhausted. Many of our soldiers are killed and the few surviving ones are still doing their best to keep on the show. I'm sure our kingdom is sure to be seized within a short time. We will fight to the last breath of our life. But that won't help. Colonel Malcolm may come and capture you. We simply cannot imagine the dire consequences to all of us, especially to you and the members of your family. Before such a tragedy happens, I pray to you, Sarkar, to escape from Naragund to some safe place. There's no time even to think about anything. Your life is more precious than the kingdom or the palace for us."

Babasaheb could see the tremour in Visnu Kulkarni's voice and tears trickling in his lachrymose face. The Commander bowed down once again to Babasaheb and said,

"Sarkar, I shall rush to the main gate to see what is happening. Meanwhile, you please leave the palace immediately."

He rode back to the main gate where the fight was going on and tried to enhearten the soldiers to fight until their last breath.

After the departure of Commander Visnu Kulkarni to the battlefield, Babasaheb grew deeply introvertive about his own condition and taking stock of what had happened in the past guess what might happen in future to him and to his mother and wife. He leant his face against his palms and sat in a drooping position. He closed his eyes for a few minutes and thought about what decision to take about himself in this dire condition. "I have angered these British fellows by troubling them in many ways. If they defeat our soldiers and take charge of Naragund, they are sure to ill-treat me and the members of my family. It's but natural for them as for any enemies to do so. Many chiefs of *Samsthans* have written to me that they would extend their help to me in this fight against the British. If these letters are found by the British, they are sure to harass these chiefs. I must not land them into trouble because they have tried to help me during this emergency. I must, therefore, burn all the letters written by them to me. Likewise I should alert my mother and wife and ask them to escape from here to save their honour. Then I must flee from Naragund and go away from the enemies." After deliberating like this, Babasaheb opened his eyes and got up from his royal seat. He, then, mounted his horse and rode towards the kitchen where the food for the soldiers was to be cooked. As he went near the kitchen, the cooks and the other attendants stood up in respect. Babasaheb went to the oven in which fire was burning mildly. He took out all the letters from the bag and consigned them to fire. Soon the flames covered the letters and turned them into a big heap of dark ashes. Babasaheb stood there watching until the letters were completely burnt. Now he heaved a sigh of relief. Then he mounted his horse and rode towards his palace. His bodyguards were of course, following him close by.

Yamunabayi and Savitribayi were also suffering from anxiety about the result of the war with the British people. They were aware of the fight that was going on between the native army and the British army. Both of them were praying to Lord Venkateswara to grant victory to the king of Naragund. By that time they heard the footsteps and guessed that Babasaheb was coming into the chamber. Within a few seconds Babasaheb entered their chamber. Savitribayi stood up as usual to respect her husband. Yamunabayi sat erect on her seat and asked him with loving affection,

"Dear son, how is the battle going on? How are the signs? Are we likely to win?"

Babasaheb, was deeply disturbed by his mother's innocent question. With a lot of pain in his heart he looked at the mother and replied,

"Mother, how shall I answer your question? This fight has no meaning. Our small native army is overpowered by the large army of the Britishers. Within a short time our story will come to an end. Our soldiers are dying very fast in the battle. That is the reason why I rushed to you to brief you about the matter. I feel it's better to run away from here than being caught by the enemies. Once arrested by them, we are sure to be separated from one another. Before such a dire thing happens, I think it is better to save our honour and follow the path as shown by the God Almighty. While passing through the thick forests, we may be devoured by the wild animals. But I think, even that is far better than being arrested by the enemies. I feel I must escape from the palace now. Similarly I would like to suggest to both of you to pursue the path that you deem fit for saving your life, *dharma* and honour. There's no time now for procrastination or to depend upon one another. Please don't tarry now. There's no time now even to discuss any of these things."

On hearing these unexpected words from the lips of Babasaheb, both the mother and the wife were shocked so much that they felt as if the skies were rushing down upon themselves. They felt as if they would suffer from sudden blackout of consciousness. Especially his wife Savitribayi was so sad that she could not speak out anything immediately. She began to sob loudly and uncontrollably. She burst out, "Oh Lord Venkatesa, what is the sin we have committed that you are so angry with us?" She then began to think of the future course of action that she should take along with her mother-in-law. But the mother-in-law Yamunabayi tried to control her sorrow and tried to reason with Babasaheb, "Dear son, you had said that the other chiefs of neighbouring kingdoms would come to your help. What happened to their promise? Did they force you to be in the forefront and let you down at the critical time? Please don't hide anything from us. We have got to accept whatever is meted out to us by the Lord. But I would just like to know the truth however bitter it is."

Babasaheb cleared his throat and replied in a steady voice, "Mother, the neighbouring kings have promised me seriously that they would help me with their armies. But that requires at least another four days time. But the cunning British fellows have preponed the war just to harass me. We can't, therefore, wait for them now. Even then we could have fought with the enemies, but those treacherous fellows like Krishnya Joshi and Baniya Bapu have rendered our gun-powder useless by mixing oil and *ragi* in it. These traitors have eaten our salt and betrayed us. They have not only leaked out all our confidential ideas and decisions, but tampered with our gun-powder. Mother, there's no time now to think of or consult one another. I am so helpless now that I cannot take you with me. Please don't prevent me from fleeing from here. Nor should you both stay here lest you should be ill-treated or dishonoured by the enemies. Please don't bother about kith or kin, land or palace or gold or money or anything. Honour is more important than anything. Please rely upon the Lord and follow your own path together. Mother please accept my last salutation and bless me and permit me to go away from here. You may take your daughter-in-law also with you."

With these pathetic words, Babasaheb fell prostrate at his mother's feet and sought her blessings. Yamunabayi was so much overcome with sorrow that she felt a big lump in her throat and words could not come out of her lips. Tears began to pour down along her cheeks. She lifted up Babasaheb's face and hugged him affectionately. She smelt his pate and stared at his face. She blessed him in her tremulous voice,

"Dear son, I understand the calamity that has befallen you and all of us. I don't want to prevent you. Please go away from here. May Lord Venkateswara bless you. May the same Lord guide us the two women also. For who else should protect us when we are so helpless? We shall leave the palace as soon as you have left. May Lord Venkateswara bless you, my son."

Although Yamunabayi spoke these consolatory words to her son, she could not release him from her affectionate arms. She was still thinking of the consequences. Time was fleeting fast. Babasaheb helplessly released himself from her hug and said,

"Mother, don't tarry now. There's hardly any time for thinking."

Savitribayi who had to part with her beloved husband could not control herself. She hugged him and sobbed with a loud voice. Babasaheb felt a sudden darkness in his consciousness for a moment. He did not know what to do or say now. Yet he controlled himself and spoke to her,

"Dear Savitri, what's this? If you behave like this, I cannot go ahead even a single step. Just think about the emergency. If I stay here for a little more time, I'm sure all of us will be captured and insulted by the enemies. Please don't behave like a child. You listen to the mother and do according to her advice. You have a lot of understanding about life. How better shall I convince you?" With these words of consolation Bhaskararao tried to disentangle himself from his wife's arms. But Savitri did not release him from her grip of arms. "No my dear sir, I cannot live without you. Either you kill me before you go or allow me to follow you like a slave," she cried at a high pitch. Hearing her wail even the diamond hearted Bhaskararao melted. His shoulder was drenched by the incessant flow of her tears. Yet Bhaskararao tried to reason with her about the emergency,

"My dear Savitri, do you think you are an ordinary woman to lament over the situation that has arisen so unexpectedly in our life? Please remember that you are the heroic wife of a king and as such, you should never cry about such situations that are common in a royal household. You should know how to behave in such contingent situations. If God willing, we shall be reunited and can lead a happy life in future." But Savitri was not in a position to listen to his words. She sobbed and continued,

"Lord, please don't leave me alone here. Please save me from worrying about your plight when you are away from me. It's better to die than be burnt in the fire of separation."

Bhaskararao was nonplused by his wife's wailing and argument. For a moment he did not know what to say to her. His mother was also observing their plight silently shedding her tears. For a few seconds, there was total silence. Then Savitri heaved a deep sigh and questioned him,

"What's there to think about so seriously, my lord? Don't you remember the story of the Rajput king Johar told by a brahmin who visited our palace in the past? Those Rajputs used to settle the problem of their wives and children by killing them before they themselves died? Why don't you follow their model?"

Bhaskararao was silenced once again by her heroic suggestion. His hairs stood on end. He felt a horripilation even in that sorrowful condition. He gathered his thoughts and tried to convince her,

"Dear Savitri, do you want to teach me a lesson? Have you ever thought about the matter seriously?" Those Rajput kings were heartless enough to throw their wives and children in the pyre and kill them. Then they used to wear the mourning gown of yellow colour and go to the battlefield only to die. But our condition is different from theirs. Nor are we heartless like them. We are likely to be reunited in future. Please remember that we are tender hearted brahmins. We can accomplish only those things that can be done with the use of intelligence and discrimination. I don't want to do the inhuman things done by the Rajputs. You are a lady with some understanding. You must know what is happening to Naragund now. Within no time the enemies will take charge of this palace and put their soldiers to bar our exit. We must flee very quickly now." With these words, Bhaskararao tried to disentangle himself from his wife's arms. But to his surprise Savitri suddenly sagged to the floor. When he looked into her eyes, he understood that she had fainted. At the sight of his fainting wife, Bhaskararao seemed to freeze as it were. He did not know what to do. Time was fleeting very fast. Yamunabayi tried to dab Savitri's eyes with cold water. After a few seconds Savitri recovered her consciousness and exclaimed, "Have you decided to desert me lord?" Bhaskararao stood silent and helpless. Yamunabayi who had a good deal of maturity understood the plight of her son and convinced her daughter-in-law,

"Dear Savitri, this is not the right time for troubling your husband. Now allow him to go. If God wills we shall all meet once again. Let's wait for that lucky day. Now we have to act boldly and save our honour. If we delay now there will be worse consequences for us. We have got to endure whatever is offered by God. Please let him go."

These words of the mother-in-law affected Savitri very deeply. She understood the plight of her husband. She, therefore, fell prostrate to her husband's feet and said,

"My lord, my parents had offered me to you in the presence of gods, brahmins and the holy fire. Accordingly you have protected me with boundless love until now. I had thought this happy life would continue for ever. But God has willed it otherwise. I am fated to be separated from you. There is no other way. I, therefore, will not prevent you from going away from me now, though there is no guarantee that I will be alive after your departure."

Hearing the rational words of Savitri, Bhaskararao felt happy even in the midst of deep sorrow. He bowed once again to his mother's feet and sought her permission and blessings. Yamunabayi blessed him,

"Dear son, have a long life. Wherever you may be, you protect your life and do only the right thing."

Then Bhaskararao addressed his wife, "Dear Savitri, be always with your mother-in-law and do as you both think fit." With these words and a very heavy heart, Bhaskararao walked out of the chamber. When Babasaheb came out of his palace and mounted his horse in order to flee from Naragund, he happened to see Raghopant Limaye. Although the latter was his enemy Babasaheb requested him, "Please protect the royal family." Then he together with his close associates like Gangadhar Chintamani, Anna Sahasrabuddhe, Puranik, Basappa Tambe, Hanumanta Hongal, Babaji Zambia, Kashiram Nalavade, Visnu Kulkarni, Raghopant and others left the palace and rode out of Naragund through the secret route.

After the departure of Bhaskararao, the whole palace looked deserted like a cemetery to Yamunabayi and Savitri. Both of them burst into loud and uncontrollable wail. The maid servants were trying in vain to hold them and console them. Savitri intuitively felt that it was a permanent separation from her husband and fainted once again. Yamunabayi again treated her with cold water and embraced her affectionately. Although Yamunabayi was outwardly trying to console her daughter-in-law, she was inwardly thinking as to what course of action she should take in that moment of emergency. The entire palace appeared like a large grave to them. They could not stay there for any longer.

After the departure of Bhaskararao, the whole palace appeared to be empty for his mother and wife. There was hardly any time for thinking or planning. Yamunabayi did not bother about the gold and silver or about the land or other property of Naragund. She asked Savitri,

"Come on, daughter-in-law, get ready. Let's also leave the palace."

"Where shall we go, mother-in-law?"

"I really do not know where we should go. First let us leave the palace and run out of Naragund. Then let us do as guided by Lord Venkatapati."

"All right, mother-in-law."

Savitri changed her dress and put on a different sari, bodice and her usual ornaments. They asked their confidant servant and the nearest relative called Ramachandra who was about twenty years or so to accompany them. Yamunabayi, Savitri and Ramachandra left the palace through the secret underground exit and hastened out of Naragund unnoticed by anyone. Even the other inmates of the palace did not know about their departure immediately.

*****

Visnu Kulkarni was quite happy to know that Babasaheb Sarkar and his family had escaped from the palace and were prevented from being ill-treated by the British enemies. But yet he could not afford to neglect the battle. He rushed to the main gate and enheartened his soldiers. Since all the cannons had failed, the soldiers of Naragund had grown helpless. The British soldiers shot at the native enemies with their double-bar guns. The soldiers of Naragund had to use only the swords supplied to them by the King. Before they could go very near the British soldiers and strike them, they used to be shot dead by the enemies. When the soldiers of Naragund learnt that they had lost more than half of their strength, they began to flee from the battlefield. The soldiers of Sir Malcolm felt encouraged by the helplessness of the native soldiers. They, therefore, entered the city of Naragund through the main gate and rode towards the palace of Babasaheb.

Virabhadra Nayaka stood near the palace along with his troop. As the British soldiers rode near his troop, he stood ready to fight with them. He rushed towards them and struck at them heroically. He ran his sword through the belly of a British soldier who fell to the ground with a piteous yell. Then another British soldier tried to aim his gun at Virabhadra Nayaka, but before that

Virabhadra Nayaka knocked his gun with his large blood thirsty sword and smote at the enemy's neck which was severed from its trunk and fell to the earth. By this time a bullet hit the belly of the horse on which Virabhadra Nayaka was saddled. The horse began to lose its strength and sagged to the earth. But Virabhadra Nayaka jumped off the horse and held it tightly with his left hand thereby preventing it from sagging and fought with his right hand degladiating his sword at the enemies. He struck another enemy at the right flank with such a force that the latter tumbled down to the earth with a thud. By that time Sir Malcolm's soldiers were terribly irritated by Virabhadra Nayaka's heroic show. One of the British soldiers aimed at him and pulled the trigger and lo : the bullet hit Virabhadra Nayaka in the chest and burst out of his back thereby creating a gory hole in his body. Virabhadra Nayaka felt an irritation in his chest. He did not back out. He rushed to a wooden casque lying nearby, took out a palmful of grease and applied it to the hole in his chest bored by the enemy's bullet. Then with a renewed anger, he lifted up his blood stained sword and brought it down on the British soldier and ripped his belly deeply. The enemy yelled piteously and slid down from his horse thereby falling into the pool of his own blood. The British soldiers were exasperated beyond measure by Virabhadra Nayaka's pertinacity. Two of them, therefore, rushed from two opposite directions and shot at Virabhadra Nayaka simultaneously. Virabhadra Nayaka could not immediately guess the directions from which the bullets were shot at him. As the two bullets hit him in his flanks he sagged down to the earth with a thump. His horse lay beside him in convulsions. Alas! Virabhadra Nayaka had laid down his life heroically on the battlefield for the love of his king Babasaheb and his native land of Naragund. Even when his life was ebbing out of him, his lips remained tightly pursed showing his patriotic determination. The bird of his life flew peacefully to Heaven after having done its duty to the master. When the soldiers of Virabhadra Nayaka's troop saw their leader being killed, they began to run for their life. By that time darkness descended everywhere. The dead bodies of the native soldiers lay in picturesque disarray in pools of blood. The British soldiers soon surrounded the palace and stood guard at all the gates. They wanted to capture Bhaskararao Bhave at the earliest possible hour as per the orders of Sir Malcolm.

*****

When the army of Sir Malcolm took hold of the palace of Naragund, he ordered his soldiers to search for Bhaskararao and the members of his family and capture them. Accordingly the captains and majors rushed into the main gate of the palace and entered the court hall of the palace which looked empty and deserted. But they were struck by the beauty of the wall painting there. They descended to the ground floor and went into the large rooms where there were many wooden cots and cushions and silken bedsheets, but there was nobody around there. The British soldiers were walking with their boots on producing a pat-pat sound on the stone floor. Then they searched in the kitchen where large vessels and cooking utensils lay helter-skelter. They opened the cupboards and boxes to see if anyone had hidden himself there. After a thorough search they felt happy that they had achieved a very easy victory over the enemy but were unhappy to know that the latter had escaped from their hands. Sir Malcolm was very happy to take possession of Bhaskararao's palace and posted soldiers at every important gate of it.

At night when the news that Babasaheb's palace was captured by the British circulated in the city, the native civilians of Naragund were scared out of their wits. For they could never believe that Babasaheb could be defeated by the British or any other enemy. But now the most unexpected tragedy had happened. People were more worried about their lives than about their property, gold or money. Women who were cooking their food left the ovens burning and ran out of their homes with their parents, men folk and children rushed out of Naragund in the overwhelming darkness. The women who were pregnant were aborted by the shocking news of the arrival of the British soldiers into Naragund. Even in their weakness they mounted the carts to flee the town along with their men folk and children. The people who were eating their dinner left their food and began to flee from Naragund for their safety to the other villages and towns where they could live securely. They did not bother to take their gold or silver or money with them, nor did they bother about locking their boxes or doors. Everybody was in a hurry to save his life. They managed to jump over the high walls of the city at midnight time and wended their ways in the encircling darkness. They ran without caring for the thorns or bushes or rocks or rivers and brooks on the way. They ran and ran until the break of day when they could decide which direction to follow for reaching their destination.

Raghopant, the close confidant of Bhaskararao, had also run away with his master nobody knew where. Raghopant had a big family with about thirty members in it. He enjoyed a lot of respect in the society because of his close connection with the royal family. Although the kith and kin of Raghopant knew that their master was busy with the military activities connected with Bhaskararao's fight with the British they did not take it very seriously as it was part of his regular job. On the contrary, they were busy with the preparations for the wedding of a relative in the family. All the men, women and children were preoccupied with their respective jobs. The women were preparing various kinds of spices for the wedding dishes and singing many benedictory songs. In another room small girls were playing chess, *chavanga* and marbles with tamarind seeds and enjoying themselves. In other big halls the relatives who had came to Naragund to participate in the wedding were playing separately various games like chess, *letta* and *ganjipa* etc., and deeply immersed in the entertainment. The women were busy preparing *karachikayi*, parched rice, sweetballs and other snacks and sweetmeats. There were several children in Raghopant's family. One of the children asked his mother, "Mummy, I'm very hungry. Please give me something to eat." The mother said, "Wait child, I shall cook the vermicelli *payasam*." She then kept the vessel on the oven and began to put water, ghee, sugar, vermicelli and condiments into it and stirred them. When the liquid reached the boiling point, it began to send out very sweet flavour all around. All these members of Raghopant's family were enjoying themselves in the festive mood of matrimony.

All these members of Raghopant's family were flabbergasted when a servant rushed in and burst out "God! The worst tragedy has befallen us all." The members in the outer room were rather surprised to hear his unusual words. "What nonsense are you talking fellow? Hope your health is all right." "Oh, the most unexpected thing has happened!" Again the elders of the family were irritated by his general remarks. One of the elders thundered at him, "Fool why are you exclaiming like that? Please tell us clearly what the matter is." Then the servant composed himself and hesitatingly said, "Sirs, you know the palace of Naragund has been captured by the British army. Babasaheb Sarkar and our master Raghoji Pant and other confidants have run away from the palace and the city itself." When the members of Raghopant's family heard these words they were really shocked out of their wits. The elderly man who had first disbelieved in the servant's general exclamation could not stand the shock. He fainted and sagged in his own seat. Soon the festive atmosphere gave place to a tearsome and mourning atmosphere. The womenfolk began to sob and wail in-between their exclamations "When the master of the family has run away from us, who can protect us here?" The confusion and fear whipped up everybody. Without knowing what to do they began to leave the house, escape from Naragund at night without being caught by the British soldiers who may harm them or do unmentionable insults to them. The women who were cooking in the kitchen left the vessels on the ovens. They did not have time even to feed their hungry children. The vermicelli *payasam* was still boiling in the vessel on the oven, but the mother dragged her child out of the house and began to run along with others in the darkness. They did not know the routes that they were following. They blindly followed any path that they could find in the darkness. They were not in a position to think of any plan.

Ramarao, who was another Lieutenant of Naragund army was also fleeing the city now. In that terrific hurry he had taken his wife and a small boy called Krisnarao along with him. Krisnarao was the eldest son of Govindarao belonging to Raghopant's family. This boy happened to be a precocious child who was affectionately called as Krisnarao by Bhaskararao himself. They were following one direction not knowing which direction the other relatives were following in the dark. Likewise Govindarao had taken his wife and two children along with him. Thus all the relatives of Raghopant's family were scattered in the encircling darkness and trying to find some place of safety for their stay or temporary hiding. Govindarao's two daughters were luckily safe in their in-laws' places like Vayi and Gurlahosur. In his hurry he had not taken his eldest son.

The next day 2nd June 1858 the British soldiers were directed by Sir Malcolm to take possession of the palace of Bhaskararao. The soldiers were accordingly doing the job assigned to them. They were very thrilled by the unexpectedly easy victory over the king of Naragund. A couple of soldiers climbed the roof of the palace and brought down the banner of Bhaskararao and threw it to the ground contemptuously. Then they hoisted the Union Jack on to the flagpost. As their banner began to flutter in the morning wind, they felt proud of themselves. The flag hoisting was, of course, accompanied by their national anthem to the accompaniment of drums, bugles and trumpets. By the morning time almost all the natives of Naragund had deserted the city for fear of being killed or wounded by the enemies. They had left their houses, coffers, cellars and storehouses unlocked, as they thought their own lives were more precious than any wealth which they could earn if alive. Their priorities had been instantly decided in the feverish hurry at night.

Now the British soldiers who were overjoyed by the easy success over Bhaskararao began to indulge in the pleasure of looting the houses of the natives. It was a pleasant surprise for them to find that most of the houses of farmers, merchants and labourers were not locked or properly closed. The platoons of soldiers who were camping near the outskirts of the city during the previous night, entered the lanes of Naragund with joyous yells and shouts. They began to barge into the wayside houses and loot all the precious clothes, corns, flour, gems, jewels, gold, silver, fruits and eatables etc., without any objection as the masters and inhabitants of those houses had fled from Naragund. They entered the houses including the puja rooms with their boots on and without caring for the feelings of the absent owners of houses. They threw about the things helter-skelter before making their own selection. They drank the milk and curds in the kitchen and ate the sweet cakes and butter etc., which were kept in covered vessels. A group of soldiers entered somebody's house and found silken clothes with filigree work worth nearly four thousand rupees and large quantities of silver and gold. Later it was learnt that the house belonged to one Govindarao. They also found a large quantity of pearls in his house.

Then the soldiers entered a big storeyed mansion which happened to be that of a courtesan called Bhimasani who also had left the city at night for her temporary safety. They rummaged all the cupboards and boxes and found countless and very valuable items like silken garments, silvern vessels, golden ornaments and large quantities of silver and copper coins. They were simply thrilled by the large wealth which they could lay hands on so easily. They felt that their life had become very meaningful as they could earn so much wealth so unexpectedly. As they were told by the native Indians elsewhere, they thought that there was some gold or silver or coins hidden in the earth in the houses of native people. The soldiers, therefore, greedily began to dig the floor of the deserted houses for the possibly hidden wealth there. There was nobody to check them anywhere in the city. Thus the enormous wealth of Naragund was looted within a couple of days. But the only piece of luck for Naragund was that there was no slaughter of native inhabitants or molesting or raping of women. Some soldiers rushed into the temple of Lord Venkateswara, broke the idol and collected all the golden ornaments on the idol as well as those buried beneath the holy shrine. Then they rushed into the famous library called Saraswati Bhandar (Treasure of Knowledge) and burnt all the valuable Sanskrit books and manuscripts. Some of them took sadistic pleasure in butchering the cows on the sacred yard of the temple.

*****

Ramarao had escaped from Naragund at night along with his wife Sitabayi and the small boy of about eight years called Krisnarao, son of Govindarao. But Govindarao had escaped to some other village where he lived with his relatives. He had only two sons of his with him but could not take Krisnarao also with him in that terrific hurry. Now there was no contact between Ramarao and Govindarao. Ramarao lived in same village along with Krisnarao anonymously. He did not want even his neighbours to know his exact identity. They were just pulling on without knowing what was in store for them. One day Ramarao introspected about his own situation and future which appeared to be rather bleak to him. "I happen to be Karbhari and chief lieutenant of Babasaheb Naragundkar. The British fellows have, therefore, kept an eye on me. They are sure to search me out. Not only that. They may destroy my whole family. In such a situation it is not advisable to have Krisnarao with me. His presence with me may prove ominous for me. I must send him to his parents living in that small village." When his own doubts became clear to him, Ramarao called his wife to his room and told her all about his plans. Sitabayi also opined, "It is better to send Krisnarao away from here." After taking the approval of his wife Ramarao moved about and made indirect enquiries with people and finally searched the address of Govindarao's whereabouts.

The very next day, Ramarao got up early in the morning and completed the ablutions and took the boy Krisnarao with him. The boy asked him,

"Uncle, where are we going now?"

"I am taking you to your parents, Krisna."

Krisna felt very ecstatic about the prospects of meeting his parents after the unexpected separation. He began to walk very enthusiastically with Ramarao. While they were treading the path Ramarao was thinking about whether he should meet Govindarao and reach him his son Krisna or not. He deliberated inwardly, "If I meet Govindarao now and leave his son with him, I'll, no doubt, have some satisfaction. But what will be the consequences for him later when the British fellows come to know about my meeting with him? Poor fellow he will have to suffer a lot under the British hands, and may even lose his life along with his wife's and children's. I must, therefore, not meet him at all, but leave his son Krisna as near his place as possible. The rest will be taken care of by Lord Venkatapati." After thus taking an inward decision, Ramarao continued his journey. On the way he bought some fruits for Krisna to eat. Both of them sat beneath the shade of a mango tree and ate their bananas. They took rest for a while. Then they continued their journey. Krisna was dreaming of what to say to his father and mother and how to be with them in a strange home and all that. The sun was growing hotter and hotter. They continued their journey for some more time. Then they reached a small hill. Both of them sat beneath a big banyan tree for rest. The shade was very cool and comfortable for them who were scorched in the hot sun and were tired of walking continuously for half a dozen miles. The shepherds were grazing their sheep on the grassy side of the hill. The occasional bleating of sheep and goats could be heard in the silence of the afternoon. Although Ramarao was feeling a lot of pain in his heart to desert the small boy Krisna, he could not do it so easily. But yet he had to do so because of the dire circumstances of his life. He was inventing some kind of pretext of disappearing from the boy. He noticed that Krisna was dozing against the trunk of the tree. He, therefore, said to him,

"My dear Krisna, you just have a nap here. I shall relieve myself beyond that boulder and come back after I am through with it."

"Please go and come, uncle. I shall be resting here."

Ramarao thought this to be the golden moment to desert the boy. He pretended to go towards the boulder rather briskly. But inwardly his heart was crying for the boy. Krisna thought his uncle was going behind the boulder for nature call. He, therefore, leant against the trunk of the tree and closed his eyes because of the fatigue of walking for a few miles. Ramarao went near the boulder, stood for a moment, turned back and observed what Krisna might be doing. He saw that the boy was dozing against the trunk of the tree. Tears gathered in his eyes. Yet he hardened himself and began to walk fast towards his own village where he was camping with his wife for the time being. After reaching his place he felt very guilty and tried hard to compromise with his own conscience. His wife also did her best to console him. But, nonetheless he spent a sleepless night that day.

When Krisna woke up after his siesta he looked around him for his uncle who had gone beyond the boulder for nature call. The sun was inclining in the western sky, the heat was still very intense. He thought his uncle must be still attending to nature call or must have gone for the second time. Meanwhile, he felt like drinking some water. He walked slowly to the nearby brook where the cool water was purling and murmuring in the shade of trees. He stood at the brink of the flowing water and splashed it on his face and felt a very cool and comfortable feeling. Then he cupped his palms and drank the cool water until he was satisfied. He walked back to the banyan tree and sat there waiting for his uncle. The intensity of the sun grew noticeably less. The boy noticed that quite a long time had elapsed after his uncle had left him to attend to nature call. He muttered to himself,

"Why did the uncle not return from nature call? Let me wait for a little more time."

He sat observing the birds flying in the sky and the wild flowers on the bushes. Again for a few moments he forgot himself in observing the colourful birds. Then he remembered his uncle again and exclaimed,

"Does the uncle take so much time to relieve himself! This time let me go near the boulder and peep and see if he is still sitting there." He got up quickly and walked towards the big boulder behind which his uncle had gone. He jumped over the thorny bushes and waded through the grass and reached the spot where the big boulder stood. He stood by the side of the boulder and stealthily peeped behind it lest he should be caught seeing him. There was nobody. He, therefore, thought that the uncle must be sitting farther back. He walked boldly ahead and examined the spot and did not find the uncle. Now he felt rather confused. He held his palms around his mouth, raised his voice and shouted 'uncle', with all the force in him. It was instantly echoed by the hillside. He repeated it for the second time. But there was no answer. He repeated it for the third time and heard no answer. Now he was certain that his uncle was nowhere around him. He noticed that evening was advancing fast. He did not even guess where his uncle must have gone and that too leaving him alone on the deserted hillside. Tears gushed into his eyes. He began to cry 'uncle, uncle,' and sat beneath a tamarind tree.

As Krisna wiped the tears in his eyes with his fingers, more and more tears gathered in his eyes thereby blurring his sight. As the evening grew darker and darker gradually, he also grew more and more apprehensive about himself and his nocturnal stay. By that time he saw a flock of sheep moving past him followed by a couple of dogs and a tall shepherd with a black woolen blanket slung across his right shoulder. He held a thin but long staff in his right hand. He saw the fair boy of about eight years crying alone beneath the tamarind tree. Out of curiosity he asked the boy :

"Hullow, boy, why are you crying alone here? What's the matter?"

"My uncle has left me here and gone somewhere I don't know", replied Krisna weepingly.

The shepherd felt a bit puzzled and wanted to know the whole story of the boy. He, therefore, asked further,

"Where did your uncle say he would go?"

"My uncle said he would go for nature call beyond that boulder. So I waited beneath that banyan tree for a long time, but he did not return so far," said Krisna and began to cry again.

Now the shepherd sat on a stone and asked him his name and other details,

"What is your name, which is your place, who are your parents?"

"My name is Krisna. My uncle is called Ramarao who left me here. My father is called Govindarao."

Then Krisna narrated all the details of how his uncle had brought him there with the promise of sending him to his parents and how he had left him in the lurch there.

The shepherd had forgotten his flock of sheep which had gone far ahead of him. He noticed that dusk had been growing into night now. He understood from the boy's description that he must be from a very noble family and that something unexpected had happened to the boy and his uncle. After studying the boy's plight, the shepherd's humanity awakened in him. He thought it inhuman to leave the boy alone there in the dark and therefore, wanted to help him out of the unexpected difficulty. He assured the boy,

"Krisna, don't you cry now. You come with me to my house where you may have your meal and sleep. Tomorrow let's search for your uncle."

Krisna felt quite assured and happy to know that his problem of shelter was solved at least for that day. He followed the shepherd silently. He thought inwardly that Lord Venkateswara himself must have sent the shepherd to help him out of the difficulty. He thankfully offered his salutations to the Lord. When he reached the shepherd's house, he was received with affectionate curiosity by the members of the shepherd's family. The shepherd explained to his wife and children how he found the boy crying near the hill and why he brought him home.

Krisna washed his face, hands and legs and rested for a while on the woolen mattress. He was feeling out of his element in the house of a nonbrahmin which appeared so different from his own. He had his own inner puritanical reservations about having to eat his dinner in a shepherd's house. But his hunger was growing so acute that he did not want to bother much about purity and pollution. The sweet flavour emitting from the kitchen was appetizing Krisna's hunger. After a little time the shepherd's wife brought a brass plate with jowar rotis, vegetable curry and thick curd and said :

"Son, have your meal. You must be very hungry, aren't you?"

"Yes, auntie, I really am very hungry."

After the shepherdess went back into the kitchen, Krisna felt free and began to taste the food. His hunger was so intense that he began to enjoy the items which were different from the ones he used to eat in his own house. After he was through with his meal, he was served a big bowl of hot steaming milk which he quaffed quite eagerly.

After the meal he went back to his bed and relaxed on it. He thanked Lord Venkatapati for looking after him in such a distress. He inwardly prayed to the Lord,

"These shepherd and shepherdess have fed me like my own parents. May their family prosper ever."

After the prayer Krisna fell asleep as he was extremely tired of the long journey the whole day.

The next morning Krisna got up fresh and had his breakfast of hot rotis and chutney and curds. He began to play with the other boys of the shepherd's family. The shepherd had heard that a few families had come to his village and camped there. He went to one such family and told them how he had brought a small boy who belonged to Naragund. Govindarao and Satyabhama felt curious to know who that boy must be. They were themselves feeling very nostalgic about their own son who was staying with Ramarao in some other village. They, therefore, walked briskly and curiously to the shepherd's home and found to their great surprise that the boy was none other than their own son Krisna. Tears of joy gathered in the eyes of Govindarao and Satyabhama. "Where are you, my son? How did you come here? Who brought you here?" exclaimed Satyabhama and hugged him tightly. Govindarao also shed tears of joy and caressed the boy on his back. After the excitement was over, the parents talked coolly with their son. Krisna narrated in a graphic manner every detail of what had happened to him and how Ramarao brought him and deserted him at the hillside.

He concluded, "Uncle Ramarao deceived me very cleverly, mother." But the mother burst out, "Don't you worry my son. Lord Venkatapati is far greater than that uncle Ramarao. He has brought us all together." Both Govindarao and Satyabhama thanked the shepherd profusely and prayed to the Lord that his family should ever prosper as he had shown such a great gesture of humanitarianism. Krisna also saluted the shepherd. Then the parents took the boy to their own home in the same village. They thanked their stars and thought that their son was reborn to them as it were.

That day Satyabhama remembered what the astrologer had predicted when the boy Krisna was born to them. She told her husband "Do you remember what the astrologer had told us after scanning his horoscope?" Govindarao tried to recollect it but could not. "I am not able to recall the details, do you remember them?" asked he. Then Satyabhama cleared her throat and said, "The astrologer had told that this boy would earn the love of people and limitless wealth by his precocious intelligence and heroism; that he would do very responsible jobs and defeat the enemies. He had also predicted that he would die at his twentieth year of age. Another thing he had said was that the boy would pass through a dangerous situation but would escape from that by his sheer intelligence." Govindarao could visualize every detail as it was narrated by his wife. He exclaimed, "This must be that dangerous time from which our boy has escaped now. Anyway, we must thank our Lord Venkatapati for the miraculous recovery of our son." Thus both Govindarao and Satyabhama were thanking their family deity.

*****

Both Yamunabayi and her daughter-in-law Savitri left the palace of Naragund through the secret underground exit and emerged out of the hill of Naragund and walked into the bordering woods in the hot sun. They were accompanied by their poor but very confidential servant-cum-relative namely Ramachandra. He was following them at a short distance. Tears were trickling incessantly in the eyes of both mother-in-law and daughter-in-law. Neither of them was used to any of these hard ways. Both of them had never been scorched in the hot sun in their entire life. Neither of them had any practice of walking on the hard or slushy earth as they always used to be carried in royal palanquins properly shielded from the scorching sun or biting cold or pouring rain. Now both of them had to undergo most unexpected torture, in addition to great mental agony and humiliation. By the time they descended the hill, they felt tired and their knees began to ache. Savitri requested Yamunabayi, "Mother-in-law, please go a little slow. My heels are already aching. I simply cannot step ahead. Let's take rest for a short while at least." She puffed out a deep sigh and sat on the ground fanning herself with the end of her sari. Yamunabayi who was also used to a very royally cozy life felt it very difficult to walk the distance. She understood the daughter-in-law's plight and sat there by her side. She gazed at Savitri's face which had grown red with the fatigue of walking and dotted with beads of perspiration. She was panting heavily. Yamunabayi hugged Savitri tightly in order to console her. Yamunabayi also started crying at the sight of her daughter-in-law. Now Savitri said in-between her sobs, "When both of us are undergoing the same suffering who should console us except each the other? It was so painful for me to see the blood gush out of your foot when Ramachandra pulled out the sharp thorn from it a little while ago." They thus rested for a few moments. Yamunabayi said to

Savitri "My daughter, you are an intelligent girl. You know very well what a terrible test God has put us to. You who had walked on the silken carpet in the palace have to tread the thorn covered road now. I simply cannot stand this sight. What's this-blood oozing out of? Oh God! The outer skin of your feet in torn. How do you bear this pain, daughter?" Then Yamunabayi rent a strip of cloth from the hem of her sari and tied it to Savitri's feet in order to prevent the further loss of blood. They could not wait there for long. Savitri, therefore, said, "Mother-in-law, let's go now talking something or the other so that we may forget the fatigue of walking and cover some distance." Ramachandra was standing near them, without any enthusiasm. Then both of them got up and began to walk ahead, he followed them. Being moved to tears by their plight, he exclaimed inwardly, "Oh Lord. Is this your sport? You have made these poor women wander in the wilderness — these women who had never seen the sunlight; who never walked on the earth but ever traveled in palanquins; whose feet were washed by servants? Have you made them walk on thorn infested ground? O God, should you not think if they have the ability to bear this sorrow? I simply can't bear the sight of these poor women. O God you are all-seeing lord. Can you not see their suffering?" Ramachandra was praying to Lord Venkatapati inwardly while he was following them.

Savitribayi was also praying to Lord Venkatapati inwardly, "O Lord, why are you troubling us like this? Are you not a dealer of justice to human beings? My husband started the war with the British people only to protect our people, our temple lands and our brahmin priests. If you did not like him to start this war, you should have appeared to him in dream and directed him not to indulge in it. You could have prevented this carnage and bloodshed, tragedy and loss. You like my husband wandering in wilderness in disguise? I don't know what terrible sin we had committed in the past lives that we are reaping the consequences now. Oh God, I am worrying only about myself. I don't know how my darling husband is suffering in strange places and forests now. May Lord Venkatapati protect him from all dangers." Thus was Savitri worrying about herself, her husband and mother-in-law. As these unbearable thoughts rushed into her mind, she could not bear it any longer. Her pace slackened. Her mother-in-law was walking ahead a few paces. Ramachandra was nearly forty steps behind Savitri. Savitri felt suddenly weak in the knees. Then she fainted and sagged to the earth with a thump. Yamunabayi heard the thump and looked back and lo Savitri had fallen down on earth. She rushed back towards her daughter-in-law and found that she had fainted. She squatted on the ground and placed Savitri's head on her lap. She wiped the perspiration off her face and began to fan her with the end of her sari. When Ramachandra saw he rushed to them and stood there silently not knowing what to do. Yamunabayi said to him, "Ramachandra, our Savitri has fainted. You go to some pit or pool and get some water by soaking your upper dhoti in it. Don't stand here silently like a fool."

Ramachandra went away in search of water. Yamunabayi tried her best to awaken Savitri from her swoon. She, first, wiped her limbs with a piece of cloth torn from her own sari. Then she fanned her gently. Even then Savitri did not wake up from her swoon. Now Yamunabayi hugged her daughter-in-law to her chest and addressed her, "Wake up daughter-in-law. Don't you know that there's no well-wisher for me except yourself? Why do you sleep like this? Please open your eyes and speak with me at least a single word." She kissed her daughter-in-law affectionately. Even then Savitri did not wake up. She then burst out, "Lord, should you not come to my rescue? Who else can help me except you, O Lord Venkatesa?" When she was crying like this, she saw Ramachandra bring the dhoti soaked in water. The old lady instantly wrung the water from the soaked dhoti and applied the water to Savitri's pate and eyes. When the cool water touched Savitri's head and eyes, she opened her eyes very gently and recovered her consciousness fully. Now Yamunabayi felt a temporary relief and noticed that the hot sun had ascended the zenith of the sky. The earth was scorching. She, therefore, said to the boy, "Ramachandra, it is very late now and the sun has already reached the top of the sky. We cannot wait here any longer. I shall lead Savitri to that tree and we shall be sitting beneath the shadow of it. You go and bring some more water in leafy cups and by soaking your dhoti. We need some water if she feels thirsty." "Yes, mother, I shall get the water," said Ramachandra and walked away into the nearby bushes. "Mother-in-law, why do you trouble that brahmin boy? I don't need any water now. I shall walk up to the tree along with you." Savitri, then, walked slowly by holding the hand of her mother-in-law. Both of them rested under the cool shade of the tree. Mentally they were comparing their present suffering with the past happiness. After resting for a while, they felt a little ease and began to think of what to do next.

Savitri asked her mother-in-law, "Where shall we go now, mother-in-law? I don't think there is any place safe for us." Yamunabayi thought for a second and said, "Savitri we are walking along the bank of the river Malaprabha. Don't you understand?" Savitri was rather surprised. "How could I recognize the river, mother-in-law? Although I have bathed in the river many times in the past on festival days, I am not able to identify it or the route to it. This is the first time that I am coming to it by this route." "Daughter-in-law, this is going to be the last time also," said Yamunabayi. Savitri thought inwardly that Goddess Malaprabha herself might show them a way out of their difficulty. While they were walking slowly, Savitri was brooding about her husband's plight. "I am worrying only about myself. I don't know how much my lord might be suffering at this time. He used to ride his horse even when he had to go to the temple for *darsan*. But now he has to wander stealthily like a thief. What an insult to his stature? He never used to be away from me. He used to wake up at the slightest jerk of my hand from his. I don't know how he would live without my company now. Is there any possibility of our reunion? If no, what is the use of brooding over it? The only way of escape from this emergency is to end my life by drowning myself in the Malaprabha." Thus the idea of death crept into her consciousness.

Ramachandra suggested to them, "Let's take some rest under these mango trees as the sun is very hot." All the three of them sat under the umbrageous shelter of a huge mango tree and felt a temporary relief. After a few moments Ramachandra remembered that his two mistresses had not eaten any thing since morning. He, therefore, stood up and said, "Mother, you two, have not had your breakfast, or lunch. You must be very hungry now. I shall bring a few mangoes for you to eat. Until then you rest under the tree." Without waiting for their approval, he walked away from there to bring the mangoes from nearby trees.

Now Savitri began to share her intimate thoughts, with her mother-in-law. She said, "Mother-in-law, the British officers have grown terribly angry with my lord after knowing that he murdered Manson. They are now like a wounded snake waiting for revenge. They might kill our menfolk by cannon fire or by sword. But if womenfolk like us are captured by them, they are likely to insult us in various ways. It is better to end our lives than being insulted by the enemies." Yamunabayi was secretly happy to note Savitri's way of thinking and felt that she could broach her inner feelings to her boldly now. "My daughter-in-law," said Yamunabayi, "we simply cannot imagine in how many ways the enemies will be insulting us if we are captured by them. I, therefore, have a suggestion. If you like it, we can be eternally free from the anxiety. There's no way simpler than that."

By that time Ramachandra returned with a few mangoes tied in his dhoti-end and offered them to the hungry mistresses. "Mothers, please eat these fruits and satisfy your hunger," said Ramachandra to them. But Yamunabayi said to him, "Ramachandra, you must be very hungry. You please eat them and rest for a while. Our belly is filled with sorrow. Let's go to some safe place before sunset." Ramachandra who was extremely tired of the continuous journey, spread his dhoti and stretched himself on it. Lo, he fell into a sound sleep instantly. He began to snore immediately. Now the two royal women felt free to exchange confidences. Savitri noticed his sound sleep and remarked, “See, mother-in-law, how our Ramachandra is sleeping so soundly even at this time.” “That’s a sign of carefreeness, daughter. Evil time has come to us and not to him. Otherwise he would not have slept so peacefully. Let it be. Savitri, even his sleep would be very convenient for our next action.”

Savitri remembered her own plight and asked Yamunabayi, “Mother-in-law, what is the easiest way to get out of this crisis?” Then Yamunabayi looked around and confirmed the fact that Ramachandra was sleeping. She then lowered her voice and said, “See, my daughter-in-law, I have decided that we must end our life by plunging into this river. That’s why I have brought you here. If this suggestion is agreeable to you, we shall do so together. Otherwise, you may suggest some other plan.” Now Savitri was really touched by Yamunabayi’s catholicity. “Mother-in-law why do you ask for my approval? Have I ever disagreed with you in any respect? You are both mother-in-law and mother for me. All that you have to do is only order me. Don’t you remember that my lord has ordered me to obey your words for getting out of this crisis? I am ready to do whatever you suggest to me.” Yamunabayi was extremely happy to have the concordance from Savitri. She, therefore, burst out, “Savitri, I am really proud of having a daughter-in-law like you. I knew inwardly that you would agree with me. Yet I wanted to know your opinion about the greatest sacrifice such as this. In that case you better remove all your golden ornaments and give them to the poor brahmin. What is the use of these ornaments after we are dead? People who come to conduct our funeral may hesitate to do it if they see these golden ornaments and mistake us to be rich ladies. We must give them an impression that we are very poor women so that they might conduct our funeral without fail. Our spirits would then be really satisfied. Besides, our Ramachandra is really a very poor brahmin boy who has served us all these years. He has accompanied us even in such an emergency. If we give him these ornaments, he can overcome his poverty and live happily everafter. He would remember us thankfully all through his life. What’s your opinion?”

"Why do you ask for my opinion, mother-in-law? You have only to order me," said Savitri and took off all the golden ornaments like bangles, armbands, necklaces, nose-rings and ear-rings except her sacramental *mangalasutra* and piled them before the mother-in-law. Yamunabayi was extremely happy to notice such an extraordinary sense of resignation in her young daughter-in-law and readiness for timely action. Now, Yamunabayi also took off her own ornments and put them together with the daughter-in-law's. They looked at Ramachandra who was stirring and yawning sleepily. Yamunabayi asked him, "Ramachandra, are you awake now? You rub your eyes properly and listen to me carefully." Ramachandra got up suddenly and sat properly and said, "Mother, I am fully awake now. Kindly order me what to do."

"Ramachandra," said Yamunabayi, "you take all these golden ornaments and go back to your home in the village. We two have to be in the guise of poor people until this mutiny is over. Now we don't have any use for these ornaments. We shall return to your home as soon as these disturbances come to an end. But, don't hesitate to sell these ornaments for your day-to-day needs of life. Your coming with us will not help you in any way. Now you go away from here. Live happily with your family. May God bless you."

Ramachandra who was a duffer by nature could not understand the full implication of the words of the elderly matron. Yet he requested them out of courtesy, "Mothers, you could have come to my home in my village where nobody could have identified you." But Yamunabayi said, "No, Ramachandra, you do not understand the gravity of the consequences later. We have to face hundred and eight problems. We have, therefore, to be in *incognito* until they are solved. You please don't pester us unnecessarily in this regard. You rush back to your village and tell people that you fled from Naragund as soon as mutiny started there. Don't divulge anything about us or where we went. Be happy in your life." Now Ramachandra was disarmed by the matron's words. He, therefore, collected all the golden ornaments and tied them in a bundle with his scarf and grew ready to leave them. He knelt and bowed to both the royal ladies. He could not control his emotions. Tears gushed into his eyes and he felt a lump in his throat. Yet with his tremulous voice he managed to say, "Mothers, I'll never be happy except in your service. I am going away from you only because I am ordered by you to go. I am going very unwillingly. Kindly take care of your health. As soon as you feel safe, kindly don't hesitate to come to my home in my village." The two ladies nodded their heads just to get rid of him. But Ramachandra mistook it for their real approval and walked away from them with a heavy heart and a lachrymose face.

Then Yamunabayi asked Savitri, "Daughter, Goddess Malaprabha is our last resort now. Our Ramachandra was a hindrance for us until now. You secure your sari tightly around you so that it shouldn't be loosened by the current of water. Besides, the encircling darkness is very convenient for us." Accordingly Savitri secured the knot and the tuck of her sari very tightly and stood ready to follow her mother-in-law. Likewise Yamunabayi also tightened the knot and tuck of her sari properly. "Shall we go?" said each to the other. Both of them walked slowly towards the river. Yamunabayi said to Savitri, "Daughter, our life span is coming to a close now. Or rather, we are going to cut it short now just to protect ourselves from further humiliation or torture. There seems to be no other way out of this crisis. O Lord God kindly forgive us for this unnatural end of our life. My dear Savitri, I have always looked upon you as if you are my own daughter. Please excuse me if I have ever hurt you in any way in our house. Come on, let's forget that we are mother-in-law and daughter-in-law and think that we are close friends. Let's jump into the river together. Let's pray to Lord God until we reach the river so that He may grant us true liberation from the mortal bondage." Savitri was embarrassed by her mother in-law's request for forgiveness and covered her ears with her palms. Then she said to Yamunabayi, "Mother, we have always lived and loved each other like mother and daughter.

Please don't embarrass me by such talk. On the contrary, I request you to forgive me if I have hurt you because of my inexperience and ignorance. I don't think we have done any injustice to anyone in this life to deserve such a tragedy. I believe it is all due to our past *karma*. We have got to suffer it. Besides, I don't think we are committing sin by jumping into the river. I remember the Brahmin pundits preach that man may follow any path during the time of emergency and that it shall not be considered as a sin. Let's pray to Lord God to forgive us for this act."

Both of them washed their faces in the water and stood facing the east with joined palms and repeated the prayers. Yamunabayi prayed, "Oh Lord God, I have never committed any sin in my life. Forgive me if I have crossed your will. I have two sons who are the heads of two *samsthans*. You have given such a suffering to the mother of two illustrious sons. I do not grudge it. Isn't everything part of your will? O God, I pray to you to keep my two sons happy by helping them out of the crisis. Likewise, give shelter to this forlorn girl Savitri into your lotus-feet." At the same time, Savitri was also praying, "O God, kindly forgive me if I have ever committed any sin unwittingly either against you or against my husband. God, kindly keep my husband happy by protecting him from the firangi enemies. Kindly accept the two of us, the helpless women unto your care. This is my last request."

Now it was growing dark all-around them. So they joined the ends of their saris and tied them together into a tight knot and descended into the water which was very shallow near the bank. They had held each other's hand tightly. The waves of the water were splashing against their legs. Then they walked further into the deeper waters of the river. Now the cool water came upto the level of their chests. Even in the dim darkness, they could listen to the murmur of the ripples spreading around them. Yamunabayi felt sorry for her daughter-in-law's plight. She, therefore, tried to reason with Savitri, "My dear daughter, I am so sad to force you to such an unnatural and premature death. I have done so only to prevent ourselves from being humiliated further. I know you are a young lady with all the hopes and desires of life. If you wish to live, you may untie the knot and walk back from the river. But I have decided to die in the belly of the River Goddess Malaprabha." Savitri was nonplused by her mother-in-law's words and counter questioned, "Mother why do you speak like this now, that too after bringing me here? Would I have come here if I had wished to live? Don't test me unnecessarily." Now Yamunabayi was convinced about Savitri's firmness and courage. She, therefore, said, "Daughter, our speech will be silenced if we go ahead by one more step in the water. Come on, let's embrace each other and be united both in life and in death. May Lord Venkateswara be with us." With these words Yamunabayi hugged Savitri tightly and they together walked ahead in the midwaters of the river. And lo, the sandy bed of the river seemed to slip from beneath their feet. The torrential current of the water pushed them ahead mercilessly along with it and stopped their respiration. The two poor women felt a sudden black out of consciousness and knew not, what happened to them further. They gurgled the water rushing into their nostrils and were soon silenced when their life ebbed away from their mortal bodies. All through the night their deadbodies floated along with the rushing water of the river unnoticed by any human being.

*****

The dead bodies of the two royal ladies floated on the surface of the water of river Malaprabha from Sangala village for nearly twenty-eight miles continuously until they were stuck up in the thorny bushes in the slush of the river bank near the Budihal village belonging to Naragund taluka. Mallanagouda of Budihal village got up in the early morning and went towards the river for nature call. Dim light was spreading in the eastern sky and birds were chirping in the trees. After washing himself in the water, he stood up and secured his dhoti in a tuck behind his back. When his eyes roamed around the landscape there, he descried a dark spot near the thorny bush in the slush of water near the river bank. Goaded by sheer curiosity, he waded through the mire and scanned the dark object and lo, to his surprise he learnt that they were two dead bodies of good-looking ladies torn and pecked at by thorns and birds. Their saris were torn at many places. Mallanagouda thought, "These ladies must be from a very high family. They must have committed suicide because of some emergency." Then he walked briskly to his home and told his wife and children what he had seen near the river. Then he ordered his servants to bring the dead bodies to the ground. The servants accordingly hitched up their dhotis above their knees, walked into the slushy mire. With the help of rough clothes they lifted the two bodies and carried them on to the bank. By that time the natives of Budihala flocked to the spot and began to express sympathy for the dead women. They began to shed tears sympathetically. One exclaimed, "Look at these poor women, what must have been the emergency which has driven them to this suicide!" "God alone knows it" said another woman. "They seem to belong to a very cultured family. They are so pretty. Do you think they are mother and daughter?" asked the third woman. "I don't think so. They do not resemble each other in facial features. I suspect they must be mother-in-law and daughter-in-law," opined the first woman. Then they all shed tears silently until men folk came there and began to conduct the *panchanama* of the dead bodies under the supervision of the Gowda of the village. Then the Gowda sent the news to the brahmin officer who was appointed by the British Administration. The brahmin officer rushed to the spot and saw the dead bodies of the two women who seemed to be of very highly cultured family belonging to brahmin caste. He, therefore, wanted to arrange for the cremation of the dead. But he thought it proper to intimate the same to his higher authorities and get their formal permission.

The brahmin officer grew helpless and had to hold up the cremation of the dead bodies until he got the permission. He accordingly arranged for the funeral pyre of fuel and saw to it that the dead bodies were kept on the square pile of the fuel.

When a servant was about to kindle the funeral pyre a messenger came and handed another envelope to the brahmin officer. But the latter did not wish to read the letter until he had cremated the bodies. He, therefore, asked a servant to ignite the pyre. The servant took a long burning stick and held it at the bottom of the pyre of faggots. Soon the faggots began to burn with a crackling sound. The flames enveloped the whole mass of wood. Within a few minutes the skulls of the two dead bodies cracked with a splutter. The people were gaping at the scene with silent sorrow. Then the brahmin officer opened the letter which read, "You are hereby instructed not to hasten the cremation of the two women as we suspect them to be belonging to Bhaskararao's family. Please wait until further orders." The brahmin officer thought inwardly, "This message is just what I guessed it to be." Then he wrote a reply to his officer as follows : "As per your first order I arranged for the cremation of the dead bodies. They were already burnt to ashes before I received your second order." Then the brahmin officer sent the letter to the office. The people were still crying and saying, "What a tragedy has befallen to the mother and wife of Bhaskararao!" Then a brahmin pundit present there tried to console them, "Although these ladies belonged to the royal family, their dead bodies were in a forlorn condition here. We have the satisfaction of having done our *dharma* according to the formula : *Anathapreta samskaram kotiyajna phalam labhet.* It is no use grieving over their death. Let's pray that their souls may rest in peace. In a way it is good that they have escaped from the hands of the enemies. Otherwise, they would have been humiliated by the *firangis* in a number of ways. It is good that they have protected their honour and dignity in their own ways." All the spectators were impressed by the brahmin pundit's words and seemed to agree with him silently. Then they heaved a sigh of relief and returned to their homes.

When the messenger went to the office and handed over the letter to the British officer sent by the brahmin officer, he opened it and glanced through the contents. He was rather disappointed to learn that the cremation had already taken place. He could not blame the brahmin officer for the action as he had discharged his duty very conscientiously according to his first order and the second order had reached him rather late.

*****

Ramachandra, who was an impecunious fellow all through his life was overjoyed by the golden ornaments gifted away by his two magnanimous mistresses Yamunabayi and Savitri. He estimated the ornaments at about twenty thousand rupees worth. He was so much surprised by these gifts that he doubted if it was a reality at all. He pinched himself to confirm that he was not in a dream world. He never knew that such a miracle would happen in his life. He had led a life of extreme poverty. His wife Janakibayi used to curse him constantly for his incurable poverty. On top of all these difficulties, he used to get an issue almost every year without fail. Consequently the family could not even get two square meals per day. His wife therefore, used to go away to her parents' home to have at least temporary relief from poverty at her husband's home. Now Ramachandra felt that Lord Venkateswara had turned his grace on him. He wanted to have a good look at the golden ornaments. He, therefore, looked around him and confirmed that nobody was watching him. He, then, untied the scarf bundle and examined the glittering ornaments, glistening pearls and gems and shining tassels. His eyes appeared to be blinded by the glitter of the ornaments for a moment. He felt as if he wound faint for joy. He wondered, "I have suddenly become so rich. I do not know if this will remain with me forever." Then he took out three signet rings and a few toe rings which he wanted to sell for his expenses and tied them in a small bundle. He put all other ornaments in the end of dhoti and tied it in a separate bundle.

Ramachandra continued his journey on foot until he reached a relatively big town. There he went in search of a *saraf* and expressed his desire of selling some of the ornaments. The *saraf* weighed the glittering ornaments in his balance and tested them by rubbing them on the teststone and confirmed the purity of gold. Then he calculated the total amount and said that he would give eight hundred rupees for them. Rantachandra was inwardly overjoyed by such a big sum. Without a second word, he agreed to it and accepted the amount and left the shop. The *saraf* was a bit surprised at the customer who unlike many others, never higgle-haggled about the price.

Ramachandra felt like fainting at the possession of a very big sum of eight hundred rupees. Never in his life had he handled such a big sum. He felt ecstatic about it. He spent part of that amount for his tiffin, lunch and dinner on the way to his native village where his wife lived. He walked blithely towards his village. When he reached his house, it was already dark. He opened the main gate of the verandah dexterously without making any noise. He found that his wife and children were already sleeping. The door of the house was locked from inside. So he thought of hiding his newfound golden ornaments in the earth. He took up a tall hoe and dug the earth at three different spots and hid the ornaments there and covered the pits with the earth in such a way that nobody could easily identify them. Then he knocked at the door and sounded the chainbolt. After a few minutes his wife opened the door and was quite happy to see him. She asked him smilingly, "Did you remember us now at least? I deem it as our goodluck." Ramachandra entered the house, bathed and had his dinner before retiring to his bedroom with his wife.

Although he was feeling sleepy, Janakibayi did not allow him to sleep. She engaged him in conversation. "At last you remembered us, didn't you? Have you ever thought about my condition here in the village, that too with all these children with me without any money? As for you, there must have been no end of pleasures in the royal family of Naragund. See how I am fated to lead the life of a *pativrita* even when you neglected me completely."

Ramachandra was listening to her non stop dialogue. He knew that his wife was very smart in mind though not formally educated in school. He wanted to tease her and asked her, "Are you sure that you are a *pativrita?*"

Janakibayi was nettled by his innocent question. She rebuffed, "What do you mean? Do you neglect me for so long and yet suspect my character?" She stood up and turned her face away from him in a sulking manner. Ramachandra understood that she was hurt by his remark which he had made just for joking. He, therefore, went near her and caressed her cheeks and tried to console her, "You fool, why do you take it so seriously? I just wanted to tease you, Don't take it seriously. Come on, my darling." With these words he drew her into his arms and kissed her gently. He then asked her, "Tell me now how you lived here in my absence?"

Janakibayi answered, "How shall I describe the suffering that I and my children have passed through? You must have had a grand gala time there at Naragund having regular feasts, handful of fees and the company of call girls. How is it possible for you to remember us poor creatures?"

Ramachandra was touched by her words and the sorrow concealed behind them. "What could I have done, my darling? I was rather helpless. Now you take these seven hundred rupees and feel happy." Janakibayi took the coins and counted them happily and kept them back in the cloth bag. Yet she tried to tease her husband,

"What's the use of giving me money now? Did you think of us for the past four years? Did you send us any money?"

"My dear, I sent you two hundred rupees twice. Don't you remember it?" asked Ramachandra.

"Do you think that money was sufficient for our maintenance?" "What could I do, my dear? I was also helpless. I couldn't do anything else. At least now you feel happy that I have given you seven hundred rupees."

"Do you think we have grown into rich people by possessing these seven hundred rupees? Haven't you heard that even a bowlful of gold will not be enough for a man who eats without working? Don't you remember our liabilities? We have to conduct *munjavi* for two sons and arrange the marriage of a daughter. People have already started commenting on us."

This was how she tried to remind him of his responsibility for the family. Then she bolted the door of the bedroom and clung to him. As she was away from him for the last four years, she was burning with passion for him. She, therefore, clung to him and caress his hungry limbs. As he was also aroused, he began to explore her undulations. He hurriedly interlocked himself in her entwining limbs and started the slow rhythmic penetration. Gradually he quickened the rhythm of strokes until he felt he was reaching the peak of paradise and experienced a sudden release of tension and a great relief. The couple were saturated with sweetness and fell into a very sound sleep.

The next day they spent the time in the routine work. Ramachandra played with his children with great affection in order to compensate for his long absence from home. In the evening they chatted for a while until food was ready. Then they finished their meal and retired to their respective rooms. The children slept in a separate room whereas the couple rested in their bedroom. Janakibayi who was a very clever young lady, began to nag her husband about their future, especially about the arrangement of marriage of their eldest daughter. Ramachandra wanted to give her some satisfaction and, therefore, told her,

"My darling, I have a surprise for you. You need not worry about our daughter's marriage."

"What is the surprise?" asked Janakibayi rather disinterestedly.

"You know, I have suddenly become rich by an unexpected turn of luck."

"How can you become rich, dear husband? Do I not know what an impecunious brahmin you are?" she taunted him.

"Do you think I am joking? I am serious. I mean what I say."

"What do you mean exactly? Don't speak in riddles."

"I have got all the golden ornaments of Yamunabayi and Savitribayi gifted away to me in their last moments." Janakibayi's curiosity was aroused conspicuously. She straightened up and asked him the how of it. Then Ramachandra narrated the whole episode in such a vivid fashion that Janakibayi cocked her ears and listened to the whole story with rapt attention. Tears were gushing out of her eyes as she learnt the details of the tragic plight of the two royal ladies of Bhaskararao's family. When he finished his story, Janakibayi burst out in-between her sobs, "What a terrible pain they must have felt in their heart when they had to run away from their royal palace? Lord Venkateswara should not have brought them to such a terrific condition." Tears were gushing out of Ramachandra's eyes also. Both of them were crying silently for a considerable time until they fell into sleep.

The next night Janaklbayi cajoled her husband and learnt the fact that he had hidden the golden ornaments in three different pits in their own verandah. As she was very clever by nature, she fed her husband very sumptuously whereas she took only a light meal. As soon as Ramachandra began to snore, she sneaked out of her room and dug the earth in the verandah with the help of an iron rod. As the pits were made very recently she could easily locate the pits on the very sight of the loose soil there. When she searched in the depth of those pits she was flabbergasted by the heavy golden ornaments which once belonged to Savitribayi and her mother-in-law. She took them inside the kitchen and examined them in the dim light of the wick-lamp there. The ornaments dazzled her eyes even in that unclear light of the kitchen. She felt like fainting for joy. She could not control the flutter of her heart for a few seconds. As she knew that the night was advancing, she bundled them in a sari piece and hid them on the shelf of the kitchen behind the earthen pots and pans. She was so impatient that she felt it very difficult to wait until morning so that she could wear them to satisfy herself. She then returned to the bedroom and slept beside her husband who was still snoring in his deep sleep. She slept dreaming about the golden ornaments.

The next morning Ramachandra got up and completed his routine ablutions. He noticed that the pits in which he had hidden the gold were looking as if they had been tampered with by somebody. He felt rather shocked and nervous to think of even the possibility of some theft. But he confirmed to himself that he had not told even his wife clearly about the spot of the pits. He rushed to the kitchen to ask his wife about it. But lo, his wife had already put on the golden ornaments around her neck and flaunting them before him. For a moment she looked like Goddess Laxmi herself to his eyes. The ornaments dazzled his eyes. He recovered his sense of surprise and shock and asked her,

"How did you come to have them, dear? I did not show you the spot where I had hidden them."

"Do you think I am a fool? Yesternight I dug up all the three pits and took out all these extraordinary ornaments. See how my luck has turned now!"

Ramachandra felt rather helpless and did not know what to do. He knew that his wife was very clever and could not be controlled so easily. He feared that she did not understand the gravity of the situation and that she was excited by the unexpected possession of golden ornaments. He was, however, reconciled to his lot and began to attend to his daily domestic chores. As days went by, Janaki could not resist the temptation of wearing the golden ornaments on her person. "Why should I be afraid of wearing them when my husband has brought them? What are the ornaments meant for if not for wearing, that too when one is quite young? Can a woman wear them and flaunt them when she is a decrepit old woman?" Thus did Janaki argue with herself inwardly and decided to wear them on her person.

The next day Janaki decked herself with a necklace, bangles, nose rings and ear rings and even toe-rings and took a round in the lane meeting her neighbours and friends and talking with them with some pretext or the other. Naturally the eyes of her friends and neighbours were dazzled by the brilliance of her golden ornaments. They noticed them with silent envy but could not ask her as to how she came to acquire them lest the question should embarrass her. Janaki went on flaunting her gold for about a week's time. One day when Janaki had gone to the village temple for *darsan,* one of her friends made bold to ask her,

"My dear Janakibayi, you look like a veritable goddess Laxmi in these ornaments."

"Do I?" replied Janaki and felt bloated with pride and a sense of achievement. She even blushed.

"By the way, how did you come to have all these ornaments all of a sudden?"

Although Janaki was rather baffled by the direct question darted at her by her friend, she instantly thought of something and replied,

"O that's a big story. To tell you briefly, my husband got these ornaments by way of brahmanic gifts."

"Is that so?" exclaimed the friend by keeping her right forefinger on her lips.

Janaki thought that she had convinced her friends and neighbours with her fake answer and, therefore, rested in ignorant peace and carefreeness.

After a few days when the womenfolk of the village gathered near the village tank for fetching water in earthen pitchers, they began to discuss Janaki's golden ornaments. The young Tungabayi who felt jealous of Janaki asked her friend,

"Hullow Santabayi, have you seen how many ornaments Janaki has been wearing nowadays?"

"Yes, I have seen them. They are so excellent."

"Do you know how she got them?"

"Janaki replied that her husband got them as brahmanical gifts from some rich family," replied Santabayi.

"Do you believe such a blatant lie and myth, Santabayi?"

"How then do you think her husband came by them, Tungabayi?"

"Can't you simply guess it? He must have stolen them from somewhere. Otherwise how can anyone gift so many valuable ornaments?"

Santabayi felt puzzled by such an answer. But she felt the possibility of such an action and replied,

"It is quite possible, Tungabayi. I have not thought along these lines."

'That is the only possibility for a poor brabmin like Ramachandra." Santabayi kept quiet for a few seconds. Then they descended into the water of the tank and filled up their pitchers and began to ascend the bank. Then Tungabayi said again,

"One day or the other his theft will be reported to the Sarkar and he will be punished properly."

"Yes, friend. He may be punished in due course. However let's not bother about it. It does not concern us."

The womenfolk went back to their respective homes. But the news circulated in the neighbouring village with a speed that was greater than that of wind. People began to feel jealous and angry at the same time about Ramachandra's unexpected acquisition of wealth. The jealous people thought that Ramachandra must have stolen the golden ornaments from the royal family of Babasaheb in Naragund. They were circulating the news wherever they went. They had also heard rumours that the British Government were planning to capture all those who had fled from Naragund after the mutiny had been quelled by the British army. There was an atmosphere of doubt and fear everywhere.

The news of Ramachandra's arrival into the village traveled fast among the other villagers and ultimately reached the British authorities who lost no time in sending their police constables in search of him. One day when Ramachandra was loitering near the village temple he heard the rumour that the British officers had come to his village asking for him. No sooner had he heard the news than his legs began to tremble with fear. His heart began to palpitate. He began to invoke the spirit of his family deity Lord Venkateswara and prayed for his safety. He rushed to his house through the back door and explained the whole matter rather briefly to his wife. He collected all her ornaments in a hurry and unearthed a small pit in the backyard and buried them and covered them with earth not to be easily identified by any strangers. He then pretended to be quite normal and sat chatting with his wife. Within half an hour or so the British officers sent word to Ramachandra. The messenger came to Ramachandra's house and asked him,

"Who is Ramachandra in this house?"

Ramachandra stood up and replied, "I am Ramachandra. What's the matter?"

"You are ordered by our officer to see him in the village *chavadi*."

"All right, come on let's go."

Ramachandra followed the messenger to the village *chavadi*. His heart was palpitating with fear about the possible loss of gold and even of his life. He ascended the steps of the *chavadi* with tremulous legs and joined his palms in salutation exhibiting a sense of humility. The British officer who was clad in an official uniform took off his hat mechanically and asked him,

"Are you Mr. Ramachandra?"

"Yes, Sarkar, I am Ramachandra."

"Very good. We wanted some information from you. Don't tell us any lies."

"I shall tell you whatever little I know."

The officer in the uniform cleared his throat and asked him in an outlandish Kannada,

"We are told that you lived with the royal family of Babasaheb at Naragund."

"Yes Sarkar, it's true that I stayed there in their service."

"Then you'll have to come with us to Naragund, for an official trial right now."

"Sarkar, I'll definitely come there, but before that I would like to see my wife and children. Kindly allow me to do so."

"All right, we shall allow you half an hour's time. Our guard will come with you. You meet your wife and children and return to this *chavadi* within half an hour."

Ramachandra recovered his little courage and returned home followed by the guard. The guard sat on a pedastal stone outside the house. Ramachandra rushed into his house and locked the door from inside and began to tell his wife with fearful anxiety. His wife and children hugged him and began to cry with the fear that he may he hanged or shot at with the cannon fire. He consoled them until their sobbing subsided to a considerable extent. Then he said to his wife,

"See, my dear, I shall try my best to wriggle out of this situation by telling them lies. But if I suspect any danger to my life I shall tell the truth even if it costs us all the gold I have brought here. Why should I unnecessarily lose my life? If I am alive, we may try to survive somehow or the other."

Janaki who was deeply depressed was exasperated by the words of her husband. She roared as if she were a lioness,

"What do you mean? Have you lost all your sense? Don't tell them anything about the gold. Don't fear even if you have to lose your life. You will have to die one day or the other. Please, for heaven's sake don't give them any hint about the gold. You tell me if you have hidden any more gold elsewhere in the backyard. It shouldn't go unnoticed by us in future. Are you a man at all who fear for the inevitable death? Don't you fear death. I shall send with you many sweetcakes and *dasamis* for your food on the way. But don't leave us your wife and children impecunious here. You face your own fate. I shall look after myself and my children. If you come back safe by the grace of God, then there's no problem. Let's hope for that."

When Ramachandra heard these words, he was shocked out of his wits. He did not know what to do or say to his wife. He decided not to confide anything about the other money that he had hidden in the earth. He did not bother even if it went a waste in the earth, but he did not want his callous wife to know about it. He silently took departure from his wife and walked out of his home. The guard who was waiting for him outside his home took him to the *chavadi*. From there he was taken by the British officers to Naragund for further enquiry.

The next day he was called from the prison to the trial in the palace. When he saw the palace where he had once served his master Babasaheb and his Rani and mother, he could not control his tears. He wiped them with the back of his palms. The British officers in uniforms were seated in their chairs. About three hours after the sunrise the prison guard took Ramachandra to the chamber where the officers were waiting for him. He walked slowly and saluted them with joined palms and stood waiting for their questions. Then the officer asked him in stilted Kannada,

"Mr. Ramachandra we learn that you were serving your master Babasaheb and his family here. Would you mind telling us where the master and his family have gone?"

"Sarkar, Babasaheb Sarkar had already left the palace when the battle began. I do not know where he went."

"But you were staying with Babasaheb's mother and wife. You also left with them, didn't you?"

"Yes, Sarkar. It's true that all the three of us left the palace and rushed out of Naragund. But on the way we separated in the woods for fear that we may be caught by your soldiers. I followed my own way and reached my present village. I do not know where the Sarkar's mother and wife went away," replied Ramachandra tremblingly.

"When you went out of Naragund you were with them, weren't you?"

"It was true that I was with them. But as we were treading the unfamiliar path in the woods and as night was advancing we could not keep track of one another. I was pursuing my own path in the overwhelming darkness and fell into a deep sleep on the way. When I woke up birds were already chirping in the trees. I again began to run for my life until I reached some village where I had my food and from where I returned to my native village after three years gap and joined my family."

"You are sure that you do not know the whereabouts of the other leaders of Babasaheb's army?"

"When I was running for my own life, how could I think of any leader, Sarkar?"

"All right you may go now."

Ramachandra was led back to the prison by the guard. He was worrying about the consequences of this trial. He suspected that his last moments were fast approaching. He tried to remember his wife and children whom he could not perhaps see again. Tears gushed out of his eyes. The whole night he spent in the meditation of Lord Venkateswara. The only happy thing about the enquiry was that not a single question was asked to him about the golden ornaments. He was saved from the sense of embarrassment and the possible self-betrayal. He remembered how a few so-called criminals of Naragund had already been hanged to death. He feared to imagine himself being led to the noose of death waiting for him. The very idea of death gave him a trepidation. He felt a continuous palpitation which he could not control in spite of will power. He went on worrying about it late into the night until he fell into a sleep out of sheer exhaustion. The next day also he spent in worrying about his possible death and wondered at the strange working of his fate. But on the third day when the guards came to his room he began to shiver thinking that he would be taken to some other place for hanging. But when the prison officer told him,

"You have been acquitted of your so-called crime. The jury have declared that you are innocent and not involved in any anti Government activities. You are released now on condition that you will not involve yourself with any of the political activities connected with Babasaheb of Naragund."

Ramachandra really felt so much surprised that he did not believe his own ears. He walked out of his prison room and thanked Lord Venkateswara inwardly. He saluted the prison officer with joined palms and walked briskly towards his village. On the way he exclaimed, "O Lord Venkateswara, strange are your ways! You got me imprisoned and now again you got me released. Nobody can understand your *lila*!" He felt ecstatic and began to walk fast towards his village and wanted to teach a good lesson to his arrogant wife.

*****

Now that the Britishers had taken charge of the administration of Naragund, they wanted to take stock of the whole mutiny preceding the seize of Naragund. The British authorities were searching diligently for Babasaheb who was said to have escaped from there along with his confidants. Meanwhile the other participants in the mutiny were captured for trial and possible punishment or release. Two large buildings were earmarked for housing the so-called 'criminals' who were fiery patriots of Naragund. One building was meant for all those natives who were suspected to be associated with the mutiny. The other building was meant for those who were confirmed to be active participants in the mutiny. Although Naragund palace had been seized by the British authorities and most of the leaders including Babasaheb had fled the city and some of the natives had run away for life to their nearest relatives in the far-off villages, there was no sense of fear in the city for about fifteen days. Then the natives slowly began to return to their houses which they had deserted in the terrific time of war. The Indian and British spies were sent out to all the neighbouring villages to search for the so-called culprits whose masterlist had been prepared by them. At both the places the culprits were called for trial before the jury. Several natives used to gather there as spectators out of a sense of curious fear. Every day the enquiry used to begin at about 10 o'clock in the morning until 4 o'clock in the evening. If the so-called crimes were proved or confirmed by the jury, then the culprits used to be punished with death sentences or loss of property or banishment from the borders of Naragund. The next day early in the morning the culprits used to be led to the foot of the hill blindfolded and shot dead or hanged to death from the large banyan trees. Thus a terrific fear entered into the city of Naragund. The parents, the widows and the children of the mutineers who were hanged to death began to wail and cry endlessly but to no purpose. The natives simply did not know when their turn would come for trial or death-sentence. Eagles and owls gathered in the city of Naragund to feed themselves or sing their sepulchral songs. Hence the natives developed an unprecedented kind of *vairagya* and realized the utter meaninglessness of their lives. For many of them their life was more precious than any property or gold or land. They began to desert their homes and go in search of their relatives elsewhere.

But the British Government was very alert with their techniques of espionage. Their soldiers were able to arrest several mutineers of Naragund and the other villages with the help of their spies and used to try them and punish them severely. Their search continued ceaselessly. They were able to capture many important mutineers except only four including Babasaheb. The authorities, therefore, sent out the towncriers to announce fat prizes of cash or land for those who helped the Government to capture Babasaheb and his companions by informing them the whereabouts of the absconders.

Within a couple of months Raghopant was captured and put behind the bars for enquiry. Later the British authorities came to know that Ramarao had sent the boy Krisnarao to Govindarao. After a few days their spies were able to get information about the village in which Govindarao was living with his wife and children. That village was inhabited mainly by the people of shepherd community. The other inhabitants of the village also lived as simple a life as that of the shepherds. As soon as the British authorities came to have some information about the village in which Govindarao was supposed to have been living, they sent an officer along with soldiers to capture him and his boy. Accordingly the officer and the soldiers with guns slung across their shoulders went in search of the village trudging across the countryside.

When the villagers saw the British officer and the soldiers enter their village they felt nervous. The news instantly got circulated in the village. The womenfolk and children began to cry and wail for their men folk who would be likely to be arrested by the soldiers out of mere suspicion. They began to invoke the name of their family gods and goddesses. "Oh God, kindly protect us from these incarnations of Yamaraya," was a common prayer muttered by them. After a few minutes the villagers received a more definite piece of news that the soldiers had come there in search of Govindarao. This news was also circulated very fast in the village and finally it reached the ears of Govindarao also. Satyabhama was busy preparing the lunch and feeding her children. The other villagers also who were busy preparing their lunch grew scared and set aside their plates and began to think of how to escape from the clutches of these soldiers. Govindarao grew pale with fear and Satyabhama was so nervous that she forgot the feeding and sat petrified against the wall. Krisnarao was sitting on her lap and looking at his mother's face. Tears were gushing out of her eyes incessantly. Govindarao also started shedding tears. When the other two children Ganapatrao and Sakharamapant saw their parents crying, they also started crying instinctively. Krisnarao also saw others crying and tears began to trickle in his eyes also. Yet because of his precocious mind he did not lose courage. He tried to reason with his father. His younger brothers Ganapatrao and Sakharamapant were too small to understand the gravity of the situation. Krisnarao tried to engage his father's attention. He asked his father,

"Father, what if the soldiers come to our village and to our house? Why should we be afraid of them? What harm have we done to anybody?" Gavindarao tried to convince his son and said, "Dear son, we haven't done any harm to anybody. These people can arrest us and even punish us with death simply because of suspicion. What can a child like you understand?"

"Of course I am only a child, father. But will they not enquire into everything before punishing us? Can we not convince them of our innocence? Let's therefore, not fear anything. Let's go with the soldiers voluntarily so that they can understand our innocence and later help us to live by ourselves."

"Dear son, what you say may be true during peace time. But these days are full of suspicion and danger. People naturally behave irrationally and consequently we may have to suffer. Even then there is some truth in what you say. Let's therefore go out and meet the soldiers before they come to our door. You put on your shirt and cap. I also shall get ready by putting on my *pagoti*."

Thus when the father and son got ready to go out to meet the soldiers, Satyabhama raised her voice and began to wail. She hugged Krisnarao tightly and caressed his back. She appealed to Govindarao, "Please do not hand over my moon-like child into the hands of Yamaraya. I implore you not to desert me like this." This heart-rending appeal of Satyabhama made Govindarao dumb with sorrow. Tears trickled in his eyes continuously. Krisnarao saw the whole thing and tried to console his mother.

"Mother, why do you cry like this? Seeing you cry father starts crying. Seeing both of you crying the two small brothers start crying. The danger cannot be avoided simply by crying. Mother, please be bold. Both father and I shall go to Naragund and convince the British authorities that we have no connection at all with the mutiny and return within three or four days."

Both Gavindarao and Satyabhama were pleased and consoled by their son's words and caressed him affectionately. They controlled their feelings and got ready to face the situation boldly. Then Satyabhama told her husband, "Please look after your health and the son's on the way. I shall give you a packet of snacks for consumption. Eat them whenever you feel hungry. I shall also give you a packet of ten or twelve wheat *dasamis*."

Govindarao was pleased to note the change in his wife's behaviour. He told her, "All right, do as you please. Keep everything ready in the cloth-bundle. First, we shall go out and meet the British officer and his soldiers. If our going to Naragund is confirmed I shall send somebody here so that you may send with him our packets of sweet balls, *dasamis* and my dhoti, holy scarf, pots, pans and the *Bhagavad Gita*."

After instructing his wife about these things, Govindarao went out of his house with Krisnarao in order to meet the British officers. The soldiers were also coming towards them. The leader of the soldiers accosted Govindarao,

"Hullow Mister, do you know where Mr. Govindarao and Master Krisnarao stay in this village?"

Now Krisnarao walked ahead and replied boldly, "Sir, I am the very Krisnarao whom you have been asking for. The man standing behind me is my revered father. We heard that you were searching for us. That's the reason why we came here to meet you."

Hearing the eloquent words of the small boy the soldiers were really surprised as well as pleased. The chief officer developed immense affection for the intelligent boy. He took him by the hand, made him sit on his lap and talked to him gently,

"My dear boy, don't be afraid of us. We have been searching for the *karabhari* of Naragund Mr. Ramarao. Do you know him? Please tell us all that you know about him. We'll not harm you in any way." Then the boy seemed to think for a few seconds and replied, "Yes, I know him. In fact I stayed in his own house. But I don't know where he has been living these days."

The British officer thought inwardly that the boy might divulge many details about Ramarao and therefore tried to please him and take him into confidence by offering him *pedhas*. "My dear boy, you eat these sweets. If you reply to my questions, I shall give you more sweets. Don't be afraid of us. Whom did Ramarao enrust you after bringing you away from his home?"

"Saheb, Ramarao did not bring me upto this village at all. He cheated me very systematically. He asked me to wait for him in the woods and went away somewhere. I sat there waiting and waiting, but he never turned up."

Hearing these words from the boy, one of the soldiers cross-questioned him, "Look here, boy don't you tell lies. How far away is that woods from here? Who brought you here from that woods?"

Now the boy affected a sort of mock anger and counter-questioned him,

"Who are you to question me like this? When I am replying to this *saheb* who are you to interfere like this? Do you want to threaten me?"

The soldiers looked at one another meaningfully. The soldier on whose lap the boy sat was the leader of the group of soldiers. He felt happy to be addressed as saheb especially in the presence of his own colleagues. Then the leader beckoned to his colleagues not to interfere and coaxed the boy to answer his querries, "Now tell me boy if Mr. Ramarao did not bring you to this village and entrust you to your father."

The boy was very alert as well as intelligent. He instantly replied, "Why saheb, did you forget what I told you a few moments ago? Didn't I tell you that Ramarao did not come upto this village but left me in the lurch in the woods? Would he ever return to me when he seemed to have planned to desert me?"

The leader confirmed the truth of the boy's repeated statement. He said to the boy, "My dear Krisna, I grant what you say. But now tell us about the person who actually brought you to your village." Krisna replied instantly, "Saheb, please listen to me carefully. When Ramarao left me in the woods, I dozed for an hour or so. When I woke up and waited for him, he did not come to me at all. I searched for him behind the trees and boulders. But there was no sign of him anywhere. Then it began to grow dark everywhere. Fear gripped me and I began to cry.

Then a shepherd heard my cry and took pity on me. After learning from me the details of my parents he brought me to this village and entrusted me to my parents. May God bless that shepherd."

All the soldiers were pleased by the clear-cut answers of Krisnarao though they were rather disappointed not to elicit any information from the boy about Ramarao. They talked among themselves in English, "The boy appears to be very intelligent and bold as well. But he is so clever that he is not giving us even a single hint about Ramarao's whereabouts." "Why not cross question the boy?" suggested one of the soldiers to their leader. Now the leader asked Krisnarao, "Let it be, boy. Could you tell us what Ramarao told you before leaving you in the woods? I mean where did he wish to go?" Now Krisnarao waved his right palm as if he was waving an *arati* ironically and said, "Ha, ha. *Saheb*, your memory power appears to be very weak. Did you already forget what I told you a little while ago? Do you think a man who wanted to cheat me would tell me where he would be going? Why are you asking me the same question over and again *Saheb*, please note that I do not know anything beyond this."

Now the soldiers were really disappointed and did not know what to do next. They were quite good and sober by nature unlike many other soldiers. They did not want to arrest people unnecessarily. They had heard the rumour that Krisnarao who was living now with Govindarao was living with Ramarao as his secretary and that Krisnarao was a grown up man. But to their dismay they had discovered that Krisnarao was only a slip of a boy yet. They could not get any hint or trace of Ramarao's whereabouts. They were also convinced beyond any doubt that these two persons *i.e.* father and son were not connected with any crime. The leader, therefore, said to Govindarao,

"Mr. Govindarao, we are fully convinced that you are innocent. You need not be afraid of any punishment. The very fact that we are not putting shackles on your wrists shows that you are not guilty of anything. Our officer might be pleased with the sweet talk of your boy Krisnarao. We also speak well about you to our officer and see that you are not arrested and kept in prison. You and your son will have to come with us to Naragund. If we leave you here we'll have very serious consequences for us. That's why we have to show Krisnarao to our officer who will be convinced by the words of this boy. Please, therefore, get ready to come along with us."

Govindarao and Krisnarao understood the situation and were mentally ready to go to Naragund, but as the news of their departure circulated in the village, the villagers began to worry about their safety. The womenfolk requested their men folk to prevent the boy Krisnarao from being arrested by the soldiers. The men folk, therefore, gathered before the leader of the soldiers. The leader asked them, "Why did you come here?" The villagers joined their palms in salutation to the soldier and requested, "*Saheb*, this small boy Krisnarao is a very smart one in our village. We all the villagers love him and enjoy listening to his sweet talk. Please don't arrest this boy and sadden all of us. You may take a fine if you like but please spare this innocent boy." Then the womenfolk of the village brought Satyabhama with them to the leader and the elder ones requested him with joined palms, "*Saheb*, please don't take away this smart boy. We all implore you humbly. You may take off all the golden ornaments from the boy's limbs, but please spare the boy." They began to wail piteously for the boy. Seeing all this the soldiers also felt pity for the men and women of the village. Since their intention was not to harm the boy or his father they convinced the villagers through Govindarao himself and asked both of them to accompany them to Naragund. The leader convinced the villagers, "Don't you worry about these two persons of your village. We shall bring them back safely after showing them to our officer at Naragund."

Even then the villagers began to cry. Satyabhama could not control herself and fainted and fell on the ground. The women sat fanning her to awaken her. When she woke up from her faint, Krisnarao tried to enhearten her, "Mother, how can we go to

Naragund if you faint like this? Please think properly. If we refuse to go with them now, we may have to lose our lives. There'll be no fear for us if we go with them now. We'll return within three or four days. Don't cry, do you?" Although convinced by the son's sweet talk, Satyabhama kept on crying and said to him in-between tears, "Please return with your father safely." Thus Govindarao and Krisnarao finally left the village for Naragund along with the soldiers.

The women also dispersed after the departure of father and son to Naragund. Satyabhama sat with only a couple of close friends in her house. She went to the niche and lit a lamp to their family deity and prayed for the safety of her husband and son. She took a vow that she would feed hundred brahmins if they returned safe. She began to count her hours.

As Govindarao and Krisnarao were treading the path along with the soldiers towards Naragund, Govindarao felt deeply humiliated and began to introspect his own plight, "Once upon a time we used to enjoy all the honour and glory in our own kingdom. But now in the alien province we are as useless as cowries. Hara, Hara! we have fallen into such a trouble that we could not even experience in our dreams. We simply do not know what is in store for us. We had to run away from Naragund at the midnight time deserting all the near ones and dear ones without even being able to talk with them. Now we are fated to return to the same city like strangers. Like the handle of an axe destroying its own source our treacherous fellows Krishnaji Pant and Baniya Bapu brought about this tragedy for all of us. Consequently countless people had to leave their homes and lands and seek shelter in the forests. We somehow escaped from Naragund and were living peacefully, but badluck has hunted us out here also." As these memories crowded in his mind, he broke into tears and began to sob. Krisnarao who saw this, tried to console his father, "Father, it's true that some unexpected danger has come to us, but don't be discouraged simply on that account. God is great and I am sure He will protect us and mete out justice." Govindarao was listening to his son's words of encouragement. He wiped his tears and tried to recover his drooping spirit.

The soldiers were also listening to the dialogues between the father and the son. They were also pleased by the sweet talk of the boy. One of the soldiers lifted the boy on his shoulder and made him ride on him and covered the distance by cracking jokes and talking lightly. In the light talk of the soldiers, Govindarao could not feel the fatigue or the boredom of covering the distance. Finally they reached Naragund. At the very sight of the leonine shaped hill of Naragund decked with the beautiful spire of the Temple of Lord Venkateswara, Govindarao's heart began to palpitate with nervousness and excitement. The soldiers took them straight to the precincts of the temple and asked them to relax there. Then they went to their office and explained to their judge the whole thing including the goodness and innocence of the two persons. So the judge allowed the two captives to stay wherever they liked provided they attended the enquiry regularly in their court at about 10 o'clock every morning. The soldiers came back and conveyed their officer's special order to Govindarao and Krisnarao who felt a little happy.

*****

When the news spread in the city that both father and son were captured by the British authorities, they could not resist the temptation of seeing them and consoling them if possible. They flocked to the temple in order to see them. Others discussed among themselves. One man said,

"The real culprit was Ramarao, and not these innocent fellows."

"But the truth will be out soon. The Britishers are a very vindictive race. They will definitely trace the criminals." said another man.

"I don't know what punishment these innocent people will be given," said the third man.

Talking thus they reached the temple and walked slowly towards the room where Govindarao and the precocious boy Krisnarao sat. They felt like crying at the sight of the innocent father and son sitting together helplessly in the temple room. They inwardly prayed to the Lord,

"Lord, kindly save these two innocent people. After all, what right have the British to try these people!"

Then some elderly man made bold to talk to Govindarao in spite of the presence of the soldiers there,

"Why Govindaraya, why are you sitting here in the temple. You could as well have stayed in your own house?"

Govindarao who was touched and stirred by the question and concern shown by his fellowman of Naragund replied in a very pathetic manner,

"Dear friend, how can I stay in that house now when it is no longer mine? Once upon a time countless members of the family stayed there. But now nobody stays there. It must be looking like a haunted house now. Can I control my feelings if I stayed there now? It's better for me to camp at this abode of God."

Govindarao controlled his rushing tears and tried to raise his tremulous voice.

"Dear Govindarao, take it easy. God is great. He would never allow injustice to continue for long. Have faith in God," said the elderly man.

"What else can I do? Everything depends upon His mercy."

Then the other natives and well-wishers of Govindarao threaded their way through the crowd and tried their best to console and enhearten them.

The soldiers went to their officer and told him, "Sir, we have brought Govindarao. But we could not trace Ramarao. Instead we have a small boy of twelve called Krisnarao from whom we can elicit some information." The officer was pleased to note that at least some information could be gathered from these two captives. He therefore ordered them, "Then bring them to my office for trial."

These soldiers had already spoken well about Govindarao to their officer. That's the reason why the good captives were allowed to stay at the temple precincts rather than in prison cells. The natives of Naragund had also wondered at this special arrangement done for Govindarao and his boy. The officer had been briefed about the goodness of the captives. But Govindarao did not notice anything special about his arrest. For him being arrested itself was a great humiliation and did not know what to do. He had heard reports about other suspects who were tried everyday and were either sent for death sentence at the gunfire or put behind bars for years together. He simply did not know what would happen to him. Most probably he will have to die at the hands of the British soldiers.

That morning about 10 o'clock a large number of natives of Naragund had gathered at the court hall to hear the judgment about these innocent captives. The natives were very curious to know what kind of judgment would be passed on these brahmins. At the scheduled time the judge came into the hall and sat majestically on his chair. Then the soldiers brought Govindarao and the boy Krisnarao into the hall. The crowd of people began to whisper and murmur among themselves. The police officers hushed them into silence. Then the Chief Officer explained to the judge by pointing to the captives,

"Your honour, we had gone to a particular village for searching for Ramarao, but we could not find him out. But when we were about to search for Krisnarao, this boy and his father volunteered to come to us and narrated certain things which prove that they are quite innocent. We offered eatables to the other children of the village and asked them about Ramarao, but they also told us what this Govindarao and Krisna had told us. We have brought this boy so that you may clarify your doubt about Ramarao and others."

Now the judge was convinced about the innocence of Govindarao as it was confirmed by the Chief Officer. But he just wanted to tackle the small boy Krisna who was hardly twelve years or so. He asked the boy to be seated by his side and caressed his back quite affectionately. He then asked him very casually,

"My dear young boy, do you know Mr. Ramarao?"

The boy Krisna was not at all afraid to be questioned by the British judge. He replied without any hesitation or ambiguity,

"*Saheb*, how do I not know Ramarao with whom I have been living since my fifth year? I know him very well."

The judge was really struck by the boy's boldness and asked him further,

"My dear boy, if you know Mr. Ramarao, could you tell us when he sent you to your father?"

Then the boy Krisna replied in very clear cut words, "Saheb, do you think Ramarao brought me to my father's house to leave me there? No. Never. Saheb. Rather he deceived me very systematically. He brought me to a nearby wooded hill and asked me to wait near a boulder until he returned from his nature call. I waited and waited, but he never came. It was already growing dark and therefore, I grew fearful and started crying. Then a shepherd came there with his sheep and asked me why I was crying. I told him the whole thing. Then he took me to the village where I met my father accidentally and began to live with him."

The judge was really impressed by the eloquent answer of the boy who spoke so well and so fearlessly. He felt really very happy and wished to hear the boy's sweet words further. He therefore asked him,

"My dear boy, who gave you all the ornaments that you have worn on your person?"

The boy replied, "Saheb, some of these ornaments have been given to me by Bhaskararao and his queen and some by Ramarao. One day at about 2 o'clock at night Ramarao's wife was whispering something to him. The same night Ramarao took me to the hill and left me in the lurch."

The judge was more than convinced by the verity of statements coming from the mouth of the innocent boy.

The judge then turned to Govindarao and asked him several cross questions in order to elicit more information about Ramarao and others like Raghopant. He asked him,

"Mr. Govindarao, please tell us whatever you know about Mr. Ramarao, Mr. Raghopant and about their whereabouts."

"Saheb, I swear by our family god Venkateswara that I do not know anything about them."

"But you were living very close with them. You were in the palace when the mutiny broke out."

"It's true that I was in the palatial quarters. And we were all busy with some matrimonial ritual at home not even caring to know the gravity of the war. When we heard the news that our beloved Babasaheb had fled the palace we were not in a position to care for anybody or anything. We simply ran for our life. In that fearful confusion I could not even try to keep track of others. I simply do not know where they went."

The judge felt a ring of sincerity in the words of Govindarao. He guessed that the boldness of Govindarao's speech was enough evidence of his conviction. Now that the judge could not get any information from Gavindarao nor could he incriminate him, he tried to use the last weapon of temptation,

"Mr. Govindarao, if you help our Government to capture Ramarao and Raghopant, we shall grant you some land for permanent enjoyment. Would you mind helping us?"

"Saheb, whatever grant we already have by the grace of God is more than enough for us. There is nobody alive now to enjoy the land. I simply have no desire for any land from you. I do not know where my kith and kin are scattered. In that terrific confusion reaching my wife and other children was itself a great task for me. I was able to get my son Krisna only because of the shepherd's mercy. I felt that my lost son was reborn for us."

The judge was really very pleased with the boy's words. He expressed his anger against Ramarao openly and said loudly so that all the people gathered there could hear him distinctly,

"Both the father and son are quite innocent. This boy is a very smart guy. He is as handsome as his eloquent speech. Ramarao must have kept this boy with him because of the precocious intelligence of this boy. That is the reason why he must have given him all these ornaments. But see how irrational Ramarao must have been to desert this boy in the forest instead of reaching him to his parents! What if some robbers had killed the boy for the sake of his precious ornaments! Look at the utter selfishness of Ramarao! Mr. Govindarao you are really very lucky to get back your son that too safely. Now onwards don't send him anywhere away from you. The boy is unusually intelligent. Let him be with us so that we could educate him well and appoint him in our office in future." The judge was affectionately caressing the back of the boy seated on his lap. Then he seemed to remember something and said again to Govindarao,

"Mr. Govindarao, since you are free from any crime, we have no objection to your coming back to Naragund and staying in your own house. You can always enjoy your ancestral property without any fear. It is only those lands which were granted by Babasaheb will be recovered by our Government. So far I have seen many boys but never one as intelligent as yours."

Then he turned to the boy and asked him again tenderly, "My dear boy, please tell us what you want. Do you wish to stay with us?"

The boy Krisna replied in a very pleasant and touching manner, "Saheb, when both father and I started for this place, my mother began to cry and wail continuously suspecting some danger to both of us. She will not be happy until both of us return home. Therefore, I request you to kindly permit us to go home. I also request you not to punish any of our relatives who happen to came to you. This much is the only request that I make to you."

The judge was again pleased by the sweet words of the boy. He gently kissed the palm of the boy and assured, "My dear boy, I grant your wish whole-heartedly. Mr. Govindarao, please don't have any fear about the mutiny. You may return to your home in Naragund and stay here. That will be quite profitable to you."

Govindarao who remained silent so far made bold to reply quite gently,

"Saheb, I cannot stay alone with my wife and children in the house in which I once stayed with hundreds of kith and kin. We will definitely return here if all of us are reunited once again by the grace of God. Until then I prefer to stay with my wife and children in the village. If we have your good will, that is more than enough for us."

After hearing Govindarao's words, the judge ordered his soldiers to send back the father and the son to their home in the village. All the spectators of Naragund who had gathered there in the court hall felt happy at the release of Govindarao and his son. They were also surprised at the humanity shown by the so-called cruel British authorities.

Then Govindarao left the court hall along with his son Krisnarao accompanied by the soldiers. His well-wishers and friends also followed him. They all went back to the temple of Lord Venkateswara with a sense of relief and satisfaction. Govindarao desired to celebrate his release by arranging for a brief service called *Laghu Rudra* for Lord Venkatapati. Likewise he arranged for the distribution of sweets to all the well-wishers and gifts to the brahmin priests of Naragund. Then he saluted all his friends and well-wishers and took leave of them and set out for his village where his wife Satyabhama was eagerly waiting for him. He and his son were, of course, accompanied by the soldiers. They all trudged their way slowly and patiently. The strain of walking for miles together was eased by the happy memory of his being exonerated from crime by the British judge.

They reached their village nearly two hours before sunset. When the villagers saw the soldiers again in their village they were frightened. But when they saw Govindarao and Krisnarao coming behind the soldiers they felt relieved. Satyabhama was leaning against the wall shedding tears incessantly. Her eyes were dimmed by the crying and wailing. The villagers were standing at a safe distance and watching everything with curiosity as well as anxiety. As Govindarao and his son went near their house, Krisnarao ran ahead into the house and hugged his mother affectionately. Satyabhama grew so ecstatic about the unexpected arrival of her husband and son that she naturally began to cry for joy. She hugged her son and kissed and caressed him repeatedly as if she was seeing him after an interval of several years. Govindarao explained to his wife how he and his son were exculpated by the grace of God very easily.

That night Govindarao arranged a grand feast and fed the soldiers who had escorted them to their village and the other brahmins and neighbours. Then the soldiers took leave of them. That night Govindarao and his wife and son were so happy that they could not sleep at all for joy. Throughout the night Govindarao sat in his verandah and narrated the story of what had happened to him in three days in Naragund and the humanitarian way in which they were treated by the British judge and his subordinates. The willing listeners sat through the night just for the pleasure of listening to such a happy turn of events which was normally unheard of so far in the British administration.

*****

Bhaskararao had left his palace after briefly requesting his mother and wife to take care of themselves in a befitting manner. He had simply no time to think about anything except his own safety. He had mounted an unsaddled horse and rode out of Naragund through the secret underground tunnel. He was accompanied by his confidants like Visnu Kulkarni, Raghopant and another four well-wishers. They rode recklessly until they crossed the borders of Naragund kingdom when darkness descended everywhere. Then they rested for the night in some valley. The next day they started their onward journey early in the morning so that they should not be detected by anyone connected with the British Government. Like this they rode away from Naragund. Then they let their horses free and began to walk the distance. They thought that their horses might be identified by the spies of the British Government and they might be arrested merely on suspicion. They therefore, decided to trudge their path laboriously. Every evening they would rest at some forest and continue their directionless journey in the early morning. Thus they covered a very long distance. One day when they were running like this, they were all utterly tired. Bhaskararao, therefore, suggested, "Come on friends, let's rest for a while. We are all dead tired." He walked to the nearest tree and sat under the shade. The others also followed him and sat near him and fanned themselves with the fringes of their dhotis to ward off the terrible heat of the midday sun. They remained speechless for a few moments on account of their panting and fatigue. Then Bhaskararao reminisced something and said, "Raghunatha, did we ever dream that we would have to suffer like this? If those treacherous fellows had not adulterated the gun-powder, would our patriotic soldiers have run for their life like cowards? As our fort was impregnable we had no fear about its being broken so easily by the enemies. Our gunmen and cannon operators were great experts in their jobs. Besides the stock of gun-powder was also inexhaustible. In spite of all these facilities our efforts came to nought simply because of the betrayal by our own people. What shall I do? If those ungrateful fellows were to be found by me, I would have hacked them to tiny pieces and satisfied my anger. How can we ever go ahead when our own men betray us like this? Even then I believe that those treacherous fellows will be properly punished by God. Don't you think Raghunatharaya? Because of their selfishness those two fellows ruined the lives of thousands of innocent people and their lands and homes. They mixed food with mud and rendered it useless. God will not pardon them. Whatever was written in our destiny came to happen. We could not control it. But we cannot sit crying over that. Don't you remember what happened to Bhima and Arjuna in *Dwapara Yuga?* Were they ever cowardly? There were none who could defeat them in the normal course of life. Yet they were deceived in the dice by the evil fellows like Duryodhana and others and sent to be exiled in the forest? If such a tragedy could happen to great kings and warriors, what about the ordinary fellows like us?"

Then Raghopant replied, "Maharaj, Pandavas' case was quite different from ours. Though exiled in the forest, they enjoyed the grace and full cooperation of Lord Krisna. But we don't have such a privilege. Nor can we hope for such a support in the *Kaliyuga*. We who were known for our heroism have been behaving like helpless women here in the forest. In that great confusion we did not have the presence of mind to bring our weapons along with us for self-protection. When our own men betray us like this, there's simply no meaning for our life. It's better to renounce the world and live like saints on hills and dales meditating upon the Lord God."

Bhaskararao listened to him carefully and exclaimed, "Raghopant, there is a truth in what you say. We are all simply disillusioned with life as we are betrayed by our own people. We fed those two fellows who turned out to be dangerous vipers. Our Kingdom is also surrounded by enemies. Our people have lost all the pride of caste or kingdom. What can we do in such a situation? What can we ever do anything? Let's leave everything to the will of God-Almighty."

"Maharaj, what you say is right. Sorrows come in our life in a chain fashion. We simply do not know how and from where they come. Now I remember something which I can neither hide from you nor express it before you," said Raghunatharaya with a deep sigh.

"In our present condition both sorrow and happiness are of equal importance. We can be neither elated with joy nor depressed with sorrow. What you intend to tell me seems to be a sad news. Don't worry. Tell me what it is. Don't hesitate," said Bhaskararao. But Raghopant hesitated to say it, "Maharaj, how shall I tell that?"

"Came on, my Raghunatharaya, why do you hesitate? We have to face the harsh facts of life."

Then Raghopant hardened his heart and controlled himself from breaking down and said in a tremulous voice, "Maharaj, we learnt from reliable sources that both *matosri* and *attige* repaired to Heaven by drowning themselves in the Malaprabha river. Their funeral was arranged in Budihal village."

Bhaskararao was shocked out of his wits. For a few seconds he sat dumbfounded. He felt that there was a sudden and inexplicable emptiness in his soul. He felt a sudden blackout of consciousness. He could not speak anything for a few seconds. Raghopant and his companions were watching their king and his reaction. Bhaskararao gulped down the spittle in his mouth and spoke rather weakly, "Raghunatharaya, in a way my burden is lightened a bit now. When I left the palace in a hurry I had told them to take care of themselves in a befitting manner and see that they won't tarnish the honour of the family or our religion. Now and then I used to worry about them and try to learn what they had been doing. Now I am free from that worry. We could not imagine how much they would have been tortured by the enemies if they had been caught by those monsters. My mother and wife have been wise enough to save the honour of the family as well as of our religion. I am really happy about them now. As for me I am willing to face any danger that is in store for me. Whatever is stored in our destiny cannot be avoided. Any other news? Is any other leader captured?"

Raghopant remembered a few other bits of news that he had collected. He said, "Maharaj, the British fellows learnt that our boy Krisnarao was in the care of Ramarao and started searching for him. Ramarao had deserted the boy in a forest, but luckily the boy was able to join his parents. Then both Govindarao and Krisnarao were brought to Naragund for trial. The smart boy Krisnarao gave the answers very boldly. He told them that he did not know anything about Ramarao. Since the British officers were convinced by the boy's clear-cut answers, they released them and sent them back to their village. This is what I have learnt from our servants and this is what I wished to present before the *Sarkar*."

"What is this Raghunatharaya? Why do you address me as *Sarkar* now? I am no longer the *Sarkar*. You address me simply as a friend. I have lost all my honorifics and title along with my kingdom."

"How is that possible *Sarkar*? What if the kingdom is lost? Our lives are not lost. As long as we are alive, we have the hope of earning or regaining our prosperity. As long as we your servants are alive you are the only *Sarkar* for us."

"All right, Raghunatharaya, let it be as you please. In a way I am really happy to learn that my mother and wife have ended their lives in a befitting manner without being caught by the British officers. Similarly the intelligent boy Krisnarao has been able to escape from the hands of the enemies by his bold and clever answers. These two events have indeed given me a sense of relief. Now let's us think of ourselves. Although we have not committed any crime, still we are criminals in the eyes of the Britishers. They will not keep quiet until they are able to search for us and capture us by using various strategies like bribing our own people. Then they are sure to kill us after giving us picturesque trouble. I, therefore, think that each one of us should follow his own path. For the past few days I am having very bad dreams. But don't think that I'm afraid of them. At the same time I feel that the dreams that we see in the early morning will never be false. I am telling you my feelings very frankly because it is my duty to tell you so. Every one of you tell me what you really want to do. Otherwise, keeping quiet will be tantamount to self-deception."

After listening to Bhaskararao's words, all the companions grew rather depressed. They began to think seriously about what to do. For a few seconds there was complete silence. Occasionally there was heard the twitter of birds in the surrounding trees. The terrible heat of the midday sun aggravated the atmosphere. Though every one was thinking in his own way nobody had any concrete suggestion as none except Raghopant had any clear-cut ideas. Nor had they any courage to express their views. Finally Raghopant made bold to express himself thus, "Maharaj, looking to the gravity of the situation, I feel that our moving together will be very risky for all of us. It would be easy for our enemies to catch us if we keep on moving in a group like this. What I humbly suggest is that we should disperse and follow different paths and finally join one another in a safe place. In my opinion, there is no place for us safer than Nepal. We shall all go there separately and meet together in Nepal."

Everyone found Raghopant's views acceptable. They therefore decided to change their appearance, but did not know which guise to adapt. For though they were expert politicians, they did not have the art of *bahurupis* to assume any guise according to the situation. But since they were all brahmins, they dressed themselves as poor brahmin mendicants. They did not have the necessary garments to assume any other guise. Since Visnupant was a clever man, he disguised himself as a *bairagi*.

Raghopant addressed his companions including Bhaskararao, "Maharaj, let's all reach Nepal separately and then meet in Nepal and join the company of Nanasaheb there." Everyone assented for that. But when the moment of separation came nearer, Bhaskararao felt lonely and alienated by the prospect of moving alone. Tears gathered in his eyes. The veins of his throat were swollen with sorrow. He could not speak easily. Even then he managed to say, "My dear Raghunatharaya and Visnupant, are you all leaving me alone in this forest? Siva, Siva. There is no other remedy. Will I be happy after your departure? O God! I who used to protect innumerable people have become helpless myself and not able to protect even half a dozen companions like you. O Lord of the Universe, why don't You better kill me than keep me in this anxiety? Friends please tell me when you are going to see me in future? If we are destined not to meet again, this happens to be our final meeting. Raghunatharaya and Visnupant, we have been like friends here in spite of our hierarchy." With these words Bhaskararao rushed towards them and hugged them one after the other. Tears were gushing out of his eyes. Visnupant controlled himself and said, "Maharaj, why are you so excited? Please don't be disheartened. The kind God may bring us all together in future. Don't you remember that kings like Nala, Rama and Yudhisthira saw better days after their exile? We must leave everything to God and seek our individual paths. What would people say if we sit here crying like helpless women?"

After listening to Visnupant's words of encouragement, everyone wiped his tears and decided to scatter from one another. Even then they felt that they could not keep their steps ahead. Bhaskararao stood there without being able to move an inch. Again Visnupant tried to console the king, "Maharaj, why are you so depressed? I shall accompany you if you like."

"No, no, friend, Visnupant. Don't you worry. Your accompanying me will not help me in any way. I shall face the consequences of my ill-luck all by myself." Then they all went away from one another rather slowly. Bhaskararao said, "Raghunatharaya, please remember to meet me in Nepal." Raghopant who was away from Bhaskararao seemed to hear the faint words of Bhaskararao and fainted and fell down on the earth. Bhaskararao also sagged to the earth in a swoon. Visnupant saw this and rushed to them and tried to awaken them by sprinkling water on their heads. He fanned both of them with the end of his dhoti. The other companions also were fanning them. After a few seconds both of them woke up from their swoon. Then Raghopant said in a weak voice, "Maharaj, it is only because of my deep love for you that I fell unconscious like this. Our proposed separation is really intolerable. Yet separate we must. That's why I have hardened myself. You also harden your heart. I fall prostrate to your feet. Kindly bless me for the last time." Raghopant got up to fall prostrate at Bhaskararao's feet, but Bhaskararao hugged him tightly to his chest and began to cry, Raghopant released himself from Bhaskararao's hug and said, "See you again, Maharaj," and walked away briskly with a special effort of his mind.

Seeing Raghopant going like this, Visnupant also fell prostrate on Bhaskararao's feet and requested, "Maharaj, lucky will be the day when we meet again." Bhaskararao lifted him up and hugged him tightly and exclaimed, "Are you also going away from me Visnu?" Then Visnupant controlled his tears with great difficulty and replied, "Maharaj, there is no other way now for us. I really don't want to go away from your feet, but I have got to go." Visnupant walked away from Bhaskararao who began to cry loudly like a child. He cried for a few minutes and allowed his other ministers to go away from him.

Thus everybody departed from one another with heavy hearts. They were looking at one another until they were invisible. Then they began to think of the way they had to follow. Though they had decided to go to Nepal, they did not know the route. Nor had they thought of the answers they had to give to the people who would ask them "Who are you?" Bhaskararao was accompanied by Anna Sahasrabudde. Both of them exchanged the dress and began to wander from place to place.

One day Babasaheb and Anna Sahasrabuddhe were walking slowly along the outskirts of the village. As usual they were very cautious about the soldiers of Company Government. They were discussing their own plight in a low pitch. When Anna Sahasrabuddhe heard the clop-clop of horses' hooves, he turned back and saw that the soldiers were rushing towards them. He grew alert and requested his master, "Sarkar, the soldiers are rushing towards us. You better hide yourself somewhere here." There was no time even to think. Babasaheb saw a haystack of rice paddy near him. He instantly rushed to the haystack and covered himself with a mass of rice paddy. Anna Sahasrabuddhe felt relieved that his master escaped from the danger at least temporarily. He began to walk slowly. Within a few seconds the soldiers surrounded him with drawn swords. Anna Sahasrabuddhe felt very helpless. One of the soldiers asked him, "We know, you are one of the companions of Babasaheb. You tell us where your master is." Anna Sahasrabuddhe pretended ignorance and replied, "Dear friends, I do not know where

Babasaheb Sarkar is." The soldiers were irritated by the answer. "We have clear information that you accompanied Babasaheb when he left the palace of Naragund. How can you pretend ignorance now?" "It's true that I accompanied him initially. But later we scattered into different directions. I really do not know where Babasaheb went away," replied Anna Sahasrabuddhe. "No, you are telling us a blatant lie," complained the soldier. "No friends, please believe me. I really do not know his whereabouts," said Anna Sahasrabuddhe. "You have to lose your life if you don't divulge Babasaheb's whereabouts," threatened the soldier. "How can I divulge the secret when I don't know it at all," repeated Anna Sahasrabuddhe. "Come on, you are under arrest. You will be properly dealt with by our higher officers," said the soldier. Then they took him to Dharwad and kept him in the jail. After a few weeks they tried him in the court and ordered him to be hanged to death as they could not get any information from him about the absconding Babasaheb.

*****

After wandering in the woods, the Sanyasi reached Bellary area where he heard people discussing the greatness of his Holiness Raghavendra Swamiji. "Why not we go there and stay in his monastery for a few days?" thought the Sanyasi. He instantly decided to go to Mantralaya and spend a few days free from tension. He, therefore, began to travel across the country without entering the villages. In the evening he would rest in some *dharmasala* and resume his journey in the early morning. The Bellary area was very hot and dry studded with rocky hills. As he continued his journey in the direction of Mantralaya he felt tired and weak. But there was no helping it. After a few days he reached Mantralaya and went to the monastery where the evening *puja* was going on. Bells and gongs were sounded to the accompaniment of the *arati* service. The smell of incense wafted through the air. The Sanyasi was instantly reminded of the grand service rendered to Lord Venkateswara at Naragund regularly. Tears trickled in his eyes, but he wiped them instantly lest somebody should notice it. He stood in the *puja* hall with joined palms and watched the holy service. After the service was over he joined the other brahmins and had a proper dinner with them. For many days he had lived only on fruits and roots. The proper food that he had in the monastery gave him some satisfaction. Then he slept in the big hall of the monastery along with other brahmins.

Next morning he was awakened by the sweet notes of the vina recited by somebody. The Sanyasi wondered if he was not dreaming. But now he heard a beautiful melodic pattern suitable to morning time. He asked the brahmin near him, "Dear friend, where do these sweet notes of the vina come from and who is playing upon the instrument at this time of the morning?" The brahmin was a bit surprised by the question. "Are you a stranger here?," he counter questioned. "Yes, I am a stranger here," replied the Sanyasi. "You see, the vina is played by His Holiness Raghavendra Swamiji every day. He is an expert in playing it before the morning puja," explained the brahmin. Then the Sanyasi understood it and kept quiet.

Next evening the Sanyasi went to see His Holiness Raghavendra Swamiji in the hall and bowed to him and introduced himself as a sadhu from the northern part of the country. He then requested, "I would like to stay in your monastery for some time. Kindly permit me to do so and also assign me some duty." His Holiness was a very kind hearted man. He, therefore, said, "All right, dear brother, can you wash the rice clean in water every day before it is cooked for the devotees of the monastery?" The Sanyasi replied, "All right, Your Holiness, I shall do it gladly." Then the Sanyasi bowed to His Holiness and went back to his resting place. In the evening he began to clean the rice by dousing it in water in big vessels. The brahmin residents of the monastery accepted him as one of the regular inmates. The Sanyasi felt at home with the whole atmosphere of the sacred complex. A couple of months went by like this in satisfaction and comfort. But he knew that the British officers were moving about all over the southern part of India.

He thought it not safe to stay in any one place for long. He, therefore, decided to leave the monastery. In the evening he had a *darsan* of His Holiness Raghavendra Swamy at the time of puja. In the night he had his dinner with other brahmins in the monastery and slept in the hall. Until he could stay awake at night he thought of his future plan. He woke up in the early morning and walked out of the monastery and continued his way in the northern direction.

*****

After capturing the fort of Naragund, the British officers began to arrest all the mutineers and try them. Then they would either hang them to death or feed them to the cannon fire. Every day the wayfarers could see at least four to six dead-bodies hanging from the gallows or eight to ten dead bodies hanging in front of the cannon bars. They could also see several mutineers mounted on the gallows led to the cannons. Those who were to be hanged or fired to death used to be crying and wailing remembering their parents, wives and children. It was indeed a very heart-rending scene for every wayfarer. Thus the human carnage went on for several days. But the British officers were rather unhappy as they had not been able to capture the main leaders of the mutiny including Bhaskararao. They, therefore, circulated notices in all the surrounding villages and sent out town-criers to announce fat prizes for those who would help the British Government to capture Bhaskararao and his companions. But the patriotic people of the land did not pay heed to these announcements as they were very unhappy with the British monsters who had put to death several of their friends and relatives. Soon the British officers realized that their announcement of the prize did not work well with the native patriots. They, therefore, thought of alternative plans. For example they appointed Mr. Frank Seutor to trace the main criminals. Frank Seutor took nearly two hundred native soldiers of British Government and began to wander with them in different part of the kingdom in various guises in order to spy on the mutineers. The news of the British espionage also circulated in the areas very soon. Though Bhaskararao and his confidants were also in disguise, they developed a sort of fear thinking that they might be captured in spite of their alertness.

When fate is against a man, his very efforts to escape from danger will drag him into it. Though Bhaskararao and his companions were wandering in the countryside in various disguises, they could be easily contradistinguished from the commonalty on account of their refined speech and behaviour. The common people could easily detect them as superior ones in ordinary apparels. As Frank Seutor's soldiers were moving about in deserted forests and crowded towns in various disguises, they were able to detect many mutineers and capture them. Then they used to send them to Naragund where the mutineers were identified by the treacherous pair Krishnaji Pant and Baniya Bapu who would advise the British officers what punishment to prescribe for the so-called criminals. Thus Krisnaji Pant and Baniya Bapu enjoyed an unprecedented glory and importance in their life.

One evening some travellers camped in a *dharmasala* of a village. They arranged their bags and rolls properly and began to discuss the current affairs of the land. Some of them opened their tobacco pouches and started smoking their pipes. Some others began to chew tobacco. In-between they were discussing the latest news that they had heard from friends and strangers. One of them said, "The other day I happened to be at Naragund and saw the treasurer of Bhaskararao's court being given the death-sentence. The British Saheb sitting in a chair consulted a brahmin sitting in another chair by his side and declared the death-sentence. Before declaring the punishment the Saheb tempted the treasurer with many gifts and awards if the latter was ready to divulge some details of the whereabouts of Bhaskararao and his companions. But the patriotic treasurer stuck to his principles and pleaded his ignorance about it. Poor fellow, he could have saved his life had he supplied some information!" Hearing these words, another man in the guise of a *bairagi* said in Hindustani, "Dear friend, tell me who has the courage even to stare at a British officer?" He inhaled his pipe deeply once and continued, "Last year I was traveling in the northern part of India and saw how arrogantly Nanasaheb was behaving there. It was beyond any description. But when the hat-wearing British soldiers erected their tents at various places and began to blow their bugles and play their bands, Nanasaheb retired to the woods like a mouse running away from the spot where it hears the miaw of a cat. Since I was moving with the native sepoys, I did not feel any trouble or difficulty. There seems to have happened a bit of mutiny on a very small scale in this area. And you have been exaggerating it so much."

Another traveler who had opened his pouch and eating his *pan* and betel got angry. He jerked his pouch and reacted strongly, "O Sadhu, please don't talk like this. People of this side are not cowards. They are as courageous as the northern Hindustanis. If all the mutineers had gathered here at the right time, then the true colour of the hatted fellows would have been revealed. They would have feared to think of the brahmin king of Naragund even in their dreams. But what to do! The hatted fellows attacked Naragund before the mutineers could gather here at the scheduled time. Then they would have tasted the sword of the brahmin king. Now everything has misfired. That is very unfortunate." There was deep excitement in his words.

When the conversation was going on like this among the travelers in the *dharmasala*, an anonymous person clad in half portion of a dhoti with silken brim and covered with the other half of the same soiled dhoti was lying there silently listening to them. Their words used to affect him inwardly and excite him with a variety of feelings which was not observed by the chatters. He used to puff out sighs of relief now and then. One of the travelers was staring at the anonymous person attentively on the sly and watch the changes in the facial expression of the person and feeling quite happy and confident. He accosted the person lying in the corner of the *dharmasala*, "Maharaj, where are you coming from and where are you going to? We feel really very sad to see you clad and covered in two halves of the same dhoti." "Please don't ask me that question. Whenever man is in trouble he has to make do with whatever little he has. How can he get additional things? When I was traveling from my village to Belagavi, a few thieves attacked me and forced my fellow rider to get off his horse and killed him mercilessly. Then they asked me to get off my horse. I, therefore, instantly got down from my horse and surrendered all my golden ornaments except this one dhoti. Then they spared my life. Otherwise they would have robbed my dhoti also and left me semi-naked in a loin-cloth. For the past two days I am lying in the corner of this *dharmasala*. Whenever I feel thirsty I go to the nearest brook to quaff some water. Because I don't have even a small bowl to carry water with me."

The travelers felt pity for the half-clad person. Then one of them asked him further, "Who are you, sir. Where do you wish to go?" He felt this question to be very absurd and even suspected that they must be the spies of the British Government. He grew rather apprehensive but did not want to betray his real feelings. By that time another traveler said, "Come on friends, let's sleep now as the night is advancing. We shall talk about it tomorrow." Everybody spread his blanket and lay down and soon fell into deep sleep. But the anonymous person in half a dhoti could not sleep at all. Because he was none other than Raghopant who began to introspect his own plight, "How strange is our destiny! We lost all our pomp and glory so suddenly and unexpectedly. How I have been reduced to the level of a beggar, no, like a thief avoiding people one after another! If I am caught by chance I am sure to be fired to death by the cannon." He felt a deep fear in his mind and a cold wave went up his spine. He slowly sneaked out of the *dharmasala* and began to walk briskly in the starlight. After walking for an hour or so he sat beneath a big tree. As the memories of his past glory rushed into his mind, he could not control his feelings. He burst into crying loudly until all the tears in him were exhausted.

Then he resumed his journey in the dark. On the way he began to ask himself the fundamental questions which he had never asked in his past life, "Who indeed am I? What has happened to me? Why has this happened to me?" He continued walking and trying to answer himself, "I am Raghunatharaya who used to be respected by one and all including Bhaskararao himself and his mother and wife. What's wrong with me in being loyal to my master? But now I am considered to be a criminal for the very virtue of my loyalty. If I am found out, I am sure to be shot dead or hanged. Now my fate is very cruel to me. I should not wander like this in the deserted forests lest I should keep on brooding about my plight. I must go into the midst of people. But where shall I go now? But what if those people detect me and report it to the British Government? O God! I can't get any clear idea about what to do! Lord Venkateswara, you guide me and save me from the clutches of the enemies. It's better to be mangled to death by wild animals than be killed by the cannon fire of the enemies."

Introspecting like this Raghopant came near a village and sat beneath a tree. He wondered, "Which village this must be? If I go in this guise people may identify me and take me to the *chavadi* and get the fat prize for capturing me. Shall I then remove these clothes? If I did so, how shall I protect myself from this cold? What a plight? Either way I have to suffer. O lord Venkatapati! I have never been false in my trust in you. Should you not have any pity on me? O God! This must be the effect of my wife's curse. She had warned me before the mutiny had started and suggested that we might go away to Kashi on a pilgrimage and be free from liabilities. But her suggestion was not palatable to me then. I was overconfident of my power and personal heroism. O my dear wife, now I realize the relevance of your suggestion! Had I listened to you, I would not have been stranded like this. I had sworn before the brahmin priests in our wedding ceremony that I would protect you all through life. But I left Naragund even without searching for you. I did not think of you in the moments of danger. Now I remember you and feel terribly guilty. I cannot search for our kith in this situation. The only relative who can give me protection is Govindarao, but I don't know how to reach him. I feel that I am going mad. While fleeing from Naragund I could at least have brought a small bowl. What's the use of this precious *pagoti*? This will certainly help the villagers to identify me as some officer. If somebody had seen me in the court of Babasaheb at Naragund, he would definitely identify me. It is better to throw away this *pagoti.*" He then unwound the silken turban and threw it away on the grass. He tore his dhoti into two halves. He clothed himself in one half and used the other half as the turban for his head. His dhoti was naturally soiled because of his continuous traveling. He did not dare enter the village. He, therefore, sat there in the forest until it grew dark. After the evening he entered the village and rested in a corner of a temple.

He had grown weak by constant traveling. Besides for the past six days he had not eaten a single morsel of food. As he was very tired, he did not bother about the consequences. Instantly he fell into a deep sleep.

*****

In the morning when the travelers woke up they found that the anonymous person clad in a dhoti with a silken border was absconding from the *dharmasala*. These travelers were none other than the spies in disguise appointed by Sir Frank Seutor. They were really disappointed to know that the bird had flown out of their hand. They grew angry with one another for having neglected their duty. "No we cannot idle away our time like this. Come on, let's go about in the countryside and search for that brahmin," said one of the spies. Then they left the *dharmasala* and set about their business of spying.

*****

Raghunatharaya woke up after a *Prahara*. He felt very thirsty. He did not know what to do. He walked out of the temple and climbed a tree and observed all around to see if there was any source of water. Luckily he saw a sugarcane field nearby. He climbed down the tree and walked to the sugarcane field. The farmers had set their sugarcane press to prepare the lumps of jaggery. No sooner had the farmer seen the brahmin than he brought a bowl full of sugarcane juice and offered it to him along with a little cream jaggery. Raghopant felt very happy. He ate the jaggery and drank the juice which gave him a temporary relief from the monstrous hunger he was suffering from. He then thanked the farmer and walked to a nearby mango tree and lay down there beneath it. The sugarcane field belonged to the village called Hosur.

A little time after Raghopant had slept beneath the tree, some travelers happened to come there rather unexpectedly and sat chewing tobacco. Some of them began to smoke *ganja*. Then they called the farmer and asked him to get some jaggery and sugarcane juice. Raghopant was suddenly awakened by the noise of the travelers. He sat up and stared at them and to his surprise recognized them as the ones who had talked with him in the *dharmasala*. Then suddenly one of the travelers who was staring at him stood up and walked up to the brahmin and said, "*Namaste*, *Rayare*, you said you were going towards Belagavi. But why did you come here?" Then he held the brahmin's hand and said, "*Rayare*, now you will have to came with us to Naragund." As soon as the brahmin heard their words, he grew pale with fear and his heart began to palpitate wildly. He also grew angry with the traveler whom he suspected to be a spy. He could not avoid them at all. He invoked his God mentally and helplessly surrendered himself to them. They handcuffed him gently. He followed them as he now realized that they were native sepoys in the pay of the British Government and acting as spies in the guise of travelers. They followed him with their hidden weapons. On the way he tried to reason with them, "Dear friends, you are our countrymen, though you may be in the service of the British Government. You know very well that we have not done anything harmful or unjust either to our people or to the Britishers. What do you gain by arresting me? You can gain as well by releasing me. You please leave me by myself if you have any patriotism in your blood." "But, *Rayare*," continued the head sepoy, "like you we are also helpless. If we fail to take you to Naragund we'll have to lose our lives. What to do?" Raghopant was really nonplused by their answer. Realizing the futility of arguing with them he followed them silently. Since the sepoys also knew his earstwhile status and dignity, they did not ill-treat him at all. On the contrary they took him to Naragund while giving him due respect that he deserved.

When the news of the arrest of Raghopant circulated in Naragund, the natives of the city began to visit him with a sense of helpless sadness. But they were not allowed even to see him let alone talk with him. Raghopant who was sitting in the prison in his own native kingdom was introspecting about his plight, "Once upon a time all these people used to dance attendance on me and wait for my orders, but now they have become my jailers. What a great paradox! Most probably within a matter of three or four days they would fire or hang me to death. There's no doubt about it at all. O God, do you want me to suffer like this? If that's your will, let it happen as you wish. I am indeed ashamed of myself. Once I accept it I will be permanently happy." He was looking ferocious like an angered but caged tiger. Meanwhile his wife and children rushed to the spot to see him, but the soldiers did not allow them. But after a lot of effort and appeal from them they were allowed to see Raghopant. The soldiers showed the spot to his wife and children. They walked near him and at the very sight of him broke into tears and began to wail and cry. His wife knew that that was her last sight of her husband, she rushed into his arms and hugged him and shed her tears on his shoulders. She burst out, "Maharaj, what's this condition of yours? Should God almighty keep me alive to see you in this predicament? Should your hands which had rendered several meritorious deeds be handcuffed in iron shackles now? O God, is there any justice in your world? Should you who had never harmed even a single creature in life suffer like this, for no reason? My dear sir, how emaciated you have grown within these fifteen days! Your toes are bleeding, your face has grown so pale and your eyes have sunk so deep. I cannot see you in this condition. O God, please close my eyes forever before his judgment takes place. O God, receive me into your lotus feet." With these words she fell into a swoon. Her clasp loosened from his chest. Then his children hugged him and began to cry piteously. Raghopant controlled himself and advised his children, "My dear children, why are you crying like women? First you sprinkle some water on her head and awaken her from her swoon." So they rushed to somebody and brought some water and sprinkled it on her face. She opened her eyes slowly and could not speak immediately. Raghopant asked them to sit beside him and advised them in a calm voice, "Please don't cry like this. Go back home and live without any worry about me. If you cry like this here the prison guards will begin to laugh at us. You know what is going to happen to me and how I am going to die. My dear son, please see that my dead body is not polluted by the touch of *mlenchas*. You conduct my funeral according to our holy custom. There is simply no escape from this. No amount of crying will save my life. After the mutiny is over, some good fellow may help and provide for you. You all be happy. My life is over. That's all that I can advise you at the last moment of my life." By this time the prison guard came there and told Raghopant's wife and sons, "Now hurry up. The time allowed for your meeting is over." But they lingered there shedding tears. Raghopant was also crying silently. "Come on, get up and clear from here. Do you think it to be your home to sit crying here?", thundered the prison guard. So the wife and sons of Raghopant walked out of the prison helplessly looking at him again and again until they could not see him.

After the departure of the members of his family, Raghunatharaya felt very sad. Everyday he used to remember the past days of his life in Bhaskararao's court. The natives of Naragund tried their best to meet him, but the British authorities did not allow anyone to see him as he happened to be one of the chief criminals in their eyes. He was kept under very strict watch. Meanwhile they were also searching for the other criminals. The British officer thought of arranging the trial of the minister of Naragund at the earliest and pass his judgment on him. The date of trial was fixed.

*****

On the scheduled morning the court met in the cool hours. The treacherous Krishnaji Pant had already briefed the British officer about Raghopant's role in the mutiny. Raghopant was led by the soldiers to the court hall and made to stand before the judge. Since the judge had learnt many details from Krishnaji Pant he did not ask him many questions. He clearly knew how important a role Raghopant had played in the mutiny. Still then he remembered the boy Krisnarao's request not to trouble his kith and kin if they were to be tried. He, therefore, asked him, "Mr. Raghojipant, do you happen to know the boy Krisnarao?" "The boy Krisnarao is my close relative, how do I not know him? Besides, why do you refer to that boy here in my case?" asked Raghopant. The judge composed himself and said, "No Mr. Raghopant, that boy Krisnarao had requested us not to harass any of his relatives. We want to oblige him. But since you are one of the main criminals, we are also helpless in this case. If you try your best and help us capture Mr. Bhaskararao and Mr. Visnu Kulkarni, we will do our best to get you exculpated and spare your life. We will grant you some *inam* for your livelihood. We feel that such a course will be better for you." The judge had spoken very gently and calmly. Raghopant caught the spirit of his words and replied, "Saheb, I simply do not know where our king Bhaskararao went. Nor do I know anything about Commander Visnu Kulkarni. Our boy Krisnarao is a very intelligent boy. You oblige him if you will. Otherwise you do whatever you like. You are promising to give me some *inam*. Please know that I have no desire for any *inam*. Also please note that our King Bhaskararao has no mistake in indulging in this mutiny. He is not a criminal. I am telling you the truth. It was I who was mainly responsible for the mutiny. You might ask me how I could do all these things without Bhaskararao's permission. That is because I enjoyed a special respect and importance in our court. People used to obey me unquestioningly. That's why I took this decision. King Bhaskararao is not responsible for this. He is totally away from all this. I have told you the naked truth. I have nothing more to tell you. You may take any action you like," Raghopant did not talk after this.

Listening to Raghopant's words, the British judge felt that this person was a real patriot who wanted to prove his king to be an innocent man. He exclaimed inwardly, "Bravo, Mr. Raghopant, your patriotism and loyalty are indeed incomparable!" But he also felt that this person could not go unpunished for his anti-British activities. The court hall was crowded with the natives of Naragund who had come there to watch the proceedings of the court on that day. Since most of them had benefited from Raghunatharaya's munificence in the past, they had come there to pay their homage to him. But in that crowd they could not see the face of Raghunatharaya. They were straining their necks to have a *darsan* of their beloved minister. Meanwhile the British judge was scribbling his judgment. After he finished writing his judgment, he handed it over to the *Sirastedar* to read out the judgment. The Sirastedar took the piece of paper and glanced over it once and then read out the judgment loudly to be heard by most of the people in the court hall, "Mr. Raghopant is given the punishment of being hanged to death on account of his rebellious and anti-British activities." All the natives of Naragund and well-wishers of Raghopant were shocked and saddened by the plight of their once beloved minister. Immediately the soldiers brought Raghopant out of the court hall. All the friends and well-wishers of Raghopant raised their voice and began to wail piteously and helplessly. The soldiers tried to scare the crowd of people away from the criminal

At the scheduled time, Raghopant was taken to the spot where the criminals of the mutiny were to be murdered officially. The British officers made Raghopant climb the wooden scaffolding and stand there. Now Raghopant was fully visible to all the gathering of people who had come there to watch their beloved minister. Then an officer read out all the charges leveled against him loudly and the kind of punishment that was given to him. Then he turned to Raghopant and said, "Mr. Raghunatharaya, you salute your people and say good-bye to them. Raghopant turned towards the natives of Naragund and saluted them with joined palms. Immediately the hangman who was standing by his side covered Raghopant's face with a black cap and slipped the noose around his head. The crowd of people began to cry and shout out of pity for their beloved minister. Then the hangman climbed down the wooden scaffolding. Then the other servants suddenly dragged the scaffold aside with a thud. Raghopant began to hang limply from the noose. The close relatives of Raghopant saw the scene and fell into a swoon. The others began to attend to the relatives who fainted. By the time the relatives were woken up, the process of hanging was complete. Raghopant's soul was released from the mortal body to be united with God. Then his dead body was offered to his sons. His relatives took charge of his body and conducted his funeral rites according to the brahmanical customs. The funeral ritual was carried out by his eldest son.

That day all the natives of Naragund attended his funeral ceremony. They were all so depressed by the pathetic death of Raghopant and the injustice perpetrated by the British people in India that they did not have their meal at all. For a whole week they did not take their meal properly. The mood of depression pervaded the whole city of Naragund. For several months people could not forget him and his golden virtues. They remembered sadly all his virtues like altruism, patriotism, efficiency, responsibility and loyalty. They felt that life had no meaning at all and that everybody will have to die one day or the other one way or the other.

*****

Frank Seutor's soldiers continued their espionage in different guises in different villages and mix with local people to indirectly elicit information about the missing leaders of the mutiny. Bhaskararao was wandering from forest to forest and used to take rest in the temples there. One day when he was resting in a temple, half a dozen travelers came and sat there. They tried to engage him in conversation in a very clever manner. He could make out the fact that they were not real travelers, but must be spies of the British Government. When the suspicion arose in his mind, his head reeled with uncontrollable anger. He, therefore, pounced upon them and gave them ferocious punches on their chests, faces and backs indiscriminately. He tumbled them to the earth and pounded their chests until they vomited blood and gave up their ghosts. After thus killing all the six of them, Bhaskararao thought it was not safe to stay on in that area and decided to go into Nizam's state. He could not travel in the daylight in the thickly populated areas or villages. He had to travel only in the darkness of night. He could not get his proper meal for a stretch of three or four days. He had to satisfy his hunger only with roots and fruits to be found in the forest. One day, he slept in a Gowda's house at night. But when he woke up in the morning, he was surprised and shocked to learn that his shoes were stolen by somebody. Bhaskararao enquired the Gowda about the missing shoes. Accordingly the Gowda also ordered for the search of the shoes, but was not able either to trace or recover them. Bhaskararao felt very sad, but could not wait for their recovery. He, therefore, continued his journey barefooted. He was so sad that he introspected about his own unprecedented plight, "O God, for whom shall I flee like a thief like this? What's the use of my living when I have lost everybody who was near and dear to me? It would be very good for me if I die in this very forest, so that birds and beasts might satisfy their hunger by feeding on my flesh. The enemies are dead set on capturing me and killing me. But I do not want to die like that. I, who used to feed countless people in my palace, am reduced to begging for a bare meal now! I, who used to wear silken slippers and walk on embroidered and silken carpets, am reduced to tread the prickly path in the forest now. I who used to be clad in woolen clothes and covered in woolen blankets, am reduced to wearing a tattered dhoti. O God. No man should have such a plight as I have. Now I am disturbed even by the slightest sound and begin to imagine the enemies around me. What a difference in my own behaviour! All this tragedy happened only because of those two betrayers Baniya Bapu and Krishnaji Pant. O God, please keep them at least happy." Bhaskararao continued his journey like this introspecting his own past and present conditions. As his feet were bleeding profusely and as the earth was very hot because of the midday sun, he would not simply step ahead. Several blisters were seen beneath his feet. He grew pale with fatigue and starvation. Bhaskararao exclaimed, "O God, I cannot tolerate this inconvenience and pain. Kindly close my eyes permanently!" He walked ahead and rested under the cool shade of a tree and fell into a deep sleep in spite of his monstrous hunger.

When he woke up he felt fresh though his hunger and thirst were intolerable. He walked up to the nearest tree and plucked a few fruits and ate them quickly. Then he drank some water from a small pool. He felt relieved temporarily at least. He felt a freshness. Now there was a new determination in him. In spite of the memories of the past glory and betrayal by his own people he decided to do his best to escape from the British monsters and hold on to his life. He did not wish to commit suicide as he deemed it to be a cowardly act. He continued his wanderings in lonely places and thick woods. On the way some of his confidants met him and exchanged their feelings with him. Finally they decided to move along together in disguise. Because of the company of his confidants Bhaskararao made bold to enter cities and villages.

*****

Sir Frank Seutor and his two hundred spies were busy wandering the streets and villages in search of their main enemy Bhaskararao Bhave. Sir Frank Seutor had made it a point of prestige and had decided to capture the anti-British king at any cost. Most of his spies were wandering in different guises and mix with civilians in crowded gatherings of secular as well as religious nature. As soon as they caught some mutineer or the other they used to send them either to Belgaum or the nearest British jail for trial and suitable punishment. This work was going on in a very speedy fashion.

One day Bhaskararao and his companions traveled a very long distance and camped in a temple of Lord Maruti at a small village. As they had not had proper food or water for the last four days, they were feeling utterly tired. All of them lay on the floor of the temple. But Bhaskararao was suffering from high fever. He lay on his half-piece dhoti spread on the hard stone flooring of the small temple. He did not bother about his food or anything. He just fell into deep sleep.

One of his companions said to another, "Dear friend, Master is sleeping soundly. This place is quite warm. Let us leave him here and go into the village and try to get some food." "You fool," asked the other one, "Who'd be so good as to offer us food at this time of night?" Then the first one said to his companions, "One of you be here with the Maharaj, the other should accompany me. Let's go into the village. If we could find out at least one brahmin family, we'll be able to get something to eat." Thus one companion sat beside Bhaskararao in the temple whereas the other two went into the village. The one who sat beside Bhaskararao heard his master sleeptalk indistinct words because of high fever. The companion felt very sad for the plight of his master and exclaimed, "O Lord Venkatapati, what's this? The king who protected thousands of people, who fought for his religion and kingdom is lying here like a beggar in the most pathetic condition. O Lord, should you not open your compassionate eyes at him and show him your grace?" The companion sat there silently thinking about his master. Then the two companions returned from the village after having their food in a brahmin family. One of them sat now beside the master as guard and the first one went out with the other companion to have his food. After a little while the two of them brought some food in leaf plates for their master and waited for his awakening. After a few minutes Bhaskararao's fever seemed to subside and he felt a little relieved of the indisposition in the body. He, therefore, slowly opened his eyes and looked at his companions. "I am very thirsty, please give me some water" said he to his companions. But they persuaded him to have some food before offering him water. Bhaskararao ate a few morsels of food and drank a little water. Now he felt more energetic and therefore sat up erect against the wall. There was silence everywhere except for the occasional barking of dogs.

Just then a few Gosais came into the temple and sat there. One of the Gosais saw the brahmins sitting around a sick one. He said to his own companions, "Came on friends, let us spread our beds here for the night and take rest. Let's start our search in the morning," in Hindi. They opened their rolls of bedspreads and blankets and got ready to sleep. One Gosai brought out a small candle and lit it in the temple. The dim light enabled them to see one another. The Chief Gosai occupied his seat in the middle against the wall. The assistant Gosais kept water for him in small tumblers. Then all of them opened their bags of dry snacks and chapatis and ate them. They drank water. Now that their hunger was satisfied, they turned their attention to the brahmins resting in another corner of the temple. One of the Gosais asked one of the brahmins who was still awake, "Hullow, brahmin sir, how many are you here and where do you come from?" The brahmin replied, "We are five brahmins. We have been wandering for our livelihood. One of our group has fallen sick. We have been taking care of him with great difficulty." Then the Gosai assured him, "Don't have any fear about that. God is great and He will listen to our prayers." By then another Gosai prepared the pipes by filling them with tobacco. They sat in a circle and began to puff at their pipes. The smoke rose in small spirals to the ceiling of the temple before vanishing in the open air. The brahmin who was still awake walked up and down a few paces in the temple and finally lay down.

One of the Gosais said in-between his puffs, "What to do! We could not detect the fellows. We have been wandering from here to there and from there to here. Yet we have not been able to capture the criminal." The Chief Gosai tried to console him, "Don't you worry man. We shall be able to capture him today or tomorrow. How long can he dodge us?" He, then, cleared his throat and said in a low pitch, "Look at the brahmins lying in the corner here. There is a sick brahmin among them. I have overheard the other brahmins address him as *Maharaj*. I have my own doubts about them. One brahmin said that the *Maharaj* was very sick and that they should have brought some hot water for him. The other replied that it was a foolish suggestion because the woman had done them more than a favour by drawing water from the well at night time and that they were deeply worried about their *Maharaj*. They were talking these things in a very low and whispering tones. Yet I covered myself with a blanket and overheard their conversation." I have a strong suspicion about these brahmins. Please check them up in the morning," said the Chief Gosai. "Yes, sab. We shall check them up in the morning. If we capture the criminal by the grace of Allah, he simply cannot escape from the gallows," replied the Jamadar in the guise of Gosai.

The Chief of Gosais said with satisfaction, "Very good brother. If according to your intuition we can capture that fellow Bhaskararao, we can stop this futile wandering. Now the night is very advanced. Let's sleep now, but you keep two guards on duty while we all sleep. We must get up early in the morning." The Jamadar ordered two of his companions to be on duty as guards while all others lay down on their beds.

That night Bhaskararao slept soundly for a little while as he had suffered from fever that evening. Then he woke up as he felt thirsty. His companions were still awake and offered him some water to drink. After drinking a little water he slept again. But he was awakened completely by three o'clock at night. He was sweating heavily. He sat up and shook his companion this side and that in order to awaken him, but the companion removed the blanket from his face partially and said, "Sarkar, it is still night time. Kindly don't sit up in the cold night." But Bhaskararao could not wait as he was feeling the pressure of the bowels. He got up and stood ready to walk out of the temple. The Chief of Gosais who was also awakened by now, saw the brahmin and asked him, "Brahmin sir, where are you going? It is still night time" and stood before him. Bhaskararao did not know the stranger and therefore asked him, "Who are you brother?" in Hindi. The Chief of Gosais replied, "I am a Gosai." Then Bhaskararao spoke to him gently, "Maharaj I have been suffering from high fever. In this cool night I wish to go around and clean my bowels. You are a sadhu. Kindly guide me to a spot where water is available."

The Gosai walked out of the temple and requested Bhaskararao, "Please come with me, brahmin sir. I'll show you where water is available. But please bring a small vessel with you for use." Bhaskararao took a vessel from the side of his companion and followed the Gosai who walked with him for a little distance and showed him the spot where water was available. Then the Gosai returned to the temple in the moonlight. Bhaskararao went behind the bushes and eased himself. Now he felt a little better. He returned alone to the temple and sat there. The Gosai asked him gently, "Brahmin sir, now go to sleep." But Bhaskararao did not wish to sleep as he knew night was drawing near dawn. He, therefore, sat crooning the morning *ragas*. The Gosai also completed his morning ablutions and lay down on his bed. But since Bhaskararao was singing the morning tunes, the Gosai also sat up and asked him casually as it were, "Maharaj, where do you intend to go in the morning?" Bhaskararo replied, "No definite direction for our travel. We have to go where we can get some food for our belly. By the way, where are you going?"

The Gosai replied, "We are going to Gokarna for a *darsan* of the deity there. But on the way we have been visiting many shrines at Kolhapur, Wadi, Kurandawad, Jamakhandi etc." Bhaskararao was not convinced by the answer given by the

Gosai. The words rang rather false. He therefore wanted to test the Gosai by cross questioning him, "Gosai Maharaj, where is your monastery? I mean in which country? Whose disciple are you? Could you kindly tell me?" The Gosai immediately thought of some name and without betraying his hesitation replied, "Why not brahmin sir, I'll tell you definitely. The disciple will always have a lot of pleasure in spelling the name of his Guru. Our monastery is situated in Allahabad. Our head monastery is in Calcutta. The name of our Guru is Nischaladasji Maharaj who resides in Allahabad." "Very good," said Bhaskararao and questioned him further, "Gosai Maharaj, the disciples have several names. May I know what your name is ?" Now the Gosai was really confused because he had started betraying his ignorance about the religious order to which he said he belonged. He could not concoct further details about the monastic order. He wanted to wriggle out of the situation by giving an evasive answer and said, "Brother, I have forgotten the name, but what I remember is only the lotus feet of my Guru Nischaladasji." Now Bhaskararao was confirmed in his suspicion about the Gosai and learnt that he must be a fake one. He wished to expose the fellow and said, "Come on brother, tell me. You don't know any other detail? He who becomes a Gosai very recently does not see the intricate differences. He can renounce his faith as easily as he clings to it."

Now that the Gosai felt that he was exposed he tried to divert the attention of the brahmin and said, "Say what you like. We the sadhus go on visiting many holy shrines and meet several people. Therefore, we tend to forget the details of our own monasteries." But Bhaskararao was more than convinced about the fakeness of the Gosai, and did not want to show it openly. He tried to round up the conversation with the concluding remarks, "All right, Gosai sir, what you say is indeed true." Now the Gosai was nonplused by the exhibition of his ignorance and did not have the face to show to the brahmin asking him penetrating questions. He remained silent in the corner of the temple.

Bhaskararao also grew introspective. He suspected that these Gosais must be none other than spies. He thought that he would have severed their heads as he had done in the past if he had the strength in his hands. But alas he could not do so because of extreme weakness caused by the fever and fatigue. He tried to control his anger in a helpless manner.

As the early morning breeze was very cool the Chief Gosai and his companions fell into sound sleep. Even the guards fell into a sweet sleep on account of the cool and gentle breeze. Bhaskararao who noticed them sleeping, awakened his own companions and gently sneaked out of the temple. After crossing the border of the temple they walked briskly and disappeared into the woods. They walked for four or five hours and were nearing the village called Toragal. By that time the sun had risen considerably high in the eastern sky. Now Bhaskararao and his companions were tired so much that they could not walk any further. Bhaskararao remembered the Gowda of the village whom he knew very intimately. He, therefore, went to his house along with his companions. The Gowda opened the gate of his compound and saw the brahmins and could not identify them immediately. He looked at them askance but before asking them any questions Bhaskararao beckoned to him to be silent and whispered into his ears his name and the purpose of his visit. Now the Gowda understood everything and closed the gate immediately and took them into the house and made arrangements for their stay in separate rooms in the interior of the house. He made arrangements for their food.

*****

At the break of dawn the Gosais were awakened by the twitter of birds. They rubbed their eyes and looked around them. Alas, the brahmins had fled from the temple. The Chief Gosai lost his temper and began to shout at his companions especially the guards in the choicest of abuses. He gnashed his teeth and looked daggers at his own companions. All of them felt so helpless with anger. Now they folded their Gosai garbs and put on their tunics and shirts and caps. Within a few minutes everybody was dressed up as a sepoy and rushed out of the temple in search of Bhaskararao and the other brahmins. They had grown desperate to capture the criminal and longed for a period of rest.

*****

The Gowda of Toragal had a son of ten years who knew that Bhaskararao and his followers were camping at his house. He was playing in front of his house in the evening. A little before that he had seen his father offering mangoes to Bhaskararao in the interior room of the big house. Bhaskararao and the Gowda were discussing some thing pleasantly and eating the mangoes leisurely. By this time Frank Seutor and his spies had entered the village of Toragal and were searching for the Gowda's house. They passed through the narrow lanes flanked by the mud built houses making enquiries about the Gowda's house. At last they came near the Gowda's house and saw the ten year old boy playing with other children there. Frank Seutor asked the boy, "Boy, where is your father Mr. Patil?" The boy did not know anything about the background. He, therefore, replied without any hesitation, "Babasaheb Nargundkar has come to our house. My father is eating mangoes with him." Frank Seutor felt extremely happy to learn the news of Bhaskararao's presence there. He asked the boy further, "Very good. Boy, please tell me where they are sitting?" Then the innocent boy conducted Frank Seutor to the interior room and showed him the spot where Bhaskararao and his father were savouring the mangoes. When the Gowda and Bhaskararao and his companions saw Frank Seutor they were all shocked out of their wits. Frank Seutor said rather maliciously, "*Salaam*, Babasaheb. Where can you escape now? Come on, let's go to Belgaum" and held Bhaskararao's hands. Though Bhaskararao was very weak now because of his sickness, he could not control his terrible anger. He instantly stood up and kicked Frank Seutor and felled him to the floor. But Frank Seutor's soldiers surrounded and overpowered Bhaskararao because of the very strength of their big number. Thus they arrested Bhaskararao and took him to Belgaum. The Gowda and his family felt so sad that they did not have their food at all for a couple of days.

On the way to Belgaum, Frank Seutor and his soldiers humiliated Bhaskararao by their abuses and irrational taunts. Though deeply hurt by their inimical words and behaviour, Bhaskararao did not retaliate because of his own helplessness as well as of the futility of doing so with the irrational people. Like Bhaskararao, his companions also followed the British authorities silently. Their anger and humiliation were simply beyond speech. Finally they reached Belgaum on June 2, 1857. They took Bhaskararao straightway to the jail and kept him under strict guard. His companions were also kept in other cells of the jail. The murky atmosphere of the jail rooms seemed to constrict Bhaskararao and gave him a suffocating experience. He felt deeply depressed. The news of his arrest circulated among the native population with the speed of air and made them agitated. Gloomy clouds seemed to surround the whole kingdom of Naragund. The natives were scared of the new British administration started at Naragund in the palace of their beloved king Bhaskararao as they feared that they might be arrested any time for any or no reason.

From the day when Bhaskararao was imprisoned, the jail officers sent him dry provision like floor, rice, chilly powder, salt etc. He was expected to cook his own food for his survival. But Bhaskararao who had led a royal life was not used to cook anything for himself. He kept all the provision supplied by the jail officers in the corner of his room and starved continuously. Later when the officers noticed it, they brought it to the notice of the higher authorities who thought about his biographical background and appointed a local brahmin called Sankara to cook food at his home and supply it to Bhaskararao twice a day *i.e.* in the afternoon and in the evening. It was only after this arrangement was made that Bhaskararao began to accept his frugal meal especially because it was cooked in a brahmin family.

The British authorities notified that the trial of Bhaskararao the ex-King of Naragund and the arch enemy of the Company Government would be on a particular date and gave it wide publicity. All the public were allowed into the court hall of trial. People were eager to watch the proceedings of the enquiry. They had also heard rumours that Baniya Bapu and Krishnaji Pant also were to be properly punished on that day.

On the day scheduled for the trial of Bhaskararao, the court hall was overcrowded with the native patriots who had come from all the surrounding villages. There was a big din of mutual conversations echoed in the large hall. At about 9 o'clock the tall British judge stalked into the court hall and sat in his big chair. His assistants brought the files and kept them on the table. The judge appeared to be a stern man without any trace of smile on his face. As soon as he entered the court hall, the loud din subsided into a hushing whisper. Within a few minutes Bhaskararao the criminal was brought by the soldiers into the court hall. Bhaskararao walked erectly without caring for anyone or fearing for anything. People were straining their necks to have a proper view of their beloved leader and silently praying for his release from prison.

The enquiry began when a bell rang. The British judge began the enquiry with preliminary remarks, "Mr. Bhaskararao Bhave, you have been accused of a number of illegalities committed against the British Government. Please say whether you plead guilty or not." Bhaskararao who was flanked by two soldiers with guns in hands replied firmly, "No, I do not plead guilty at all." The British judge was really floundered by the bold negative answer given by Bhaskararao. For a moment he did not know how to deal with this patriotic criminal. A few moments went by in silence. Then the judge collected himself and said, "Mr. Bhaskararao, you have committed the great crime of organizing a mutiny against the Company Government in India. Don't you know that?" Bhaskararao replied curtly, "That's because your

Company Government tried to snatch away our natural freedom and our right to adopt children of our choice for our properties." "But don't you remember that the Doctrine of Lapse prevents you from adopting any child?" asked the judge. "But your Doctrine of Lapse is itself an illegal rule unnaturally imposed on our people," replied Bhaskararao. "You cannot say like that. The law had been passed by Lord Dalhousie in the British Parliament," said the judge. "No, it is not applicable to our country. Our laws are different from yours," replied Bhaskararao. "Our laws are applicable to you because we have conquered your country" said the judge. "No, you have not conquered the country. You came here only for business purposes but later on gave up your scales and took up swords to fight with us. You have cheated our countrymen." Now the judge's blood was up. "You can't complain against what has happened in the past. You cannot alter the history. Your duty is simply to be governed by the law that is prevalent now." "No, we the patriotic Indians refuse to abide by your laws," replied Bhaskararao excitedly. Now the judge did not know how to proceed. He tried to consult his file and then asked him further, "You have murdered Mr. Manson in cold blood. Don't you think you have committed a heinous crime against the Company Government?" "I had to murder Mr. Manson because he refused to grant me permission to adopt a child. I refuse to be governed by the alien law. We have to go by our own native laws," replied Bhaskararao full of emotion. "Further, you have been guilty of organizing the other kings of the area against the Company Government," said the judge. "No," replied Bhaskararao angrily, "I have not instigated them. They were also naturally against the Company Government. They wanted my cooperation. That's all." The British judge could not proceed further because his legal questions were nullified by Bhaskararao's patriotic logic.

Now the judge tried to change his strategy and tempt him. He, therefore asked Bhaskararao, "Mr. Bhaskararao, if you tell us the names of other Samsthanikas who had agreed to take part in the mutiny, we'll not only release you but give up part of our land along with your own." Now Bhaskararao lost his temper and shouted, "I am not a man to be tempted by the offer of your land or anything. Do you think a landlord will be tempted to receive land from others? Do you think I am such a fool as to receive it from you? No Samsthanika has instigated me to start this mutiny. Nor has anyone helped me in this. I started this all by myself. You Britishers forgot your original policy of doing business in our country and took up administration of our country. You went back on your words. Hence I had to start the mutiny to show you how wrong you were to snatch our freedom and country from us. At least now you may follow the path of truth and justice so that the target of my mutiny will be fulfilled." Now the judge who listened to the fiery and patriotic words of Bhaskararao felt completely disarmed by his argument. He even admired the passionate patriotism and self-respect of Bhaskararao. He inwardly said to himself. "Hats off to your admirable patriotism." The people who listened to the words of their beloved and dauntless king felt a thrill of horripilation.

The British judge who was bound by his own rules and professional requirements had to pass his final judgment after tallying the charges against the so-called criminal and the answers offered by him in the trial. The judge consulted his colleagues and the other files. Finally he took up the quill, dipped it into the inkpot and scribbled his final judgment. Then he signed it and gave it to his colleagues for counter signature. Then they handed the judgment copy to the court clerk who read it aloud for the public to hear, "Mr. Bhaskararao Bhave, the arch enemy of the Company Government has been sentenced to death by hanging for all the crimes he has committed against the British Government." Bhaskararao who listened to the judgment that was read out by the clerk stood without any change in his feelings but with a sense of complete resignation. The public who heard the verdict were deeply agonized and began to shed tears and sob piteously for their beloved king who had nourished them in a selfless manner. Then the British judge stood up and walked away from the court hall briskly. The soldiers led Bhaskararao back to his dungeon.

*****

Sankara was a kind brahmin who used to take lunch and dinner to Bhaskararao in the jail everyday. The sentries had no objection to his entry or departure from the jail building as he had officially been permitted to do so. That day Sankara felt very sad to learn that Bhaskararao was going to be hanged the next day. It was during the afternoon time when he was relaxing but he could not have his siesta because his mind was preoccupied with Bhaskararao's death by hanging. Sankara thought that he was going to cook his food only for one and a half day. His mind was flooded by a variety of thoughts and guesses. As he leant against the wall he thought within himself, "Bhaskararao is the only true hero who took up arms against the Britishers without ever caring for his life. He happens to be the only real patriot. His life is worth crores of lives like ours. If a man like this lives he can make countless people happy. There is no meaning in cowards continuing to live on this earth. They'll be simply burdens to the earth. How to save the precious life of Babasaheb? Ha... Why not offer my life for saving his? What's wrong with that? We have eaten his salt all through life. Whatever money or happiness we have had was only due to his munificence. Should we forget him so easily when he is in such a dangerous situation? If I sacrifice my life for him I will definitely attain Heaven after my death. I must release him from this tonight itself." Thus Sankara consolidated his ideas and came to a firm decision. He felt a new enthusiasm after taking a positive decision to pay the debt of his master. He packed the lunch box and walked briskly towards the jail. The sentries allowed him into the building without any fuss as they knew his appointment. He went into the cell and placed the plate of food before Bhaskararao and stood aside. Bhaskararao ate his food rather mechanically and washed his fingers. Sankara did not take the plate back from Bhaskararao but stood silently with a serious appearance. In fact he was very eager to talk with his master although the latter had turned a taciturn these days. Bhaskararao felt that something was the matter with the brahmin. He, therefore, asked Sankara Bhatta, "Why, Bhatta sir, why are you standing there with joined palms? What's the matter? You seem to be preoccupied with something. Why do you hesitate? Tell me frankly whatever you think."

Sankara Bhatta felt very happy to be talked to by his master Bhaskararao. He looked around and confirmed that no sentry was watching them. Then he said gently, "Maharaj, you must be knowing that you are going to be hanged tomorrow." "Yes, I know it fully well. But why do you worry so much about it?" replied Bhaskararao. "Maharaj, I am worried about my service to you," said Sankara Bhatta. "Bhatta sir, why do you bother about the service when I am going to leave the mortal world for good?" asked back Bhaskararao. "But Maharaj, I feel so sad for your plight. I cannot sit silently watching your suffering," said Sankara Bhatta. "Bhatta sir, why do you talk like this? I am thankful to you for this sympathy. What can you ever do other than sympathizing with me? I am facing the consequences of my past karma. I, therefore, request you not to worry about me."

Now Sankara Bhatta felt a very deep sorrow for Bhaskararao. He felt a great urge for expression of his inner wish. He said, "Maharaj, I pray to God that your life should be saved. I am sure that God will fulfil my desire." "God will save me from all the cares and worries of life once I am hanged tomorrow," said Bhaskararao philosophically. "Siva, Siva, please don't talk such inauspicious words, Maharaj. Lord Supreme will save you from danger." "Yes, yes, Lord Supreme will save me from all these mortal anxieties. I'll be released," said Bhaskararao. Sankara Bhatta thought it unnecessary to argue with Bhaskararao, but decided inwardly to help him out of the danger at the nick of time. "May I go now, Maharaj?" asked Sankara Bhatta. "Yes, you may," said Bhaskararao. Sankara Bhatta collected the pots and bowls and walked out of the jail after saluting the master.

After the departure of Sankara Bhatta, Bhaskararao sat on the floor of his cell against the wall and introspected, "That brahmins are kind by nature is very true. This poor brahmin Bhatta is feeling so sad to learn that I am going to be hanged tomorrow. But what can the poor fellow do except sympathize with me? At the most he may take interest in conducting my funeral rites after my death. What else can he do? But even then he was the one man who used to see me every day when I was in trouble. That at least is of some satisfaction to me. I may be alive for another six *praharas*. Why should I grieve now? What do I possess now? I lost my kingdom and the glory. All the ministers scattered away from Naragund. My reverend mother and beloved wife went to Heaven. What's the meaning of my living in this mortal world when I have lost everything? It is simply absurd and foolish. I can be rid of all the anxieties once I leave this mortal world. I will be free from fear. Until then I should spend my time in the meditation of God Almighty." Bhaskararao started praying to Lord Venkatapati. Consequently he forgot his sorrow and the mortal desires. "Lord Venkatapati, you did not keep even a single soul alive to keep company with me. You are my only companion now until I leave the world tomorrow." This is how he prayed with the whole of his heart.

Bhaskararao did not remember that it was already growing dark. Lamps were lit at every corner of the jail building. The overwhelming darkness of the jail was relieved by the dim oil lamps placed at regular intervals. But the soul of Bhaskararao was still gloomy. He did not have enthusiasm to do anything. By then a jail officer came to him and asked him, "Maharaj, do you wish to eat or drink something special?" "Not at all. I don't feel like eating or drinking anything tonight," replied Bhaskararao. The jail officer felt a great pity for Bhaskararao and tried to cheer him up by his words, "Maharaj, you know very well that whatever is destined in our fate is bound to happen. Nobody can change the course of our fate. What is the meaning in rejecting food or water? Kindly eat and drink as much as you can and be cheerful until the last moment. Everything is happening according to God's will. We have no choice. Look here, your cook is coming. I am going. Please have your food with a cheerful mind." With these words the jail officer went away from there.

Sankara Bhatta came there and placed the plate of food and requested him, "Maharaj, kindly have a few morsels and wash your fingers. Now let's exchange our garments. You quickly escape from here. I'll sit here in your place. Kindly be quick, there's no time for thinking." Bhaskararao was really taken aback by the words of Sankara Bhatta. He could not believe his own ears. "What do you mean Bhatta sir? Do you want to die for me? Never. It's impossible. Why should you die for my sake? I don't wish to push an innocent man like you into the jaws of death. I have to face my fate. But I am very grateful to you for this extraordinary sympathy. Bhatta, sir, I have no mind to have my food tonight. Please take it back." But Sankara Bhatta had made up his mind to save his master. He clasped the feet of Bhaskararao tightly and requested him, "Maharaj, all through my life I have eaten your salt. The gold and money that you have given to me in the past will suffice to take care of my family. If you are alive you can protect countless people like me. Kindly listen to me and take my garments and give me yours. There's no time now even for thinking. You escape from this jail with this food packet and run as far away from Belgaum as possible until sunrise tomorrow. Don't be caught by these mean fellows. I shall die for you my master." With these words he took off his garments and gave them to Bhaskararao and Bhaskararao who was to do it out of necessity took his garments and put them on. Now their roles were changed. Sankara Bhatta looked like Bhaskararao and vice versa. Sankara Bhatta touched Bhaskararao's feet and asked him to hurry out of the jail. Bhaskararao got tears in his eyes and caressed his face. He took up the food packet and walked slowly out of the jail building. No soldiers objected to his departure from the jail as everybody mistook him to be the brahmin Sankara Bhatta. Sankara Bhatta sat in the cell in the guise of Bhaskararao in a fake dignified suffering. Since both Sankara Bhatta and Bhaskararao had a physical resemblance nobody could identify or differentiate between them easily. Sankara Bhatta had a sense of fulfilment as he was going to sacrifice his own life for his master's sake by way of clearance of debt. Bhaskararao walked out of the jail without any difficulty and began to run hectically until he was beyond the borders of the Belgaum city. Once he was out of the city, he entered the woods and ate his food at some pond and began to walk briskly towards the north. He was wondering at the strange quirks of his own fate.

*****

The next morning Bhaskararao was scheduled to be hanged. In the morning the soldiers came and took Bhaskararao and led him to the jail office for formal identification and discharge of the criminal to the hanging spot called the Haystack Hill. All the officers had gathered in the hall. Bhaskararao was made to stand in the middle of the platform opposite the British officers including the judge. The clerks came, read out the name of the criminal Bhaskararao and the so-called crimes he had committed against the Company Government. One of the officers pointed out Bhaskararao to another British officer and asked him, "Do you identify this person as Bhaskararao Bhave?" The other officer looked at the figure standing there with all pride and arrogance. When Bhaskararao heard these words he wanted to confuse them and therefore suddenly jerked his head a little back. When he did so, his turban slipped a little ahead and covered his forehead completely. The British officer scanned his figure attentively and found a complete agreement between Bhaskararao's features and those described in the office papers. His garments and the high stature, the arrogant behaviour and the proud face with twirled mustaches were the very embodiments of the mutinous figure of Bhaskararao. The British officer therefore said, "Yes. This is the person whom I identify as Bhaskararao Bhave of Naragund." Then the other officers who had never seen Bhaskararao personally in the past signed the papers and allowed him to be taken to the Haystack Hill.

Accordingly Bhaskararao was led out of the building where a cart was waiting for him. As the British people wanted to insult Bhaskararao until the last moment by defiling his brahmanical pride and purity, they made him mount the cart and sit in it. They placed a makeshift crest of thorns on his turban to humiliate him. Bhaskararao looked like a very comic figure. They laughed at him maliciously. Then twelve untouchables of Holeya caste clad in dhotis were ordered to push and pull the cart simultaneously through the main routes of Belgaum including the market. The cart pullers were bare bodied and thick mustached. As they pushed and pulled the cart, their sweat was dripping from their limbs. The crowd of Bhaskararao's admirers followed him at a safe distance beyond the soldiers' cordon. Bhaskararao thought that that was the worst and final humiliation he had to suffer at the hands of mlencha officers. He tried to control his emotions with great effort.

All the natives of Belgaum and surrounding villages who happened to be Babasaheb's admirers had gathered at the Haystack Hill where the hanging had to take place. When the cart carrying Bhaskararao reached the Hill, the people began to murmur and whisper among themselves. The cart was led near the spot where the noose was hanging ready to kill its victim. Bhaskararao was made to dismount from the cart and walk towards the scaffold. Since he was surrounded by the soldiers, he could not be seen by the crowd of people. Nonetheless they were trying their best to have a glimpse of him by straining their necks. By then one of the officers came there and read out the name of the criminal and the list of his crimes. Then they asked him to offer his last salute to the gathering of people. Bhaskararao, therefore, joined his palms and raised them above his head to be visible to all the onlookers and admirers. People began to shout and cry out of pity for their master. But who would ever care for their feelings? One of the servants mounted the scaffold and slipped a black cap around his head. Now people could not see his face. Then another servant slipped the noose around his neck and stepped down. Now the third servant pulled the wooden scaffold from beneath the feet of Bhaskararao. They had expected that the corpse of the criminal would hang limp in the air. But no, their expectation was frustrated. As soon as the scaffold was removed from beneath the feet of Bhaskararao, the rope from which the noose was made snapped suddenly and Bhaskararao fell to the ground. When people saw this, they were overjoyed and thought that their beloved leader would be saved from the calamity of death. But the servants brought another rope and put it around the neck of Bhaskararao, but it snapped for the second time also. Again there was a big furor in the crowd who shouted "Victory to Babasaheb Maharaj. But the British officers were terribly infuriated by this comic failure. One of the officers shouted, "Our order is that he is to be hanged to death. Therefore try another stronger rope." Soon a stronger rope was procured by the servants. The servant put the noose for the third time around the neck of Bhaskararao and removed the scaffold from beneath his feet. This time they were successful in their effort. Now the dead body of Bhaskararao hung limp from the noose with a downward face. The large gathering of people began to shed tears and sob for their beloved master. They exclaimed, "At last our great master ascended to Heaven. May his soul rest in peace." Then the people unable to control their tears walked home with heavy hearts. The dead body of Bhaskararao was lowered by the servants and laid on the stone platform. The official doctor walked to the spot and examined the pulses, heartbeat and respiration. Then he formally declared him to be dead and gave his permission for the arrangement of funeral. The soldiers busied themselves with the task of consigning the dead body to the pyre. In course of time the hanging of Bhaskararao was published in the Gazette. The Company Government heaved a sigh of relief after the hanging of the great mutineer of Naragund.

*****

But Bhaskararao who had escaped from the prison in Sankara Bhatta's garments was feeling very sad for the poor man's great sacrifice which had come as the most unexpected boon to him. He wondered at the quirks of his own fate which had transformed his would-have-been-tragedy into an unbelievable comedy as it were. Bhaskararao leant against a big tree in the woods and wondered at the turn of things in his life. He introspected, "I had been running from place to place like a thief to escape humiliation from those British monsters. But this poor brahmin came forward to sacrifice his own life. Though it has already happened, I cannot believe it. It looks like a miracle. Could it be that Lord Venkatapati listened to my prayer and saved me in the form of a poor brahmin? O Lord Venkateswara, great indeed is your *lila*! But nonetheless I feel very sorry for the poor Sankara Bhatta. I also admire his extraordinary loyalty and humanity. I could never believe that such great humanity could be experienced side by side with the terrible inhumanity of the British fellows. May his soul rest in peace and may God keep his family and all his descendants happy forever." Bhaskararao prayed to Lord Venkateswara inwardly and shed hot tears for the poor brahmin Sankara Bhatta who had done the greatest sacrifice for his master. After offering his condolences to the late Sankara Bhatta, Bhaskararao made a very diligent effort to go towards Nepal in different guises. He crossed the diverse rivers and brooks and climbed many hills and mountains all through the journey until he reached the borders of the Himalayas where he felt he was quite safe.

*****

Now that the palace of Naragund was seized and Bhaskararao Bhave hanged to death by their beloved British officers, Baniya Bapu and Krishnaji Pant felt exulted and began to dream of the bright future promised to them by Sir Manson and Sir Malcolm. They were happy to know that they were consulted by the British officers whenever an important or dangerous mutineer of Naragund had to be hanged to death. They saw to it that many of their own personal enemies were declared as mutineers and hanged to death by the British Government. They felt elated to be given such an important place by the alien officers. They tried to visualize themselves as seated on royal thrones and enjoying unprecedented pleasures in their life. They waited for a couple of weeks. Until Naragund was captured by the British officers, these treacherous persons enjoyed the shelter at the British headquarters as they had no courage to face either Babasaheb or his followers. But as soon as the fort of Naragund was seized by the British Government, they returned to Naragund and started arrogating themselves to the poor natives of Naragund. They had succeeded in having everyone whom they did not like hanged to death under the pretext of involvement with the mutiny. Now they began to think of their own future and reward for helping the British with very valuable intelligence against Bhaskararao and his patriots.

One day, both of them exchanged their views confidentially and arrived at a decision to put forth their demands to the British officers. They, therefore, entered Sir Malcolm's chamber and saluted him in the British fashion. Sir Malcolm said to them with a warm smile,

"Come on, sirs. How are you? What brings you here?"

Krishnaji Pant made bold to say, "We are very happy to know that you have seized the palace of Naragund and hanged all the troublesome mutineers to death."

"Ahem, yes. That's right?"

Baniya Bapu nudged Krishnaji Pant gently and whispered something into his ears. Krishnaji Pant cleared his throat and requested Sir Malcolm rather nervously,

"Dear Sir, kindly give us the reward that you promised us."

Sir Malcolm stared hard at them and asked them, "You want the reward. What for?"

"For helping your Government with intelligence against our king Bhaskararao Bhave and his companions."

"Oh I see. You want a reward for betraying your king to us."

"Yes, sir. You are able to seize the fort of Naragund only with our help."

Sir Malcolm stared hard at them for a second and replied,

"That's good. I fully agree with you. You have betrayed your own beloved king whose salt you have eaten all through your life. Besides, you belong to the caste of your beloved king, don't you?"

Baniya Bapu and Krishnaji Pant felt ashamed of themselves for a few seconds and quickly recovered from it as they were very practical in their approach to life. Baniya Bapu made bold to say, "Sir, you had promised to give us a some jahagir and ample gold for supplying intelligence. Now that you have achieved everything you wanted, we request you to grant us a Sannad regarding half the portion of land belonging to Bhaskararao and some gold." Sir Malcolm was flabbergasted by the demands of Baniya Bapu. He looked up at the ceiling and thought for a few second. Then he said, "Mr. Baniya Bapu, I never made you any promise about the property or gold."

Krishnaji Pant then made bold to make a rejoinder to Baniya Bapu's request, "No sir, you did not make the promise. The promise was made by the late Sir Manson and his officers. We request you to fulfil the words of your own officers."

Then Sir Malcolm said, "See, Mr. Baniya Bapu and Krishnaji Pant, I know you have helped us in many ways. We thank you profusely. As for the jahagir I have no powers to make any gifts. I shall consult my superior officers and make arrangements for the proper rewards. You may go now."

Both Baniya Bapu and Krishnaji Pant saluted the British officer and walked back to their residences. They hoped that a miracle might happen turning both of them into *lakhapatis*. They waited for several days. Meanwhile Sir Malcolm wrote to the higher authorities confidentially about these two persons and received some answer.

After a fortnight's time, Baniya Bapu and Krishnaji Pant went to the office of Sir Malcolm again and reminded him of their demand. This time both of them were hoping for a miracle to happen. They had told their wives on that day that they would get memorable gifts from the British Government for the help they had rendered to them. When both of them stood before Sir Malcolm, he was rather cold this time and replied to them,

"Don't you worry. An appropriate gift will be given to you."

Baniya Bapu and Krishnaji Pant felt very happy and began to dream of their future and looked at each other meaningfully with smiles. Then Sir Malcolm said to them, "Dear friends, you have betrayed your own beloved king to our Government for the sake of your petty selfishness. Then what guarantee is there that you would not betray our Government to others? You know that the British Government will not have any place to treacherous people like you."

Baniya Bapu and Krishnaji Pant felt rather unnerved by the embarrassing answer. Yet Krishnaji Pant made bold to explain it, "No saheb, we did all that to help your Government. You have gained more than we two ever can."

But Sir Malcolm replied, "I am just a servant of my Government. I have to obey the instructions given by my superiors. I am sorry to tell you that you are to be punished properly. Krishnaji Pant, you are given the blackwater punishment. And Baniya Bapu, you have to stay in dungeon at Dharwad." He pressed the bell and the soldiers appeared in his room. He ordered them, "Arrest them." Hearing these strange words, Baniya Bapu and Krishnaji Pant felt a sudden black out of consciousness. They did not know what to say or how to react. Before they could overcome their sense of shock they were shackled and led by the soldiers to the dark dungeon of Naragund.

As they were led by the soldiers, they were shedding tears incessantly. "Is this the reward for our hard work? Is it for this loss of our lives that we betrayed our own beloved king

Bhaskararao?" They thought like this inwardly. They had not even told their wives that they could have such a treatment at the hands of the British officers. Their wives had been dreaming of better prospects in their life. Then they were pushed into two separate dark rooms of the stone building and locked up.

All through the night, Baniya Bapu and Krishnaji Pant wondered at their own strange quirk of fate. Krishnaji Pant thought about the malicious nature of the British officers. He thought how they used both of them for their intelligence and were now harassing them. In the other room Baniya Bapu also wondered at the treacherous nature of the British officers. He genuinely felt that they should not have betrayed their beloved king Bhaskararao. But everything was over now. They could not do anything now. Thus both of them brooded about their strange fate.

As per the 1858 Act IV Colonel Malcolm had ordered for death sentence for thirty people, *phatka* for nine people, black water punishment for thirty-four people; hanging for five people and *sakta majuri* for thirteen people.

*****

The spies of Company Government had discovered the fact that Vishnubhatta Ghodse had distributed the farman of Dondopant Nanasaheb Peshwa among all the Kings, Chiefs and Zamindars of the south. The Government therefore tried Vishnubhatta Ghodse in the court. During the trial Vishnubhatta Ghodse had confessed that he had visited Subbannabhatta in Melodi village. Vishnubhatta Ghodse's crime was confirmed and therefore he was hanged publicly by the Company Government. During the trial Subbannabhatta happened to camp at Vasai, busy with the editing of Sanskrit poetry along with Ramachandrabhatta. As per the Government order, Subbannabhatta was arrested and taken to Dharwad for further enquiry. Two soldiers took Subbannabhatta to Lieutenant Thomson's office.

Martanda was shocked out of his wits when he heard about his own father's arrest. He, therefore, rushed to Dharwad office. He clasped the feet of Lieutenant Thomson and requested him to forgive his father who, he said, was innocent. Thomson felt fuzzled for a moment. He did not know what to do. He remembered the fair brahmin youth whom he had met on the way to Melodi village, a few months ago.

Lieutenant Thomson thought about what to do. He wondered if Subbannabhatta did not have a hand in the conspiracy against the British Government. At the same time he felt that he could not trust the brahmins completely. But when he thought of the young Martanda, he felt pity for him. He remembered how Martanda had helped the English Government by abetting Krishnaji Pant and Baniya Bapu to mix cowdung in the gunpowder at Naragund when Babasaheb was busy fighting the enemy. He also remembered how the fort of Naragund could not have been easily captured by the Britishers without Martanda's secret help and how the British soldiers would have died like butterflies in the fire of cannons of Naragund. Thomson knew that although Martanda was a servant of the lowest position, he had rendered enormous help to the Company Government.

Subbannabhatta stood as a criminal in front of Lieutenant Thomson. Martanda also stood near his father. Thomson had respect for Subbannabhatta's learning. He was in a dilemma as to whether he should forgive him or punish him. He gazed at Martanda's face and felt like exculpating Subbannabhatta. But his professional duty did not allow him to do it. He, therefore, thought of subjecting the culprit to rigorous enquiry. Martanda was sobbing continuously. Lieutenant Thomson tried to console Martanda, "My dear Mr. Martanda, you know, we must try your father. He will definitely be released if he is found innocent. Don't you worry." Martanda stood helpless.

Lieutenant Thomson began the enquiry formally. He asked Subbannabhatta a number of questions and cross questions. Subbannabhatta composed himself and answered boldly. He boldly stated that Vishnubhatta was his disciple and had stayed in his house for a night and that he did not know anything more than that. Lieutenant Thomson asked him many cross questions and confirmed that Subbannabhatta had not participated in the distribution of Nanasaheb Peshwa's farmans. Finally he wrote a favourable report about Subbannabhatta and sent it to Magistrate Oglivey at Dharwad. When Mr. Oglivey glanced through the report, he remembered the enormous service rendered by Martanda to the Company Government and generously exculpated Subbannabhatta. As per the Magistrate's order, Subbannabhatta was released from the prison. Martanda grew overjoyed to learn that his father was free now and thanked Mr. Thomson, Mr. Oglivey and the entire Company Government. His faith in the British officers and their Government was doubled. He took his father to Navalagund in a very happy mood.

*****

Bhaskararao felt sorry for Sankara who sacrificed his own life for the sake of his master. The British Government easily believed that they had captured the real mutineer Bhaskararao and hanged him to death. As the British officers believed in their own efficiency, they gave wide publicity to the news of the execution of Bhaskararao Bhave and printed it accordingly in their gazettes. The large majority of the common people believed in the so-called execution of Bhaskararao Bhave and shed tears and paid him rich tribute posthumously. Though the real Bhaskararao was sorry for Sankara, he also admired his extra-ordinary loyalty. But now he had no time to think of the past. He was worried about the future and contemplating vengeance against the British Government. As he was in touch with Nanasaheb he wanted to consult him for further activities in the country. He knew that Nanasaheb was staying in Nepal where he was relatively free from the British hold, he decided to go there. But he did not want to be caught by the British officers this time especially after escaping from the noose of death prepared by them for him. He, therefore, disguised himself in the ochre robes and held a copper bowl and an arm-rest in his hands and proceeded on his journey towards Nepal. He trudged long distances meticulously. As he was in the guise of a sanyasi, people could not detect his real identity. He crossed the Marathi-speaking area and entered the desert area of Madhya Pradesh after crossing the Vindhya mountains. He saw different kinds of people at the different spots. After the lush greenery of the Marathi area he entered the arid and sandy area where people talked Gujarathi. He used to travel during the day time and rest in the evening in some temple or *dharmasala* and eat whatever food was locally available. After a month's continuous journey he crossed the Gujarathi-speaking area and entered the Hindi-speaking area. There he befriended many sanyasis and crossed the Ganga river and visited many temples. Then he mended his way towards Nepal and began to climb the slopes of the Himalayan range until he was in the midst of Nepal. He saw the Nepalis with tiny eyes and yellowish complexion busy with their daily chores. Many Nepalis happened to be Buddhists who used to visit their holy *pagodas* which differed from the Hindu temples in shape and size. Bhaskararao felt that he was in a relatively safer land. He took a couple of days to adjust himself with the new atmosphere, people and their day-to-day life. He used to sit near the local *pagodas* and watch the Buddhist monks performing their daily meditation and rotate the wheels on the precincts of the Buddhist temples. After making preliminary enquiries about the place where Nanasaheb Tantyatopi was staying, Bhaskararao traveled a long distance through the deserted hilly area thickly covered with wild plants and trees. He took nearly a week's time to reach the place where Nanasaheb was camping. He went near the large thatched hut and asked the guards there, "Is His Highness Nanasaheb present inside?" The guards who observed the ochre robes of the sanyasi carefully replied, "His Highness is resting inside. May we know who you are so that we can inform him?" Then Bhaskararao replied, "Please tell His Highness that a sanyasi from South India has come to see him personally." The guard requested the sanyasi, "Please be seated on this wooden plank here. I shall inform His Highness," and went inside. The sanyasi leant against the

the wooden seat and closed his eyes for a moment as he was sufficiently tired of the journey. After a few minutes, the guard came out of the thatched hut and said, "His Highness is waiting for you, please come in," and conducted the sanyasi toward the seat where Nanasaheb sat. The sanyasi joined his palms in reverence and said, "Namaste, huzoor." Nanasaheb had not seen the sanyasi ever before but yet wished him back by saying, "Namaste, please be seated." Then the sanyasi asked, "Huzoor, could you identify me?" Nanasaheb answered, "Not exactly. But I guess you belong to some south Indian monastery." The sanyasi laughed mischievously and said, "In a way you are right. Now I deserve to enter a monastery permanently." Nanasaheb was rather puzzled and asked him, "What do you mean? You have already been staying in a monastery, don't you?" "No, Maharaj, you have not recognized me yet. You used to write to me before. I am Bhaskararao Bhave of Naragund Samsthan in South India." The sanyasi uttered these words in a low pitch. Then Nanasaheb jumped out of his seat and hugged him and exclaimed, "What a surprise! You are our bold Bhaskararao of Naragund who fought with those British monsters!" Both of them were deeply excited and could not talk for a few moments. Then Nanasaheb recovered himself from the sense of excitement and patted on the back of Bhaskararao and said, "I heard vague reports about your fight with the British people. You have done the right thing. I am really proud of you. But why are you clad in these monastic robes?" Then Bhaskararao narrated everything about the mutiny and how he had been betrayed by his own treacherous people and consequently lost his entire kingdom. Then he finished his saga of suffering, they realized that a couple of hours had gone by. The sun had risen high at the zenith of the sky. Nanasaheb was deeply touched by the story of Bhaskararao's heroic deeds. At last he exclaimed, "My dear Bhaskararao, though I pity you for your loss of kingdom, wife and mother, I admire your extra-ordinary courage and self-respect. If our country had kings like you the British monsters would not have snatched our own land from us. You are a model for the Indian mutineers who wish to light the lamp of freedom."

Bhaskararao felt a deep sense of satisfaction when he found a kindred soul in Nanasaheb who could understand the noble purpose behind his patriotic fight. "Come on my dear Bhaskararao, it is already midday. Let's have our lunch together and relax until evening," said Nanasaheb. The cooks began to make arrangements for laying their plates. Both of them had their lunch and relaxed in separate tents. In the evening they discussed several details of the causes and consequences of the mutiny and the opportunistic behaviour of the British rulers in India.

Bhaskararao spent a couple of days with Nanasaheb and felt a sense of relief by sharing the patriotic views of his inspirer who also had undergone the same plight as he himself. Then Bhaskararao took leave of Nanasaheb and started his journey back to Varanasi. He walked long distances of Nepal and saw the peculiar habits and customs of the local people there. He observed the multi-gabled spires of their holy pagodas and their daily meditations in the temples. He used to talk freely with the Buddhist monks as and when he could meet them. He was really impressed by their piety and seriousness about their principles. Whenever he went out of the cities and was wandering in the wilderness, he used to observe the beautiful hills and valleys with multicoloured plants and trees which provided a sharp contrast to the Indian landscape with which he was quite familiar. After a couple of weeks, he reached Kashi, the city of countless temples along the banks of the great river Ganga. He stepped into the holy water of the Ganga and bathed leisurely. The chime of temple bells, the chanting of mantras and the general din of the pilgrims in the temples and *dharmasalas* was audible to him. He felt quite soothed by the sacred sound. He instantly remembered the sweet notes of *nagaswararn* which used to be regularly played at Naragund at the time of holy service rendered thrice a day to Lord Venkateswara. He got tears in his eyes. He simply could not control them. He was standing in the chest deep water of the Ganga. The ripples of water used to spread wider and wider from around him as he washed himself. Then he walked up the steps and sunned himself dry on the parapet there and changed his ochre robes. He felt a freshness. He smeared his forehead with *vibhuti* and slowly walked towards the famous temple of Lord Viswanath along with other pilgrims. After nudging his way through the crowd of devotees, he finally came to the *sanctum sanctorum* and stood before the idol of Lord Viswanath. He joined his palms and prayed, "O Lord, my life is at the mercy of your will. I have to do everything according to your great will. I have nothing in my hands to change it or question it. Lord, you know how to protect me and guide me." Then he sprinkled some flowers on the idol and walked back slowly. After crossing the precincts of the temple, he accosted a few sanyasis and asked them about the local temples, worships and sacrifices etc. One of the sanyasis guided him to the nearest *dharmasala* where both of them had their lunch of sweet cakes, rice and sambar and rested in one of the rooms for the afternoon siesta. In the evening Bhaskararao went around in the nearby lanes along with the other sanyasis to familiarize himself with the holy city. Thus he got himself adjusted to the new life and began to live there in the presence of Lord Viswanath. A couple of months went by. Luckily he was not detected by anyone because of his ochre robes and long beard and mustaches. He could speak Hindi expertly with the north Indian sanyasis. As he himself was a good scholar in Sanskrit lore, he could easily discuss *Vedas* and *Brahma Sutras* with the other scholars.

*****

One morning Bhaskararao was walking towards the temple of Lord Viswanath. He saw a middle aged lady with a young girl by her side coming in front of him after having their *darsan* of the deity in the temple. Bhaskararao stood for a moment and watched her attentively. Their faces appeared to be quite familiar and their garments were those of Marathi-speaking area. When he noticed them, they also looked at him for a moment and seemed to identify him as a *sanyasi* from south India. But the two ladies could not dare to speak with him because of their shyness. But the two of them nudged each other and whispered something into each other's ears and walked ahead. Bhaskararao also did not want to talk with them on his own accord lest he should be mistaken. He went into the temple, had his *darsan* and went back to his *dharmasala* to attend to his daily chores. He saw those two women three or four times again in the morning at the same time. Still he controlled himself. Each time there used to be ocular but silent encounter between the two parties. Thus there grew a silent but unspoken intimacy between them.

One morning when Bhaskararao was walking towards the temple, he saw the two women coming in front of him. This time, the women came straight towards him and accosted him. The elder of the two wished him "Namaste, Maharaj." Bhaskararao also wished them back with "Namaste, amma." "Maharaj" said the elder lady, "we have been seeing you almost regularly in this temple. We guess that you have come from southern part of the country. We just wanted to confirm it sheerly out of curiosity." "Yes, amma, I come from south India." "By the way, where are you from?" "We have come from a town called Naragund in the south." Bhaskararao's heart fluttered for a moment at the very mention of Naragund. He controlled it with some effort of the will and asked them further, "What family you belong to there, amma?" "My name is Kashibayi Mane, but I was living with my brother Tadmiri at Naragund." Bhaskararao knew very well as the latter served as Jamadar in his office. He was eager to know more details about the happenings at Naragund after his departure from there. "Let's go to a nearby spot where we can sit and talk leisurely" suggested Bhaskararao. Accordingly all the three walked a little distance and sat on a platform beneath the large banyan tree. Bhaskararao asked her, "Come on tell me, amma, where Tadmiri is now and how you are related to him." Kashibayi's face grew pale with the rush of sad memories. "How shall I recount all that, Maharaj? Bhatt alias Tadmiri was my brother who was working as Jamadar in the court office of Bhaskararao Bhave at Naragund. Since I had lost my husband early in my life, I had been living with my brother's family at Naragund. He has a daughter. But during the riots at

Naragund people began to flee from Naragund overnight for fear of losing their life. Some were arrested and hanged to death. In that turmoil my brother disappeared all of a sudden. We did not know for certain whether he fled somewhere or was hanged by the British people. His daughter and I were left alone in the house. Without my brother in the house, I felt very nervous and disillusioned with this life itself. I, therefore, brought my niece with me to Kashi by way of pilgrimage. Since then we have been living here. We have no desire to return to Naragund or anywhere. I would like to have my *mukti* here only on the ghat of Ganga." Kashibayi narrated this brief story with sobs and tears in-between. Her niece was also shedding tears silently. Bhaskararao felt deeply annoyed to see how many people had lost their lives or properties on account of the mutiny in Naragund. Tears trickled in his eyes also for all the unfortunate people who had suffered in the insurgence.

A few moments passed in silence. Bhaskararao visualized all the tragedy that must have happened to the luckless participants in the mutiny. He had heard about how several people had been hanged to death. After the disturbance of his heart subsided, he cleared his throat and asked her, "Amma, where do you both stay here in Kashi? Is this your niece?" Kashibayi introduced her niece to the sanyasi. The niece joined her palms in reverence to the sanyasi and sat silently with her face bent down. The sanyasi scanned the face of the young girl and felt a deep pity for her plight and furlornness. Kashibayi replied, "Maharaj, we both of us live in a small room in a nearby lane. Kindly bless us the poor creatures by visiting our house once." "Don't you worry, amma, I shall definitely come to your house next time." With these words they departed.

*****

About fifteen days went by after their first meeting. The next time Kashibayi met the sanyasi and enquired after his health and well-being. The sanyasi replied that he was all right. Both of them stood aside on the precincts of the temple and made way for others. As usual the chime of puja bells and the din of pilgrims could be heard from inside the temple. This time she was not accompanied by her niece. After the usual amicabilities, Kashibayi requested the sanyasi, "Maharaj, last time you promised to visit us in our poor house. But so far you did not come. Today I request you to come to our house and partake of the meal prepared by me and my niece." The sanyasi remembered the fair girl whom he had seen last time along with her aunt. He enquired about her, "How is your niece? Why has she not come today?" "She wanted to come with me, maharaj, but I asked her to stay back at home. She is attending to the daily cooking and other chores." "She appears to be a very quiet and nice girl," said the sanyasi. Kashibayi liked the compliment offered by the holy sanyasi about her niece because she thought it augured well for her niece. She persuaded the sanyasi further, "Yes, maharaj, kindly come along with me. I shall show you my poor house. Kindly have your meal there and bless us." The sanyasi was really touched by her genuine affection for him. "All right, amma, I shall come to your house today," said he and accompanied her. He carried his bowl and the arm-rest in his hands. They went on discussing the local customs and habits.

As the sanyasi reached the little house of two rooms, he was offered hot water for washing his face, hands and feet. He washed his limbs clean and rested on the string cot put near the wall against a cotton pillow. Kashibayi sat on the floor in front of him and talked with him with affectionate intimacy. The sanyasi felt a strange kind of familiarity in the house of this widow. After the mutiny he had been wandering from place to place without any security anywhere. Here he felt a peculiar satisfaction which had characterized his early life of comfort and pomp. The sanyasi enquired, "Where is your niece?" "She is cooking the meal inside, maharaj." By then the niece brought a tumbler of hot and sweet milk and offered it to the sanyasi who took it and drank it leisurely. He felt as if he was staying with his own family. He emptied the tumbler of milk and kept it aside. Then Kashibayi asked him, "Maharaj, you say you are a sanyasi belonging to some monastery of south India." "Yes, amma, I come from south India," replied the sanyasi. "But, somehow you look exactly like our Babasaheb Sarkar of Naragund. That's why I felt a special reverence for you, maharaj. I told my niece also the first time I saw you." These words awakened a sense of embarrassment in the sanyasi. Still he tried to control his real identity. He said, "Yes, might be. Sometimes it happens that two persons look alike. Now Kashibayi, tell me what are your plans for the future. Don't you want to return to your native place?" "No maharaj, I have no desire to return. I have come here to stay until my death. My only anxiety is about my niece. I am a widow and have no desires of any kind. But my niece is very young. She has several dreams about her future. I want to see her settled in life, but I don't know how to manage it all by myself. Nor do I know anybody here. It's all right for her as long as I am alive. But I am worried about her security after my death." When Kashibayi spoke these words her face appeared to be pale with uncertainty and apprehension. The sanyasi tried to console her, "Don't you worry amma. God is there. He will definitely show some way out." Then Kashibayi's niece came out from the kitchen and said, "The meal is ready." Kashibayi then requested the sanyasi to partake of the meal prepared by them so reverentially. The sanyasi enjoyed the homely food after a long interval of several years. He was reminded of his past royal life at Naragund. He was thinking inwardly that there was nobody now to think of him or take care of him. Nor was there anybody left whom he could love or take care now. But he was deeply touched by their purely humanitarian concern shown to him, although they never knew who he was in the real sense of the term. After the meal Kashibayi offered him edible leaf, betel and lime. The sanyasi felt so satisfied that he thought he could not return their debt. Then he relaxed on the stringed cot for a couple of hours. When he got up, it was late evening. He said, "I think, I must be going back to my *dharmasala*, amma." Kashibayi requested, "It's already late evening, maharaj. Why do you want to return to the *dharmasala*? Think this to be your own home and stay here tonight." "I don't want to trouble you, amma. You have already done a lot for me," said he. "It's not a trouble at all, maharaj. we earn a lot of *punya* by serving the holy men like you. Kindly stay here for one more day," requested Kashibayi. "If you are going to be happy on account of my presence, I will definitely stay for one more day," said the sanyasi.

After the dinner, the sanyasi and Kashibayi sat talking late into the night. The whole city of Kashi was sleeping. There was pindrop silence except for the occasional barking of dogs. The niece was sitting inside the kitchen and listening to their talk. The sanyasi broached the subject gently, "Amma, this morning you said that I look like your Babasaheb of Naragund. Didn't you? Come on, tell me why did you have such a doubt?" Kashibayi replied, "Maharaj, I had seen our Babasaheb Sarkar riding his stallion at Naragund many times. He was tall like you. His eyes were as bright as yours. He had bushy mustaches like yours. The only thing he lacked was the beard like yours. That's why I was immediately reminded of our beloved Sarkar." The sanyasi felt very happy to listen to her description of her king. "Where did your Sarkar go? What happened to him? Please tell me whatever you know." Then Kashibayi cleared her throat and told him, "Maharaj, our Babasaheb Sarkar was a very patriotic king who fought against the *firangi* fellows. He was betrayed by his own people who were shamelessly treacherous. He, therefore, ran away from the palace riding a naked horse. Then his mother and wife drowned themselves in the Malaprabha river. Later we heard rumours that Babasaheb Sarkar was arrested by the *firangi* fellows and hanged to death." Kashibayi sobbed and whimpered in between this brief narration. The sanyasi also got tears in his eyes while listening to the tragic story. There was a long silence before either of them could continue to speak. The sanyasi decided to reveal the truth gently after making some preparatory remarks. He said, "Strange are the ways of Lord Venkatapati, amma. We do not know what happens to us when and where." Kashibayi felt a bit puzzled by the sanyasi's reference to Lord Venkateswara. She made bold to ask him, "Maharaj, you mentioned Lord Venkataswara just now. The temple of Venkatapati is there at Naragund. How come did you know it?" "Should I not know the holy temple which I maintained with all the land grants and appointment of worshippers and dancers?" asked the sanyasi. Kashibayi felt still more puzzled. "But maharaj, how do you remember all these details? Were you one of the worshippers there by any chance?" interrogated Kashibayi. "How can the King of Naragund be a mere worshipper in his own temple?" Kashibayi did not know how to respond. She was utterly confused by the direction of the conversation. "Maharaj, Babasaheb Sarkar was the King of Naragund. And according to reports, he was hanged to death. But how do you know all these details?" She was breathless with confusion and anxiety. The sanyasi chuckled for a moment and said, "Amma, you have not identified me yet. Perhaps my saffron robes have misled you. You have not noticed that the King of Naragund is sitting before you." Kashibayi felt dumbfounded with confusion. But yet she recovered her sense of surprise quickly and said, "That means, Maharaj you are none other than our Babasaheb Sarkar!" "You are right, amma. I am glad to know that you have identified me at last," replied Bhaskararao. Kashibayi stood up and fell prostrate at the feet of Bhaskararao Sarkar and begged him, "Sarkar, kindly forgive me. I did not understand you. I treated you as an ordinary sanyasi. You are our guardian who has fed all the members of our family at Naragund." Bhaskararao tried to pacify her, "Take it easy, amma. Don't be surprised at these unexpected things. Everything happens according to the Divine Will. We have nothing in our hands." Kashibayi felt a new excitement at the revelation of the true identity of Bhaskararao Bhave, the King of Naragund sitting right in front of her and enjoying her hospitality. She even felt proud of it for a moment. "But Sarkar, we heard the rumours that you were taken to the jail and later hanged to death. Isn't that true?" asked Kashibayi. "Amma, whatever you have heard was true. But just a day before I was to be hanged, something unexpected happened. And consequently I came to this part of the country in the guise of a sanyasi." Then Bhaskararao narrated several other details of his escape from the Britishers. When he completed the saga of his suffering, birds had already started chirping. Kashibayi could not believe her own ears. All of them fell asleep in the early morning as they had spent a sleepless night.

*****

The second day Bhaskararao completed his morning chores and had his breakfast of milk and fruits. Then he said to Kashibayi, "Amma, you took care of me for two days so affectionately. Now it is time for my return to my *dharmasala*." After hearing the entire story of Bhaskararao's suffering from his own mouth the previous night, Kashibayi had compared herself with him and felt that her suffering was nothing in comparison with that of a king of the whole kingdom. She felt not only a great sympathy for him, but felt that she could spend the rest of her life serving her master thereby earning some *punya* for the future life. These ideas flashed across her mind with the speed of a lightning. She, therefore, folded her palms and requested Bhaskararao, "Sarkar, now that I know the whole story, I will not allow you to step out of my poor home. How can a king like you stay in a *dharmasala* and wait for somebody's mercy there for every sundry thing? No, no. Sarkar. You stay in our house and I shall serve you until my last breath. My niece also will serve you as your faithful servant. We have nobody now to think of. Nor have you any. Let's stay here together and scrape through." Although such a humanitarian invitation had come rather unexpectedly, Babasaheb felt touched by it. But still he did not want to be a burden on those two forlorn women. He, therefore, said, "Amma, I am very grateful to you for this kind gesture. But how shall I burden you with such a liability? My conscience does not agree to do this." Kashibayi got tears in her eyes and implored, "Sarkar, please do not mistake my request. Kindly do not feel obligated at all. You have fed my brother and his family in the past by giving him employment in your office. We have eaten your salt directly or otherwise. You have a moral right to demand service from us. Even if you hesitate to do so, we do not allow you to go away from here. It's our moral duty to serve you and take care of you. Luckily or unluckily we have been brought together by Fate. Let us make the best use of it. Sarkar, kindly stay with us permanently until we die." Bhaskararao was deeply touched by her request. His respect for Kashibayi increased suddenly. He thought that he was a small man when compared to her nobility of feeling. He contemplated about it for a few minutes silently. "All right, amma, I would oblige you just to give you some satisfaction. I will go to the *dharmasala* and bring back my clothes and other belongings." Kashibayi and her niece felt some satisfaction when he agreed to stay with them. Then Bhaskararao went to his *dharmasala* and brought back his little things and clothes. He thus settled himself in Kashibayi's humble house and felt as though he was one of them since the beginning. Outsiders never detected his true identity as he continued to wear his ochre robes. They addressed him as a sanyasi as he normally moved among the fellow sanyasis and had regular discussion with them on matters of *Veda* and *Vedanta*. But Kashibayi treated him as her master and served him with all the concern and affection of a mother. Bhaskararao would secretly wonder at the strange quirks of his fate. Being a king he never wanted to take any help from anybody without returning their debt in some form or the other. That was his royal philosophy of life. He did not know how to repay the debt that Kashibayi and her niece had implicated him in. He also knew that they were serving him purely from a selfless motive. But yet he wanted to do something for them, though he was not quite clear about how to do it. Now he felt the homely atmosphere after a long interval of time when he lost everything including his kingdom to the British Government. A couple of months went by like this in ease and comfort. He was absolutely free from anxiety or liabilities. The only thing he was waiting patiently for was death.

One day Bhaskararao and Kashibayi sat chitchatting after their midday siesta. Bhaskararao was filled with a sense of gratitude for the selfless lady. He, therefore, said to her, "Amma, you have been serving me with such care and affection that I do not know how to repay your debt." "Why do you think like that Sarkar? Please don't think along those lines," replied Kashibayi. "No, amma, I am so helpless that I would not be able to clear the debt in this lifetime." "Sarkar, I have a request. If you promise to grant it, I shall place it before you," said Kashibayi. "Amma, why do you hesitate? I shall certainly do something for you, if it lies in my hands," assured Bhaskararao. Then Kashibayi made bold to request him, "Sarkar, you know that I have nobody to think about except my niece. I am already growing old. After my death, there will be nobody to take care of my niece. I, therefore, request you to do something about it." "I understand your anxiety, amma. I shall search for a bridegroom for her as early as possible." 'That's not what I want from you Sarkar," replied Kashibayi. "Then, what do you want me to do?" asked Bhaskararao. "Sarkar, I request you to marry my niece yourself." Bhaskararao was really surprised by her odd request. He tried to convince her and asked her back, "Amma, don't you think, your suggestion is a bit absurd? Your niece is a budding young woman with all the youthful dreams about her future. I am already past sixty now. Will it be an ideal match? Don't you like your niece marrying a youngman and being happy with him?" Kashibayi was ready with her own answer as she had given a lot of thought to the problem. She said, "Sarkar, kindly don't put forth the arguments which are desirable in the normal course of life. But we are in a strange situation. Our life is so uncertain. I am really worried about my niece. I want to see her settled so that I can spend the rest of my life in the meditation of God. I have seen several old men marrying very young girls not for any physical relationship but for other legal and social reasons. I know that you have crossed sixty, yet you are a kind man. I request you to give the goodluck of *mangalya* to my niece so that I shall be free from tension and she will get a direction in her life. Kindly give her security by holding her hand. I fall to your feet, Sarkar. Please don't disappoint me." Bhaskararao could detect the agony of her soul in her tremulous voice and the tears that had gathered in her eyes. He was deeply touched by her request. He also thought inwardly that that was the only way her request. He also thought inwardly that that was the only way of repaying her debt and making her happy. "Don't you cry, amma. I can understand your difficulty. I only put forth my views and suggested better alternatives. If my marriage with your niece gives you so much satisfaction, I shall definitely do so. Please feel free now at least." Kashibayi really felt happy and heaved a deep sigh of relief.

After two days Kashibayi arranged for the private ritual of marriage in her own house. Bhaskararao and the bride put on new clothes after taking bath. Kashibayi lit the wick lamps before the deity. Then Bhaskararao secured the sacred *mangalyam* around the neck of the bride. Then both of them garlanded each other. Kashibayi waved the *arati* circularly around their faces and wished them a happy life. Now that Kashibayi was equal to his mother-in-law, Bhaskararao bowed down to her feet. Then the bride bowed down to the feet of her husband and her aunt. There was no witness other than the Lord God himself for their marriage. Thus was their sacred marriage solemnized privately on the basis of mutual trust and need. Then Kashibayi prepared a variety of sweet dishes and offered them to the newly married couple.

In the early night Kashibayi served a feast to the couple. Then she arranged the bed with new bedspreads and strewn it with jasmines for the ritual of first night for the couple. Bhaskararao entered the room and sat waiting for his new wife. Then Kashibayi sent her niece into the room with a tumbler of milk for her husband. Then Kashibayi closed the door and bolted it from outside. The young wife walked gently towards her lord and bowed down to his feet and gave him the tumbler of hot and sweet milk. Bhaskararao sipped half the milk and made her sip the other half. He was playing the role of a new husband with a sense of resignation and moral duty and not out of any infatuation. The dim wick lamp was flickering in the niche. Bhaskararao gently drew her into his arms and planted a few kisses. When touched by his masculine body, she felt a sudden thrill and her hairs stood on end. Being an experienced man, he the erotozones. For his wife, it was an unprecedented experience. In spite of her extraordinary shyness, she yielded herself to him whole-heartedly. As both of them entered into the experience of sweet sensuousness, the wife felt as if she was floating in the sky of inexplicable bliss. Bhaskararao thus initiated her into the joys of matrimony and offered her a new security in life.

The next morning the couple got up a bit late which was quite understandable. Kashibayi examined the bedsheet and felt satisfied with the blood stains on it. The couple had their bath. The niece of Kashibayi felt that her body was still tingling with the pleasures of the previous night and enjoyed remembering it again and again. Not only that. She even began to look forward to it the next night. Kashibayi was really very happy to notice that her niece was happy with her husband. Now that her responsibility was over, she thought she could spend the rest of her lifetime in the meditation of God. She thanked Bhaskararao inwardly for relieving her of her anxiety.

As a couple of months elapsed, Kashibayi noticed that her niece was growing more and more cheerful and healthy. She had developed a slight bulge in the belly and began to vomit frequently. Kashibayi felt very happy that her niece was pregnant and that Bhaskararao was going to be the father of a child, perhaps a son. She conveyed the news to Bhaskararao who felt extremely happy about it. Kashibayi thought that now at least her niece had found a direction in life and that she herself could die a peaceful death. Bhaskararao exclaimed "Strange are the ways of God. I could not believe that I at the age of sixty-two could beget a child on a youngwoman. I really wonder at my own fate." Bhaskararao began to treat his young wife more affectionately and tenderly. Kashibayi also busied herself in giving extra attention to her pregnant niece who was carrying the seed of a rebellious Raja. She really felt proud of her niece.

When Bhaskararao's wife completed nine months and nine days of her pregnancy, she was delivered of a male child. Bhaskararao was waiting outside of the little house, whereas Kashibayi and a midwife were attending to her delivery.

Bhaskararao was a little doubtful about whether the baby could be male or female. After about half an hour Kashibayi came out of the house and announced, "Sarkar, you have got a beautiful son." Bhaskararao felt ecstatic and inwardly thanked Lord Venkatapati of Naragund and Lord Visveswara of Kashi for granting him a son at last. After a little more time Kashibayi brought out the newborn baby swaddled in white clothes and showed it to Bhaskararao. The child was indeed very beautiful and resembled Bhaskararao himself in all the facial features. The baby smiled at him as he tickled and caressed it. Then Kashibayi took it into the room of confinement. As Bhaskararao sat beneath a tree near the house, he introspected the strange course of his life, "How strange is the *lila* of the Lord Almighty! O Lord, you did not grant me a son when I needed one very badly for my kingdom. I lost everything including my kingdom, mother and wife simply because I did not have a son. How much I had to struggle with the British fellows for this reason. O God, you have given me a son only now when I have nothing to offer him. I do not understand what is there in your design. The only satisfaction that I have now is that I am a father of a son. All right, I shall accept it as a divine blessing and live according to Your Will now."

*****

One day a sanyasi rode into the lanes of Naragund. The natives looked at him with awe and curiosity, but could not identify him properly as it was dusk time. The dogs followed him barking and snarling as long as they could and grew silent. Darkness was descending everywhere on the city. The wick lamps began to flicker in the houses. He crossed the potters' lane and rode past the house of Thakurdas. Then he turned towards Deshpande's house and waited near the gate. A servant came out of the compound and asked the sanyasi, "Your Holiness, where did you come from and whom do you wish to see?" "Bhayya," replied the sanyasi, "I have come from Kashi. I would like to see Keshar Prasad. Is he at home?" "Yes, Your Holiness, he is very much there. He is sitting in his inner room. You may ride right into the compound," replied the servant. Then he opened the gate, thereby letting in the sanyasi on the horse and closed it again. Then the servant conducted the sanyasi through the labyrinthine but palatial building and showed him the room in which Keshar Prasad was playing with his grandchildren. The sanyasi asked the servant to tether the horse to a peg and walked towards the room. Keshar Prasad was rather surprised by the unexpected arrival of a sanyasi who was a perfect stranger to him. He stopped playing with his children, stood up and welcomed the sanyasi with formal reverence. He sent in his grandchildren and therefore, there was nobody inside the big hall. He said formally, "Your Holiness, kindly be seated on this cushion" and stared at him interrogatively. He was not able to identify the guest properly. The sanyasi asked him, "How are you Keshar Prasad? Is everything all right? Hope you recognize me?" "Yes, Your Holiness" fumbled Keshar Prasad. "Do you recognize me? Can you tell me where we met each other?" asked the sanyasi. "I think we met each other in Satara," replied Keshar Prasad. "Then, it clearly means that you have not recognized me." "Frankly speaking, no." replied Keshar Prasad. "Ha, ha, ha, ha." The sanyasi burst into a guffaw which embarrassed Keshar Prasad. The sanyasi looked around him and confirmed that nobody else was around there. He lowered his pitch and said, "Why you cannot recognize your own king?" Keshar Prasad was puzzled a bit and said, "You mean, you are our Babasaheb Sarkar? How strange! I was really misled and confused by your beard and saffron robes. They instinctively rushed into each other's arms and hugged tightly for joy of reunion. Keshar Prasad got tears in his eyes for the unexpected pleasure of meeting his beloved king. Then the sanyasi released himself from his arms and said, "Keshar Prasad, I have one very important request to you. Please oblige me. That is, please don't reveal my identity to anyone including the members of your family. Just tell them that I am a sanyasi from Kashi. Will you?" "All right, Sarkar. Don't you worry about it. I shall keep it a secret even from the members of my family. I promise you and swear by

Lord Venkatapati." Then Keshar Prasad sent for his younger brother Madan Prasad and introduced the guest to him.

They arranged for a grand feast of sweet cakes, rice, curry, saltchips and pickles etc., for the rare and honourable guest. Bhaskararao who had almost forgotten his royal food for the past several years enjoyed the delicacies with real gusto and remembered his past nostalgically. After the dinner, edible pan, betel, lime, cardamom and cloves were served to Keshar Prasad, Madan Prasad and the guest. By that time the whole city was sleeping peacefully. Keshar Prasad, Madan Prasad and the guest closed the door of their hall and shared several confidential news to their hearts' content. Then both of them slept for about two hours.

They woke up early in the morning when they heard the sweet notes of *nagaswaram* from the rampart of Venkateswara temple. The sanyasi, Keshar Prasad, Madan Prasad completed their morning ablutions and rode to the templeyard in the darkness of early morning. They tethered their horses to the rings. Then they went round the temple once and entered the central hall and fell prostrate before the well-decked icon of Lord Venkateswara. The sanyasi watched the priest waving *arati-lamp* before the deity and tinkling the brass bell. As the priest brought the *arati* before them, the sanyasi and Keshar Prasad held their palms upon the wick lamps and touched their eyes with them. The sanyasi felt happy to learn that the holy service to Lord Venkateswara was rendered regularly without any hindrance. They dropped a few coins on the *arati* platter and bowed to the deity once again by folding their palms reverentially. Then the sanyasi suggested to Keshar Prasad, "Let's go now." Then both of them walked out of the temple. The sky in the east was growing rosier and rosier every moment. They came back to the place where they had tethered their horses. Keshar Prasad said, "Let's go home now. You may take one more day's rest." "No, my dear friend. This is not the time for me to stay here. I must rush back now towards Kashi. I shall come in future whenever it is possible. I must cross the borders of the city of Naragund before the human traffic starts." With these words the sanyasi mounted his horse and rode away towards the north of Naragund along the hillside. Keshar Prasad bid him farewell and stood watching him until his figure disappeared in the horizon. Keshar Prasad returned home with a heavy heart.

*****

When Queen Victoria took over charge of India in 1858 and issued the *Jahirnama*, all the life prisoners were released. Accordingly Baniya Bapu was released from the prison at Dharwad and returned to Naragund. He stayed in his old house for a few years. He died in the second half of January 1863. But those who were sent out for black water punishment were totally forgotten.

*****

Bhaskararao began to spend his old age years in the company of his newborn son. His wife was extremely happy to give a son to her husband and felt proud of herself. Kashibayi began to spend all her time in cuddling her niece's baby. They all affectionately named the baby as Ganeshpant. After a couple of months had gone by, Bhaskararao and Kashibayi and his wife felt that it was not desirable for them to stay in Kashi any longer. They had found some direction in this life and felt that they could settle down peacefully in the midst of their own cultural group. Accordingly one day they left Kashi and moved towards the south. After crossing the desert like land of Gujarathis, they entered the Marathi-belt and settled down in a place called Vasai like ordinary people. They were happy to know that they were not specially noticed by anybody in that town. Bhaskararao was watching the growth of his child Ganeshpant over the months and years with a sense of satisfaction. He had reached sixty-six years by now. One day he slept after his lunch. In the evening he did not get up as usual. His wife, therefore, went to his bed to wake him. She shook him this way and that, but alas! his face fell to a side. Bhaskararao was no more. His wife screamed and fell on his chest and began to cry. Her child Ganeshpant did not understand anything, but yet he began to cry simply because his mother was crying. Kashibayi was also crying piteously because her carefreeness had disappeared once again. Soon the neighbours gathered and made preparations for the funeral of the late Bhaskararao.

Kashibayi and Bhaskararao's widow began to live their life rather mechanically. They had no wish except bringing up their four year old child Ganeshpant. She tried her best to console her niece, "My dear niece, don't you cry over your late husband. Try to forget him by nourishing his beautiful son. Your husband's spirit will be happy if you bring up his son properly. What else can you do in this life?" The niece was consoled and convinced by her words and tried to concentrate her attention on her son who was growing beautifully like the moon.

After the lapse of a couple of years, the widow of Bhaskararao was inflicted with plague. She vomited continuously and could not be cured. No medicine was of any help to her. After a few days of suffering she also died. Her son Ganeshpant became a forlorn once again. Kashibayi felt disheartened by the death of her niece. She requested the local brahmins and arranged for the funeral of her niece. Now the entire responsibility of bringing up the child fell upon her shoulders. Besides, she felt terribly lonely in Vasai. She, therefore, traveled to Bombay and settled in Baykala with the intention of educating her grandchild. As Ganeshpant grew into a boy of about six years, she sent him to a local school.

*****

A Sanyasi clad in ochre robes reached Bankapur situated near Shiggaon. He was very tired and therefore relaxed under a big banyan tree. The sun was blazing fiercely in the afternoon. He fell into sound sleep. He had been wandering for several days without revealing his true identity to anyone or trusting anyone. For a couple of hours he was oblivious of all his fatigue and anxiety. He was awakened by the chirping of sparrows and the twitter of birds on the tree. He gently opened his eyes and looked at the sky. The sun was already descending in the western sky. He had the satisfaction of having slept well for a couple of hours after so many days. The terrible heat had disappeared from his body now. He was feeling cool and calm all over. But he heard a deep rumble in his belly and realized that he was very hungry. He remembered that he had eaten some wild fruits in the morning. Now he was really very hungry. But he did not know anyone in this village. He did not even know which village he had come to. He got up and tidied his ochre garment. He then collected his copper bowl and the arm-rest and began to walk into the heart of the village. Cows were walking towards their respective homes raising the dust behind them. The Sanyasi accosted the cowboy, "Hullow, brother. Could you tell me what this village is called?" The cowboy leant against his big staff, stared at the sanyasi and answered, "This village is called Bankapur, *Buddhi*. May I know from where you are coming?" asked the cowboy. The Sanyasi replied, "Brother, I am coming from Kashi in the north. Could you tell me if there is any *dharmasala* or monastery here where I can have some shelter for the night?" The cowboy scratched his head for a moment and thought something for a while. Then he remembered something and replied, "*Buddhi*, there is no *dharmasala* in this small village of ours. But there is a small monastery over there where you can rest for the night. People of that monastery are very good in hospitality." "All right, brother. I shall go there," said the Sanyasi. The cowboy ran behind the cows which had gone ahead of him when he was conversing with the Sanyasi. Then the Sanyasi walked towards the monastery from which he could hear the chime of bells. He entered the main gate of the monastery and asked a youngman about the manager of the institute. The youngman conducted the Sanyasi to the manager who wore a buff coloured dhoti and a scarf across his shoulders and who wore prominent triple ash-marks on his forehead. He asked the Sanyasi, "*Buddhi*, where do you come from? What can we do for you?" The Sanyasi replied, "Brother, I have returned from Kashi after a long stay there. I would like to have some shelter here for a few days if your monastery can accommodate me." The manager replied instantly, "For food and shelter, there is absolutely no problem here. You need not worry about that. It is part of the function of the monastery to conduct *dasoha* and provide free food to the needy believers. And we cannot have a better guest than you." The Sanyasi felt very happy to have such a welcome from unfamiliar people and said, "I am very grateful to you, brother." The manager then led him to a big room and requested him, "*Buddhi*, you may stay here in this room. I shall provide you bed and blankets and pillows." He then offered the Sanyasi some water to wash his hands, face and feet. The Sanyasi rubbed his hands and face with a towel offered by the manager. He sat on a mattress and leant against a pillow and asked the manager, "By the way, what's the name of this monastery?" The manager replied, "*Buddhi*, this monastery is called Jeragatti Matha. We had two swamis here in the monastery who happened to be great penants and yogis. We constructed their *samadhis* after their merger into the Absolute Linga. But even after their death several believers visit this monastery and offer grains, crops and money for the maintenance of the institute." Then the Sanyasi observed everything carefully and confirmed the fact that the monastery did not belong to his own caste. He therefore asked the manager, "Brother, you know, I am a Sanyasi. And there's no caste for a sanyasi. Still out of curiosity, I would like to know to which order this monastery belongs." The manager said, "*Buddhi*, there's nothing wrong in knowing the details of our institute. Our monastery belongs to Lingayat order and we are very liberal in our views and treatment of visitors to our institute. In fact we practise the humanistic ideals of our faith laid down by Basaveswara and other *Saranas*." Now that the doubts of the Sanyasi were cleared, he sat silent. The manager beckoned to his servant who brought a few bananas and a bowl of hot milk and placed them before the guest. The manager requested, "*Buddhi* you must have been very tired and hungry. Please have these fruits and this milk so that you may have temporary relief. Then you may relax until the dinner time." The Sanyasi peeled the bananas gently and began to swallow them. Then the manager excused himself to attend to the other things of the monastery. That night the Sanyasi had a very sumptuous meal after a long interval of time. He remembered his early days of family life when he had enjoyed life to the lees. But now he could not share his experiences or grievances with anyone because of the fear of betrayal to the British Government. He slept a very carefree sleep that night. The next day he familiarized himself with the details of the monastery and learnt a bit more about its history and the early saints who lived there. He noticed that the monastery enjoyed a great popularity among the natives of Bankapur. He did not feel any difficulty in living in that monastery although it did not belong to his own caste. He felt the real practice of humanism in that monastery. He thought inwardly that there was nothing greater than humanism in human life. After all, wasn't humanism the essence of all religions of the world? Thus he developed a special attachment to the monastery. But he was doubtful if the people of the monastery would allow him to stay there for more days.

One day the Sanyasi finished his breakfast of sweetballs and fruits and told the manager, "Dear brother, I am very grateful to you for all the hospitality shown to me. Now please allow me to take my leave and seek shelter elsewhere." When the manager heard these words he grew rather sad. He went to his colleagues and other members of the faith and told the news of the departure of the Sanyasi. The people were so fond of the Sanyasi that they rushed to him with folded palms and requested him, "*Buddhi*, what are you doing? Do you want to seek shelter elsewhere when we are alive here and so eager to serve you? It's a shame on our part if we are to lose such a holy man." All of them spoke in a chorus. The Sanyasi said in a convincing tone, "No, brothers. My intention is not to hurt your feelings. I simply felt that I should not be a burden to you or to your institute. That's why I wanted to go elsewhere." Then the eldest of the believers said, "*Buddhi*, we request you with folded palms not to leave our monastery, but to stay here until your last breath. We'll look after you to the best of our abilities. Your very presence adds glory to our monastery." Others repeated the same request in different ways. The Sanyasi was deeply touched by their humanistic concern and appeal. He, therefore, changed his decision and promised them, "All right, brothers. I am indeed overwhelmed by your heartfelt request. I shall stay here as long as you want me." The believers were all so happy to learn that the Sanyasi had changed his decision according to their request. They were so jubilant about it that they arranged a special feast to celebrate it.

The Sanyasi settled down in his room of the monastery. He had a long beard and flowing hair which were turning gray. He had a fair complexion and a royal luster on his face. The devotees of the monastery had noticed that he had some very valuable items with him which no ordinary Sanyasi could afford to have with him. He, for example, had a folding fan of sandal wood which looked like the tailspread of a peacock when unfolded for use. It had very intricate pattern of carving on it and smacked of something royal. His robes also happened to be silken rather than of cotton. Sometimes he used to smoke his pipe in his room. Some boys who had peeped through the creeks of the door panel, had seen him putting some precious things along with tobacco into his pipe and smoking it leisurely. He had hidden some of his belongings in his cloth bag, but nobody had dared to check it or question him about his belongings. They all had such reverence for him.

Quite a few years elapsed since the Sanyasi settled down in the monastery of Bankapur. He had become part and parcel of the institute and the natives revered him as if he was their own man, although they knew that he belonged to a caste not their own. The Sanyasi knew inwardly that he did not belong to their caste. The Lingayats bury their dead whereas the Brahmins burn their dead. Now that he was living an impersonated life of a Sanyasi he could not divulge his real identity to anyone. He knew what had happened to the mutineers and the persons of the royal household of Naragund. Now he thought of his last days. How should his funeral be conducted? thought he. Should it be according to Brahmanical rituals or to Lingayat rituals? It was a dilemma for him. He had grown sufficiently old now. His skin had shriveled all over and he had grown weaker than before. He suspected that his last days were fast nearing him. His disappointment and the strange quirks of his fate had made him really detached from the worldly life now. He felt that he was aging very fast these days. He knew that he could not have a Brahmanical funeral ritual simply because he could not give any clue to anybody about his identity. The contingencies of life had compelled him to reject the rigidities of his caste and to adjust himself with the society around him. He thus made up his mind.

One day he was chatting with a few elders of Bankapur including the staff of the monastery. He became serious all of a sudden in the course of his conversation with them. One of the elders asked him, "*Buddhi*, you grew suddenly serious while we were chatting. May we ask for the reason? Are you feeling all right? How's your health?" Then the Sanyasi said, "Dear brothers, I suddenly became conscious of my death. Now that I have grown very old, I am likely to die any day. I have a special request to you all. Will you oblige me?" "Is there anything in the world which we have refused to give you, *Buddhi*?" counter questioned the elder. Then the Sanyasi said in a serious way, "Dear brothers, so far you have all treated me with great care and affection. I have never felt that I am an outsider with you. Now my last request to you all is that you bury me here on the precincts of the monastery and build a *samadhi* near the old ones. But do not forget to keep my pipe in my *samadhi*. That's all. That happens to be my last wish in this mortal life." Hearing these words of the Sanyasi, the elders grew sad and tears gathered in their eyes. One of the elders said in his lachrymose voice, "*Buddhi*, you don't have to request us for that. Instead you should command us to do it. Is there anything holier for us than to oblige you? You don't have any doubt about it. It is our bounden duty to arrange for everything meticulously according to your desire." They all prostrated to his feet and dispersed. The Sanyasi had a very carefree sleep that night. He was indeed overwhelmed with gratitude to all of them for their affection and reverence for him. "I am receiving boundless love and affection from the most unexpected corner. How strange are the ways of God!" wondered he.

The Sanyasi led a contented life in the monastery and had a regular chat with the staff and devotees of Bankapur. He seemed to have forgotten all his earlier frustration in life as he had cultivated true *vairagya* now. He never felt the onward march of time because of his ascetic contentment. About six months went by like this. One day, the manager of the monastery noticed that the Sanyasi had not woken up at the regular time and therefore, went to his room and gently pushed the door which opened with a creak. The manager thought that the Sanyasi might have been sleeping after completing his nature call and that the door was not bolted from inside as the night was advancing towards dawn. He went back to attend to routine matters of the monastery. After the lapse of another hour he went to the room and noticed that the door was kept ajar as he had left it. This time he could not control his curiosity and wished to check whether the Sanyasi was feeling well or not. He, therefore, opened the door boldly and did not care even for the loud creak of the door. He walked gently to the bed and said in a loud voice, "*Buddhi...Buddhi.*" But there was no response. He thought that the Sanyasi might be sound asleep. He, therefore, shook him by the shoulders. Again there was no response. Then he tried to shake the head of the Sanyasi, but found that the head lay limp on one side. "*Buddhi*, did you leave us all as forlorned!" burst out the manager. Soon the staff of the monastery rushed into the room and saw that the Sanyasi's spirit had left the mortal body and merged into the Absolute. They all scanned his face carefully and saw a great serenity on his face. Soon the devotees of Bankapur began to cry loudly and mourn his departure. The elders remembered the last wish of the Sanyasi. They, therefore, bathed the dead body of the Sanyasi and arranged it in a sitting posture on a wooden platform and decked his body with holy-ash marks, flower-garlands and *bel*-leaves and performed the last *puja* to his person. The *Bhajan*-singers sang the devotional and philosophical songs to the accompaniment of drone-box, drums and stringed instruments. The entire village flocked to the monastery to pay their last homage to the holy man. The *Bhajan*-singing continued upto the evening. In the evening, the decorated dead body of the Sanyasi was mounted on a hearse and carried by the devotees around on the main roads of the village. Finally the dead Sanyasi was buried on the precincts of the monastery according to the Lingayat rituals. The devotees did not forget to bury the Sanyasi's smoking pipe also along with him in the *samadhi*. They all felt a deep blankness in their hearts for several days and months and remembered him with a nostalgic agony.

A month after the death of the Sanyasi, the staff of the monastery arranged for the proper construction of a *samadhi* with polished stones. The masons busied themselves with stone-cutting and building it with great care. The construction of the *samadhi* was completed within a fortnight's time. Then they got it painted white and decked it with floral garlands and *bel*-leaves. Thus they performed a reverential *puja* to the *samadhi* of the Sanyasi who had endeared himself to the whole village of Bankapur.

One day the staff and elders of the monastery sat chatting among themselves on the outside platform of the monastery. They remembered their past days with the Sanyasi with nostalgia. One of the elders asked the other one, "Dear friend, did you notice that the Sanyasi never divulged any detail about his past life or personal life?" The other elder counter-questioned, "Didn't he tell us that he had come from Kashi?" "But, my question is why did he have to come from Kashi? Since he knew Kannada very well, he must have been a man from the Kannada speaking area. Besides, he never looked like a poor saint. He had a royal appearance and had costly belongings like the smoking pipe, the sandal-fan and other golden rings etc. I have my own doubts about him." "Who do you think he was?" asked the third man. "Why could he not have been Bhaskararao in disguise? Don't laugh at my inference. This is only my wild guess," replied the second man. Then the fourth man said, "Your guess is a nonsensical one. As we have all heard, Bhaskararao Bhave was hanged to death by the British authorities." "That's what we have heard. But the truth is that Bhaskararao escaped to Nepal and lived somewhere there. It was some surrogate who was hanged in the name of Babasaheb." "Then our Sanyasi might not be Babasaheb," said the third man. "I think," said the second man, "our Sanyasi must have been one of the mutineers preferably belonging to the blood relatives of Babasaheb. It could be Visnu Kulkarni or Govindarao." "Anyway we all suspect that the Sanyasi was not a professional one but one who turned ascetic under duress," said the first man. "Don't you know that it's a sacrilege to know the origin of a Sanyasi as also of a river?" interrogated the second man. "Let's not commit that sacrilege and spoil our faith. Let's only remember our sweet days spent in his company," said the third man and clinched the matter.

GLOSSARY OF NATIVE WORDS

Abhiseka	:	Holy bath rendered to deities or icons
Aksata	:	Rice grains mixed with turmeric powder and sprinkled on bride and groom during the wedding ceremony or on holy persons.
Arati	:	Wick lamps waved in a circular fashion.
Attige	:	Elder brother's wife.
Bahurupi	:	An actor who can play multiple roles.
Bairagi	:	Saint
Bhajan	:	Devotional song.
Buddhi	:	Honorific used to address a holy man/Your Holiness.
Chawadi	:	Village office.
Chitti	:	Eight seers/about 10 kilos.
Dak Bungalow	:	Circuit house
Dal	:	Pulse
Dasami	:	Chapati.
Darsan	:	Sight/Vision
Desai	:	Ruler or administrator.
Deshpande	:	Registrar/record keeper
Deshmukh	:	Petty administrator
Dharmasala	:	Charity hall
Dunk nagari	:	Twin drums facing each other at an angle.
Farman	:	Order/instruction
Firangi	:	Foreign
Ganja	:	Narcotic drug
Ganjipa	:	A pack of cards

Garuda vahana	:	Riding on the back of an eagle.
Golandaj	:	Cannon operator.
Gosai	:	Religious mendicant of Saiva or Vaisnava faith.
Gowda	:	Village chief.
Huzoor	:	Respected Sir.
Inamdar	:	Landlord.
Ingreji	:	English.
Istalinga	:	Tiny icon symbolizing God.
Jagirdar	:	Landlord.
Jahagir	:	Land-grant
Jahirnama	:	Public proclamation.
Kaffir	:	Agnostic : Non Muslim.
Karachikai	:	A fried sweet dish.
Lambani	:	Tribal people.
Lagna	:	Central combination of planets in a horoscope.
Lakhapati	:	Lakhier.
Letta	:	Dice, chess, gambling.
Lila	:	Frolic play of God.
Mangalya	:	Holy wifery.
Mangalyam	:	Sacred necklace of tiny black beads symbolizing wifehood.
Mantra	:	Spell.
Mlencha	:	Sudra, heathen.
Mukti	:	Liberation from this worldy life.
Munjavi	:	Brahmanical initiation through the wearing of sacred thread.
Nagari	:	Large drum.
Nagaswaram	:	Wood instrument producing very mellifluous notes.
Naikwadi	:	A city administrator.

Navaratri	:	Nine holy nights.
Pagadi	:	Turban.
Pagoda	:	Buddhist temple.
Pagoti	:	Turban.
Pan	:	Edible leaf.
Panchamrita	:	A compound made of five substances like milk, curds, ghee, honey and sugar.
Panchanama	:	Public enquiry and registration.
Patel	:	Village chief.
Pativrita	:	Chaste wife.
Pedha	:	Sweet condiment.
Phatka	:	Vigorous caning or slapping.
Prahara	:	Duration of eight hours.
Prasad	:	Consecrated food.
Puja	:	Holy service.
Punya	:	Merit.
Puskarini	:	Lotus pond.
Pausya	:	The month of December-January.
Ragi	:	Millet.
Raksasa	:	Demon.
Rayare	:	O Sir.
Saheb	:	Sir.
Saktamajuri	:	Capital punishment.
Samadhi	:	Grave.
Sambar	:	Curry.
Sannad	:	A charter or grant.
Saraf	:	Jeweler.
Sarana	:	Virasaiva saint.
Sarkar	:	Government, 'Your Highness'.
Shetsundee	:	Native collector of the revenue of a division of villages or land.
Sirastedar	:	Revenue clerk.

Sola Somawar Vrita	:	A vow to be observed for sixteen consecutive Mondays.
Tirtha	:	Holy water.
Uppittu	:	A dish of samolina.
Vairagya	:	Detachment; passionlessness.
Vibhuti	:	Holy ash applied on forehead and other limbs.
Vilayati	:	Foreign.